"Suppose I refuse?"

The light around him seemed to pulse, as if in anger. "As I told you, it has already happened—in this timeline. You have found Ahriman. You have saved the human race. All that you need to do now is to play out the part that our history shows you played."

"But if I refuse?"

"That is unthinkable."

"If I refuse?" I insisted.

He glittered like a billion fireflies. His face became grim. "If you do not play out your predestined role—if you do not stop Ahriman—the very fabric of space-time itself will be shattered. This timeline will crack open, releasing enough energy to destroy the universe as we know it. The human race will disappear. All of space-time will be shifted to a different track, a different continuum. The planet Earth will be dissolved. This entire universe of space-time will vanish as though it had never existed."

He was utterly convincing.

Look for these other TOR books by Ben Bova

ORION

BEN BOVA

A TOM DOHERTY ASSOCIATES BOOK

ORION

Copyright © 1984 by Ben Bova

Portions of this book previously appeared in *Analog Science Fiction/Science Fact Magazine* as "Floodtide."

A TOR Book

Published by Tom Doherty Associates
8-10 West 36 Street
New York, N.Y. 10018

Cover art by Boris Vallejo

First TOR printing: April 1985

Second printing/April 1985

ISBN: 0-812-53215-5
CAN. ED.: 0-812-53216-3

Printed in the United States of America

To the inimitable Alfred Bester

PART ONE:
PHOENIX

CHAPTER 1

I am not superhuman.

I do have abilities that are far beyond those of any normal man's, but I am just as human and mortal as anyone on Earth.

The core of my abilities is apparently in the structure of my nervous system. I can take completely conscious control of my entire body. I can direct my will along the chain of synapses instantly to make any part of my body do exactly what I wish it to do.

Last year I learned to play the piano in two hours. My teacher, a mild, gray little man, absolutely refused to believe that I had never touched a keyboard before that day. Earlier this year I stunned a Tae Kwan Do master by learning in less than a week everything he had absorbed in a lifetime of unceasing work. He tried to be humble and polite about it, but it was clear that he was furious with me and deeply ashamed of himself for being so. I left his class.

My powers are growing. I have always been able to control my heartbeat and breathing. I thought everyone could until I began reading about yogis and their "mystical" abilities. For me, their tricks are child's play.

Two months ago I found myself sitting in a restaurant in midtown Manhattan. I tend to be a solitary man, so I often take my lunch hour late enough to avoid the noisy crowds. It was after 3:00 p.m. and the restaurant was almost empty. A few couples were sitting at scattered tables, speaking in hushed tones. A middle-aged pair of tourists were studying the French menu warily, suspicious of food they had never heard of before. A couple of secret lovers sat well toward the rear, holding hands furtively, glancing up toward the door every few seconds. One young woman sat alone, not far from my own table near the front of the restaurant. She was beautiful, with dark hair curling at her shoulders and the strong, classic facial features that marked her as a photographer's model.

She happened to glance in my direction, and her calm, intelligent eyes penetrated to my soul. Her eyes were large, gray as a polar sea, and seemed to hold all the knowledge of the world. Suddenly I realized that I was not merely a solitary man; I was a lonely man. Like a love-struck puppy, I wanted desperately to go over to her table and introduce myself.

But her gaze shifted to the door. I turned to see a man enter, a strikingly handsome, gold-maned man of that indeterminate age between thirty and fifty. He stood by the door for a moment, then went to the bar up by the curtained plate glass window and took a stool. Even though he was wearing a conservative gray business suit, he looked more like a movie idol or an ancient Greek god than a Manhattan executive who was getting an early start on the cocktail hour.

My gray-eyed beauty stared at him, as if unable to pull herself free of his spell. There was an aura about him, a golden radiance. The air almost seemed to glow where he was sitting. Deep inside me, a long-buried memory began to nag at me. I felt that I knew him, that I had met him long ago. But I could not remember where or when or under what circumstances.

I looked back at the young woman. With a visible effort, she tore her gaze away from the golden man and looked toward me. The corners of her lips curled upward slightly in a smile that might have been an invitation. But the door opened again and she looked away from me once more.

Another man entered the restaurant and went directly to the bar, sitting around its curve so that his back faced the curtained window. If the first man was a golden angel, this one had the look of a midnight netherworld about him. His face was heavy and grim; his muscular body bulged his clothing. His hair was jet black and his eyes burned angrily under heavy, bushy brows. Even his voice seemed heavy and dark with fury when he ordered a brandy.

I finished my coffee and decided to ask for my check, then stop at the model's table on my way out. I started to look for my waiter among the four of them loafing by the kitchen doors in the rear of the restaurant, conversing in a mixture of French and Italian. That is what saved me.

A bald little man in a black coat popped out of the kitchen's swinging door and tossed a black egg-shaped object the length of the restaurant. A hand grenade.

I saw it all as if it were happening in slow motion. I realize now that my reflexes must have suddenly gone into overdrive, operating at a fantastically fast rate. I saw the man ducking back inside the kitchen, the waiters stiffening with surprise, the couples at the other tables still talking, not realizing that death was a second or two away. The young beauty a few tables away from me had her back to the grenade, but the bartender stared straight at it as it clunked on the carpet and rolled lumpily along to within five feet of me.

I shouted a warning and leaped across the intervening tables to knock the young model out of the

way of the blast. We thudded to the floor, me on
top of her. The clatter of dishes and glassware was
lost in the roar of the explosion. The room flashed
and thundered. It shook. Then—smoke, screams,
the heat of flames, the acrid smell of the explosive.

I got to my feet unharmed. Her table was splintered and the wall behind us shredded by shrapnel.
Smoke filled the room. I got to my knees and saw
that the young woman was unconscious. There
was a gash on her forehead, but she seemed otherwise unharmed. I turned and saw through the
smoke the other people in the restaurant mangled
and bleeding, sprawled on the floor, slumped
against the walls. Some were moaning. A woman
sobbed.

I took the young model in my arms and carried
her out to the sidewalk. Then I went back in and
brought out another couple. As I stretched them
out on the pavement among the shards of glass
from the blown-out window, the police and firemen began to arrive, sirens shrieking. An ambulance was right behind them. I stood aside and let
the professionals take over.

There was no sign of either of the two men who
had been sitting at the bar. Both the golden one
and the dark man seemed to have disappeared the
instant the grenade went off. They were gone by
the time I had pulled myself up off the floor. The
bartender had been cut in half by the blast. His
two customers had vanished.

As the firemen extinguished the smoldering blaze,
the police laid out four dead bodies on the sidewalk and covered them with blankets. The medics
were treating the wounded. They lifted the model,
still unconscious, onto a stretcher. More ambulances arrived, and a crowd gathered around the
scene, buzzing.

"Goddamned I.R.A.," grumbled one of the cops.

"Cheez, they're tossin' bombs around here, too, now?"

"Coulda been the Puerto Ricans," another cop suggested, his voice weary, exasperated.

"Or the Serbo-Croatians. They set that bomb off in the Statue of Liberty, remember?"

They questioned me for several minutes, then turned me over to the medics for a quick checkup at the back of one of the ambulances.

"You're lucky, mister," said the white-jacketed medic. "You didn't even get your hair mussed."

Lucky. I felt numb, as if my whole body had been immersed in a thick enveloping fog. I could see and move and breathe and think. But I could not *feel*. I wanted to be angry, or grief-stricken, or even frightened. But I was as calm as a stupid cow, staring at the world with placid eyes. I thought about the young woman who was being taken off to a hospital. What made me try to save her? Who was responsible for the bombing? Were they trying to kill her? Or one of the men at the bar?

Or me?

Two TV vans had arrived by now, and the news reporters were speaking to the police captain in charge of the scene while their crews unlimbered their mini-cameras. One of the reporters, a sharp-faced woman with a penetratingly nasal voice, interviewed me for a few minutes. I responded to her questions automatically, my mind dull and slow.

Once the police let me leave, I pushed my way through the milling crowd that had been drawn by the excitement and walked the three blocks back to my office. I told no one about the explosion. I went straight to my private cubicle and shut the door.

As evening fell, I was still sitting at my desk—wondering why the grenade had been thrown and how I had escaped being killed by it. Which led me to wondering why I have such physical abilities and whether those two strangers who disappeared from the bar had the same powers. I thought again about the young woman. Closing my eyes, I recalled from my memory the image of the ambulance that had taken her away. St. Mercy Hospital was printed along its side paneling. A quick check with my desktop computer gave me the hospital's address. I got up from my desk and left the office, the lights turning off automatically behind me.

CHAPTER 2

It wasn't until I pushed through the revolving door of St. Mercy's main entrance that I realized I had no idea of the name of the woman I had come to see. And as I stood there in the middle of the frenetic, crowded, bustling lobby, I saw the foolishness of asking any of the harried-looking receptionists for help. For a few moments I was at a loss; then I spotted a uniformed policeman.

Step by step I went from one police officer to another, asking for information about the people brought in from the bombing earlier that day. I told them I was from the restaurant's insurance company. Only one of the policemen, a burly black man with a handsome mustache, eyed me suspiciously and asked for identification. I showed him my group insurance card; he barely glanced at it, but it looked official enough to satisfy him. Perhaps my air of utter confidence also helped to convince him.

In less than a half-hour I entered a ward that contained sixteen beds, half of them empty. The nurse in charge led me to the bed where the young model lay, eyes closed, a flesh-toned plastic bandage taped to her forehead.

"Only a few minutes," the nurse whispered to me.

I nodded.

"Miss Promachos," the nurse called softly, leaning over the bed. "You have a visitor."

The young woman's eyes opened. Those lustrous gray eyes that seemed as deep as eternity.

"Only a few minutes," the nurse repeated. Then she walked away, her soft-soled shoes squeaking on the tiled floor.

"You . . . you're the one who saved me, in the restaurant."

I could feel my heart throbbing wildly, and I made no effort to slow it. "Are you all right?" I asked.

"Yes, thanks to you. Only this cut on my forehead; they said I won't need plastic surgery, it won't leave a scar."

"That's good."

Her lips curled upward slightly. "And a few bruises on my body and legs from being knocked down."

"Oh. I'm sorry . . ."

She laughed. "Don't be! If you hadn't knocked me over . . ." The laughter faded. Her lovely face grew serious.

I stepped closer to the bed. "I'm glad you weren't hurt seriously. I . . . I don't even know your name."

"Aretha," she said. "Call me Aretha." Her voice was a low, soft purr, totally feminine without being high-pitched or shrill.

She didn't ask me my name, but instead looked at me with a gaze that seemed perfectly calm, yet expectant, as if she were waiting for me to tell her something. Something important. I began to feel uneasy, confused.

"You don't know who I am, do you?" she asked.

My mouth felt dry. "Should I know?"

"You don't remember?"

Remember what? I wanted to ask her. Instead, I merely shook my head.

She reached out and took my hand. Her fingers

felt cool and calming on my skin. "It's all right," she said. "I'll help you. That's why I'm here."

"To help me?" My mind was whirling now. What did she mean?

"Do you remember the two men who were sitting at the bar this afternoon?"

"The golden one . . ." His image was burning in my memory.

"And the other. The dark one." Aretha's face was somber now. "You remember the other one?"

"Yes."

"But you don't remember who they are, do you?"

"Should I?"

"You must," she said, gripping my hand tightly. "It is imperative."

"But I don't know who they are. I never saw them before today."

She let her head sink back on the pillows. "You *have* seen them. We both have. But you can't remember any of it."

I heard the squeak-squeak of the nurse's footsteps approaching. "This is all very confusing," I said to Aretha. "Why was the restaurant bombed? Who's behind it all?"

"That's not important. I'm here to help you recall your mission. What happened this afternoon is trivial."

"Trivial? Four people were killed!"

The nurse's hissing whisper cut through our conversation, "That's all, sir. She needs her rest."

"But . . ."

"She needs her rest!"

Aretha smiled at me. "It's all right. You can come back tomorrow. I'll tell you about it then."

Reluctantly, I bade her good-bye and left the hospital.

As I walked slowly through the hospital's busy maze of corridors, I paid no attention to the people rushing along beside me. Their individual tales of grief and pain were as far from me as the most distant star. My mind was boiling, seething, from the tantalizing scraps of information that Aretha had given me.

She knew me! We had met before. I should have remembered her, and the two men who had been at the bar. But my memory was as blank as a darkened, empty computer screen.

By the time I was walking down the front stairs of St. Mercy's, looking up the street for a taxi, I decided not to go home. Instead, I gave the cabbie the address of my office building—where my personnel record was on file.

The externals are easy. My name is John G. O'Ryan. That had always made me feel slightly uneasy, as though it wasn't the proper name for me, not my real name at all. John O'Ryan. It didn't feel right. I am the chief of marketing research for Continental Electronics Corporation, a multinational firm that manufactures lasers and other high-technology equipment. My personnel file, as I searched through it on my desktop computer, said that I was thirty-six years old, but I've always felt younger. . . .

Always?

I tried to remember back to my thirtieth birthday and found with a shock that I could not. My thirty-third birthday was clear in my mind: that was the night I had spent with Adrienna, the boss' private secretary. It was a memorable occasion. Adrienna was transferred to the company's London office a few weeks later, and ever since then I seem to have spent all my time with the computers and my work. I tried to recall Adrienna's face and could not. Nothing came to my mind except the hazy recollection of dark hair, a strong, lithe body, and lustrous gray eyes.

Beyond my thirty-third birthday my mind was a blank. I frowned in concentration so hard that my jaw muscles started to ache, but I still could not remember anything more than three years back. No knowledge of who my parents were. No memories of childhood. I did not even have any friends outside the small circle of acquaintances here at the office.

Cold sweat broke out all over my body. Who am I? *Why* am I?

I sat in my little office for hours as evening deepened into darkness, alone in my quiet, climate-controlled, chrome-and-leather cubicle, behind my sleek desk of Brazilian mahogany, and stared at my own personnel file on the desktop computer screen. There was not very much in it. Names. Dates. Schools. None of them made sense to me or touched the faintest wisp of memory.

I looked up at the polished chrome mirror on the wall across from my desk. John G. O'Ryan looked back at me: a stranger with thick, dark hair, an undistinguished face that had a slightly Mediterranean cast to it (why the O'Ryan, then?), just under six feet tall, with a trim build dressed in an executive's uniform of dark blue three-piece suit, off-white shirt and carefully knotted maroon tie.

The personnel file said that I had been a good athlete at school. I still felt strong and solid. But totally "average." I could fade into a crowd and become invisible quite easily.

Who am I? I could not escape the feeling that I had been put here, placed into this life, only three years ago by some power or agency that had wiped clean all memory of my earlier life.

I realized that I had to find out who, or what, had put me here. And Aretha was the key to my past; she knew, and she wanted me to know. My heart was pounding now, my breath fast, almost panting. I was feeling some emotion now, and for several minutes I reveled in it. But then, with a deliberate effort I lowered the adrenaline level in my blood, slowed my heartbeat and breathing rate.

Somehow I knew that the grenade had been meant for me. Not Aretha or anyone else. Me. Someone had tried to kill me. With the total certainty of truly in-built instinct, I realized that to try to discover my origins would mean mortal danger for me. Death. But I could not turn back. I had to know. And I realized that whoever I was, whatever my past had been, it must have involved not only Aretha but those two men as well—the angel and the dark spirit. One of them, perhaps both of them, had tried to kill me.

CHAPTER 3

The morning after the restaurant bombing I strode into my office exactly at nine, a bit later than usual for me. I had to brush aside questions from my secretary and several co-workers who had either seen the story on the evening TV news or were brandishing morning newspapers with a front-page photograph of me standing amid the injured and the dead.

I slid behind my desk and told my computer to phone St. Mercy's Hospital. The hospital's answering computer told me, in the warm tones of a trained human actress, that visiting hours were from two to four p.m. and six to eight in the evening. Ms. Promachos was listed in good condition. She could not come to the phone; the doctor was examining her at the moment.

I left a message saying that I would be there at two. Then I did a day's work, and more, that morning. For some foolish reason I felt wonderful. It was as if a veil had been lifted from my eyes or a window had suddenly opened to reveal a lovely landscape to me. Yes, I was aware that my memory was virtually a blank, that I did not know who I was or why I was here. I realized that my life was probably in the gravest sort of danger. But even that knowledge was wonderfully exhilarating. Twenty-four hours earlier I had been an emotionless automaton; I hadn't even guessed that most of

my memory had been erased. I was merely going
through the motions of being alive. I breathed, but
I didn't *feel*. Now it was like coming up to the
beautifully sunlit surface of the sea after spending
much too long in the murky darkness of the depths.

I worked right through the nominal lunch hour;
I was much too excited to eat. Like a teenager
running eagerly to his first date, I left the office
just before two o'clock and hailed a taxi down on
the crowded, rushing avenue and fidgeted impa-
tiently as the cab wormed its way through the
afternoon traffic to St. Mercy's Hospital.

"Ms. Promachos," said the nurse behind the desk
at the entrance to Aretha's ward, "checked out
about half an hour ago."

I felt stunned. As if someone had clubbed me
between the eyes. "Checked out . . . ?"

"Yes. Are you Mr. O'Ryan?"

I nodded mutely.

"She left a message for you." The nurse handed
me a folded scrap of paper. My name was penciled
on it, in what looked like swift, rushing strokes.
She had misspelled O'Ryan. I opened the tablet
sheet and read: *No time. The dark one* . . . Then, in
an almost undecipherable scribble, *Underground.*

I crumpled the sheet in my hand.

"When did you say she left?"

The nurse was an experienced old bird. The look
in her narrow eyes told me that she did not want
to get involved in a lover's triangle.

"When?" I repeated.

She glanced at the digital clock on the panel in
front of her seat. "Twenty-eight minutes ago, to be
exact."

"Who was with her?"

"I didn't get his name. She signed herself out."

"What did he look like?"

She hesitated. I could see a struggle going on

inside her head. Then: "A big man. Not quite as tall as you, but . . . *big*. Y'know? Wide as a bus. Like a Mafia hit man, only worse. He looked . . . *threatening*. Scared you just to see him."

"Dark complexion, black hair, bushy brows."

"That's him." She nodded. "Only . . . Ms. Promachos didn't seem to be afraid of him. *I* was, but she didn't look scared at all. Acted like she knew him, like he was a member of her family."

"Some family."

The nurse had no idea where they had gone. It was against hospital rules for her to give me Aretha's home address, but she did it anyway, with only the slightest urging from me. The dark one had truly frightened her.

I took another taxi to the address the nurse had given me, far downtown, near the Brooklyn Bridge. The driver, a Latino from Central America, was quickly lost in the maze of Lower East Side streets. I paid him off and walked several blocks, searching for Aretha's apartment.

There was no such address. The information was fake. I stopped on a street corner, beginning to feel conspicuous in my business suit where everyone else was wearing jeans, fatigues, tee shirts, even shawls that had once been tablecloths. I wasn't afraid of being mugged; I suppose I should have been, but I wasn't. I was concentrating too hard on trying to figure out why Aretha had given the hospital a phony address. I was certain that the nurse had told me the truth; it was Aretha herself who had falsified her address.

Underground. What did she mean by that? Underground. I looked at the time. She had left the hospital nearly an hour ago. In an hour they could have gone anywhere in this vast, teeming city.

"Hey, that's a nice watch you got, man."

I felt the prick of a knifepoint against my back

as the foul breath of the man who held it warmed my neck.

"I really like that watch, man," he said, low, trying to sound menacing.

I was in no mood to be mugged on a busy street corner in broad daylight. This fool was standing close behind me, pressing his knife into the small of my back, trying to rip me off without letting anyone walking past know what was happening.

"Just gimme the watch, shitface, and keep your mouth shut."

I lifted my hands as if to slip the watch off my wrist, then whirled and gave him an elbow in the abdomen and a backhand chop across the bridge of his nose. The knife clattered to the pavement. The blow to his middle had cut off his wind so he couldn't even yelp. He sank to his feet, nose broken, blood gushing over his ragged clothes and spattering the cement. I grabbed a handful of his filthy hair and jerked his head back. His face was covered with blood.

"Get out of here before I lose my temper," I told him. With my left foot I kicked his knife into the gutter.

Gagging, wide-eyed with pain and shock, he staggered to his feet and limped away. A few passersby glanced at me, but no one said a word or lifted a hand to intervene. The city at its finest.

Underground. I heard a subway train rumble beneath my feet, its wheels screeching on the iron rails. *Underground* is a British word for subway. There was a subway station just outside the hospital's main entrance. Looking across the street from where I was standing, I saw the entrance to another station. I dashed across the street, leaving a chorus of bleating horns and cursing drivers behind me, and raced down the steps. In the grimy, urine-stinking underground station, I went from one map of the subway system to another until I found one that was readable beneath the spray-can graffiti. Sure enough, a red line connected the station at the hospital with this station downtown.

Underground. They had come down here on the subway and gotten off at this station. I was certain of it. That's what Aretha's hastily scribbled message meant.

Now what? Where had they gone from here? A four-car train pulled in, roaring and squealing to a stop. The cars were decorated with bright graffiti paintings, cartoons and names of the "artists." I found myself scanning the words on the sides of the cars, looking for a message. Foolish desperation. The doors hissed open and everyone got out. I started toward the first car, but a black man in a Transit Authority uniform called out to me:

"End of the line. This train's goin' t' the lay-up. Next train uptown in five minutes. Next train over th' bridge on the other level."

The doors hissed shut and the train, empty of passengers, lumbered away from the platform and screeched around a bend in the track. I listened as carefully as I could, filtering out the other echoing noises in the station: the conversations, some kid's radio blaring rock music, high-pitched laughter from a trio of teen-aged girls. The train went around that curve, out of sight, and then stopped. "The lay-up," the Transit man had said. Trains taken out of service are kept there, down the track, until they are needed again.

I looked around. No one was paying attention to me. I walked to the end of the platform, vaulted easily over the padlocked, heavy wire gate that barred entry to the tracks, and went down the steps that led to the floor of the tunnel. The steps, the tunnel walls, the railing I touched were coated with years of filth, of grease and accumulated grime. The floor of the tunnel was like a sewer with tracks. In the dim lighting I saw that the electrified third rail, which carried enough current to drive the trains and kill anyone who touched it, was covered by wooden planking. I stepped up onto that; my shoes were already dank from the foul-smelling wetness of the tunnel floor.

In the distance I heard a train approaching. The walls were scalloped with niches for a man to stand in, and as the train's headlamp glared at me and its whistle hooted, I pressed myself against the grimy wall and let the juggernaut whoosh past. Despite myself, it took my breath away to have the train roar past just a few inches from me.

I pulled myself together and headed along the track after the train had passed. Sure enough, around the bend there were a dozen or more trains standing quiet and idle, side by side. Each of them was decorated with graffiti from one end to another. The overhead lights were spaced far apart; they threw weak pools of dim light into the grimy darkness that enveloped the lay-up.

They're here, I told myself. They're in here somewhere. I stopped and held my breath, listening. Eyesight was of little use in this darkness.

A scampering, slithering sound. The scrape of something hard sliding across the metal tracks. Then a squeaking, chittering noise. Something brushed against my ankle and I jerked my foot away involuntarily, almost losing my balance on the sagging planks above the electrified rail.

Rats. I peered into the darkness and saw baleful red eyes glaring back at me. Rats. Many of them.

But then I heard voices. I couldn't make out the words at first, but I could hear that one voice was a woman's and the other the harsh, ugly, menacing kind of voice that I instantly knew belonged to the dark man I had seen so briefly in the restaurant.

I followed the voices, moving as silently as a wraith, ignoring the evil red eyes of the rats that hovered in the darkness around me.

"What did you tell him?" the man's voice insisted.

"Nothing."

"I want to know how much you told him."

"I didn't tell him anything." It was Aretha's voice, no doubt of it. But then I heard her gasp and give out a painful, frightened sob.

"Tell me!"

I abandoned all attempts at stealth and ran along the warped, loose planks toward their voices. Aretha screamed, a strangled, agonized cry, as I dashed between two of the idle trains and finally saw them in a circle of light.

They were at the end of the tunnel. Aretha was sitting in the filth of the floor, her arms pinned behind her back, the bandage still on her forehead. The dark one stood off to one side, half in shadows, staring down at her. She was surrounded by dozens of rats. Her feet and legs were bare and bleeding. Her blouse was ripped open and a huge rat, malevolent as hell itself, was standing on its hind legs, reaching for her beautiful face.

I gave a wordless roar and charged straight for them. I saw the dark one turn toward me, his eyes as red and vicious as the rats' own. He seemed to recognize me as I charged down the tunnel toward him, and he backed away into the shadows.

Weaponless, I kicked wildly at the swarm of rats around Aretha, bent down and grabbed one of them in each hand and threw them with all my might against the walls. Turning, wheeling, kicking, flailing, I scattered them in every direction. They fled, screeching, into the protective darkness.

Suddenly they were all gone, and the man with them. I looked down at Aretha. Her eyes stared up at me blindly. Her throat had been ripped out. Her bright red blood spattered my grimy shoes and trousers.

I dropped to my knees and lifted her from the filth. But I was too late. She was dead.

CHAPTER 4

I spent the next two days in a sort of rage-induced state of shock, clamping down on my emotions so hard that I felt nothing. Police interrogations, lie detector tests, medical examinations, psychiatric tests—I went through them all like a robot, responding to questions and stimuli without an outward trace of emotion.

For some reason I told no one about the dark man who had killed Aretha. He had murdered her, somehow controlling the rats that had torn out her jugular vein, using them the way another man would use a gun. But I made no mention of him. I merely told the police and the doctors that I had followed Aretha from the hospital and found her as the rats attacked her in the subway lay-up. I was too late to save her. At least that last statement was the truth.

Something buried deep inside my consciousness warned me not to mention the darkly evil man. Far down within me, where the fires of fury lay banked and smoldering, I knew that it would cause me more trouble with the police and the psychiatrists if I mentioned his existence. But more than that, I wanted to track him down and find him myself. I wanted to deal with him with my own hands.

So I withheld the facts. The police detectives I spoke to were no fools. They knew that a woman does not wander into the subways to be attacked by rats and followed by a stranger who had met her only the day before—when they had both been victims of a terrorist bombing. They made it clear that they didn't believe me and that they wanted to use the lie detector on me. I agreed, as coldly indifferent to their questions as if they had been asking me the time of day or the color of the sky. The lie detector told them what I wanted it to, of course; controlling my pulse rate and perspiration was no great feat for me.

After an overnight at Bellevue for psychiatric observation, the police reluctantly released me. I went home to my apartment and telephoned my employer that I would be in for work at the normal time the following morning. He sounded surprised, asked me how I was feeling after two ordeals in the same week.

"I'm all right," I said.

It was the truth. I was physically unharmed and emotionally under tight control. Perhaps too tight.

"You sure you don't want to take the rest of the week off?" my boss asked me. His normally gruff features looked quite solicitous in the telephone's small picture screen.

"No. I'm fine. I'll be in tomorrow morning. I hope my being away hasn't fouled things up too badly around the office."

He attempted to lighten the situation. "Oh, we can get along without you—for a while. We'll all look forward to seeing you tomorrow."

"Thanks."

By the time I had replaced the phone in its cradle, my mind was away from the office and onto the problem of finding Aretha's murderer. The dark one. He and the golden man. The two of them were part of—what? My own life, from what Aretha had hinted at.

I tried to remember how they had behaved at

the restaurant. They had not said a single word to each other; I was certain of that. They had barely looked at each other, now that I thought of it. But the one glance they had exchanged was not in friendship. Their eyes had locked for the briefest fraction of a second in a link forged by pure hate.

They knew each other. They hated each other. I realized that if I could find one of them, I would certainly find the other close by.

How do you find two individual men in a city of seven and a half million? And what if my conclusions were wrong? Was I insane? Had I caused Aretha's death, as the police detectives had insinuated during their long interrogation of me? Why couldn't I remember anything further back than three years ago? Was I an amnesia victim, a paranoid, a madman building murderous fantasies in his mind? Had I invented the two men, created imaginary creatures of light and darkness within the tortured pathways of my own brain?

There was one answer to all these questions. It took me a sleepless night of thinking to find that single, simple answer, but I have never been much of a sleeper. An hour or two has always been sufficient for me; often I have gone several nights in a row with nothing but occasional catnaps. My fellow workers have sometimes complained, jokingly, about the amount of work I take home with me. Once in a while the jokes have been bitter.

The next morning, once I said hello to the office staff and fended off their questions and wondering stares, I went to my cubicle and immediately phoned the company physician. I asked him to recommend a good psychiatrist. On the phone's small picture screen the doctor looked slightly alarmed.

"Is this about the trouble with the police you've been caught in for the past few days?" he asked.

"Yes," I said to him. "I'm feeling ... a little shaky about it."

Which was no lie.

He peered at me through his bifocals. "Shaky? You? The imperturbable Mr. O'Ryan?"

I said nothing.

"H'mm. Well, I suppose having a hand grenade go off in your soup would shake up anybody. And then that girl dying that way. Pretty grisly."

I said nothing and kept my face expressionless. He waited a few seconds for me to add something to the conversation, but when he saw that I wasn't going to, he muttered something to himself and turned aside slightly to check his files.

He gave me the name of a psychiatrist. I called the man and made an appointment for that afternoon. He tried to put me off, but I used the company's name and our doctor's, and told him that I wanted only a few minutes for a preliminary talk.

Our meeting was quite brief. I outlined my lack of memory and he quickly referred me to another psychiatrist, a woman who specialized in such problems.

It took several weeks, going from one recommended psychiatrist to another, but finally I reached the one I wanted. He was the only specialist who agreed to see me at once, without hesitation, the day I phoned. He sounded as if he had been expecting me to call. His phone had no picture screen, but I didn't need one. I knew what he looked like.

"My schedule is very full," his rich tenor voice said, "but if you could drop into my office around nine tonight, I could see you then."

"Thank you, Doctor," I said. "I will."

The office was quite empty when I got there. I opened the door to the anteroom of his suite. No one was there. It was dark outside, and there were no lights on in the anteroom. Gloomy and dark, lit only by the glow from the city's lights out on the street below. Old-fashioned furniture. Bookshelves lining the walls. No nurse, no receptionist. No one.

A short hallway led back from the anteroom into a row of offices. A faint glow of light came from the half-open door at the end of the hall. I followed the light and pushed the heavy door fully open.

"Doctor?" I didn't bother speaking the name that was on the door. I knew it was not the true name of the man in the office.

"O'Ryan," said that rich tenor voice. "Come right in."

It was the golden man from the restaurant. The office was small and oppressively overfurnished with two couches, a massive desk, heavy window drapes, thick carpeting. He sat behind the desk, smiling expectantly at me. The only light was from a small floor lamp in a corner of the room, but the man himself seemed to glow, to radiate golden energy.

He wore a simple open-neck shirt. No jacket. He was broad-shouldered, handsome. He looked utterly capable of dealing with anything. His hands were clasped firmly together on the desktop. Instead of casting a shadow, they seemed to make the desktop brighter.

"Sit down, O'Ryan," he said calmly.

I realized that I was trembling. With an effort I brought my reflexes under control and took the leather armchair in front of his desk.

"You said you have a problem with your memory."

"You know what my problem is," I told him. "Let's not waste time."

He arched an eyebrow and smiled more broadly.

"This isn't your office. It's nothing like you. So, since you know my name and yours is not the one on the nameplate on the door, who are you? And who am I?"

"Very businesslike. You have adapted to this culture quite well." He leaned back in the swivel chair. "You may call me Ormazd. Names really don't mean that much, you understand, but you may use that one for me."

"Ormazd."

"Yes. And now I will tell you something about your own name. You have been misusing it. Your name is Orion . . . as in the constellation of stars. Orion."

"The Hunter."

"Very good! You *do* understand. Orion the Hunter. That is your name and your mission."

"Tell me more."

"There is no need to," he countered. "You already know what you must know. The information is stored in your memory, but most of it is blocked from your conscious awareness."

"Why is that?"

His face grew serious. "There is much that I cannot tell you. Not yet. You were sent here on a hunting mission. Your task is to find the Dark One—Ahriman."

"The man who was in the restaurant with you?"

"Exactly. Ahriman."

"Ahriman." So that was his name. "He killed Aretha."

"Yes, I know."

"Who was she?" I asked.

Ormazd made a small shrug. "A messenger. Unimportant to the . . ."

"She was important to me!"

He gazed at me with a new expression in his pale golden eyes. He almost looked surprised. "You only saw her once at the restaurant . . ."

"And in the hospital that evening," I added. "And the following day . . ." My breath caught in my throat. "The following day I saw her die. *He* killed her."

"All the more reason for you to find the Dark One," said Ormazd. "Your task is to find him and destroy him."

"Why? Who sent me here? From where?"

He sat up straighter in his chair, and something of his self-assured smile returned to his lips. "Why? To save the human race from destruction. Who sent you here? I did. From where? From about fifty thousand years in the future of this present time."

I should have been shocked, or surprised, or at least skeptical. But instead I felt relieved. It was as if I had known it all along, and hearing the truth from him relaxed my fears. I heard myself mutter, "Fifty thousand years in the future."

Ormazd nodded solemnly. "That is your time. I sent you back to this so-called twentieth century."

"To save the human race from destruction."

"Yes. By finding Ahriman, the Dark One."

"And once I find him?"

For the first time, he looked surprised. "Why, you must kill him, of course."

I stared at Ormazd, saying nothing.

"You don't believe what I have told you?"

I wished I could truthfully say that I didn't. Instead, I said, "I believe you. But I don't understand. Why can't I remember any of this? Why . . ."

"Temporal shock, perhaps," he interrupted. "Or maybe Ahriman has already reached your mind and blocked some of its capacities."

"Some?" I asked.

"Do you know the capacities of your mind? The training we have lavished upon you? Your ability to use each hemisphere of your brain independently?"

"What?"

"Are you right-handed or left-handed?"

That took me off-guard. "I'm . . . ambidextrous," I realized.

"You can write with either hand, can't you?
Play a guitar either way."

I nodded.

"You have the ability to use both sides of your
brain independently of each other," he said. "You
could run a computer and paint a landscape at the
same time, using your right hand for one and your
left for the other."

That sounded ridiculous. "I could get a job as a
freak in the circus, is that it?"

He smiled again. "More than that, Orion. Far
more."

"What about this Ahriman?" I demanded. "What
danger does he pose to the human race?"

"He is evil itself," Ormazd said, his golden eyes
blazing up so brightly that there was no doubt in
my mind of his sincerity. "He seeks to destroy the
human race. He would scour the Earth clean of
human life for all time, if we allow him to."

Strangely, my mind was accepting all this. It was
as if I were re-learning the tales of my childhood.
Distant echoes of half-remembered stories stirred
within me. But now the stories were real, no longer
the legends that elders tell their children.

"If I actually came here from fifty thousand years
in the future," I said slowly, as I worked it out in
my mind, "that means that the human race still
exists at that time. Which in turns means that the
human race was not destroyed here in the Twentieth Century."

Ormazd sighed petulantly. "Linear thinking."

"What does that mean?"

Leaning forward and placing his golden-skinned
hands on the desktop, he explained patiently, "You
did save the human race. It has already happened,
in this space-time line. Fifty thousand years in the
future, humankind has built a monument to you.
It stands in Old Rome, not far from the dome that
covers the ancient Vatican."

It was my turn to smile. "Then if I've already saved humanity . . ."

"You must still play your part," he said. "You must still find Ahriman and stop him."

"Suppose I refuse?"

"You can't!" he snapped.

"How do you know?"

The light around him seemed to pulse, as if in anger. "As I told you, it has already happened—in this time line. You have found Ahriman. You have saved the human race. All that you need to do now is to play out the part that our history shows you played."

"But if I refuse?"

"That is unthinkable."

"If I refuse?" I insisted.

He glittered like a billion fireflies. His face became grim. "If you do not play out your predestined role—if you do not stop Ahriman—the very fabric of space-time itself will be shattered. This timeline will crack open, releasing enough energy to destroy the universe as we know it. The human race will disappear. All of space-time will be shifted to a different track, a different continuum. The planet Earth will be dissolved. This entire universe of space-time will vanish as though it had never existed."

He was utterly convincing.

"And if I do cooperate?" I asked.

"You will find Ahriman. You will save the human race from destruction. The space-time continuum will be preserved. The universe will continue."

"I will kill Ahriman, then?"

He hesitated a long moment before answering slowly, "No. You cannot kill him. You will stop him, prevent him from achieving his goal. But . . . he will kill you."

I should have realized that when he'd told me

about the monument. I was to be a dead hero. It had already happened that way.

Suddenly it was all too much for me to bear. I shot up from my chair and lunged across the broad desk, reaching for his arm. My hand went completely through Ormazd's shimmering, gleaming image.

"Fool!" he snapped, as he faded into nothingness.

I was alone in the psychiatrist's office. I had seen holographic projections before, but never one that looked so convincingly solid and real. My knees were weak from the weight Ormazd had placed upon me. I sank back into the leather chair, totally alone with the knowledge that the fate of all humankind depended on me. And the only human being I really wanted to save was already dead. I could not accept it. My mind refused to think about it.

Instead, I found myself searching the office for the holographic equipment that this trickster had used to project his image. I searched until dawn, but I could not find a laser or any electrovisual equipment of any kind.

CHAPTER 5

For many days I simply refused to consider what Ormazd had told me. It was too fantastic, I kept telling myself. Yet all along, I knew it was true. Every atom of my being knew it was true. I was merely postponing the inevitable.

And deep within me, I burned to find the Dark One, the man who had murdered Aretha. My soul raged to seek him out and destroy him. Not for the cosmic drama that Ormazd had described to me. I wanted my hands around Ahriman's throat for a very simple, very human reason: justice. Vengeance for my dead love.

Finally, a wisp of memory put me on Ahriman's trail. I remembered (*remembered!*) the origin of the names the golden man used: Ormazd, the god of light and truth; Ahriman, the god of darkness and death. They were from the ancient religion of Persia, Zoroastrianism, founded by the man the ancient Greeks called Zarathustra.

So the golden one considered himself a god of light and goodness. He was at least a time traveler, if he had been telling me the truth. Was he indeed the same Ormazd who appeared to Zoroaster long millennia ago in Persia? Had he been struggling against Ahriman even then? Of course. Then and now, future and past, the track of time was becoming clear to me.

I brooded about the situation for days, not knowing what to do, waiting for some clue, some indication of how to proceed. Then a new memory stirred me, and I understood why I had been placed in this moment of time, why I had been sent to this particular company and this exact job.

I closed my eyes and recalled Tom Dempsey's long, serious, hound-dog face. It had been at the office Christmas party last year that he had told me, a bit drunkenly:

"The Sunfire lasers, man. Those goddam' beautiful high-power lasers. Most important thing th' company's doin'. Most important thing goin' on in th' whole fuckin' world!"

The lasers for the thermonuclear fusion reactor. The lasers that would power a man-made sun, which in turn would provide the permanent answer to all the human race's energy needs. The god of light made real in a world of science and technology. Where else would the Dark One strike?

It took me nearly a week to convince my superiors that the time had come for me to do a new market forecast for the laser fusion project. Continental Electronics was building the lasers for the world's first commercial CTR—Controlled Thermonuclear Reactor. By the end of that week I was on the company jet, bound for Ann Arbor, where the fusion reactor and its associated power plant were being built. Tom Dempsey sat beside me as we watched the early winter cloudscape forming along the shore of Lake Erie, some thirty thousand feet below our speeding plane.

Tom was grinning happily at me. "First time I've seen you take an interest in the fusion project. I always thought you couldn't care less about this work."

"You convinced me of its importance," I said, not untruthfully.

"It *is* damned important," he said, unconsciously playing with his seat belt as he spoke. Tom was the kind of engineer who was compulsively neat; yet he could never keep his hands from fiddling with things.

"The fusion reactor is ready for its first test run?" I led him on.

He nodded enthusiastically. "Yep. We've had our delays, but by god we're ready to go now. You put in deuterium—which you can get from ordinary water—zap it with our lasers, and out comes *power*. Megawatts of power, man. More power in a bucket of water than in all the oil fields of Iran."

It was an exaggeration, but not much of one. I had to smile at his mention of Iran—modern-day Persia.

The flight was smooth, and the company had a car waiting for us at the airport. As we drove up to the fusion lab building, I was surprised at its modest size, even though Dempsey had told me that CTRs could eventually be made small enough to fit into the basements of private homes.

"No need for electric utility companies or any other utility except water once we've got fusion. Turn on the kitchen tap and filter out enough deuterium in five minutes to run the house for a year."

He was a happy engineer. His machines were working. The world was fine.

But I saw that there were pickets marching along the wire fence in front of the lab. Most of them were young, students and the like, although there was a sprinkling of older men and more than a dozen women who looked like housewives. The placards they carried were professionally printed:

WE DON'T WANT H-BOMBS
IN OUR BACK YARD!

PEOPLE YES! TECHNOLOGY NO!
FUSION POWER HAS TO GO!

RADIATION CAUSES CANCER

Our car slowed as we approached the gate. The driver, a company chauffeur, said over his shoulder to Dempsey and me, "The lab security guards don't wanna open the gate. They're afraid the pickets'll rush inside."

There were only a few dozen of them, but as our car stopped before the gate, they seemed like a larger mob. They swarmed around the car, shouting at us.

"Go back where you came from!"

"Stop poisoning us!"

In a flash they all started chanting, "People yes! Technology no! Fusion power's got to go!" They began pounding the car with their placards and rocking it.

"Where are the police?" I asked the driver.

He merely shrugged.

"But they've got it all wrong," Dempsey said, his face showing that he felt personally hurt by the crowd's lack of appreciation for his machines. "Fusion power won't produce enough radiation to hurt anybody."

Before I thought to restrain him, he pushed open the car door on his side and wormed out among the demonstrators shouting, "There's no radiation coming out of the reactor! The major waste product of fusion is just plain old helium. You can give it to your kids so they can blow up their balloons with it."

They wouldn't listen. They clustered around Dempsey, screaming in his face, drowning out his words. A couple of youths, big enough to be varsity football players, pushed him against the side of the car and pinned him there.

I began to get out as our driver, muttering to himself, swung his door open hard enough to hit somebody and produce a yelp of pain. As I ducked out on the other side of the car, somebody swung a fist at me. I blocked it automatically and pushed the youngster away from me. Out of the corner of my eye I saw one of the housewives bring her placard down squarely on Dempsey's head. He sagged, and then one of the football players punched him in the midsection. Dempsey went down face-first on the blacktop. The chauffeur tried to wrestle the placard away from one of the women demonstrators while she yelled and tried to squirm out of his grasp. Several of the students swarmed over the chauffeur and began to pummel him.

"Let's teach 'em a lesson!"

I raced around the back of the car and dove into the crowd, yanking bodies out of my way until I was straddling Dempsey's prostrate body, next to the wobbly-kneed chauffeur. His nose was bleeding, his mouth open wide, lips pulled back over his teeth in rage.

I took a punch on the side of my face. Before the snarling young man who threw it could pull his arm back, I had him by the wrist and elbow and flung him against the others, knocking them down like ten pins. Everything happened very quickly. Suddenly the crowd melted back and started running away from us, except for the five on the ground with concussions or fractures. The others dropped their placards and fled down the street.

The security guards opened the front gate, almost falling over themselves to apologize for not moving more swiftly. In the distance I could hear the wail of a police siren approaching—too late.

The guards took us to the lab's infirmary, where I met their security chief, a waspish little man named Mangino. His skin was the color of cigarette tobacco; his eyes narrow and crafty.

"I just don't get it," he grumbled as Dempsey's head was being bandaged. "We never had a speck of trouble before today. This bunch of nuts just pops up out of nowhere and starts parading up and down in front of the main gate."

They were meant for me, I knew. A welcoming committee from Ahriman. But I said nothing.

"Our public relations people have been telling the media for years that this reactor won't be like the old uranium fission power plants," Mangino went on. "There's no radioactive waste. No radiation gets outside the reactor shell. The thing can't melt down."

Dempsey, sitting atop the infirmary table while a doctor and a pretty young nurse wrapped his head, spoke up. "You can't talk sense to people like that. They get themselves all worked up and they don't listen to the facts."

"No," I corrected him. "They don't get themselves all worked up. Somebody works them up."

Mangino's eyes widened for the barest flash of a second. Then he nodded. "You're right."

"It would be a good idea to find out who that somebody is," I said.

Mangino agreed. "And where he comes from. Could be the Arabs, or the oil companies, or any one of a dozen nut groups."

No matter who it was, I knew, Ahriman was behind it.

CHAPTER 6

It was not difficult to find the headquarters of the demonstrators. They belonged to an organization that called itself STOPP, an acronym for Stop Technology from Over Powering People.

STOPP's headquarters was an old four-story frame house across the main avenue from the university campus. I parked my rented car in front of the house and sat watching it awhile. Plenty of students went walking by, and more of them congregated around the pizza and hamburger shops down the street. This side of the avenue had once been a row of stately Victorian houses. Now, with the growth of the university across the way, the homes had been turned into apartments and offices. Many of the houses' street fronts had been converted into stores.

Across the avenue was academia: a lovely campus of gracious buildings, neatly tended hedges, and tall trees that reached bare branches toward the gray winter sky. This side of the street was dedicated to the greed of landlords: seedy, bustling, noisy, lucrative. And all along the avenue there was the constant rush of traffic: cars honking, growling, moving endlessly; trucks, buses, motorbikes, even a few electrically powered bicycles.

I got out of the car, convinced that the best approach was the direct one. I walked up the wooden steps and across the porch that fronted the house, pushed the antique, rusting bell button. I heard nothing, so I opened the front door and stepped inside.

While the outside of the house was Middle-American Victorian and rather tasteless, the inside was decorated in Neo-Student-Activist style. Yellowing posters covered most of the walls in the front hallway, featuring personalities as diverse as Martin Luther King and Jane Fonda. The newest of the posters, and it was already fading, demanded U.S. OUT OF BRAZIL! NO MORE EL SALVADORS! A library table stood to one side, heaped high with pamphlets. I glanced at them. Everything from abortion to disarmament, but none of them mentioned the fusion laboratory.

Doors were open on the right and left of the hallway. I looked left first, but the big high-ceilinged room was devoid of people. A couple of old sofas, three tattered Army cots, a big square table with a battered, well-worn word processor on it. But no people.

I tried the room on the right. A bright-looking young woman was sitting behind an ultramodern portable telephone switchboard, which rested incongruously on a heavy-legged, ornate Victorian mahogany table. She had an earphone and pin-mike combination clamped over her short-cropped blonde hair. Without breaking her conversation into the microphone, she waved me into the room and pointed to one of the rickety plastic chairs that lined the wall.

I remained standing and waited until she finished her conversation. My mind wandered, my attention shifted, and I saw Aretha's serious, finely chiseled face once more, her midnight-dark hair, her luminous gray eyes. I shut off the image in my mind and forced myself to concentrate on the gum-chewing girl at the switchboard.

The blonde ended her phone conversation and

looked up at me. Their phones had no picture screens, I saw.

"Welcome to STOPP," she said cheerfully. "What can we do for you, Mr. . . . er . . . ?"

"Orion," I said. "I want to see the chief of this operation."

Her pert young smile clouded over. "You from the city? Fire Marshal?"

"No. I'm from the CTR facility. The fusion lab."

"Oh!" That took her by surprise. The enemy in her boudoir.

"I want to see the head person around here."

"Don Maddox? He's in class right now."

"Not him. The one he works for."

She looked puzzled. "But Don's the chairperson. He organized STOPP. He's the . . ."

"Is he the one who decided to demonstrate against the fusion lab today?"

"Yes . . ." It was an uncertain answer.

"I want to know who put him up to it."

"Now wait a minute, mister . . ." Her hands began to fidget along the keyboard buttons. A barely discernible sheen of perspiration broke out along her upper lip. Her breathing was slightly faster than it had been a few moments earlier.

"All right, then," I said, easing off the pressure a little. "Who first suggested demonstrating at the fusion lab? It wasn't one of the students, I know."

"Oh, you mean Mr. Davis." She sat up straighter. Her voice took on a ring of conviction. "He's the one who woke us up about your fusion experiments and all the propaganda you've been laying on the people."

There was no point arguing with her. Davis. I had to smile to myself. With just the slightest change in pronunciation it came up *Daevas*, the gods of evil in the old Zoroastrian religion.

"Mr. Davis," I agreed. "He's the one I want to see."

"Why? Are you trying to arrest him or hassle him?" she asked.

I had to grin at her naivete. "If I were, would I tell you? No one was arrested at the lab this morning, were they?"

Shaking her head, she replied, "From what I heard, they had a goon squad out there to break heads."

"Really? I'd still like to see Davis. Is he here?"

"No." I could easily see that it was a lie. "He won't be around for a while. . . . He comes and goes."

With a shrug, I said, "Very well. Get in touch with him and tell him that Orion wants to see him. Right away."

"Mr. O'Ryan?"

"Orion. Just plain Orion. He'll know who I am. I'll wait outside in my car. It's parked right in front of the house."

She frowned. "He might not be back for a long while. Maybe not even the rest of the week."

"You just get in touch with him and give him my name. I'll wait."

"Okay," she said, in a tone that implied, *but I think you're crazy.*

I waited in the car less than an hour. It was a cold, gray afternoon, but I adjusted easily enough to the chill. Clamp down on the peripheral blood vessels so that body heat isn't radiated away so fast. Step up the metabolic rate a little, burning off some of the fat stored in the body's tissues. This keeps the body temperature up despite the cold. I could have accomplished the same result by going to the corner and getting something to eat, but this was easier and I didn't want to leave the car. Too much could happen while my back was turned. I did get hungry, though. As I said, I'm no superman.

The blonde girl came out on the porch, shivering

in the cold despite the light sweater she had thrown
over her shoulders. She stared at my car. I got out
and she nodded at me. I followed her back into the
house. She was waiting in the hallway, her arms
clamped tightly across her small bosom.

"It's really cold out there!" she said, rubbing her
arms. "And you don't even have an overcoat!"

"Did you reach Davis?" I asked.

Nodding, she replied, "Yes. He . . . came in
through the back way. Down at the end of the hall.
He's waiting for you."

I thanked her and walked to the door at the end
of the hall. It opened onto a flight of steps leading
down to the cellar of the house. *A logical place for
him*, I thought, wondering how many legends of
darkness and evil he had spawned over the span of
millennia.

It was dark in the cellar. The only light came
from the hallway at the top of the stairs. I could
make out a bulky, squat, old-fashioned coal furnace
spreading its pipes up and outward like a giant
metal Medusa. Boxes, packing crates, odd-shaped
things hugged the shadows.

I took a few tentative steps into the dimness at
the bottom of the stairs and stopped.

"Over here." The voice was a harsh whisper.

Turning slightly, I saw him, a darker presence
among the shadows. He was big, almost my own
height, and very broad. Heavy, sloping shoulders;
thick, solid body; arms bulging with muscle. I
walked toward him. I could not see his face; the
shadows were too deep for that. He turned and led
me toward the furnace. I ducked under one of the
pipes. . . .

And was suddenly in a brightly lit room! I
squinted and staggered back half a step, only to
bump against a solid wall behind me. The room
was warmly carpeted, paneled in rich woods, furnished with comfortable chairs and couches. There

were no windows. No decorations on the walls.
And no doors. Not one.

"Make yourself comfortable, Orion," he said, gesturing to one of the couches. His hand was thick-fingered, blunt and heavy.

I sat down and studied him as he slowly eased his bulk into a soft leather armchair.

His face was not quite human. Close enough so that you might not look twice at him on the street. But when you examined him carefully, you saw that the cheekbones were too widely spaced, the nose too flat, and the eyes had a reddish cast to them. His eyes! They smoldered; they seethed—they radiated a constant torment of fury—and, looking deeper, I could see other things in his eyes: implacable hatred and, mixed with it, something else, something I could not fathom. It made no difference to me. The hatred was there, burning in his eyes. Just as it was in mine.

His hair was dark and cropped close to his skull. His skin had a grayish pallor. He wore denims and a light shirt, open at the neck. He was as muscular as a professional weightlifter.

"You are Ahriman," I said at last.

His face was grim, mirthless. "You don't remember me, of course. We have met before." His voice was a whisper, like a ghost's, or like the tortured gasping of a dying man.

"We have?"

With a ponderous nod of his head: "Yes. But we are moving in different directions through time. You are moving back toward The War. I am moving forward toward The End."

"The War? The End?"

"Back and forth are relative terms in time travel. But the truth is that we have met before. You will come to those places in time and remember that I told you. If you live."

"You're trying to destroy the fusion reactor," I said.

He smiled, and it was not a pleasant thing to see. "I am trying to destroy your entire race."

"I'm here to stop you."

"You may succeed." He placed a slight, ironic stress on *may*.

"Ormazd says that I will . . . that I already have succeeded." I didn't mention the part about being killed. Somehow, I couldn't. That would make it true. That would give him strength and rob me of it.

"Ormazd knows many things," Ahriman said slowly, "but he tells you only a few of them. He knows, for example, that if I prevent you from stopping me this time . . ."

This time! Then there have been other times!

". . . then not only will I destroy your entire race of people, but I will smash the fabric of the space-time continuum and annihilate Ormazd himself."

"You want to kill us all."

Those red, pain-wracked eyes bored into me. "Kill every one of you, yes. I want to bring down the pillars of the universe. *Everything* will die. Stars, planets, galaxies . . . everything." His massive fists clenched. He believed what he said. He was making me believe it.

"But why? Why do you want to . . ."

He silenced me with a stare. "If Ormazd has not told you, why should I?"

I tried to see past his words, but my mind struck an utterly implacable wall.

"I will tell you this much," Ahriman whispered. "This fusion reactor of yours is a nexus point in your race's development. If you make the fusion process work, you will be expanding out to the stars within a generation. *I will not allow you to accomplish that.*"

"I don't understand."

"How could you?" He leaned closer to me, and I could smell the odor of ashes and death upon him. "This fusion machine, this CTR as you call it, is the key to your race's future. If it is successful, fusion will supply limitless energy for you. Wealth and plenty for all. Your people could stop playing with their puny chemical rockets and start building real starships. They could expand throughout the galaxy."

"They *have* done so," I realized.

"Yes they have. But if I can change the nexus here, at this point in time, if I can destroy that fusion reactor . . ." He smiled again. And I shuddered.

I tried to pull myself together. "The failure of one machine can't kill the entire human race."

"Yes, it can, thanks to the manic nature of your kind. When the fusion reactor explodes . . ."

"It can't explode!" I snapped.

"Of course not. Not under ordinary circumstances. But I have access to extraordinary means. I can create a sudden surge of power from the lasers. I can cause a detonation of the lithium shielding that surrounds the reactor's ignition chamber. Instead of a microgram of deuterium being fused and giving off a puff of energy, a quarter ton of lithium and heavier metals will explode."

"They can't . . ."

"Instead of a tiny, controlled, man-made star radiating energy in a controlled flow, I will create an artificial supernova, a lithium bomb. The explosion will destroy Ann Arbor totally. The fallout will kill millions of people from Detroit to New York."

I sagged back, stunned.

"Even if your leaders are wise enough to recognize that this is an accident and not a nuclear attack, even if they refrain from launching their missiles at their enemies, your people will react violently against fusion power. Their earlier protests which closed all the uranium fission power plants will seem like child's play compared to their reaction to this disaster. There will be an end to all nuclear research everywhere. You will never get fusion power. Never."

"Even so, we will survive."

"Will you? I have all the time in the world to work with. I can be patient. As the years go by, your growing population will demand more and more energy. Your mighty nations will struggle against each other for possession of petroleum, coal, food resources. There will be war, inevitably. And for war, you have fusion devices that *do* work—H-bombs."

"Armageddon," I said.

He nodded that massive head in triumph. "At the time when you should be expanding outward toward the stars, you will destroy yourselves with nuclear war. This planet will be scoured clean of life. The fabric of space-time itself will be so ruptured that the entire continuum will collapse and die. Armageddon, indeed."

I wanted to stop him, to silence him. I wanted to kill him just as he had killed Aretha. I leaped for his throat, snarling. He was real, no hologram. And he was incredibly strong. He brushed me aside easily, knocking me to the floor as if I were a child.

Standing over me like the dark force of doom, he said in his harsh, whispering voice, "Despite what Ormazd has told you, I will succeed in this. You will die, Orion. Here. You are trapped in this chamber, while I shall destroy your fusion machine."

"But why?" I asked, climbing slowly back to the couch. "Why do you want to wipe out the human race?"

He stood for a moment, glaring at me with those burning eyes. "You really don't know, do you? He never told you . . . or he erased your memory of it."

"I don't know," I said. "Why do you hate the human race?"

"Because you wiped out *my* race," Ahriman answered, his harsh voice nearly strangling on the words. "Millennia ago, your people killed mine. You annihilated my entire species. I am the only one of my kind left alive, and I will avenge my race by destroying yours—and your masters as well."

The strength left me. I sat weakly on the couch, unable to challenge him, unable to move.

"And now, good-bye," Ahriman said. "I have work to do before the first test run of your fusion reactor. You will remain here. . . ." He gestured around the tiny room. It had no doors or windows. No exits or entrances of any kind. *How did we get in here?* I wondered.

"If I succeed, it will all be over in a few hours," Ahriman said. "Time itself will begin to falter and the universe will fall in on itself like a collapsing balloon. If I fail, well . . ." that ghastly smile again, ". . . you will never know it. This chamber will be your tomb. Or, more properly, your crematorium."

"Where are we?" I asked.

"Thirty miles underground, in a temporary bubble of safety and comfort created by warping the energies of the atoms around us. Think about that as you burn—you are only a step away from the house in Ann Arbor. One small step for a man, if he truly understands the way the universe is constructed."

He turned abruptly and walked *through* the wall and disappeared.

CHAPTER 7

For long minutes I sat on the couch unmoving, my body numb with shock, my mind spinning in turmoil.

You wiped out my race . . . your people killed mine . . . and I will avenge my race by destroying yours— and your masters as well.

It couldn't be true. And what did he mean by his talk of the two of us moving on different time tracks, of having met before? Your masters? What did he mean by that? Ormazd? But he said masters, plural. Is Ormazd the representative of a different race, an alien race from another world that controls all of humankind? Just as Ahriman is the last survivor of an alien race that we humans battled so long ago?

How many times had we met before? Ahriman said that this point in time, this first test of the fusion reactor, marked a nexus for the human race. If it succeeds, we will use fusion energy to reach out to the stars. If it fails, we will kill ourselves within a generation. There must have been other nexuses back through time, many of them.

Somewhere back along those eons there was a war, The War, between the human race and Ahriman's kind. When? Why? How could we fight invaders from another world back in the past, thousands of years ago?

All these thoughts were bubbling through my

brain until finally my body asserted itself on my conscious awareness.

"It's getting hot in here," I said aloud.

My attention snapped to the present. To this tiny cell. The air was hot and dry. My throat felt raw. The room was now hot enough to make me sweat.

I got up and felt the nearest wall. It was almost too hot to touch. And although it looked like wood paneling, it felt like stone. It was an illusion, all of it.

One small step for a man . . . if he truly understands the way the universe is constructed.

I understood nothing. I could remember nothing. All I could think of was that Ahriman was back on Earth's surface, up in Ann Arbor, working to turn the CTR into a mammoth lithium bomb that would trigger the destruction of the human race. And I was trapped here, thirty miles underground, about to be roasted like a sacrificial lamb on a spit.

You are only a step away from the house in Ann Arbor, he had said. Was that a lie? A joke? His idea of a cruel taunt?

"One small step for a man," I muttered to myself. How *is* the universe constructed? It's made of atoms. And atoms are made of smaller particles, tiny bits of frozen energy that can be made to thaw and flow and surge . . .

This room had been created by warping the energies of the atoms in the Earth's crust. Those energies were now reverting back to their natural form; slowly the room was turning back into hot, viscous rock. I could feel the air congealing, becoming hotter and thicker by the second. I would be imbedded in rock thirty miles below the surface, rock hot enough to be almost molten.

Yet I was only a step from safety, according to Ahriman. Was he lying? No, he couldn't have been. *He* had walked directly through the rock wall of this room. He must have returned to the cellar of the house in Ann Arbor. If he could do it, so could I. But how?

I already had! I had stepped from the cellar into this underground dungeon. Why couldn't I step back again?

I tried doing it and got nothing but bumps against solid rock for my efforts. There was more to it than simply trying it.

But wait. If I had truly traveled thirty miles through solid rock in a single step, it must mean that there is a connection between that house and this chamber. Not only are the atoms of Earth's crust being warped to create this cell, but the geometry of space itself is being warped to bridge the thirty-mile distance.

I sat on the couch again, my mind racing. I had read magazine articles about space warps, speculations about how someday starships would be able to fly thousands of lightyears almost instantaneously. Astrophysicists had discovered "black holes" in interstellar space that warped space-time with their titanic gravitational fields. It was all a matter of geometry, a pattern, like taking a flat sheet of paper and folding it into the form of a bird or a flower.

And I had seen that pattern! I had gone through it on my way into this chamber. But it had happened so quickly that I could not consciously remember it in detail.

Or could I?

Data compression. Satellites in orbit can accumulate data on magnetic tapes for days on end, and then spurt it all down to a receiving station on the ground within a few seconds. The compressed data is then played at a much slower speed by the technicians, and all the many days' worth of information is intact and readable.

Could I slow down my memory to the point

where I could recall, miscrosecond by microsecond, what had happened to me during that one brief stride from the house to this underground tomb? I leaned back on the couch and closed my eyes. It was getting more and more difficult to breathe, but I tried to ignore the burning in my chest and concentrate on remembering.

A thirty-mile stride. A step through solid rock. I pictured myself in the cellar of that house. I had ducked under a heating pipe and stepped into darkness. . . .

And cold. The first instant of my step I had felt a wave of intense cold, as if I had passed through a curtain of liquefied air. Cryogenic cold. Cold so intense that atoms are frozen almost motionless, at nearly absolute zero temperature.

In those few microseconds of unbearable cold I saw that the crystal structure of the atoms around me had indeed been frozen, almost entirely stilled. All around me the atoms glowed dully like pinpoints of jeweled lights, faint and sullen because nearly all their energies had been leached away from them. The crystal latticework of the atoms had formed a path for me, a tunnel wide enough for my body to take that thirty-mile-long step in a single stride.

I opened my eyes. The tiny room was glowing now; the air itself seemed afire. I held my breath, wondering how long my body could function on the oxygen stored within its cells and in my blood.

I understood how I had gotten here. There was a crystal latticework of energy connecting this crypt with the house in Ann Arbor—a tunnel that connected *here* with *there*, using the energies stolen from the atoms in between to create a safe and almost instantaneous path between the two places. But the tunnel was dissolving just as this room was dissolving. The energies of those tortured atoms was returning to normal. In seconds all would be solid rock once again.

How to find the opening into that tunnel? I concentrated again, but no sense of it came through to me. I was sweating, both from the intense heat and from the effort of forcing myself to understand. But it did no good at all. My brain could not comprehend it.

My brain could not . . . *Wrong!* I realized that I had so far been using only half my brain to attack the problem. I remembered Ormazd telling me that I could consciously employ both hemispheres simultaneously, something that ordinary human beings cannot do. I had been using one hemisphere to visualize the geometric pattern of the energy warp that connected this underground chamber with the surface. But that half of my brain could *only* perceive geometrically those relationships involving space and form.

With a conscious effort I forced the other hemisphere of my brain to consider the problem. I could almost hear myself laugh inside my head as the unused portion of my mind said something like, "Well, it's about time."

And it was about time. The solution to the problem of finding the gateway to the crystal latticework of atoms was a matter of timing. All those dully glowing atoms were still vibrating slowly, unnaturally slowly, because most of their energies had been drained from them. But still they vibrated. Only when they had all moved to a certain precise formation was their alignment such that the tunnel's entrance could open. Most of the time they were shifted out of phase, as unaligned and jumbled as a crowd milling through a shopping mall. But once every second they reached precisely the correct arrangement to open the tunnel that led back to safety. The arrangement dissolved within a few microseconds.

Only during that incredibly tiny moment of time

was the tunnel open. I had to step into the crystal latticework, through the searing hot wall of the chamber, at precisely the exact moment—or not at all.

I got to my feet and forced myself close to the wall. The heat was enough to singe the hair of my eyebrows and the backs of my hands. I kept my eyes closed, picturing with one side of my brain the crystal pathway itself, while simultaneously calculating with the other side of my brain the precise moment when the lattice would be open for me to step through.

With my eyes still closed I took a step forward. I felt an instant of roasting heat, then cold beyond the most frigid ice fields of Antarctica. Then . . .

I opened my eyes. I stood in the shadowy cellar of the STOPP house. For the first time in what seemed like years, I let out my breath and took in a double lungful of sweet, cool air.

I found a back door to the cellar and stepped out into the cold night. It felt wonderful. An alley led between the house and its next-door neighbor to the street. My rented car was still there, adorned with a yellow parking ticket affixed to its windshield wiper. I stuffed the ticket into my jacket pocket and got behind the wheel, glad that no one had towed the car away or stolen it.

It took me ten minutes to get back to the fusion lab. Once in the deserted lobby of the building, I phoned for Tom Dempsey, Mangino the security chief, and the lab's director of research. It was close to midnight, but the tone of my voice must have convinced them that something important was happening. I got no arguments from any of them, although the phone's computer had to try three different numbers before it located Dr. Wilson, the research director.

They all arrived in the lab within a half-hour— thirty minutes during which I checked personally with every security guard on duty. No one had reported the slightest problem. They were on constant patrol around the laboratory, inside and out, and everything appeared to be quite normal.

Dr. Wilson was a lanky, ruddy-faced, tousle-haired Englishman who spoke softly and seemed totally unflappable. He arrived first. As I was explaining that somebody would try to detonate the fusion reactor—and he smiled tolerantly at the ridiculous idea—Dempsey and the security chief came into the lobby together. Dempsey looked more puzzled than upset. His dark hair was an uncombed, tangled mop; he must have been asleep when I called and pulled his clothes on helter-skelter. Mangino was definitely angry. His narrow brown eyes snapped at me.

"This is a lot of hysterical nonsense," he growled, when I explained my fears. I didn't tell them about Ormazd and Ahriman, of course, nor about the underground chamber I'd just escaped from. It was enough to convince them that a real danger existed. I didn't want them to bundle me off to a psychiatric ward.

Dr. Wilson tried to tell me that the reactor simply could not explode. I let him talk; the longer he explained, the longer we stayed on the scene, available to counter Ahriman's move.

"There simply is not enough deuterium in the reactor at any given moment to allow an explosion," Wilson repeated in a his soft, friendly voice. He sat slouched on one of the plastic couches that decorated the lab's lobby. I stood by the receptionist's desk. Dempsey had stretched out on another couch and apparently had gone back to sleep. Mangino was behind the desk, checking out his security patrols on the picture phone.

"But suppose," I stalled for more time, "there was a way to boost the power of the lasers . . ."

"They'd burn out in a minute," Wilson said. "We're running them at top capacity now."

". . . and an extra amount of deuterium was put into the reaction chamber."

Wilson shook his head, and a mass of sandy hair flopped down over his eyes. Pushing it back with one hand, he told me, "That simply cannot happen. There are fail-safe circuits to prevent it. And even if it did, all that would happen is that you would get a mild little poof of a detonation—not a hydrogen bomb."

"What about a lithium bomb?" I asked.

For the first time, his eyebrows knit worriedly. "What do you mean?"

"If things worked out the right way, couldn't the deuterium detonation trigger the lithium in the shielding around the reaction chamber?"

"No, no. That would be impos—" He checked himself, hesitated, then said slowly, "That would be very unlikely. *Very* unlikely. I'd have to work out the calculations, of course, but the chances against that must be . . ."

"Twenty-four, *report*." Mangino's razor-sharp voice sliced into our conversation.

I turned and looked at the security chief. He was frowning angrily into the phone's picture screen. "Dammit, Twenty-four, answer me!"

He looked up at me, as if I were responsible. "One of the guards outside doesn't respond. He's supposed to be patrolling the area around the loading dock."

"The loading dock!" Wilson shot to his feet. I could see that he had started to tremble.

Mangino held up a hand. "Don't get excited, now. I've got the area on one of the outside TV cameras. Everything looks normal. Just no sign of the guard. He might be taking a leak or something."

I went around the desk and peered at the TV screen. The loading bay was brightly lit. There were no cars or trucks anywhere in sight. All seemed quiet and calm.

"Let's take a walk down there anyway," I said.

We roused Dempsey and told him to stand guard over the phones and TV screens. He rubbed his eyes sleepily but nodded okay. Then Dr. Wilson, Mangino and I hurried down the building's central corridor toward the loading dock. Mangino reached inside his coat and pulled out a slim, flat, dead-black pistol. He flicked the safety off and then slipped it into his jacket pocket.

Lights turned on automatically ahead of us as we hustled along the corridor, and switched off behind us. The loading bay was a miniature warehouse: stacks of cardboard cartons, steel drums, packing cases, strange-looking equipment wrapped in clear plastic.

"You could hide a platoon of men in here," Mangino grumbled.

"But everything seems to be in order," Wilson said, glancing around. I started to agree, but felt the slightest trace of a breeze on my face. It came from the direction of the loading dock doors, big metal roll-up doors that were closed and locked tight. Or were they? I walked slowly toward the hangar-like doors and saw that a man-sized doorway had been cut into one of them. A person could slip in or out without needing to raise the entire rig. This smaller door was windowless. And shut. I reached for its handle.

"It's locked," Mangino said. "Electronic time lock. If anybody tries to tamper with it . . ."

I touched the handle and the door swung open effortlessly. Mangino gaped.

Kneeling, I saw that the area around the edge of the lock had been bent slightly, as if massive hands had pried it open, bending the metal until it yielded. I had felt the stray breeze through the bent area.

"Why didn't the alarm go off?" Mangino wondered aloud.

"Never mind that," I said. "He's inside the lab! Quick; we don't have a second to lose!"

We ran to the fusion reactor area, Wilson protesting all the way that no one could tamper with the lasers or the reactor to cause an explosion.

The doors to the laser control room had been pulled off their hinges. A quick look inside showed that no one was in there. The control boards seemed untouched. While Wilson inspected them, Mangino yelled into his palm-sized radio, "All security guards converge on the reactor area. Apprehend anyone you see. Shoot if they resist. Call the local police and the F.B.I. at once!"

We entered the big double doors that led to the long, cement-walled room where the lasers were housed. Again the overhead lights snapped on automatically as we crossed the doorway.

"Those doors should have been locked," Dr. Wilson said, an edge of alarm in his voice.

The lasers were long, thin glass rods, dozens of them, mounted on heavy metal stands, one over another like a series of parallel gymnasium bars. Every ten feet or so the glass rods were interrupted by groupings of lenses, Faraday rotators, and diagnostic sensors. The multiple line of lasers marched down the length of the long room and focused on a narrow slit cut into a thick, steel-reinforced cement wall. On the other side of that wall was the reactor itself, where the energy from the lasers was concentrated on micropellets of deuterium fuel.

The three of us stood there uncertainly for a moment. Then suddenly an electrical hum began vibrating through the air. I caught a whiff of ozone, and the laser tubes began to glow with an eerie, uncanny greenish light.

"They're turning on!" Wilson gasped.

CHAPTER 8

Mangino and I swung our attention to the far end of the room, where the control center was. In the shadows back there, behind thick protective glass, bulked the heavy, dark form of Ahriman.

Mangino pulled out his pistol and fired. The glass starred. He emptied the gun, finally shattering the glass. But in those few seconds Ahriman was gone.

The lights went out. All we could see was the brightening glow of the lasers, multiple paths of intensifying energy aimed at the slit and, beyond it, the reactor core. We stumbled out into the hallway. It was dark everywhere. For all I knew, Ahriman had caused a blackout throughout the region to pour power into the blazing lasers.

Over the whining hum of the electric generators I heard running footsteps. Then shots.

"They've got him!" Mangino yelled. But to me it sounded as if the running and shooting were going in the direction away from us. The sounds grew fainter. They hadn't caught Ahriman, I knew.

"I'm going after him," Mangino said, and he sprinted off into the darkness.

"We've got to turn off the lasers," I told Wilson, "before they build up enough power to set off the lithium."

In the eerie green light from the open doorway,

his eyes looked wide with fright. "That can't happen!" he insisted.

"Let's turn them off anyway," I said.

He didn't argue. We went to the laser control room, only to find that the equipment was a shambles. The control consoles had been smashed, dials shattered, metal paneling bent out of shape. Wires sagged limply from broken modules. It was as if an elephant had gone berserk inside the tiny room. And through the smashed window, we could see that the lasers were pulsing now, their light growing more intense, feverish.

Wilson's jaw hung slackly. "How could anyone . . ."

The electrical whine of the generators suddenly went up in pitch several notches and the lasers began to glow even more fiercely. I heard a glass lens pop somewhere down on the floor of the room. The light was becoming painful to the eye. I pulled Wilson away from the shattered controls and together we staggered down the darkened hallway toward the reactor chamber.

"How do we turn the thing off?" I shouted over the generators' insane shrieking.

He seemed dazed, bewildered. "The deuterium feed . . ."

"That's been tampered with too, I'll bet. We won't be able to turn it off any more than we can turn off the lasers."

He shook his head and ran a hand through his unruly hair. In the garish green light he looked sickly, deathly ill.

"Main power supply," he mumbled at last. "I could get to the main switches and shut down everything."

"Good! Do it!"

"But it will take time. Ten minutes. Five, at least."

"Too long! By then it'll be too late. It's going to blow up in another minute or two!"

"I know."

"What else can we do?" I had to shout to make myself heard over the screaming of the generators.

"Nothing!"

"There's got to be *something* . . ."

"Damper," he shouted at me. "If we could place a damper inside the reactor chamber to block off the laser light . . ."

I understood. Cut off the light that the lasers were pouring into the deuterium fuel pellets and the reactor would shut down.

"A damper," I yelled at Wilson. "All right. You find the main power switches. I'll find a damper."

"But there's no way . . ."

"Get moving!" I shouted.

"You can't go inside the reactor! The radiation would kill you in less than a minute!"

"Go!"

I pushed him away from me. He stumbled off, then hesitated as I yanked open the door to the reactor room.

"For god's sake . . . don't!" Wilson screamed.

I ignored him and stepped inside.

The room was round and domed, low and cramped, like a womb made of cement and steel and bathed in the hellish green fury of the laser light. The fetus in its center was a five-foot-wide metal ball surrounded by coiling pipes that carried lithium coolant to the spherical core. It looked like a bathysphere, but it had no portholes in it. There was no way to interrupt the laser beams from outside that sphere; they were linked to it by a thick quartz light pipe. I couldn't break the pipe without tools, even if I had the time to try.

There was one hatch in the core's sphere. Without taking the time to think about it, I yanked it open. The overwhelming intensity of light and blazing heat slammed me back against the wall. A man-made star was running amok inside that chamber, getting ready to explode.

My burning eyes squeezed shut, I groped for the searingly hot edges of the metal hatch and forced myself inside the chamber. I put my body in front of the laser beams.

I learned what hell is like.

Pain. Searing agony that blasts through your skull even after your eyes have been burned away. Agony along every nerve, every synapse, every pathway of your entire body and mind. All the memories of my existence stirred into frantic, terrified, gibbering reality. Past and present and future fused together. I saw them all melting and flowing in that single instant of soul-shattering pain, that eternally long, infinitesimal flash of time.

I stood naked and burning, skin flayed from my flesh as my mind saw yesterdays and tomorrows.

A newspaper headline blared ATTEMPT TO SABOTAGE FUSION LABORATORY FAILS.

A puzzled team of F.B.I. agents and scientists searching for some trace of my body as Dr. Wilson is wheeled into an ambulance, catatonic with shock.

Ahriman's dark presence brooding over my horizon of time, his red eyes glowering with hate as he plans his revenge.

Ormazd shining against the darkness of infinity, glowing in the depths of interstellar space, powerful, commanding, moving the chesspieces of an entire universe of space-time across the landscape of eternity.

And me. Orion. The Hunter. I see all my pasts and futures. At last I know who I am, and what, and why.

I am Orion. I am Prometheus. I am Gilgamesh. I am Zarathustra. I am the Phoenix who dies and is consumed and rises again from his own ashes only to die once more.

From fifty thousand years in Earth's future I

have hunted Ahriman. This time he escaped me, although I have thwarted his plans. Humankind will have fusion power. We will reach the stars. That nexus has been passed successfully, just as Ormazd told me it would be. It required my death, but the fabric of the space-time continuum has not been broken.

I have died. Yet still I live. I exist, and my purpose is to hunt down Ahriman wherever and whenever he is.

The hunt continues.

INTERLUDE

To mortal eyes the place might have looked like an impressionist's view of Olympus, or Valhalla, or the Heaven that Christians prayed to reach.

There were no visible limits to it; soft clouds and calm, sweet blue sky extended toward infinity in every direction. Straight overhead the sky darkened just enough to show a few scattered stars, unblinking pinpoints of light that never moved from zenith. Time itself was meaningless here. No planet rotated underfoot. No sun or moon swung across the changeless sky. Yet the air was bright, suffused with a soft light that had no visible source.

If a human being ever saw this place, it would remind him or her of being at the peak of a high mountain, above the cares and needs of the world, above the clouds that bring storm and turmoil, looking out across the clean, still air of a realm of endless calm and beauty. A domain far beyond the world of ephemeral mortals who are born in pain, struggle all their brief years, and then are snuffed out like the flickering flame of a candle.

Somewhere in this trackless realm of clouds and sky, a pinpoint star of light detached itself from the high heavens and moved downward, swelling into a globe of golden radiance until it almost touched the upper swirls of the clouds. It glowed brilliantly, but without heat, as it moved swiftly across the cloud tops and finally came to rest, for no outwardly discernible reason. Slowly the globe wavered, shimmered, contracted until it had formed the image of a man, a youthful, yet fully adult human being, handsome as a god, tall and broad-shouldered, with a thick mane of golden hair and eyes the color of a lion's tawny coat. His robe was golden, trimmed with an intricate tracery of thin red lines, like a pattern of blood vessels.

He sat on a billowing cloud, reclining like an emperor of old against cushions of cumulus, his majestic face set in intense concentration, as if he were watching something that no mortal eye could follow. How long he sat that way, it is impossible to say, for time had no meaning here.

Presently a smaller glowing sphere appeared near him, shining silver and pulsating slowly. It contracted to form a human female, a woman of lustrous dark hair and deep gray eyes, as beautiful as the golden man was handsome. Her robe was of silver mesh, metallic and glittering.

"You are becoming fond of the human form?" she asked.

The man looked up at her, unsmiling. "It seems to help me to understand them, to feel the way they feel."

"You enjoy being a god."

The man said nothing.

"Shall I call you by the name you have chosen to have them call you?" She seemed amused, almost. But beneath her words there was irony. Her lips smiled, but her gray eyes probed him coldly.

He turned away from her unblinking gaze. "You will call me whatever you wish to, won't you?"

"Ormazd," she said. "The God of Light. How modest you are with your toys."

"And what should I call you?"

She thought a moment. "Anya. That's a pretty

name. As long as we are being human, you may call me Anya."

"You're taking this all very lightly," Ormazd said.

"Not at all," replied Anya, her bantering tone gone. "I know how serious it is. I have felt what *they* feel. The terror. The pain. The incredible fear of dying—of becoming . . . *nothing*."

"You didn't have to go. I didn't want you to go."

"No, you would have activated your warrior and flung him against the Dark One by himself, without a friend, without a hope, without even memories."

"None of them understand. Why should he have been different?"

"But they *do* understand!" Anya said. "In their own dim way they perceive that a struggle is going on, that they are caught as pawns between powers far greater than they are."

Ormazd shook his golden-maned head. "They understand only what I want them to understand."

"Not so," she insisted. "Look at their scientists, how they are organizing knowledge of the universe. They are on the verge of learning the true nature of space-time . . ."

"Never. They still think of time as sequential. They still believe that cause must always precede effect."

She laughed. "Look more closely, O God of Light. Your toys are beginning to penetrate the mysteries that surround them."

"Then I'll have to change things. They mustn't learn too much. Not yet."

"No! Don't! Let them learn. You can't treat them so callously."

He stared at her. "I can treat them in whatever manner I like. I created them. They are mine."

"But you cannot control them."

"Nonsense."

"Admit it," Anya insisted. "They are slipping beyond your grasp."

"I control them."

"You built curiosity into them. The thirst for knowledge."

"That was necessary," Ormazd said. "But I balanced it with fear of the unknown."

Anya's eyes glittered angrily. "Balanced? Not so, my godlike one. You have created a terrible tension within them. They are driven by curiosity, yet afraid of anything unfamiliar. They live their lives in torment, in agony."

The one who called himself Ormazd began to contradict her, but stopped before he uttered a word. He saw what she would say. She had allowed herself to be a human being, briefly, and she had felt what the rest of his creations felt.

With a sigh he took a different tack. "They believe that their gods are all-powerful, all-knowing. They blame me for their ills, for their own shortcomings."

"They also give you credit for being merciful," said Anya. "They want to believe that you love them."

He sighed again, more deeply, wearily.

"They realize that they have been created for a purpose," she went on, "but they grope in darkness to discover what that purpose might be. They *want* to serve you, but they don't know what you expect of them."

Ormazd rose to his golden-booted feet. The radiance of his energy made the clouds glow.

"They served their purpose, ages ago. Now if the Hunter will accomplish his task . . ."

"Then you will have won it all," she said. "Then we will be safe."

"And then I can get rid of all of them, at last."

"You cannot eliminate them!"

He arched an eyebrow. "Cannot? *I* cannot?"

"Dare not," Anya corrected. "You know that our fate is inextricably linked to theirs. Creatures and creator, we all share the same continuum. If *they* are eliminated, we will cease to exist also."

"Surely you don't believe that."

"I know that it is true. Why would you have allowed them to remain, otherwise? You created them to defeat the Dark One. They did that ages ago. . . ."

"Not completely. He still exists."

"Yes." She shuddered. "And as long as he does, you need the humans, don't you? As long as the Lord of Darkness still eludes you, the humans are necessary. Your army of warriors. Your bodyguard. Your suicide squad."

"I created them to be warriors. I made them for that purpose."

"Yes, and did the job so well that when they have no one else to fight, they fight each other. They slaughter each other endlessly."

Ormazd shrugged carelessly. "Of what matter is that? There are billions of them now. They breed constantly. I built *that* into them, too. I gave them pleasure to balance out their pain."

"Again you speak of balance." Anya smiled bitterly. "I think you actually believe that you have been fair to them. Kind, even."

"They are only creatures. Toys, as you call them. I have no need to be kind or fair to them."

For long moments Anya said nothing, but her eyes showed that she was thinking furiously.

Ormazd reached out a golden-skinned hand toward her. Gently, he said, "There was no need for you to become one of them. I never meant for you to be as vulnerable as they are."

"But I did," she replied, as softly as he. "And now I can't forget it."

"My dearest one . . ."

"They're so . . . fragile," she said. "So full of hurt."

"They are very limited. You know that. I created them that way. I had to."

"Don't you feel any responsibility toward them?"

"Of course I do," he said.

"Do you know what they believe, some of them?" Before he could answer, she went on, "Some of their best philosophers believe that *they* created *us*. In their own dim, limited way, they are beginning to understand that we need them, that we cannot survive without them."

He gave a disgusted grunt. "Bah! Their philosophers have uttered every kind of wisdom and nonsense, in random order. They simply say everything that comes into their heads, and then call it intelligence."

"They are learning. And they try so hard, Ormazd! They create music, and paintings, and machines that will reach out to the stars."

"So much the better," he snapped. "That will make them more useful."

"But the knowledge they are gaining is bringing them great powers. They have weapons now that can wipe out the entire race."

"That will never happen," he said quickly.

"You are afraid it will."

"No. I will see to it that they do not kill themselves off completely."

"You built that aggressiveness into them. You made them a race of fighters, of killers."

Nodding, Ormazd admitted, "Of course. That is what I needed. Their aggressive nature is all-important."

"Even though it leads them to slaughter one another?"

"Even if they destroy their so-called civilization in nuclear war. So what? Some of them will survive. I will see to that. Their petty little civilizations have tumbled down before. The race survives. That's what is important."

"And the Dark One? I suppose, if you call yourself Ormazd, the God of Light, then he should be called Ahriman, the God of Darkness."

Ormazd bowed his head slightly, acknowledging her reasoning.

"Does he truly have the power to make an end of us?" she asked.

"He believes he does. He believes that if he can annihilate the humans, we will die along with them."

For the first time, Anya looked afraid. "Is that true? Can that happen?"

And for the first time, Ormazd appeared troubled. "I am not certain. The humans want to believe that they are the center of creation, the crux upon which the entire universe depends."

"Are you saying that they may be right?" she whispered.

"I don't know!" Ormazd shouted, his fists clenched in helpless anger. "How can anyone know? So much is hidden from us, so much is beyond our understanding!"

Strangely, Anya smiled. She stood before the gleaming, golden, angry God of Light, her smile widening until she threw her head back and laughed aloud.

"Then the humans are right! They don't need us. What have we given them except pain and grief?"

"I created them!"

"No, no, my would-be god. They created us. You may have molded them out of clay and breathed life into them, but you were doing it because they demanded it of you. They insisted on being created and you, and I, and all the would-be gods and goddesses are merely their servants."

"That's insane!" Ormazd insisted. "I *created* them! To serve *me*!"

Anya's laughter filled the air like the tinkling of a silver bell. "And you blame them for insisting on strict causality! Yes, you created them. But they created you, too. Cause and effect, effect and cause. Which came first?"

Ormazd stood there, stunned into silence.

"Does it matter?" Anya asked. Without waiting for an answer, she said, "Their struggle is our struggle. If they die, we die. We *must* help them. We have no choice."

Ormazd finally regained his voice. "I have been helping them," he insisted.

"Yes, by creating warriors to do your fighting for you, while you remain here, safe from all the pain and turmoil, pulling strings like a puppeteer."

"What would you have me do, go to them and make myself human?"

"Yes!"

"Never."

"I have done it."

"And died for it. Felt their agony and fear. Experienced death, just as they do."

"Yes, and I will do it again. And again. As often as necessary."

"Why?"

"To help them. To help *us*."

"You're mad."

"I love them, Ormazd."

He stared at her. "But they're only creatures!"

"Yes, but they're alive. Along with the pain and the grief and the frightening uncertainty of their lives, they also experience love and joy and kinship and adventure. They're *alive*, Ormazd! You made them better than you know. And I want to be one of them."

"Even though you'll have to experience death?"

"Even though I go through a hundred deaths. Or a thousand. Life is worth the price. Try it!"

"No." He took a step back away from her.

"You'll remain here while the rest of us struggle for the final victory?"

"I'll stay here," he said.

"The puppeteer." Her tone was mocking.

He drew himself to his full height. "The creator."

Anya laughed and, shimmering into a silver radiance, slowly faded from his view. He remained alone, suspended beyond space and time, wondering if the creatures he had made on that tiny world called Earth really bore the crux of the continuum on their shoulders.

Even the gods can weep, and as Ormazd stood there thinking about Earth and the strange convolutions that cause and effect can take, he began to feel very old and very much alone.

PART TWO:
ASSASSIN

CHAPTER 9

I opened my eyes and found myself standing in the Middle of a flat, empty wasteland. The soil was sandy, with scrubby patches of grass scattered here and there. The sky was cloudless, although a pall of smoke rose far off on the horizon to my right, climbing into the clear blue sky and spreading its dirty fingers outward. Something was burning. Something the size of a city, judging from the huge bulk of the smoky cloud.

The sun burned hotly on my bare shoulders. I was wearing a short skirt and a pair of sandals, nothing more. Not for an instant did I marvel that I was still alive. I remembered dying in the fusion reactor. I knew that I had not survived that inferno. This was another life. I felt strong, totally in command of myself, although my knees trembled when I thought of what I had gone through during those last few seconds back in the twentieth century.

Back in the twentieth century? Somehow I was certain that I was in a different era, an earlier time. Ahriman had said that I was proceeding through time in reverse, back from The End to The War. Although I knew he was the Prince of Lies, somehow I believed him about that.

Where was I? The desert scrubland all about me gave me no clue. The only sign of human activity was that immense pyre smoldering on the horizon. I started walking toward the tower of smoke, the

hot sun at my back throwing a lengthening shadow
before me as the weary hours wore on.

It was difficult to control my thirst. If I prevented myself from sweating, my internal body
temperature climbed to the point where I grew
dizzy and faint. But if I let my sweat glands do
their job and cool me, my body began to dehydrate.
To some extent I could draw moisture from the
plasma in my blood and from water stored in the
cells of my visceral organs, but that was a dangerous game that could lead to further, fatal dehy-
dration. Like any ordinary human being caught in
the merciless heat of the desert, I needed water.
And more desperately with each passing hour.

Off to my left I saw birds circling high in the
brazen sky. Vultures. Something, somebody, was
either dead or dying off in that direction. Animal
or human, whatever it was might have water—or
its corpse might be a source of it. I am no less
squeamish than the next man, but the desert
squeezes the fastidiousness out of you. A man dying
of thirst gives up pity before his own life.

The vultures circled lower as I stumbled over
rocks as hot as newly baked bread. Both of us were
scavengers in the merciless oven of the desert. Finally I saw what the birds had seen before me: a
family of refugees, stretched out dead on the dusty
soil; an overturned ox-cart a few yards away, with
a vulture perched on the rim of its useless wheel
and eying its prospective meal. The other birds
were swooping in low, spreading their angel-shaped
wings as they landed, making obscene sounds as
they waddled slowly toward the corpses.

I picked up a fist-sized rock, despite its searing
heat, and pegged it at the vulture on the wheel. It
hit him on the head like a rifle bullet, killing him
instantly. The other birds hardly seemed to notice,
until I threw three more rocks at them, hitting two
more of their number and finally alarming the rest

enough to make them flap angrily into the air, stirring up the dust as they departed.

The birds of death hovered above me, waiting with the patience of certainty, as I staggered toward the bodies. They had not died of thirst. The man was riddled with wounds, most of them in his back. The blood had barely congealed. It looked as if he had been shot with arrows, which his killers had then pulled out so that they could be used again. His wife and two children all had their throats sliced open. The woman, who could not have been much more than twenty years old, was stripped almost naked.

Whatever they had been carrying in the cart had been taken away; it was completely empty. The oxen were gone too. I could see the tracks of the animals in the dusty soil. Whoever had overtaken this pitiful little family placed more value on the beasts of burden than the human beings. There was no water, no possession of any kind among the four corpses. And I found that, despite my earlier certainty, I could not assault their wretched bodies any further to drink their blood, even though my life depended on it.

I squinted up at the glaring sky and saw the vultures still circling, watching silently. I wished I had the tools and the strength to bury these strangers. But I had neither. The vultures won. I turned back toward the pillar of smoke, stumbling across the stony desert, and left the filthy birds to their feast.

The day seemed to go on interminably, each moment hotter than the one before it. I walked for many hours, and still the smoke seemed no closer than it had been when I had first noticed it. Something deep inside my mind found the situation ludicrous enough to be almost funny. Certainly Ormazd had sent me here. Certainly something was going to happen at this time and place that

could alter the entire history of the universe;
Ahriman was going to make another attempt at
tearing space-time apart and destroying the continuum. And just as certainly, it seemed, I was
doomed to die ignominiously of thirst before I ever
got close to the task that Ormazd had sent me here
to perform.

And then I saw them.

Five—no, six—horsemen moving slowly across
the scrubland ahead of me. Their ponies were
lean and haggard, the riders themselves seemed
equally wiry. They wore pointed metal helmets
and carried long slim lances. Each of them also
had a small, double-curved bow and a curved sword
clinking at his side.

They saw me at almost the instant I spotted
them, stopped their ponies for a moment, then
nosed them in my direction. They approached
slowly, not out of wariness, but because they knew
that a half-naked, unarmed man on foot was not
going to escape them.

As they approached, I saw that they were oriental,
with the high cheekbones and flattened face of the
true Asian. Their skin, what little of it showed
outside their leather and metal armor, was a light
brownish tone, almost like the color of cured
tobacco. Their eyes were narrow, but not particu-
larly slanted. Mongol warriors, I thought, or perhaps some of the earliest Turks to invade the Middle
East from their original homeland in high Asia,
near Lake Baykal.

The six of them reined up about twenty yards in
front of me and eyed me as curiously as I inspected them. Their leader, the second rider from
the left, spoke to the others and I found, with a
slight shock, that I could understand their language.

"He doesn't look like the others."

"Perhaps he was one of their slaves, taken from
a different tribe."

"I've never seen anyone like that before. Look at the size of him! And his skin is pink . . . like a pig's, almost."

The rider on the leader's right gave a harsh laugh. "Maybe we should take him back to the Orkhon. He might reward us for finding such an unusual thing."

"Such a freak, you mean."

"He looks human enough, except for the strange color of him."

"His blood is red, I'll bet."

And with that, the rider who said it, the one just to the right of the leader, kicked his skinny pony's flanks and sprang into a gallop aimed right at me, swinging his lance down to aim it at my heart. The other horsemen sat calmly in their saddles to watch the sport, grinning.

My skin color might remind them of a pig's, but I had no intention of being spitted like one. I stood stock-still as the horse and lance-wielding rider dashed toward me, drawing up the little strength left in me. I could feel adrenaline surging through my body, making every sense hyper-alert. The horse and rider seemed to slow down, and I had time to notice the pony's wide eye staring fearfully at me, see its nostrils flaring as it sucked air. The tip of the rider's lance rode without a waver straight toward my heart, the barbarian horseman hunched forward in his saddle, holding the reins with his left hand, his mouth half-open in which might have been a grimace or a grin of anticipation.

At the right instant I made a toreador's sidestep, let the lance point slide harmlessly past me, grabbed the haft of the lance and jerked the astounded rider clean out of his saddle. He landed painfully on his shoulder as the horse, its head suddenly twisted around by the jerking of its reins, stumbled and thudded to the ground, raising a thick cloud of dust. The lance splintered, leaving me holding about three feet of its business end.

For a moment or two there was not a sound out of any of us. The dust drifted away and the horse scrambled to its feet and trotted a few yards away, its reins dragging in the dust. The other riders, I noticed, looked at the horse first, and only after they were satisfied that it was unhurt, did they return their attention to their companion, who got to his feet much more slowly than the pony did.

His left arm hung limply from the shoulder, but with a snarl he drew his curved saber and rushed at me before I could say anything to him. I parried his overhand cut with the shaft of the lance I still held, although his surprisingly powerful swing almost slashed all the way through the wood. As he raised his arm for another stroke, I kicked him in the midsection, doubling him over. Dropping the useless shaft of the lance, I wrested the sword from his hand and let him collapse to the ground, gasping for breath.

The leader of the little band wasted no words. He unslung his bow and notched an arrow to it. Pulling the string back to his chest, he let the arrow fly at me. I saw it all as if in slow-motion and used the sword to parry the steel-headed arrow in mid-air.

That stunned them. But not for long. They were hardened warriors, and they were not going to let an enemy escape them, no matter how well he fought. They simply began to edge their ponies around to form a circle around me. They knew as well as I did that I would not be able to parry arrows shot at me from five different directions.

"Wait!" I said. "I am not your enemy. I have come from a far place to see your Khan."

The warrior at my feet had gotten his wind back somewhat by then, and lifted himself to his knees, still sucking air through his wide-open mouth.

"I have not killed your friend, even though I

could have easily," I said to their leader. "I come in peace. I am not a warrior."

The leader eyed me suspiciously. "Not a warrior? Then god protect us from the warriors of your race!"

"I come in peace," I repeated. But I kept a firm grip on the sword.

"You speak our tongue."

"That is true. I seek your Khan, your leader."

His narrow-eyed face pinched into a thoughtful frown. "The Khan? The High Khan?"

"Yes."

"This man is a devil," said one of the other warriors. "Let's kill him." He unlimbered his bow.

"No," said the leader. "Wait."

I could see he was struggling furiously within himself to decide what to do. Barbarian warriors are seldom faced with such choices. I wondered if these six horsemen were the ones who had ravaged and killed the family I had seen earlier in the day. They seemed to be carrying no loot.

"Where are you from, stranger? What is your name?"

"I am called Orion," I said, "and I come from far to the west of here."

"From beyond the western mountains?" asked one of the warriors.

I nodded. "And beyond the seas that are beyond those mountains."

"You are an emissary, then?" the leader asked.

"Yes. An emissary from a distant land." I hoped that even barbarians treated emissaries with some vestige of diplomatic immunity.

"And you wish to see the High Khan." It was not a question.

"That is my mission," I said.

The warrior at my feet slowly got up, on legs that were still wobbly. His left arm was useless; probably the shoulder was broken. The kick I had given him would have felled a man twice his size, I knew. His midsection must be very sore; it obviously hurt him to breathe. He stared at me for a moment, then held out his empty right hand. I debated within myself for a moment, then handed him back his sword.

He took it, hefted it, smiled at me, then raised the sword over his head for a vicious slash at my neck. I stood unflinching, staring into his eyes. I knew that I had plenty of time to block his swing once he started it. This might be merely a test, or his attempt to show that he was uncowed by me.

His eyes probed mine, searching for the slightest sign of uncertainty or fear. I held my ground. The warrior's face was lean and hard; the thin white slash of a scar ran along his left cheek, down near the jaw. His leader, leaning both arms on the pommel of his high-peaked saddle, said nothing.

The warrior slowly brought his sword down until his arm hung at his side. Turning to the others, he shook his head. "He is a demon, not a true man."

The leader laughed. "He is a strange one, that is true. We will take him to the Orkhon and see what comes of him."

CHAPTER 10

They made me walk while they rode, but they were generous enough with their water. I drank from the leader's leather canteen, and then from the canteens of two of the other warriors, as the long, hot day slowly dragged to its conclusion.

We were in Persia, I was certain of that. And from the way these tough, scarred warriors spoke, they were most likely Mongols of the horde of Genghis Khan. This was the twelfth or thirteenth century, then, and these wild barbarian horsemen were ravaging the civilized world from Cathay to the plains of Poland.

I tried to ask the leader of this small troop a few questions, but he had gone silent. Apparently he had made up his mind to deliver me to higher authority, and he wished to be drawn into no further talk. He was a warrior, not a diplomat. But he had spared my life, and that was a good enough decision for this day, as far as I was concerned.

The sun touched the flat horizon of the desert and within minutes it was night. And cold. I clamped down on my body's surface capillaries and did what I could to keep myself warm, but I was not dressed for a desert night. The warriors took no notice of my shivering; they simply plodded along, with me walking beside the horse of their leader.

It was a city that had been burning all day long.

I never found out its name, but I recalled that the Mongols had no use for cities; being nomads, they preferred the open grazing lands that fed their horses and cattle. In war, if a city surrendered to them, they left it in peace, merely installing a Mongol overlord to collect taxes. If the city resisted, it was besieged until it fell; then it was methodically destroyed and all its inhabitants either killed or sent into slavery. Twentieth-century people thought that city-destroying nuclear weapons were something new under the sun; the Mongols razed cities by hand—burned them or took them apart stone by stone and in some cases even diverted rivers across the blackened foundations. And they murdered the inhabitants one by one, with swords and lances and arrows, after raping the women and pillaging every home. Of course, they also tortured anyone who looked rich enough to have hidden gold or other treasure. Compared to what I saw with my own eyes of the barbarian conquests, nuclear weapons at least have the blessing of being swift and impersonal.

The Mongol encampment was huge, even in the flickering lights of the campfires. Tents and round, felt-covered yurts—which looked like teepees mounted on ox-carts—stretched for acre upon acre across the barren ground. Thousands of horses snuffled and neighed in huge, roped-in corrals. You could smell them miles away. Women cooked in front of most of the tents, stirring heavy, black iron pots. Smoke rose from the central holes of most of the yurts, telling me that they had at least a primitive form of central heating.

The warriors marched me through what seemed like miles of the camp, through the maze of tents and yurts that had been laid out with no apparent order whatsoever. But they knew exactly where they were heading. Suddenly I saw that there was a large open space, ringed by fully armed guards, the firelight glinting off their steel helmets and jeweled sword hilts. My captors reined in their horses here. The leader dismounted and spoke swiftly to one of the guards, who cast me an utterly disbelieving look. But he nodded, and the leader of the little band of horse warriors quickly remounted his pony, grinning. The six of them galloped off, happy to be relieved of the responsibility of their strange prisoner.

The guard was obviously an officer accustomed to giving commands that were obeyed instantly.

"I am told you speak the tongue of the Gobi," he said. He was older, a trace of gray at his temples, but like the horsemen, he was almost fully a head shorter than I. Although his face was unmarred, across the back of his right hand there was a livid scar that disappeared beneath the leather cuff of his tunic. His voice was high; he would have made an excellent tenor.

"I understand your words," I answered.

"Your name is Orion; you come from beyond the western mountains, and you are an emissary sent to make submission to the High Khan."

"I have been sent to see the Khan, that is true."

He looked me over disdainfully. "You carry no gifts for him."

"The gifts I bear are here." I tapped my temple. Then, seeing the faintest flicker of a smile curl his lips, I realized that I was dealing with a very literal man. I added, "They are gifts of wisdom and knowledge, not jewels or fine pearls."

He almost looked disappointed. I believe he would have enjoyed splitting open my skull to examine it for hidden treasure.

With a shake of his head, he told me, "You cannot approach the Orkhon looking like a naked beggar. Come with me."

As I started to follow him, I said, "I have not eaten . . ." What should I say? I wondered. That I have had nothing to eat in eight centuries? ". . . for many days," I concluded.

He was like a minor officer in any army; everything displeased him, except for those important things which made him angry. Grunting and mumbling to himself, he led me to a campfire and told the woman there to feed me. I gulped a steaming bowlful of unidentifiable stew, hot enough to scald my tongue, and swilled it down with sour-tasting milk. By the time I was finished, the guard came back and dumped an armful of clothes on the ground beside me. Gratefully, I pulled on a pair of loose-fitting trousers, a rough shirt that was tight across my shoulders, and a shaggy leather coat.

The woman at the cook-pot, a straggle-haired crone who had lost most of her teeth, looked me over and laughed. "The clothes are too small. And you'll never find boots big enough for those feet."

The guard grunted. "That's his problem, not mine."

It was true. I was taller and broader than any of the Asians I had seen so far. The trousers he had given me had obviously belonged to a fat man; they were more than wide enough, but they ended halfway between my knees and ankles. I agreed with the old woman; there were probably no boots in the camp big enough to fit me. I did not care, though. I had sandals, and my new clothes were warm enough to make me feel almost comfortable, despite the itching, crawling feeling that I was not the only one living in them. Too, the crone's stew had warmed me. I was ready to face the Khan.

For more than an hour I was passed from one set of guards to another, questioned briefly by each new officer, and then sent on. The encampment, I was beginning to realize, was actually two separate camps, one within the other. In the center of the big, sprawling city of warriors and horses and camp followers was the true encampment of

the Mongol leader. The *ordu*, as they called it, was
a tent city within the larger camp where the staff
officers and royal guard were quartered. And at
the center of the ordu, in a huge tent of white silk
decked with banners and lit by huge bonfires, was
the tent of the Orkhon.

By the time I approached this magnificent central tent, I was flanked by two battle-hardened
officers who wore as much gold as steel on their
uniforms. A half-dozen warriors marched behind
me. We passed between the two big bonfires that
blazed into the dark sky as we neared the main
entrance to the white tent. I learned later that all
strangers are made to walk between those fires, on
the superstition that the heat will burn out any
devils that the stranger may harbor within him.

We were stopped at the entrance to the tent,
where two of the biggest guards I had seen searched
me swiftly and perfunctorily for weapons. These
men were almost my height, but were still as lean
and wiry as the other Mongols. Men who live in
the saddle and cross deserts and mountains on
their way to battle do not have the time to get fat.

Finally I was ushered inside the tent. I had expected oriental splendor, fine silks and Persian
carpets, wine goblets of gold encrusted with jewels,
and beautiful slave girls dancing for the conqueror
of the world. Strangely, the Orkhon was indeed
sitting on a magnificent carpet. The tent was hung
with silks and brocades. The men gathered there
were drinking from goblets heavy with precious
stones. Four women sat at the left of the Orkhon,
each of them young and slim and, I suppose, beautiful in the eyes of the Mongols. But the impression that all this gave me was not one of sybaritic
magnificence; the tent had the look of pragmatic
utility to it. The carpets and hangings kept out the
cold. The golden cups the men drank from were
booty from their battles; it seemed to me that they

were just as accustomed to drinking from leather canteens. The women—well, they too were the spoils of battle.

There was no air of decadence about the Orkhon's court. These were warriors, temporarily at rest. They had sacked and burned a city this day; tomorrow they would be on the march again, heading for the next city.

"You are called Orion?" said a tall, slim Oriental who stood at the Orkhon's right hand. He looked more Chinese than Mongol, and he wore a silk robe that covered him from neck to foot.

The officer at my side gave me a slight nudge. I took a step forward. "I am Orion," I said.

"Come forward so that my lord Hulagu may see thee more closely."

I walked slowly toward the Orkhon, who sat calmly on the silks and cushions that were his by right of conquest. He was a small man, even shorter than most of the others. His long hair was still jet black, and his body was just as slim and hard as any warrior's. I judged him to be no more than thirty-five years old. His face was utterly impassive, expressionless, his eyes fixed on me as I approached.

The Chinese raised one hand slightly and I stopped.

"You are an emissary from the West?" he asked, his voice still slightly sing-song, even though he spoke in the Mongol language.

"That is true," I answered.

"From where in the West?" asked the Mongol seated next to the Orkhon. He was older, graying, but even sitting upon the silken cushions, he vibrated eagerness and restless energy.

"From far beyond the western mountains," I said, "and beyond the seas that are beyond the mountains."

"From the land where the earth is black and

crops grow as thick as the hairs of your head?" he
asked, his eyes gleaming.

I guessed that he meant the Ukraine, the black-
earth granary of what would someday be Russia.

"From beyond even there, my lord," I replied,
thinking of space *and* time. "I come from a land
that is as distant from this place as we are distant
from Karakorum. Much, much farther."

The Mongol smiled. Distance meant nothing to
him. "Tell us of your distant land," he said.

But the Orkhon interrupted. "Enough talk of
distant lands, Subotai. The report says that this
man is a warrior of incredible strength."

Subotai. That was the name of a Mongol general,
I recalled. But the name that the Chinese gave for
the Orkhon, Hulagu, I did not recognize.

The energetic little general looked me up and
down. "He is a big one. But we were told he claims
to be an emissary, not a warrior."

"Still," said Hulagu, "the report is that he bested
a mounted warrior while he himself was afoot and
weaponless. And then he caught an arrow in his
bare hands when the *tuman* tried to kill him."

As usual, the report of my prowess had been
exaggerated. But Hulagu was obviously impressed
and looking forward to a demonstration. He ordered a bowman to stand across the tent from me.
The other warriors and officers cleared away from
the area behind me.

"My lord," I protested, "I did not catch an arrow in my bare hands, I merely deflected . . ."

"Deflect it, then," said Hulagu. And he nodded
to the bowman.

The arrow sprang from the bowstring and my
reflexes went into overdrive. The world around me
slowed and I could see the arrow, flexing almost
like a dolphin dipping in and out of the water, as it
flew languidly toward me. I knew the kinetic energy it carried, and that attempting to catch it

would be folly. So I stepped slightly to one side
when it reached me and slapped it away with the
edge of my hand against its shaft.

The Mongols gasped. Subotai half rose from the
cushions he sat upon. Hulagu managed a slight
smile.

Next he ordered a wrestler, a huge brute of a
man with shaved head and oiled body. I stripped
to the waist and took off my sandals, then chopped
the monster down with a kick that took out his left
knee and a karate blow to the back of his neck.

I bowed to Hulagu. "Truly, my lord, I am an
ambassador, not a warrior. I fight only to protect
myself."

The Orkhon did not seem pleased. "I have never
seen any man, warrior or not, possess the strength
and speed that you have shown."

"A race of such men," said Subotai gravely,
"would be a formidable enemy."

The other Mongols were muttering among themselves; they appeared to agree with the general.

"I am merely an emissary from a far-distant
land," I said, raising my voice to still their hubbub.
"I seek your ruler, Genghis Khan."

That stopped everything. The entire tent was
instantly silent. Hulagu glared at me angrily.

"He is a stranger among us," Subotai said to the
Orkhon. "He does not know that we do not speak
the name of the High Khan."

"My grandfather has been dead for more years
than the fingers of both my hands," said Hulagu
slowly, menacingly. "Ogotai now rules at Karakorum."

"Then it is Ogotai that I seek," I replied.

"Shall I send you to Karakorum," he said, "as
an emissary from a land so distant that you do not
know who sits upon the golden throne? A man
who can stop arrows with his bare hands and
break the back of the strongest wrestler? Are you

an emissary or a sorcerer? What business do you have with Ogotai?"

I wish I knew, I said to myself. To Hulagu I stated, "My instructions are to speak to none but the High Khan in Karakorum, my lord. I would be unfaithful to my ruler if I failed to carry out my orders."

"I think you are a sorcerer. Or worse, an assassin."

I lowered my voice. "I am not, my lord."

Hulagu sank back into his cushions and extended his right hand as he gazed at me through narrowed eyes. It was impossible to tell from his expressionless face whether he was afraid, worried, or angry. A man with the high-arched aquiline nose of the true Arab and the air of gentility about him handed Hulagu a golden cup. He sipped from it, still eying me suspiciously.

"Go," he said at last. "The guard will find you a place to sleep. I will decide about you tomorrow."

Something about the way he said that made me think that he had already decided.

I had enough presence of mind to bow. Then I picked up my shirt and jacket and, carrying them over my arm, followed my armed escort out of the tent. I took a last glance at Hulagu; he was staring at the arrow lying on the carpet where I had knocked it.

It was outside in the dark coldness of the night, as I was pulling the lice-ridden shirt over my head, that they attacked me. There were six of them, although I didn't know that at first. I was knocked to the ground, the shirt still tangled around my head and arms, and they were on top of me. I flailed and kicked, tore the shirt away and saw the glint of a dagger blade in the moonlight. I fought for my life without worrying that I might kill some of them as they kicked and beat me with clubs. Then the flaring pain of a knife slashing cut into my gut, again and again. I could feel my own hot blood spurting across my skin. A final blow to my head and I lost consciousness.

When I awoke, a few minutes later, the attackers had gone and I had been dragged behind a cart. I could see the cleared space that surrounded the Orkhon's white tent and the two big bonfires in front of its entrance. I clamped down on my slashed blood vessels as hard as I could, and the bleeding slowed. But I could not stop it altogether. I felt very weak, and I knew that if I passed out again, my control over the severed vessels would fade and I would bleed to death.

I heard voices from somewhere in the darkness behind me. I tried to turn, but even the effort to move my head left me giddy and sliding toward unconsciousness.

"Here, my lord," a man's whispered voice said. "They dragged him here."

I heard another man make a huffing kind of grunt. "So he is not a demon after all. He bleeds just like any man."

It took a supreme effort of will to turn my head toward the voices. I could barely make out the shadowy silhouettes of two men standing against the moonlit sky.

"Take him to Agla. Maybe the witch can keep him from dying."

"Yes, my lord Subotai."

The silhouettes melted into the darkness. The voices faded away. It seemed to me that I lay there for hours, forcing myself to remain awake. Then other men came and lifted me roughly from the ground by my shoulders and legs. The sudden flare of agony made me cry out, and then everything went blank.

I came back to a sort of semi-consciousness. I felt warm, too hot to be comfortable. My head swam and my eyes refused to focus properly. I tried to sit up but did not have the strength.

"No, no . . . lie back," crooned a woman's voice. "Be still."

I felt the touch of cool fingers against my burning cheek. "Sleep . . . go to sleep. Agla will protect you from harm. Agla will heal you."

Her voice was hypnotic. I drifted away, feeling somehow safe within the calming power of her words.

I was told later that it was two days and two full nights before I opened my eyes again. I lay flat on my back, staring up at the sloping felt walls of a round yurt. I could see a bright blue sky through the smoke hole at the top. My whole body ached, and it pained me to take a breath, but I could raise myself up on my elbows and examine my midsection. The daggers had sliced deeply, but already the wounds were healing. Within a few days there would be nothing left of them except scars, and in time even the scars would disappear. I wrinkled my nose; the tent smelled of sour milk and human sweat. The Mongols were not much for bathing, I knew.

She pushed aside the leather flap that covered the entrance to the yurt and stepped inside.

"Aretha!" I gasped.

Her skin was suntanned to a radiant golden brown, her dark hair braided and coiled in the Mongol fashion. She wore a long skirt and a loose blouse over it that reminded me of the buckskins of the old American West. Necklaces of shells and bones were strung around her neck, and a leather belt about her waist was hung with pouches and amulets.

But I recognized that beautiful goddess-like face, her lustrous dark hair, those gray eyes that a man could lose himself in.

"Aretha," I said again, my voice nearly breaking with the wonder of her being here, being alive.

She let the entry flap fall behind her and stepped

to the straw pallet on which I lay. Sinking to her knees, she stared at me silently. I could feel my heart beating within my chest.

"You have come back to us," she said. It was Aretha's voice.

"You've come back to me," I replied. "Across all these centuries. Across death itself."

She frowned slightly. Touching my forehead with the back of her cool hand, she said, "The fever is gone; yet you speak wildly."

"You are Aretha. I knew you in another time and place, far from here . . ."

"My name is Agla," she said. "My mother was Agla, and her mother was, also. It is the name for a healer, although some of the barbarians believe that I am a witch."

I sank back onto the straw. But when I reached out my hand, she took it in hers.

"I am Orion," I said.

"Yes, I know. The lord Subotai brought you to me. The Orkhon, Hulagu, tried to have you killed. He fears you."

"Subotai does not?"

She smiled at me, and the rancid, stuffy yurt seemed suddenly filled with sunshine.

"Subotai is greatly interested in you. He gave me no uncertain orders. I am to heal you or lose my own life. He has no use for those who cannot carry out his commands."

"Why is he interested in me?"

Instead of answering my question, she went on, "When they brought you here to my yurt, I was terrified. I tried not to show my fear to Subotai, but from the wounds they had inflicted upon you, I was sure that you would not live out the night. You were bleeding so!"

"But I did live."

"Never have I seen a man with such powers," she said. "There was little I could do for you except to keep your wounds clean and give you a potion to dull your pain. You have healed yourself."

I couldn't get it out of my mind that she was Aretha, the woman I had known so briefly in the twentieth century, re-created here in the thirteenth. But either she had no memory of her earlier existence (or should I say *later* existence) such as I did, or she was truly a different person who looked and sounded exactly like Aretha. A clone? How could that be? If Ormazd could bring me through hell and death with all my memories of that other life intact in my mind, why doesn't Agla recall being Aretha?

"If the barbarians knew that you have healed yourself," she went on, "they would think you are truly a sorcerer."

"Would that be an advantage for me?"

She shuddered. "Hardly. Sorcerers die by fire. Either they are burned alive or they have molten silver poured into their eyes and ears."

I shuddered. "It doesn't pay to be known as a sorcerer."

"Are you . . . ?"

"No, I'm not. Can't you see that? I'm a man, like any other."

"I have never seen a man like you," Agla said, her voice very low.

"Perhaps so," I admitted. "But what I do is not magic or supernatural. I merely have more strength than other men."

She seemed to brighten, happy to convince herself that I was not something monstrous or evil.

"Once I saw how rapidly you were healing, I told lord Subotai that your wounds were not as deep as I had at first thought them to be."

"You don't want to take credit for healing me?"

"They call me a witch, but they don't really mean it seriously. They endure me as a healer because they have need of me. But if they thought that I had used arcane powers to heal you, then I would be a sorceress, and I would face the fire or the molten silver."

We were both silent for a moment, two aliens in the camp of barbarian warriors. She *was* Aretha, but she didn't know it. How could I bring back her memory of that other life?

I thought of Ahriman, and of the reason why I had been brought to this time and place. Perhaps a recollection of him would stir her dormant knowledge.

"There is another man, a dark and dangerous man," I began, then went on to describe Ahriman as closely as I could.

Agla shook her head, the motion making her bone and shell necklaces clatter softly. "I have never seen such a man."

He had to be here, somewhere. Why else would Ormazd have sent me here? Then a new thought struck me: Was it actually Ormazd who had sent me to this time and place? Might Ahriman have exiled me to this wilderness, centuries distant from where I was needed?

But I had no time to worry about such a question. The entry flap was pushed open again, and the Mongol general called Subotai stepped into the yurt.

CHAPTER 11

Subotai entered the felt yurt alone, without guards or announcement, and without fear. Dressed in well-worn leathers, he bore only one weapon, the curved dagger at his belt. He was as lean and wiry as any warrior; only the gray of his braided hair betrayed his age. And although his round, flat face looked impassive and inscrutable, his dark eyes glittered with the eagerness and restlessness of a boy.

Agla bowed to him. "Welcome to my humble yurt, lord Subotai."

"You are the healer," he said. "They tell me you are a witch."

"Only because I can heal illnesses and wounds that would slay a warrior who has not my aid," Agla replied. She was slightly taller than the general when she stood straight.

"I have Chinese healers who perform miracles."

"They are not miracles, lord Subotai. They are merely the result of knowledge. Your warriors are brave and have great skill in warfare. We healers have skills in other arts."

"Including magic?" he asked. "Divination?"

Agla smiled at him. "No, my lord general. Not magic and not prophecy. Merely knowledge of herbs and potions that can heal the body."

He gave the same kind of huffing grunt I had heard the night I had been attacked. It seemed to indicate that he was satisfied that everything that could be was being done.

Turning to me, Subotai said, "You seem to be healing with great speed. Soon you will be on your feet again."

"My wounds were not as deep as they seemed at first," I lied.

"So it appears."

I propped myself up on my elbows and Agla hurried to stuff a pair of cushions under me.

"Did anyone catch the men who attacked me?"

Subotai sat himself down cross legged on the carpeted floor beside my pallet. But he said merely, "No. They escaped in the darkness."

"Then they are still in the camp somewhere, waiting to attack me again."

"I doubt it. You are under my protection."

I bowed my head slightly. "I thank you, lord Subotai." I was about to ask him why he had decided to place me under his wing, but he spoke before I could.

"There are times when a man in a high place—say, the leader of a warrior clan such as Hulagu—must deal with a thorny problem. Some of those times, such a leader might express the hope that the problem will go away. Other men, loyal to such a leader, might interpret the leader's words incorrectly and cause injury to the stranger who causes the problem. Do you understand?"

I could feel my forehead knit into a frown. "But what problem am I causing Hulagu?"

"Did I say I was speaking of Hulagu? Or of you?"

"No," I replied quickly. "You did not."

Subotai nodded, satisfied that I understood the delicacies of the situation. "But you yourself are a good example of what I mean. You appear out of nowhere; you are obviously an alien, and yet you speak our tongue. You say you are an emissary

from a distant land, and yet you have the strength
of ten warriors. You insist that you must see the
High Khan in Karakorum. Yet Hulagu fears that
you are not an emissary at all, but an assassin sent
to murder his uncle."

"Assassin?" I felt shocked. "But why . . ."

The wiry little general waved me down. "Is it
true that you come from a land far to the west of
here?"

"Yes." I knew that of all crimes, the Mongols
hated lying the most. Like most nomadic, desert-
honed peoples, their very existence depended on
hospitality and honesty among one another.

He hunched forward, leaning his forearms on
his bent knees. "Years ago I led my men west of
the larger of two great inland seas into a land
where the earth was as black as pitch and so fer-
tile that the people there grew crops of grain that
stood taller than a man."

"The Ukraine," I said, half to myself.

"The men there had pink skin, such as you do."

I glanced at Agla, who sat silent and still on her
heels at the foot of my pallet.

"It is true," I said. "Men of my coloring live
there, and throughout those lands, westward to
the great sea."

"Farther to the west there are kingdoms that no
Mongol has ever seen," Subotai said, eagerness
beginning to crack his impassive façade. "Kingdoms
of great wealth and power."

"There are kingdoms to the west," I admitted.
"The Russians and Poles, and farther westward
still, the Hungarians, the Germans, and the Franks.
And even beyond those lands, on an island as large
as the Gobi itself, are the Britons."

"You are from that kingdom?" Subotai asked.

I shook my head. "From farther westward yet.
From across a sea as wide as the march from here
to Karakorum."

Subotai leaned back a little, pondering that, trying to imagine such a vast stretch of water. I estimated, from the scraps of information I had heard so far and from the inner conviction that we were camped somewhere in Persia, that we were more than a thousand miles from the Mongol capital, Karakorum, on the northern edge of the Gobi Desert.

"I have placed you under my protection," Subotai said at last, "because I believe that you are speaking the truth. I want to know everything you know about these western kingdoms—their cities, their armies, the strength and valor of their warriors."

Agla gave me a barely perceptible nod, telling me that to refuse Subotai's request, or even debate it, would be a fatal mistake.

The general gave no thought to my resisting his command. He went on, "But first you must satisfy me that Hulagu's fears are groundless. Why do you wish to see the High Khan? You have no gifts with you, no tokens of obeisance. You told Hulagu that you have not been sent to offer the submission of your kingdom. What message have you for Ogotai?"

I hesitated. There was no message, of course. I had merely blurted out that I was an emissary to avoid being killed outright.

Subotai sat up straighter, and his voice became iron-hard. "I have spent my life serving the High Khans, Ogotai and his father, the Perfect Warrior whose name all Mongols revere. *They* have trusted me and I have never failed them."

The implicaton was clear. If Genghis Khan trusted this man, who was I to hesitate?

"I have come," I said slowly, thinking furiously as I spoke, "to warn the High Khan Ogotai against an evil that could destroy him and the entire Mongol empire."

Subotai's dark eyes searched my face, as if to

find the truth by sheer force of will. "What evil is that?" he asked.

"There is a man, one who is unlike any other you have ever seen, a man of darkness with eyes that burn with hate . . ."

"Ahriman," said the Mongol general.

"You know him?" The breath caught in my throat.

"It was he who prophesied our victory over Jelal ed-Din, and who told Hulagu that he will conquer Baghdad itself and crush the power of the Kalif forever."

I closed my eyes for a moment, remembering from history the tales of Haroun al-Raschid and the fabulous Baghdad of the Thousand and One Nights. All were obliterated by the Mongol tide, the flower of Islam annihilated by the merciless destructive power of the Mongols. Cities burned, gardens trampled by the hardy little ponies of the Gobi, millions massacred, an entire civilization gutted. While the knights of Europe fought their skirmishes against Islam in Spain and the Holy Land, the Mongol invaders were obliterating the heartland of the Moslems, turning the irrigated gardens of the ancient plain of Shinar into an ever-lasting desert.

"Ahriman is evil," I said to Subotai. "He will bring destruction to the Mongols."

The general gave no sign of alarm. Or belief. "Ahriman has brought us victory and good fortune so far."

"He is in the camp, then?" Perhaps it was Ahriman's men who had tried to kill me, and not over-zealous servants of the Orkhon Hulagu.

"No," Subotai answered. "He left two weeks ago."

"Where did he go?" I was afraid that I knew what the answer would be.

Sure enough, Subotai said, "Like you, he wished to go to Karakorum, to see the High Khan."

I felt a surge of strength rise in me. "And he left two weeks ago? I must catch up with him."

Subotai asked, "Why?"

"I told you. He is dangerous. I must warn the High Khan against him."

The general tugged at the tip of his mustache, the only gesture of uncertainty that I had seen in him. I turned from him to Agla, who had not moved all through our conversation. She was staring at Subotai, waiting for him to come to some decision.

"I will send you to Karakorum," Subotai said at last, "under my personal protection."

"He cannot travel yet," Agla interjected. "His wounds are not sufficiently healed."

"I can travel," I insisted. "I'll be all right."

Subotai raised his hand slightly. "You will remain here in camp until our healer is willing to let you go. And during this time I will come to you each day. You will tell me everything you know about the kingdoms of the West. I have a great need to learn of them."

Before I could even start to answer, he got to his feet—a little stiffly. It was only then that I realized this man must have been close to sixty years old, if not older, and that most of those years had been spent in the saddle, winning battles and destroying cities.

Subotai left the yurt. I glared at Agla. "I must leave at once. I can't let Ahriman reach Karakorum and get to the High Khan."

"Why not?" she asked.

There was no way to explain it. "I've got to. That's all."

"But how can this one man be so dangerous?"

"I don't know. But he is, and my task is to stop him."

Agla shook her head. "Subotai won't let you leave camp until you've told him everything he wants to know. And I don't want you to leave either."

"Are you afraid that your reputation as a healer will suffer if I go away?"

"No," she said simply. "I . . . want you to stay with me."

I reached out both hands to her and she came over and let me fold her in my arms. I held her gently and she leaned her head against my shoulder. I could smell the scent of her hair, clean and natural and utterly feminine.

"What was the name you called me?" she asked in a whisper. "The other name that you said was mine?"

"It doesn't matter," I said. "That was far away."

"What was it?"

"Aretha."

"There was a woman of that name? You loved her?"

I took a deep breath and reveled in the luxury of her soft, warm body pressing close to me. "I hardly knew her . . . but, yes, I loved her. Ten thousand miles from here and almost eight hundred years away . . . I loved her."

"Was she very much like me?"

"You are the same woman, Agla. I don't know how it can be, or why, but you and she are the same."

"Do you love me, then?"

"Of course I love you," I said, without an instant's hesitation. "I have loved you through all of time. From the beginning of the world I've loved you, and I will love you until the world crumbles into dust."

She lifted her face up to mine and I kissed her.

"And I love you, mighty warrior. I have loved you all my life. I have waited for you since I have been old enough to remember, and now that I have found you, I will never let you go away from me."

I held her tightly and felt both our hearts beating. Deep in the back of my mind, though, was the knowledge that Ahriman was on his way to Karakorum, where I must go, and that he had been living in this camp, even though Agla had told me that she had never seen him.

CHAPTER 12

For three days I told Subotai everything I knew about the Europe of the thirteenth century. Only gradually did I realize that his interest was neither esthetic nor academic, but strictly pragmatic. This general who had led conquering armies for his Khan from the windswept wastes of the Gobi across the grassy steppes all the way to the Ukraine was now intent on pushing farther west. He intended to sweep through Europe and plant the yak-tail standard of the Mongols on the shore of the great ocean that he had never seen.

"But why?" I asked him, at last. "You already share in an empire that stretches from Cathay to the Caspian Sea. Soon Hulagu's army will take Baghdad and Jerusalem. Why go farther?"

Subotai was a plain, direct man, not given to pretenses. I could imagine the answers I would have gotten to that question if I had asked it of Caesar Augustus, Napoleon, Hitler, or any of the other conquerors whom the Europeans called "civilized." But as he sat inside his own tent, dressed in leather pants, a rough shirt, and a leather vest studded with steel bolts, Subotai gave me the unvarnished answer of a barbarian.

"Since I was a young man and swore allegience to the old High Khan, the Perfect Warrior, I have led armies in conquest, it is true. But always for him or for his sons. Now I am an old man and have not many years left. I have seen much of the world, but there is still more that I have not seen. I share in the empire, it is true, but no part of it is my own. The sons of the Perfect Warrior and his grandsons have inherited the lands that I have helped to conquer. Now I wish to have lands of my own, so that my sons will have a place within the empire that is equal to those of Hulagu and Kubilai and the other grandsons of the old High Khan."

There was no trace of bitterness in his words, no hint of envy or anger. He was merely stating the situation clearly, and more succinctly than any politician ever would.

"Would not the ruling High Khan, Ogotai, give you a share of the empire for your own, so that you could pass it on to your sons?"

"He would, if I asked him for such. But that is not the best way. Better to find new lands and add them to the empire."

I thought I understood. "That way there would not be jealousy or conflict among the Orkhons, such as Hulagu."

He gave me a patient sigh. "We have no jealousy or conflict among ourselves. We are ruled by the Yassa, the laws of the High Khan. We are not dogs, to fight with one another over a bone."

"I see," I replied, bowing my head to show that I had not meant to insult him.

"It is *necessary* to add new lands," Subotai went on, in a rare mood of explaining things to an outsider. "That is the wisdom of the old High Khan. That is why we have no jealousy or conflict among ourselves. The Yassa that he gave us instructs us to conquer other peoples. As long as we do so, we will not fight among ourselves."

I was beginning to understand. The Mongols' empire was the creation of Genghis Khan, who was so revered by these warriors that they would not willingly mention his name. It was a model of

dynamic social stability: as long as it kept expanding, it would remain stable at its core. That was
why Subotai was driven westward; everything to
the east as far as the Pacific coast was already
under Mongol sway.

"Besides," Subotai added, as if able to read my
thoughts, "it makes me happy to see new lands
and strange sights. I yearn to see this western
ocean you speak of, and the lands beyond it."

It was difficult not to admire him. "But, my lord
general, the kingdoms of Europe will raise huge
armies to oppose you—thousands of knights and
tens of thousands of men-at-arms . . ."

Subotai actually laughed, a rare loosening of his
self-discipline. "Do not try to frighten me, Orion. I
have seen armies against me before. Did I ever tell
you the story of the Battle of the Carts? Or our
first battle against the host of Kharesm?"

And so it went for three days and long into each
night. In his simple and straightforward way,
Subotai was gathering intelligence and planning
his next campaign. I felt twinges of conscience in
giving him the information he needed, but I knew
from my memory of the twentieth century that the
Mongols never conquered Europe.

As our third sesson seemed to peter out to its
natural conclusion, close to midnight, I told him
that now he knew as much about Europe as I did,
and there was no point in delaying me here further.

"Ahriman has a long lead on me, and he will
arrive in Karakorum to do his evil work before I
have a chance to stop him."

Subotai seemed unconvinced about Ahriman's
evil, but, practical soldier that he was, he appeared
perfectly content to let Ahriman and me fight that
battle between ourselves.

"Ahriman heads toward Karakorum with a treasure caravan," he told me, "that is only as swift as

its most heavily laden camel. How good a rider are you?"

As far as I knew, I had never been on a horse. But I had seen others ride, and I knew that what they could do I could train myself to do in a day or less.

"I can ride," I said.

"Good. We can send you to Karakorum by the *yam*."

I was unfamiliar with the word. Subotai explained that it was a horse-post system, almost exactly like the Pony Express that would be reinvented in the American West six and a half centuries later. Barbarians the Mongols might be, but their post system was the most efficient communications network in the world. And the safest. The law of the Mongols, the Yassa, ruled the empire with a grip of steel. It was said that a virgin carrying a sack of gold could ride from one end of the empire to the other without being molested. And, I found, it was true.

When I returned to Agla's yurt that night and woke her to tell her that I was leaving in the morning, she nodded sleepily and lifted the quilted blanket that was covering her.

"Get to sleep, then," she said drowsily. "We'll have a long day ahead of us, tomorrow."

"We?"

"I am riding to Karakorum with you, of course."

"But . . . will Hulagu allow you to leave?"

If she hadn't been half asleep she would probably have been indignant. "I'm not a slave. I can go as I please."

"It will be a difficult journey. We're riding the horse-post. We'll be on horseback all day, every day, for weeks."

She smiled, closed her eyes, and muttered, "I'm better padded for that than you are." And went back to sleep.

It was a grueling trip. In the twentieth century,
travelers thought themselves rugged to endure the
ride across Asia on the Trans-Siberian Railway
from Moscow to Vladivostock. Agla and I rode
horseback the same distance, across a more difficult route, crossing deserts and high, ice-draped
mountain passes as we made our way across the
Roof of the World and into the vast wilderness of
the Gobi. By ourselves, we would have perished in
less than a week. But the entire route was marked
by a chain of Mongol posts, each a hard day's ride
from the last one, where we could get hot food,
good water, and fresh ponies. Old or crippled warriors kept each post, usually aided by a few local
youths who tended the corrals of horses. It was a
monument to the power of the Mongols that no
one ever attacked these posts. There seemed to be
no underground resistance to the empire. Probably the people, remembering the terrifying massa-
cres that accompanied the Mongol armies, were
cowed to passivity. But perhaps the laws of the
Yassa, and the tolerant rule of the Mongols once
they had conquered a territory, kept their empire
peaceful.

I had hoped to catch up with the caravan that
Ahriman had taken, but the horse-post generally
used a different, more direct route. Swift ponies
with expert riders could tackle terrain that a camel
caravan would never dare try to cross. Here and
there we crossed the ancient caravan route. Even
from miles away we could see the well-marked
path that millennia of camels, oxen, and asses had
beaten into the grassland. Twice we met caravans,
long strings of beasts of burden heaped with treasures looted from the West, tinkling and jingling
as they made their slow, patient way to Karakorum.
Only a handful of warriors rode along as guards.
No one in his right mind attacked a Mongol

caravan; whole tribes could be exterminated for such a crime.

I asked, I searched for Ahriman, but he was not in either caravan. Which meant that he was even farther ahead of me than I had feared.

One night, after we had come down from the icy passes of the Tien Shan mountains and were safely housed for the night in the rude hut that passed for guest quarters at one of the post stations, I asked Agla why she had denied seeing Ahriman in Hulagu's camp.

"I did not see him," she said.

"But you knew he was there, didn't you? Even in a camp as large as Hulagu's, the presence of such a man would be known to everyone."

"Yes," she admitted, "I knew he was there."

"Then why did you lie to me?"

Her chin went up a notch. "I did not lie. You asked me if I had seen him and I told you the truth: I had not. The Dark One stayed in the tent of Subotai. I never set eyes on him."

"But you knew he was there."

"And I knew that he had prophesied to Hulagu that you would come to the camp. And that he warned Hulagu that you were a demon and advised him to kill you," Agla said. There was no shame in her expression, no guilt. "I knew that they had almost succeeded. And I knew that as long as you were under the lord Subotai's protection, no further harm would come to you. Who do you think found you, dying in the dust behind the dung heap? Who do you think brought Subotai to you and convinced him that you were too valuable to be allowed to die?"

"You did that?"

"Yes."

"But why? You didn't know who I was or why I had come to . . ."

"I knew enough," Agla said, her gray eyes shining in the light of the fire that crackled in the hearth. "I had heard that a strange man of great power had been brought into the camp and that Hulagu was fearful enough to listen to the Dark One's warning. I knew that you were the man I have waited for all my life."

"So you saved my life and protected me until I was well."

She nodded. "As I will protect you with all my power once we reach Ogotai's court in Karakorum."

"Ahriman will be there," I said.

"Yes. And he will try to kill you again."

CHAPTER 13

Karakorum was as strange a mixture of squalor and splendor, of barbarian simplicity and Byzantine intricacy, as ever existed on the face of the Earth.

During the time of Genghis Khan this city of tents and yurts had become the capital of the world, where the conquered nobility of China and Islam came to serve the Mongols as slaves, where the treasures of all Asia flowed into the hands of men who had begun their lives as nomadic tribesmen.

While he lived, Genghis Khan had forbade the building of permanent structures in his capital. The tents and carts and yurts of old were good enough for him, in this encampment by a serene river, where good grass grew to feed his most important treasure—the herds of horses that carried his warriors to the farthest corners of the world.

It was the horses that marked the outskirts of Karakorum. Huge corrals ringed the Mongol capital, holding tens of thousands of the small, tough ponies of the Gobi. Their neighings could be heard for miles. Their stirrings raised clouds of dust that could be seen from two day's ride away. It reminded me, as we approached the capital one chilly morning, of the smoke and smog that marked industrial cities in the twentieth century.

Ogotai was the High Khan, and he ruled with the administrative aid of Chinese mandarins who

117

understood writing and record-keeping. As Agla and I neared the city, we could see that buildings of sun-baked mud and even stone were rising around the ordu, the pavilion of tents that marked the headquarters of the High Khan. Most of these new buildings, I quickly learned, were churches or temples. The Mongols were tolerant toward religions, and priests of every type crowded the bursting city: Buddhist monks in their saffron robes, turbaned imams from the Moslem lands, Nestorian Christian priests, Chinese Taoists in their silks and brocades, and many others whom I could not recognize.

We were stopped by the guards who stood on duty where the road entered the maze of buildings that marked the outskirts of Karakorum. A silk-robed Chinese examined the paper that Subotai had given me—a paper written by one of Subotai's Chinese aides—and commanded a warrior to find us living quarters. The warrior mounted his pony and led us silently through the bustling hodge-podge of Karakorum. Treasure caravans were unloading; men and women milled about everywhere. There was no order to the layout of the buildings, no preplanned streets as such, merely meandering paths of hard-beaten earth between the haphazardly constructed buildings. Every language in the world was being spoken here, and often shouted or screamed, as merchants haggled over prices or offered wares ranging from pomegranates from China to swords of Damascus steel so fine that you could bend the blade over double without snapping it.

We were installed in a small, one-story house made of adobe. Its door opened onto the broad empty space that surrounded the High Khan's ordu. From the narrow window of the front room we could see the pavilion of white tents, hung with silk and cloth-of-gold, and the warriors who stood guard before the entrances. As they had in Hulagu's camp, forty degrees of longitude to the west of here, the Mongols had two big bonfires blazing in front of the main entrance to the High Khan's tent. To ward off evil spirits.

There was an evil spirit already in this city, I knew. Ahriman must have arrived before us. Had he won the ear of the High Khan? Would I be the victim of another assassination attempt once I presented myself to Ogotai?

But even those worries failed to keep me awake. After so many weeks of hard riding, Agla and I collapsed into the feather bed and slept for almost twenty-four hours.

I awoke to a sense of danger.

My eyes snapped open and every sense was instantly alert. Agla lay slumbering beside me, her head nestled against my shoulder. Without moving my head, I scanned the little bedroom. It had no windows and only one doorway, hung with a curtain of beads, about two feet to the left of the bed. It had been a slight rustling of those beads that had awakened me, I realized.

I held my breath, listening. My back was turned to the doorway, so I couldn't see it unless I turned my head, and I didn't want to do that for fear of alerting whoever it was that was standing on the other side of the beaded curtain.

The curtain rustled again and I saw, in the dim early morning light, a gray shadow slide against the far wall of the bedroom. Then another. Two men, wearing the conical steel helmets of Mongol warriors. The first shadow raised its arm and I saw the slim blade of a dagger in its hand.

I rolled across the sagging bed and hit them both at the same time with a body block that sent them staggering into the other wall. Pushing myself up from the floor before they could gather their wits, I twisted the dagger out of the first one's hand. As it fell clattering to the floor, I swung as hard as I could at the neck of the second assassin with a backhand chop. Behind me I heard Agla scream. The first warrior was scrambling to his feet now and reaching for the sword at his waist. I punched at his heart and felt ribs breaking. As he doubled over, I drove a knee into his face. He bounced off the wall and slid to the floor.

Turning, I saw Agla standing naked on the far side of the bed, a dagger of her own in her left hand, her lips pulled back in a savage snarl.

"Are you all right?" We both asked at the same instant. Then she laughed, shakily, and I took a deep breath and calmed my racing heart.

She wrapped the bed quilt around her as I squatted down to examine the would-be assassins. Both were dead. I had driven a sliver of bone from the nose into the brain of the first one, and the second one's neck was broken.

Agla came around the bed and knelt beside me. Her eyes were round with awe.

"You killed them both, with your bare hands!"

Nodding, "I didn't mean to. I wanted to find out who sent them."

"I can tell you that. It was the Dark One."

"Yes, I think so, too. But it would be better to know for certain."

A warrior burst through the open front door, sword in hand. "I heard a scream!" Then he saw the two dead men sprawled on the floor. He looked at me, then back at the would-be assassins.

I expected that he would be angry that two of his fellow Mongols had been killed by an alien. I tensed myself for another attack. Instead, he gaped at me in wonder.

"You did this?"

I nodded.

"Alone? Without weapons?"

"Yes," I snapped. "Now get them out of here."

Agla, still grasping the quilt around her shoulders, said, "Wait. You wanted to make certain who has sent these killers."

Before I could reply, she dropped to her knees and peeled back the eyelid of one of the dead men. She stared into it intently, shuddered slightly, and then closed the man's eye again. Then she turned to the other and did the same. As I watched her, I realized that I was standing stark naked. The heat of fighting and anger was subsiding inside me; I began to feel chilled.

Agla got to her feet and clutched the quilt around her more tightly. "It was the Dark One. I saw it in their eyes."

"You can see that in the eyes of dead men?" It sounded ridiculous to me.

But she said solemnly, "I can see their entire lives in their eyes. It is a gift of the gods."

I couldn't believe that. Agla "saw" what she wanted to see. If she had believed that the assassins had been sent by Hulagu, or the High Khan, or the Man in the Moon, she would have seen that in their eyes, too.

But the warrior believed her. Wide-eyed, both at my fighting ability and at her psychic power, he dragged the two corpses out of the house and shut the door—but not before he ordered us to remain inside until an officer came to speak with us.

Barbarians they might have been, but the Mongols lived by strict laws and had much the same kind of police system that any civilized city did. Faster and more efficient than most, in fact. We had hardly finished dressing when a military officer rapped on the front door and opened it, without waiting for us to open it for him.

He questioned me, ignored Agla. I told him exactly what happened, leaving out only Agla's "examination" of the two corpses.

"Who might have sent assassins against you?"

the officer asked. He seemed truly concerned. Things like this did not happen often in the Mongol capital.

I kept my opinion to myself. "I have no way of knowing," I told him. "We arrived here only yesterday."

"Who are your enemies?"

I shook my head. "I am a stranger here, from a faraway land. I did not think I had any enemies here. Perhaps they mistook me for another."

He looked unconvinced, but he said, "Perhaps. Stay here until notified otherwise. You will be guarded by my men."

House arrest is what it amounted to. The Mongols did not like trouble in their midst, and they intended to get to the bottom of this. Two warriors parked themselves outside our door. Servants brought food and fresh clothes to us. As usual, they could find no boots large enough to fit me. I kept my sandals. They had stood me in good stead all these weeks, even when I had had to wrap them with skins and furs as we rode through the high passes of the Tien Shan.

"It is the Dark One," Agla brooded, once we were alone. "He seeks your death."

She insisted on tasting the food that the servants brought before letting me eat it. She even inspected the clothing for hidden charms or potions.

"A man can be poisoned through the skin," she warned me. "I know of a poultice that can kill a strong warrior, once it touches his skin for a few moments."

Nerve poisons in the thirteenth century? I deferred to her superior knowledge of the time. My attention focused on another matter. I agreed with Agla that no one except Ahriman could possibly want to kill me. But why? Why were we both here? My mission was to kill him, I knew. Was he under the same compulsion? Was it our destiny to hunt each other through all of time, playing an eternal prey-and-predator game for the amusement of Ormazd and whatever other gods there be?

I refused to believe that I was nothing more than an elaborate toy. Ahriman sought to kill me not merely for the sport of it, but to prevent me from thwarting his plans. He sought nothing less than the destruction of the whole human race, forever, for all of time and space, even if it meant destroying the very fabric of the continuum and demolishing the entire universe of space-time. My unalterable mission was to prevent him from doing that, and the only way I could accomplish it, unfailingly and permanently, was to kill Ahriman.

I am not an assassin, I told myself. I am not a murderer. I am a soldier, fighting for the life of the entire human race against a ruthless alien who would snuff us out like a candle flame. If I must kill Ahriman, it is because only his death can ensure the life of humankind.

But still I was troubled. No matter how hard I tried to convince myself, it still boiled down to what Ormazd had told me so long ago in the future: my mission is to find Ahriman and kill him.

How many times? I suddenly wondered. When is a man finally, unquestionably dead? Ahriman had killed Aretha in the twentieth century, and yet Agla lived here beside me. I myself had died, but still breathed and moved and loved. Is the cycle endless?

I sank onto the soft mattress of our bed, too soul-weary to contemplate an eternity of hunting Ahriman, of death after death, murder after murder. Agla, sensing my despair, tried to comfort me.

Then someone knocked at our door. A polite but firm tapping, three distinct raps.

I went to the door and opened it. It was night now, and the whole inner compound of the ordu was lit by the crackling flames of the twin bonfires. Ogotai's silken tent swayed in a breeze that was not interrupted by hill or tree for hundreds of miles.

Standing in front of me was an elderly, slender Chinese in exquisite robes of sky blue and silver. In his high, peaked hat he was almost my height. With the bonfires at his back, it was difficult for me to make out the features of his face.

"I am Ye Liu Chutsai, advisor to the High Khan," he said in the soft, high voice of an old man. "May I enter?"

CHAPTER 14

The mandarin stood patiently at the doorway. The two Mongol guards were squatting on the bare ground a few yards from the door, gobbling their supper from wooden bowls. Their lances and bows were on the ground next to them, their swords at their sides.

"Yes, of course," I said to the mandarin. "Please come in."

He had the trick of walking so smoothly that it looked as if he was standing on a small rolling cart, under his floor-length robes, and was actually being wheeled across the threshold. I introduced him to Agla, who bowed very low to him, then busied herself building the fire higher in the hearth.

Ye Liu Chutsai looked older than any man I had seen among the Mongols. His wispy beard and mustache were completely white, as was the long queue that hung down his back. He stood in the middle of the bare little room, hands tucked inside his wide sleeves.

I gestured to the only chair in the room, a heavy, stiff thing of wood. "Please sit down, sir."

He sat. Agla ducked into the bedroom and brought out two cushions. She offered them to the mandarin, who refused them with a slight shake of his head and a small smile. She and I sat on them, at the feet of the elderly Chinese.

"I should begin by explaining who I am," he said so softly that I had to strain slightly to hear him over the crackle of our fire. Its warmth felt good on my back.

Agla said, "Your name is known as the right hand of the High Khan."

He bowed his head again in acknowledgment.

"Since the original High Khan was still called by his birth name, Timujin, I have served the Mongols. I was only a youth when they swept through the Great Wall and ravaged Yan-king, the city where I was born. I was taken into slavery by the Mongols because I was a scribe. I could read and write. Although the Mongol warriors did not appreciate that, Timujin did."

"It was he who became Genghis Khan?" I asked.

"Yes, but to use either of these names before the Mongols is not wise. He is called the High Khan. He was the father of Ogotai, the current High Khan. He was the man who directed the Mongol conquest of China, of High Asia, of the hosts of Islam. He was the greatest man the world has known."

It was not my place to contradict him. The elderly mandarin did not seem like the kind who would bestow praise foolishly or insincerely. He believed what he said, and for all I knew he may have been right.

"Today the empire of the Mongols stretches from the China Sea to Persia. Hulagu is preparing to conquer Baghdad. Subotai is already on the march against the Russians and Poles. Kubilai, in Yan-king, dreams of subduing the Japanese on their islands."

"He should forego that dream," I said, recalling that Kubilai's invasion fleet was wrecked by a storm that the Japanese called The Divine Wind, *Kamikaze*.

Ye Liu Chutsai looked sharply at me. "Why do you say that?" he demanded. "What do you prophesy?"

Agla gave me a warning glance. Prophets trod a dangerous path among these people.

"I prophesy nothing," I replied, as offhandedly as I could manage. "I merely made a comment. After all, the Mongols are horse warriors, not sailors. The sea is not their element."

The mandarin studied my face for long moments. At last he replied, "The Mongols are indeed the fiercest warriors in the world. They are not sailors, true. But neither are they administrators, or scribes, or artisans. They use captives for those tasks. They will find sailors enough among the Chinese."

I bowed my head to his superior wisdom.

"The empire must continue to expand," he went on. "That was the true genius of the original High Khan. He saw clearly that these barbarian tribes must continue to move outward, to find enemies that must be conquered, or else their empire will collapse. These horse warriors are utterly brave; they live for war. If there were no enemies beyond their borders, they would fall back to their old ways and begin fighting among themselves. That was the way they lived before Timujin welded the warring tribes of the Gobi into the mightiest conquering army the world has ever seen."

"That is why the empire continues to expand," I said.

"It *must* expand. Or collapse. There is no middle way. Not yet."

"And as the empire expands, the Mongols slaughter helpless people by the tens of thousands and burn cities to the ground."

He nodded his head.

"And you help them to do it? Why? You are a civilized man. Why do you help the people who invaded your land?"

Ye Liu Chutsai closed his eyes for a moment. It made his old, lined face look like a death's mask in the flickering firelight.

When he opened his eyes again, he said, "There is but one true civilization in the world, the civilization of the land that you call Cathay, or China. I am a son of the Chin, the Chinese. I serve the Mongol High Khan so that civilization may be extended to the four corners of the world."

I felt confused. "But the Mongols have conquered Cathay. Kubilai Khan rules in Yan-king now."

The old man smiled. "Yes, and already Kubilai— who was born in a felt yurt on the grasslands not far from this very spot—already he is more Chinese than Mongol. He wears silk robes and paints beautiful landscapes and deals with the intrigues of the court as delicately as any grandson of a mandarin."

His meaning became clear to me. I leaned back and drew in a deep breath of understanding. "The Mongols are the warriors, but the Chinese will be the true conquerors."

"Exactly," said Ye Liu Chutsai. "The Mongols are the sword arm of the empire, but the civilization of the Chin is its brain."

Agla spoke up. "Then the Mongols are serving *you*, aren't they?"

"Oh no, by my sacred ancestors, no, not at all!" He seemed genuinely upset by such an idea. "We are all serving the High Khan, Ogotai. I am his slave—willingly."

"But only because the High Khan is paving the way for a Chinese empire that spans the world," Agla insisted.

Ye Liu Chutsai went silent again, and I realized that he was arranging his thoughts so that he could present them to us as clearly as possible.

"Timujin," he said softly, as if afraid someone would hear him use the revered name, "hit upon the idea of conquest as a means to keep the tribes of the Gobi from annihilating each other. It was a stroke of genius. But it requires that the Mongols constantly expand their empire."

"Yes, you told us that," Agla said.

"Of what use is all this bloodshed and misery, however?" the mandarin asked. "What purpose does it serve, other than keeping these nomadic warriors from each other's throats?"

Neither Agla nor I had an answer for that.

"On the other hand," he went on, "here is the civilization of the Chin, the highest civilization the world has ever seen. It is not warlike, so it has no way of spreading the fruits of its culture to other lands."

"The Mongols invade Cathay," I took up, "but the Chinese civilization conquers them, eventually."

"It takes a generation or two," Ye Liu Chutsai said, agreeing with me. "Sometimes longer."

"So your task is to keep the Mongol empire growing, so it won't collapse, for a long enough time to allow it to evolve into a Chinese empire, ruled by civilized mandarins who will control the entire known world."

He nodded. "A single, unified empire that girdles the entire world, from sea to sea. Think of what that would mean! An end to war. An end to the bloodletting. A world of peace, ruled by law instead of the sword. It is the goal to which I have devoted my entire life."

A Chinese empire, carved out by Mongol warriors, ruled by silk-robed mandarins. Ye Liu Chutsai saw the highest civilization in history creating a world of peace. I saw a stifling autocracy that would stamp out individual freedom.

"I share my vision with you," the mandarin said, "because I want you to understand the problem you have raised for me."

"Problem?" I asked.

He sighed. "Ogotai is not the man his father was. He is too amiable to be a good ruler, too content with the wealth he has today to understand the need to drive constantly onward."

"But you said . . ."

"Fortunately," he went on, stopping me with one upraised, slender, long-nailed finger, "the dynamics of the empire are still powerful. Hulagu, Subotai, Kubilai and the other orkhons and princes along the periphery of the Mongol conquests still press onward. Ogotai stays here in Karakorum, content to let the others do the fighting while he enjoys the fruits of their conquests. It is not a healthy situation."

"But what has that to do with us?" Agla asked.

"Ogotai is a superstitious man," Ye Liu Chutsai answered. "And his soothsayers have been warning him, lately, to beware of a stranger from the West—because he will attempt to murder the High Khan."

I said firmly, "I too have a warning for him."

"You are from the West," Ye Liu Chutsai said. "So is the one who calls himself Ahriman."

"He *is* here!" I blurted.

"You know him?"

"Yes. It is he whom I must warn Ogotai against."

The mandarin smiled vaguely. "Ahriman has already warned Ogotai against you, the fair-skinned man of great strength from beyond the western sea."

I sat there on the cushion, wondering where this would lead. My word against Ahriman's. How could I convince . . .

"There is something more," Ye Liu Chutsai added. "Something that makes the problem acute."

"What is it?"

"A threat to the empire has arisen."

"A threat?" I echoed.

"What could possibly threaten an empire that has conquered half the world?" Agla asked.

"Earlier today you used the word 'assassin' when you spoke to the guards."

"Yes, after those two men tried to kill me."

" 'Assassin' is a new word here. It comes from the land of Persia, where a cult—perhaps it is religious, I do not yet know—has sprung up. It is a murder cult, and its members are called assassins. I am told the word stems from a Persian name for a drug these men use: hashish."

"I don't understand what this has to do with me," I said.

"The man who directs this murder cult is as clever as a thousand devils. He recruits young men and promises them paradise if they follow his bidding. He gives them hashish, and no doubt other drugs as well, to show them a vision of the paradise that will be theirs after their mortal bodies perish. Small wonder that the youths are willing to give up their lives to do their master's will."

"I know of these drugs," Agla said. "They are so powerful that a man will do anything to have them."

Ye Liu Chutsai dipped his head once in acknowledgment. "The addicts are ordered to kill a man. Even though they know that they themselves will be killed as a result, they do so gladly, believing that they will awaken in an eternal paradise."

I said nothing, even though I knew that what appears to be death is not the end of existence.

"In Persia, thousands of merchants, noblemen, even imams and princes have been . . . assassinated.

The cult has merely to warn a man that he has been marked for death and so great is the terror that the man is willing to pay any price to placate the assassins. Thus the cult grows rich and powerful."

"In Persia," I said. The land of Ahriman and Ormazd, and their ancient prophet Zoroaster.

"It has grown far beyond Persia," replied Ye Liu Chutsai. "All of Islam is gripped by the terror. And I fear that assassins have made their way here, to Karakorum, to kill the High Khan."

"Ahriman is from Persia," I said.

"So he freely admits. But he says that you are, too. Which you deny."

"Assassins nearly killed me today."

The mandarin made a small shrug. "That could have been a clever ruse, to put us off our guard. The two dead men were not Mongols, despite their garb. They could easily have been Persians. You may have killed them to keep suspicion away from yourself."

"But I did not. They tried to kill me."

The mandarin's wrinkled face looked truly troubled. "I want to believe you, Orion. But I do not dare to act naively. I am convinced that either you or Ahriman is an assassin, perhaps even the very leader of the cult, the man known to the Persians only as the Old Man of the Mountains."

"How can I convince you . . . ?"

With a shake of his head, Ye Liu Chutsai said, "In a problem such as this, the Mongols would act with wonderful simplicity. They would simply kill both you and Ahriman—and possibly you, too, my dear lady—and have done with it. I, with my civilized conscience, will endeavor to determine which of you is the assassin and which is the innocent party."

"Then I have nothing to fear," I said, wishing that I actually felt that way.

"Not from me. Not yet." The mandarin hesitated, then added, "But Ogotai is not a patient man. He may apply the Mongol solution and be rid of the problem once and for all."

CHAPTER 15

Agla and I were not exactly prisoners, but wherever we went in Karakorum, the same two Mongol warriors followed us. Ye Liu Chutsai said they were guards, for our protection, but they made me feel uneasy. Day and night they were never more than a few swift strides away. I learned that Mongol discipline was relentless: these men would guard us until they were ordered to stop. If we escaped their sight, they would be killed. If one of them died while guarding us, his son would take his place in such duty, if he had a son old enough to be a warrior. If not, his closest male relative would step in.

We had the freedom of the city, except for the one place I wanted to go—the pavilion of the High Khan, the ordu of silk-draped tents that I could see from the door of our quarters each morning. Ye Liu Chutsai would not permit me to see the Khan or to come any closer to Ogotai than the edge of the wide cleared space that marked the ordu. The mandarin still worried that I might be an assassin, or even the leader of the entire cult of assassins. So I was kept from seeing the High Khan while Chinese court intrigues began to weave their way through the ordu of the Mongols.

But there was nothing to prevent me from seeking out Ahriman. For days Agla and I wandered

134

through the crowded, noisy lanes that meandered between yurts and buildings of stone and adobe, seeking the Dark One. Karakorum was a metropolis built by accident, without plan, without facilities. The Mongols saw it as merely another encampment, larger than any previous collection of yurts and carts that they had known. But they could not understand the differences that a change of scale makes. A nomad's encampment of a thousand families with their tents and ponies and livestock could live beside a river for weeks on end before it had to move on. But a city of ten thousand families, or a hundred thousand, which remained fixed in one place, was beyond the ability of the Mongols.

Sanitation was nonexistent. To these nomadic warriors and herdsmen, who rubbed animal fat on their bodies to protect themselves from winter's cold, bathing was almost unheard of. Garbage and human wastes were simply dumped on the ground, usually behind one's tent. Water was carried to the city on the backs of slaves, taken from the same river into which the runoff from the waste dumps ran. That system worked for a temporary camp, but for a permanent city it meant disease, inevitably. I began to wonder how long it would take for Karakorum to be swept away by an epidemic of typhus. Perhaps that was what eventually ended the Mongol empire.

The noise of those twisting narrow streets rivaled twentieth-century Manhattan. Nobody spoke in tones lower than a shout. Ox-drawn carts creaked and groaned under heavy loads. Horsemen clattered by, scattering merchants, women, children and anyone else who happened to be in their way. It seldom rained, but when it did, thunderbursts poured torrents on the city. Almost every storm knocked down one flimsy adobe building or another, although the round felt yurts and the big tents of

the ordu seemed to make it through the wind and
rain better than the "permanent" buildings did.
After each thunderstorm there were puddles everywhere, in which king-sized mosquitos bred.

No one I spoke to admitted to knowing of the
Dark One. Ye Liu Chutsai had met Ahriman, and
told me that he had even spoken with Ogotai before I had arrived in Karakorum. But the mandarin would give me no hint as to where to find
Ahriman.

So, day after day, Agla and I, trailed by our two
faithful warrior guards, made our way through the
bustling, noisy capital of the Mongols, shouldering
and elbowing through the thick crowds, seeking
one man in a city that must have numbered close
to a million.

I tried every church we could find, from the
foul-smelling hut of some Christian hermits to the
golden magnificence of a Buddhist temple.

After nearly a week of searching, I finally saw
what I had been looking for—a small, windowless,
squat building made of gray stone, far off on the
outskirts of the city, out near the corrals and barns
where the stench of the animals and the droning
buzz of the flies that lived off them were overpowering.

Agla's face showed her disgust at the surround-
ings. "There's nothing here but filth and smell,"
she said.

"And Ahriman." I pointed to the gray stone
building.

"There?"

"I'm sure of it." Turning to our guards, I asked,
"What building is that?"

They glanced at each other before shrugging their
shoulders and pretending not to know. Perhaps
they were under orders to keep me away from
Ahriman. Perhaps they were afraid of entering the

Dark One's domain. No matter. I headed straight for the low, wide door—the only opening in the building that I could see.

"That is not a good place to enter," said one of our guards. It was the longest string of words I had ever heard him utter.

"You can wait outside," I said, without breaking stride.

"Wait," he said, hurrying to get in front of me.

"I'm going in. Don't try to stop me."

He was clearly unhappy with the idea, but equally unwilling to challenge me. He had been told what I had done to the two assassins. He sent his partner around to check on the building's other entrances. There were none. Satisfied that he could watch the solitary door, he stepped aside.

"You must call me if there is danger," he said.

Agla replied, "I will call, never fear." But the warrior paid no attention to a woman.

I had to duck to get through the low doorway. Inside, the chamber was dark, gloomy. Agla pressed against me.

"I can't see a thing," she whispered.

But I could. My eyesight adjusted to the darkness immediately, and even though the chamber remained shrouded in murky shadows, I could make out a stone altar on a slightly raised platform, with strange symbols carved on stone above it.

"I've been expecting you," Ahriman's harsh, rasping voice rumbled.

I turned toward the sound and saw him, a darker presence among the deepest shadows in the far corner of the chamber.

"Come to me," he said. "The girl will not be harmed; you can leave her there."

Agla seemed to have frozen into lifelessness. She stood stock-still, clutching my arms, staring ahead blindly into the darkness.

"She will neither see nor hear anything," Ahriman told me. "Leave her and come to me."

I disengaged my arm from Agla's grasp. She was still warm and alive, but I could detect no breath in her, no heartbeat.

"I have merely accelerated time for the two of us," Ahriman said as I studied her. "This way we can talk without being overheard or interrupted."

I stepped across the stone floor toward him. The stones felt solid and real. Ahriman looked as I had remembered him—a dark, brooding, powerful hulking body and red burning eyes. Agla remained as lovely and as still as a statue made of living flesh.

"When you return to her, she will not know that an instant has passed. And for her, no time will have elapsed."

"You play many tricks with time," I said.

He was standing straddle-legged, his huge fists planted on his hips. He wore fur-trimmed robes and high leather boots. I could see no weapons on him, but how paltry a sword or dagger would be to a man of his powers.

"You travel through time quite easily yourself," Ahriman hissed. "And through space. It was a long journey from Hulagu's camp."

"You never rode in the camel caravan, did you?"

His broad, brooding face almost smiled. "No. I took a different mode of transport. I have been here in Karakorum for three months now. I am highly regarded as a priest of a new religion, a religion for warriors."

"You sent those two assassins."

"Yes," he admitted easily. "I doubted that they would accomplish much, but I had to see if you still possessed the powers that you had the last time we met."

"At the fusion reactor."

His heavy brows knit in puzzlement for a moment. "Fusion rea . . ." Then he took in a deep breath.

"Ah yes, of course. You are moving back toward The War. I haven't reached that time yet."

We were traveling across time in different directions, I remembered. We had met before, and we would meet again.

"Did you . . . kill me, then?" Ahriman's labored voice almost sounded worried.

"No," I answered. "You killed me."

He seemed pleased. "Then I still may accomplish my task."

"To destroy the human race."

He glowered at me. "Human. Look at the wonders that these Mongols have achieved. Observe how they slaughter their own kind by the hundreds of thousands, and how others who believe themselves to be civilized applaud such slaughter and benefit from it. Human, indeed."

"Do you count yourself better because you plan to slaughter us by the billions?"

"I plan to correct a mistake that was made fifty thousand years ago," Ahriman rasped. "For every life that is snuffed out, a life will be gained. *My* people will live; yours will die. And so, too, will your creator die—the one who calls himself Ormazd."

"The War was fifty thousand years ago?"

"You will learn," he said. "You will meet me then. You will see. Why else would Ormazd have you moving back from The End toward The War? To keep the truth from you."

I squeezed my eyes shut, trying to keep his lies from penetrating my consciousness. I formed a mental image of Ormazd, shining, glowing against the darkness of eternity. The Golden One, the giver of life and truth. Ahriman called him my creator and said that he would kill us both.

Opening my eyes, I said, "My mission is to kill you."

"I know. And I would happily kill you, as easily as you would crush an insect beneath your heel."

"As easily as you murdered her?"

"The girl?"

"Her name was Aretha . . . in the twentieth century."

"I have not been there yet."

"You will be. And you will kill her. If there were no other reason for me to hate you, that would be enough."

He shrugged those massive shoulders. "You can hate; you can love. Ormazd has programmed you quite flexibly."

I was close enough to reach out and take him by the throat. But I had felt the strength of those mighty arms before, and I knew that even with all the powers I possessed, he could toss me about like a matchstick.

"The Mongols make it difficult for us to do battle," Ahriman said, breaking into my thoughts. "They have their laws, and they will do their best to see that we obey them."

"I will gain an audience with Ogotai and warn him against you. You will not succeed here."

His almost lipless slash of a mouth curled back in a hideous smile. "Succeed? I have already succeeded. And you have helped me!"

"What do you mean?"

He shook his head. "What do you expect of me? Do you think that I am here to assassinate Ogotai?"

"You are the leader of the cult of the assassins, aren't you?"

The smile degenerated into a sneer. "No, my ancient adversary. I am not the Old Man of the Mountains. Only a true human would think of murdering his fellow humans for profit. The leader of the assassins is a Persian, as human as you are. He was a boyhood friend of someone you may have heard of—Omar Khayyam, the astronomer."

"I know the name as a poet."

"Yes, he scribbled some verses now and then. But as for the assassins, Hulagu will crush them—after he takes Baghdad and destroys the flower of Islamic culture."

"You said you have already succeeded here . . . and I helped you."

"Yes," Ahriman said, his face becoming serious again. "Come. I will show you."

He turned and walked toward the solid stone wall that had been behind him. Remembering what he had done in the twentieth century, I hesitated only a moment, then followed him.

I stepped through the wall, again feeling the chill of deepest space for an instant. And then we were in a forest, surrounded by tall, dark trees that sighed in the night wind. Wordlessly, Ahriman led me along a path that meandered through the underbrush. High above, through the leafy canopy, I could see a thin sliver of a moon racing through scudding clouds. An owl hooted in the darkness; crickets chirped ceaselessly.

We stopped at the edge of the woods, where the ground slanted downward toward a wide grassy plain. Tents were pitched there; horses were tethered in long sleeping lines. But these tents were high-pitched and square in shape, not like Mongol tents. The carts were huge and heavy compared to those I had seen in Karakorum. And the horses also looked different from the ponies of the Gobi—bigger, heavier, slower.

"The cream of Eastern Europe's knighthood," Ahriman whispered to me, "led by Bela, the King of Hungary. A hundred thousand men are camped there, knights from Croatia, Germany, the Hungarian cavalry, of course, and even Knights Templar from France."

"Where are we?"

"Down there is the plain of Mohi. Across the

river is Tokay, the wine country. That is where Subotai and his Mongols are spending the night—or so Bela thinks."

By the wan light of the moon I could see guards standing around the edges of the huge camp, and more tents pitched on the other side of the river at the foot of a stone bridge that spanned it. Neither the guards nor I noticed anything amiss as the night slowly faded and the first gray fingers of dawn began to streak the sky.

Ahriman pulled me down to a crouching position in the underbrush. I started to protest, but he silenced me with a massive hand on my shoulder.

In the predawn dimness I heard the slight snuffle of a horse. Turning, I saw through the tangled undergrowth a pair of Mongol warriors nosing their ponies slowly, silently, through the woods. Behind them were more horsemen, each as quiet as a wraith. They stopped, bows in their hands, already notched with arrows. They waited for a signal.

A shower of fire arched across the gray sky. Flaming arrows fell into the Europeans' camp, setting tents afire and terrifying the tethered horses. A horrendous roaring scream arose from thousands of warriors as the Mongol horsemen spurred their mounts and dashed into the sleeping camp from three sides. Horsemen thudded past us as we crouched in the brush, spattering us with clods of earth, shrieking their hideous war cries, bending their little double-curved bows and firing arrows into the stumbling, barely awake Europeans.

The slaughter was complete. All morning long the two armies battled, thousands upon thousands of maddened men furiously trying to kill one another. The Europeans fought with the strength of desperation; they were surrounded and had no hope of escape or mercy. The Mongols, though heavily outnumbered, remorselessly cut down their opponents with arrows, lances, and curved swords that drank the blood of nobleman and peasant equally. The Europeans never had a chance to mount their battle steeds or even don their armor. They were slaughtered in their nightclothes. The men on the far side of the stone bridge fought bravely, but soon enough the Mongols cut down the last of them and stormed across the bridge to complete the encirclement.

The sun climbed higher in the sky as I stared, horrified, at the dust and blood of the battle. Men screamed; horses whinnied: confusion and terror were everywhere.

"Here you see the human race at its finest, Orion," gloated Ahriman. "Observe the energy and passion your kind puts into slaughtering itself."

I said nothing. There was nothing I could say. The stench of blood, the sight of severed limbs and slashed bodies was making me sick.

"I have already won," Ahriman told me. "Thanks to the knowledge you imparted to Subotai, the Mongols have crushed the European army. Nothing stands between them and the Rhine now. They will sweep westward, razing cities and slaughtering whole nations. The French will make a stand before them, just as they made a stand against the Moors under Charles the Hammer. But Subotai's final moment of glory will come when he destroys the French army as thoroughly as he has destroyed Bela and his allies here today. All of Europe will be under Mongol sway—all of Eurasia, from the Pacific to the Atlantic."

"And that is what you seek?" I asked, turning away from the carnage. But I could not keep from hearing the screams of the dying.

His powerful hand squeezed my arm. "That is what I seek, Orion. And nothing can prevent it from happening. Neither you nor Ormazd can stop me now."

I closed my eyes for a moment to blot out the horror of the battle. His grip on my arm eased somewhat, and the noise and reek of the battle seemed to fade away.

I opened my eyes and it was Agla holding on to my arm, not Ahriman. We were back in the dark stone temple at Karakorum. Ahriman gave me a last parting smile, more a grimace than anything else, and disappeared once again into the shadows.

Agla stirred and drew in a breath, as if a statue coming to life. "I can't see a thing in here," she said.

"I've seen enough. More than enough." I led her out into the daylight again.

In a few weeks, maybe less, a post rider would gallop into Karakorum bearing news of Subotai's victory. The Mongols would rejoice, but Subotai would not be called back to the capital for congratulations or reward. He and his army would press on, as Ahriman had said, to desolate the heart of Europe the way they had destroyed the heart of the Moslem world.

Before the Mongols came, Persia and the land between the Tigris and Euphrates rivers had been the most heavily populated, most abundant land on Earth. Irrigation canals that had been dug in the misty time of Gilgamesh made Babylon, and later Baghdad, the center of civilization—no matter what the Chinese thought. But once the Mongols swept through that part of the world, they razed the cities, utterly destroyed the canal system, and slaughtered so much of the population that it was centuries before the area could recover even a semblance of its former glory.

Now Subotai had Europe open and defenseless before him. And his warriors would do to Poland,

Germany and the Balkans what they had done to
the Middle East. Maybe Italy would escape, guarded
by the Alps. But I doubted it. Warriors who crossed
the Roof of the World would not be deterred by
mountains that could not stop Hannibal. Italy,
Greece, the flower of Mediterranean civilization
would be crushed as utterly as all the others.

And I had helped Subotai to do this. Ahriman
had much to gloat over.

CHAPTER 16

I tried to explain it all to Agla, but she could not seem to grasp the situation in its full implications. For hours I sat in our bare little hut, telling her of Ahriman and the other lives we had both lived, of Ormazd and the titanic struggle that spanned the centuries.

"Ahriman seeks to destroy the continuum of space time itself," I said, my voice rising to drive the point home, as if speaking louder would make everything clear to her.

She listened patiently. She tried to understand. But despite the fact that she had lived in the twentieth century and in other times, Agla comprehended very little of what I told her. In this incarnation she was totally a child of the thirteenth century.

"Ahriman is a dark wizard," she said at last, giving me her explanation of how the world looked to her, "and he has powers that allow him to show you the past and the future."

"But what he showed me happened today," I insisted. "And he didn't merely show it to me; we were there—thousands of miles away."

"You never left my side." She smiled faintly.

"Yes, I did. But I moved in a different time reference. To you, no time elapsed at all. To me, I spent nearly twelve hours at the plain of Mohi."

146

"So it seems to you. He is a wizard of great powers, that much is certain."

I decided to agree with her on that and let it go. That night we made love fiercely, as if both of us feared we would never have another night together. It was close to dawn when I finally drifted into sleep. I dreamed of Ormazd, arrayed in golden armor and riding a golden palomino horse. I watched him canter along a path through a green, parklike forest. The sun shone brightly and the sky was a cloudless blue. But as I watched, the forest thickened, grew darker, and soon the sun was hidden behind thick, black boughs heavy with foliage. I knew what was going to happen and I cried out to warn Ormazd, but no sound issued from my throat. I was paralyzed, powerless to move or even speak, as tiny, dark reptiles slithered across Ormazd's path and grew into lithe, wiry Mongol warriors who clambered over the palomino and pulled Ormazd down to the blood-soaked ground and stabbed again and again and again, over and over, blood spurting everywhere, arms and legs hacked off, throat ripped open, belly sliced apart so that I could see his living bowels being ripped by the filthy warriors of darkness.

"Orion, help me!" Ormazd screamed, his voice shrieking despite his wounds. "Where are you, Orion? Help me! Help me!"

All the world grew dark and cold and I remained paralyzed, frozen in deepest starless space while the entire planet Earth dwindled and disappeared into blackness.

I awoke, sitting up on the bed. Agla lay beside me, sleeping peacefully, oblivious to the world.

Think, Orion, think! I commanded myself. How can you defeat Ahriman if you don't even understand what he is trying to accomplish?

I closed my eyes again and considered the facts that I knew. Ahriman sought to destroy the fabric of space-time, to disrupt the continuum so completely that the entire universe would shatter. He claimed that we humans had annihilated his race, and he sought total revenge, the annihilation of the human race for all time and space. That meant that he must destroy Ormazd, whom Ahriman called our creator.

There was much that I did not know, much that I could not understand. I shook my head, wondering how I could reach Ormazd and ask him for more information. But obviously he felt that I had all the knowledge I needed. He had sent me here, to this time and place, with all the powers of my mind and body, and even with an understanding of the Mongol language printed into my brain. He had also sent Agla here, as a sort of native guide, a barometer of the attitudes and understandings of the people of this era. That was her role, just as Aretha's role in the twentieth century had been to awaken me to the task of finding Ahriman.

Somehow, Ogotai was the key to everything here. I had blurted out, when the Mongol warriors had first captured me, that I was an emissary to the High Khan. Ormazd had put that into my mind. I did not know why, but I knew with utter conviction that everything depended on my meeting the High Khan face to face.

As the rising sun slanted through the front room's single window, filling the dusty bare chamber with dancing motes, I resolved to make Ye Liu Chutsai grant me an audience with the High Khan.

Agla came with me as I sought out the mandarin. Dressed in her robes and beads, she served me as a sort of radiation meter, sensitive to the nuances of this strange world that I would never pick up for myself. But she was also the woman I loved and I wanted her by my side so that I could protect her from Ahriman and all other dangers.

It took the best part of the morning for us to talk

our way past the dour-faced guards and soft-spoken Chinese administrators of the ordu. We found ourselves at last in a small tent that stood to one side of Ogotai's main pavilion. Inside, the tent was richly carpeted, and furnished with chests and cabinets decorated with intricate scrollwork and inlaid ivory and gold. Their motifs of dragons and pagodas showed them to be from Cathay.

Liu appeared from behind a seven-foot-high ebony screen, moving as smoothly and mysteriously as ever in his floor-length robes to a cushioned chair set off to one side of a long table covered with scrolls and maps. He nodded to us and smiled; taking one hand from his wide sleeves, he gestured us to the smaller chairs near his own.

After a few polite exchanges of greetings, the mandarin asked me why I sought his ear.

"To beg you for an audience with the High Khan," I said. "It is urgent that I meet Ogotai."

He toyed with his wispy white beard for a few silent moments. I focused every atom of my being, every flickering synapse along the myriad neurons of my brain, at the old man's mind. He seemed to feel it; his body stiffened slightly, and he looked up, directly into my eyes. I saw confusion in his dark brown eyes, then a widening understanding of my purpose.

"I have been protecting you from possible danger," he said, almost apologetically. "If you meet Ogotai and he decides that you truly are the menace Ahriman prophesies you to be, he will have you killed."

"There is a greater danger in waiting," I answered. "I must see him now."

"Yes," Liu said, nodding his understanding. "I shall arrange an audience for you. Wait here."

He rose from his chair like a sleepwalker and glided behind the elaborate ebony screen once more. I turned to Agla and smiled at her.

She was regarding me with a strange expression on her face. "You forced him to do your will," she said.

"I convinced him that it must be done."

She reached up to brush a stray hair back from her eyes and a *snap* of static electricity stung her fingers. "You are a wizard also." Her voice was a whisper of awe. "Why didn't you tell me?"

"I'm not a wizard."

"Yes, you are. Like Ahriman. A man of great powers. I should have known it when you healed your wounds so quickly . . ."

"My powers are for good, not evil," I said. "But I am not a wizard."

"You have no idea of how powerful you truly are," Agla insisted. "What you did to my lord Chutsai . . . I could feel it!"

I tried to downplay my little instinctive trick of hypnosis, but Agla knew better than I what was involved. "You must not let Ogotai or the guards around him see your powers. They are superstitious men, and they would kill you out of fear."

"But they allow Ahriman to live," I said.

"Yes, because he prophesies victories in battle for them. I have listened to what the women say of Ahriman. He is feared for his dark powers, but the warriors are more afraid of displeasing him and having him prophesy defeat for the Mongols. These foolish men believe that Ahriman's prophecies *create* victory or defeat."

"Doesn't that put him in much danger? Wouldn't they be likely to slit his throat one night and be rid of him?"

She shook her head, tossing that stray lock of hair back over her eyes. Again she pushed it back, this time without a shock.

"Ahriman has been very clever. He came to Karakorum, from what I hear, as a priest of a new religion. A warrior's religion. The Mongols do not harm priests; they tolerate all religions. So, even though there is great fear of Ahriman's powers, the High Khan will not allow him to be harmed—so long as his prophecies of victory continue to be true."

He was clever, I thought. More clever than I, to understand these people so thoroughly.

"Besides," Agla went on, a bit more lightly, "the Mongols do not shed the blood of important personages."

"Oh? Then what . . ."

"They strangle them, or smother them beneath carpets. The Yassa forbids bloodletting among the Mongols, but it does not overlook the need for killing."

I sat in the stiff wooden chair, digesting all that Agla had told me. I could not help seeing Ahriman's face, and his ghastly smile, as I considered the fact that not even Genghis Khan's code of laws could prevent human beings from murdering one another.

Ye Liu Chutsai returned at last, looking somewhat puzzled, as if he could not quite remember why he was doing what he was doing.

"It is arranged," he said to me. "You will be received by the High Khan tonight, before the evening meal. You will come alone."

I glanced at Agla.

"The High Khan," explained Liu, "would not respect a man who was accompanied by a woman. It is the way of the Mongols, and no insult to you, lady."

"I am not insulted," Agla said. "Merely afraid that Orion might not understand everything that happens in Ogotai's court."

"I will be there to guide him," Liu said. "He is in enough peril, with Ahriman's prophecy already working against him, to have him appear before the High Khan with a woman at his side, and a woman whom many in Karakorum know to be a healer—and perhaps something of a witch . . ." He let the thought dangle.

"I understand," I told him. But, remembering what had happened to Aretha, I added, "I would like to have the guards protect Agla while I am away from her. Ahriman, or others, might try to strike at me through her."

The mandarin bowed his head slightly. "It will be done. You are both under my protection, for whatever good that does. And you, Orion, still have Subotai's recommendation to protect you."

I smiled at him. "I value Subotai's generosity, and I treasure your own, my lord Chutsai."

That pleased him. But he warned, "A shield is only as strong as the arm on which it is worn. You have a powerful enemy here at Karakorum. Be careful."

"Thank you, my lord. I will be."

Late that afternoon, as Agla fussed nervously about our quarters and I tried to concentrate on understanding what I had learned thus far so that I could peer into the future and determine what I must say to Ogotai, a servant brought new clothes for me to wear for my appearance before the High Khan. A gift from Ye Liu Chutsai.

Agla marveled at the outfit of leather and fine cloth. "You look like a prince! A handsome, powerful prince."

I smiled at her, although it hurt my newly shaven face. Shaving in cold water with a finely honed knife is a true test of courage. Agla beamed at me like a little girl and tried not to show how worried she was. We both knew that visitors to the High Khan's pavilion sometimes came away with gifts of gold and slaves and even horses. But sometimes they came away with molten silver poured into their ears.

"You must be very careful," she warned me, staring at me with somber, anxious eyes.

"I will be."

"Let the mandarin guide you. Do not allow them to see your powers; that will frighten them, just as Hulagu was frightened."

"Will Ahriman be there, do you think?"

Her gray eyes went even wider with fear. "I don't know. Perhaps."

Someone knocked at the door.

"Well, whether he is or not," I said, "that must be the guards to escort me to the pavilion."

Agla flung her arms around my neck. "I wish I were going with you!"

"I'll be all right," I said. I gave her a swift kiss and then went to the door and opened it. A quartet of warriors stood outside, their gleaming armor and burnished helmets making our two regular guards look scruffy and mangy by comparison.

I glanced over my shoulder at Agla, gave her a final smile, and closed the door. My escort marched me to the pavilion, but not before I looked back to see her standing at the door watching me, while the two guards looked back and forth from me to her.

I walked between the two bonfires and stood patiently while the guard at the entrance to the High Khan's tent searched me for weapons. It was no perfunctory search; I have had medical examinations that were less thorough.

Finally I was allowed to enter the tent, my four escorts walking with me, two ahead and two behind. I was either an important guest or a dangerous captive; I imagined that Ogotai and his aides had not yet decided which.

The tent was much larger than Hulagu's or any other I had seen. Carpets from China and Persia covered the ground. Silks and tapestries hung along the felt walls. To one side stood a long table of what appeared to be solid silver, laden with mare's milk, fruit, meat and salt: a symbol of the nomad's generosity to guests. Warriors stood at either end of the table, and more were posted at the various entrances to the wide, long tent. Up ahead of me, on a one-step-high platform, sat Ogotai, the High Khan, flanked on his left by half a dozen of the most beautiful women I had ever seen, and by twenty or more Mongols who could only be generals and other warriors, on his right. I recognized only Ye Liu Chutsai, standing in a splendid robe of sky blue and gold, to the High Khan's immediate right and slightly behind him.

Ogotai reclined on cushions. He had no throne. He was a solid, chunky man, in his early fifties, I judged, with an open, curious expression on his round face. He was getting fat, but he did not seem to care about that. In one hand he held a wine goblet of gold, encrusted with jewels. Well behind him stood a Chinese boy, holding a gold pitcher—the Khan's wine steward.

As I marched in step with my four escorts toward the Khan's slightly raised dais, I scanned the big tent for a sign of Ahriman. I could not see him. That was all to the good, I thought.

The warriors brought me to a stop three paces in front of the High Khan. I bowed from the waist, then straightened up. I had no intention of falling on my face in obeisance. I was an emissary, not a slave.

"Most High Khan," said Ye Liu Chutsai as I stood before Ogotai, "this is the man Orion, an emissary from the land far to the west, beyond the mountains and plains and even the wide sea."

Ogotai glanced over his shoulder and the wine steward hurried forward to fill his goblet. The High Khan took a deep draft from it, then smacked his lips and gave me a long, careful study. He looked me up and down, then suddenly burst into uproarious laughter.

"Look!" he said, pointing at me. "He has no shoes!"

CHAPTER 17

The whole tent burst into shrieks of laughter, all except Ye Liu Chutsai, whose usually impassive face looked upset and embarrassed.

I was still wearing my travel-stained sandals, and they must have looked quite incongruous, in the eyes of the Mongols, with the handsome outfit that the mandarin had sent to me. Liu had included a pair of leather boots, but as usual they were too small for me. The shirt and vest were tight across my shoulders and short in the sleeve, but I had managed to get into them. The shoes had proved impossible.

Ogotai was almost hysterical with laughter, and the other Mongols joined in heartily. The High Khan might have been half drunk before I entered; I saw nothing so very funny about the condition of my footwear.

"I never saw a wizard walking around with his toes peeping out!" Ogotai gasped. And that sent him into another round of boisterous guffaws.

I felt both embarrassed and relieved. At least, it seemed to me, the High Khan was not terribly worried about me. A man does not laugh until the tears flow down his cheeks at a suspected assassin or supernatural danger.

At last Ogotai's laughter subsided and the tent grew fairly quiet once more. The guards who had been pointing at me and doubling over with glee straightened up again and grew silent. Ye Liu Chutsai stared off into a distant nowhere. Ogotai raised his cup and the wine boy hastened to fill it.

"Baibars," the High Khan called, after another draft of wine.

A young man rose from his pillows and bowed to Ogotai.

"Baibars, find a shoemaker and see to it that our guest gets a proper set of boots."

"Yes, Uncle."

"Now then, man from the West, come and share some wine with me. Your people do drink wine, don't they?"

Half a dozen slaves sprang from behind the High Khan's dais and arranged big, boldly colored pillows for me to sit at his right hand. A wine goblet appeared, almost as precious as the one Ogotai held. I sat, took the goblet, raised it in thanks to him, and sipped the deep red wine.

"The wine of Shiraz," Ogotai said. "A country not far from where you encountered my nephew Hulagu."

I said, "It is a rare treat. Even in my faraway land, the wine of Shiraz is spoken of highly." This was the wine, I knew from my twentieth century reading, that Omar Khayyam praised in his *Rubaiyat*.

Lazily, almost indifferently, the High Khan said, "I was warned against you. I was told that you are a powerful wizard—and an assassin."

I glanced up at Liu, who remained standing two paces behind his Khan.

"I am a man, my lord High Khan, not a wizard. I am an emissary from a far-distant land, not an assassin. I carry no weapons . . ."

"But you need none," Ogotai interrupted. "You kill armed warriors with your bare hands. You catch arrows with your teeth." He grinned. "Or so I have been told."

"I defend myself as best I can, O High Khan. But if a warrior shot an arrow at me, the chances are I would stop it with my flesh, the same as any other man."

"That is not what I was told."

I took a deep breath, stalling momentarily as I wondered how far I could trust his good humor.

Finally I answered, "Most High Khan, surely you have heard more wild tales of fabulous things than any man living. You know how the truth becomes exaggerated each time it is retold."

He laughed. "Yes, yes. My own prowess in battle grows with every day that I sit here! The armies I beat are larger with each telling, and the numbers that I slaughtered grow like a column of smoke rising to the sky."

"My lord High Khan," said one of the Mongols seated a few places away from us, "let us not depend on this stranger's words alone. Let us test him."

He had the gruff look of a policeman to him; probably he was the Mongol responsible for Ogotai's security.

"What do you propose, Kassar?" asked Ogotai.

"Stand him up," the Mongol waved to the open area in the middle of the tent, "and let a few of the guards fire arrows at him. Then we will see if the tales we have heard are true or false."

Ogotai looked at me before answering, "If the tales are false, we will have killed an emissary."

"Better a dead emissary than a live wizard," the man called Kassar muttered.

"Or give him a sword and let him fight Chamuka!" said another Mongol. "That would be lively."

"Or a wrestling match!" called still another.

The High Khan listened and sipped at his wine. Ye Liu Chutsai stood over us impassively, gravely, and said nothing.

I knew that if they tried to shoot me with arrows

or match me against a swordsman, I would have to defend myself. That would mean showing them that the tales they heard about me were not such exaggerations, after all. Then what would happen? A wrestling match might not be so bad, but I seemed to remember that a man might have his neck snapped or his back broken in a "friendly" Mongol match.

Ogotai looked into my eyes from over the rim of his goblet. I wondered how much of his wine-drinking was a masquerade, a prop he used to give himself time to study the situation and think.

He put the empty goblet down on the carpet at his side. As the Chinese lad hastened to refill it, the High Khan silenced the tent with a single uplifted hand.

"The Yassa commands us to be hospitable to strangers who enter our camp," he said, his voice suddenly firm and clear. "This man is an emissary from a distant land. He is not to be tested like a freshly broken pony or a newly forged blade of steel."

Kassar was not satisfied. "But Ahriman warned us . . ."

"I have spoken," said the High Khan.

That ended the discussion.

Ogotai leaned back into the mound of cushions. He glanced at the brimming wine goblet by his side but did not touch it. Nodding slightly toward the women at his left, he said, "I was told that you have a woman with you, a healer. Does she please you? Would you like another? Have you enough servants to take care of you?"

"I am quite satisfied, thank you, most generous one," I replied.

He closed his eyes for a moment, as if a flash of pain had suddenly attacked him. When he opened them again, he said, "You are an emissary from the western lands. Subotai's message said that you know much about the lands beyond the black-earth country. What is your mission here? Why have you come to me?"

Why, indeed? I knew it would be senseless to warn him against Ahriman and get into a finger-pointing contest. Ye Liu Chutsai had warned me that, when in doubt, the Mongols took the easiest way out—by chopping heads in both directions.

It was my turn to search deep into Ogotai's eyes. I saw pain there, and understanding, and something I had not expected to find in the eyes of a barbarian emperor: friendship. This man who could direct the burning of cities and the slaughter of whole populations had decided, on the strength of my shabby footgear, that I was no threat to him. I liked him. He was willing to trust me, and he was not the drunken fool that Ye Liu Chutsai had led me to believe he would be.

What could I tell him, except the truth?

Lowering my voice, I said, "My lord High Khan, may we speak where others cannot hear? What I have to say to you is for your ears only."

He thought in silence for several moments before nodding to me. "Later. I will send for you." Then, raising his voice so that the others could easily hear him, he asked, "How did you make the trip across the Tien Shan in those ridiculous sandals?"

The Mongols laughed and joked among themselves as I launched into a description of riding from Persia without a pair of boots. The night wore on and they asked me about my country and the sea that separated it from Europe. I described the Atlantic Ocean as a wild and tempestuous sea, an unpassable gulf—which, for these horsemen, it truly was.

"Then how did *you* cross it?" Kassar suddenly asked. "By wizardry?"

The tent went absolutely silent. Even the High

Khan looked at me keenly. I had talked myself into a trap.

"Not by wizardry," I said, desperately trying to find an answer. "You have seen the sailing craft of Cathay, haven't you?"

Some of the Mongols nodded. Kassar was among those who did not.

"Ships such as those could cross the ocean, if they were lucky enough not to be caught by storms." I thought of the Vikings, who had made their voyages to Iceland, Greenland, and even Labrador in their open longboats.

"Then why can't we cross in such vessels?" Kassar demanded.

"A small number of men could," I said. "But to transport an army would take hundreds of ships. Many of them would be caught by storms or whirlpools or the monsters that come up from the deep." I silently prayed that my words would not someday reach Spain and delay Columbus. "An entire army could never make the crossing without losing more men than it would lose in many battles."

Ogotai frowned. "My nephew Kubilai dreams of sending an army across the water to conquer Japan. What do you prophesy about that?"

I hesitated, unwilling to step into another trap. "I make no prophecies, O High Khan. I am an emissary, not a prophet."

He made a small, grudging grunt. He would have liked to have heard a prediction, but I had no intention of getting in the middle of court politics.

The talk went on for hours, and toward dawn, when even the unmoving Ye Liu Chutsai began to look weary, Ogotai clapped his hands and announced that he was going to his bed. The rest of us got to our feet, bowed, and drifted out of the tent. I noticed that three of the women accompanied Ogotai as he headed for his sleeping tent.

I had barely made it halfway back to my house, though, when a warrior ran up to me and told me that the High Khan wanted to see me. My escort and I made an about-face and followed the warrior to the High Khan's private tent.

He was sitting on a high bed, his legs dangling over the edge. The tent was lit only by a few candles. The women were nowhere in sight.

The warrior stopped just inside the entrance and bowed. I did likewise.

"Man of the West," said the High Khan, "I want you to know that there are six armed guards in this tent."

I peered into the shadows and, sure enough, saw the glint of candlelight on steel helmets and jeweled sword hilts.

"They are my personal guards," Ogotai went on, "and extremely loyal to me. Each of them is deaf and dumb: they cannot hear or speak. But, at the first sign of danger to me, they will fall upon you and slay you without hesitation or mercy."

"Most High Khan, you are as wise as your position among men is lofty."

"Spoken like a true emissary," he replied, grinning at me. He dismissed the warrior who had accompanied me, and then, pointing to a stool next to the bed, he commanded me to sit.

"Now then, what is this message from the West that must not be heard by anyone except me?"

"My lord High Khan, the truth is that I was sent here to kill a man—the one known as Ahriman."

"Then you are not an emissary?"

"Oh, I am an emissary, High Khan. I bring you a message from my distant land, a message that explains why I have been sent here. This message holds the key to the future of the great empire that you and your father have created."

"And my brothers," he murmured. "They have all done their share. More than I, truly."

"Great Khan," I said, "I come from a land that is not only far away in distance, but in time. I have traveled across many centuries to reach you. Seven hundred years from now, the name of the first High Khan will be known and praised throughout the world. The Mongol empire will be known as the greatest empire that ever existed."

He took the time-travel idea without blinking an eye. "And will the empire still exist in that distant time?"

"In a way, yes. It will have given rise to new nations. China will be strong because you have united the Cathayan kingdoms of the north and south. Russia will be powerful: the lands that you know as those of the Muscovites and the Cossacks, the black-earth country and much of what was once Karesm—all that will be welded together into a nation that calls itself Russia."

"And the Mongols?" Ogotai asked. "What of the Mongols?"

How could I tell him that his descendants would be a minor satellite of the Soviet Union?

"The Mongols will live here, by the Gobi, on the grasslands that have always been their home. And they will live in peace, unthreatened by any foe."

His head went back slightly and he made a barely audible hissing sound. I could not tell if he was in pain or if the sound meant satisfaction.

"The Mongols will live in peace," he whispered, as if talking to himself. "At last."

Sensing what he wanted to hear, I went on, "There will be no more war among the tribes of the Gobi, no more blood feuds between families. The law of the High Khan, the Yassa, will be revered and obeyed."

Ogotai nodded happily. "It is good. I am content."

I wondered what to tell him next, how to get back to the subject of Ahriman and my mission.

"You wonder why I am happy at the thought of

peace?" Ogotai asked. "Why the High Khan of a race of warriors does not seek further conquests?"

"Your brothers and sons . . ."

"Yes, they still reach out. While there is land for a pony to tread upon, they will battle to possess it." He took a deep breath, almost a sigh. "All my life I have spent in wars. Why do you think I spared you a test of your strength this night?"

I smiled at him. "Because I had no shoes?"

With a fleeting grin, he replied, "No, Orion. I have seen enough arrows flying through the air. I have seen enough swordplay. I yearn for peace, for an end to pain and battles."

"Wise men prefer peace to war," I said.

"Then wise men are more rare than trees on the Gobi."

"Peace will come, in time, High Khan."

"Long after I have returned to my ancestors," he said without a trace of bitterness. It was merely a statement of fact.

"My lord High Khan," I started, then hesitated.

"You want to speak about your enemy, Ahriman. What is the matter between you? A blood feud? A family quarrel?"

"Yes, you could call it that. He is an evil one, High Khan. He means you no good."

"He has served me well in the short time he has been at Karakorum. The warriors fear him, but they like his prophecies of victory."

"High Khan, anyone can predict victory for the Mongols. When have you known defeat?"

Ogotai's tired face lit up briefly. With a laugh, he said, "That is true enough. But still, even my generals want to hear prophecies of success. It makes them feel better. And Ahriman has helped me to feel better as well. He is on his way here and should arrive shortly."

"Here? To your tent?"

"I summon him almost every night. He has a

potion that helps me to sleep. It's better than the wine of Shiraz."

My mind went into a spin, trying to digest this new information.

"It would be best if the two of you did not meet," Ogotai said. "At the slightest threatening move, my guards would kill you both."

That was my dismissal. With a bow I took my leave of the High Khan.

CHAPTER 18

I could not sleep that night, although to say "night" is misleading. The sky was already pearl-gray with the coming dawn when I returned to my house from Ogotai's tent.

Agla was wide-awake, waiting for me. We talked as the sky brightened into true morning. Finally she could keep her eyes open no longer and drifted into slumber, her head resting on my shoulder. I can get along with little sleep. I lay beside her, wondering what I should do next.

I had not been placed here by mistake or misdirection. Ahriman was here, working his plan for the destruction of the human race. He saw Ogotai nightly and gave him some sort of drink to help the High Khan sleep. Medicine? Liquor? Slow poison?

Why did Ogotai need help to sleep? Did his conscience bother him? He said he was tired of wars and slaughter, but yet he ruled an empire which *had to* keep expanding, or it would collapse into tribal wars. That was what Ye Liu Chutsai had told me.

I shook my head. It made little sense to me. Ogotai lived off the wealth of all Asia, longing for peace, while his brothers and nephews spread fire and havoc in the Middle East, Europe, and China. How can this be a nexus in the space-time continuum? What did Ahriman plan to do here? How could I

166

stop him if I did not know what he was trying to accomplish?

There was one way, of course. Simply kill Ahriman. Lie in wait for him at his stone church and slit his throat. Kill him the way he killed Aretha, without mercy or hesitation.

But a countering idea struck me. Perhaps that is what Ahriman wants! He has made no secret of his presence here. He has not tried to harm me or Agla. He has not tried to prevent my learning that he visits Ogotai's tent each night. Perhaps his murder would trigger a sequence of events that would accomplish his goal here, whatever that goal might be.

I felt suspended in midair, hanging on nothingness while two powerful forces pulled me in opposite directions. I was being torn apart, but there was nothing I could do about it. I could not move, could not take action, until I learned more about Ahriman's plans.

My deliberations, and Agla's sleep, were rudely shattered by an insistent pounding on our front door.

"What is it?" Agla wondered, instantly awake.

The pounding sounded like whoever it was would break the door down.

I pulled my robe around me as I got to my feet. Agla burrowed deeper under the bedclothes, looking frightened.

Opening the door—there were no locks in Karakorum—I saw a stumpy, wizened old man with skin that looked as tough as tree bark and fists almost the size of his shaved head. He wore shabby, stained clothes and had a huge leather satchel slung over one shoulder.

"So you're awake!" he snapped at me.

I glared down at him. "I am now."

He gave a disgusted snort. "I know how long those drinking bouts go on in the ordu. And while the High Khan is in his cups people get him to promise them things."

"Who are you?" I demanded.

"The bootmaker, who else?" He pushed past me and entered the house. "A messenger from the High Khan ordered me to come to you and make you a pair of boots. As if I don't have enough to do! But do *they* care? Not them! Make this stranger from the western lands a pair of boots! The High Khan himself has ordered it! Do it quickly or we'll all lose our heads! So here I am, whether you like it or not. I may have spoiled your sleep, but by all the gods you'll have a pair of boots that will please the High Khan, and you'll have them before the drinking starts again this evening."

He sat flat on the floor of the front room and began unpacking his satchel. I had my boots by that evening, all right, and fine and comfortable they were. But I never met a worse tyrant among all the Mongols than that bootmaker.

Ogotai had taken a liking to me, and he invited me to his pavilion frequently. One day he took me riding, out beyond the bedlam of the crowded, dirty, noisy lanes of the growing city, past the vast horse corrals and cattle barns, out into the endless, rolling grasslands.

"This is the true home of the Mongol," he told me, turning in his saddle to survey the vast, empty, treeless grassland. He took a deep breath of air unpolluted by crowded buildings and people.

I told him, "Far to the west, in a land called Greece, when the natives there first saw men riding on horses—long ages ago—they thought that the man and horse were one creature. They called them Centaurs."

Ogotai smiled in the sunlight. "Truly, a Mongol without a horse is not much of a man."

We rode frequently together. At first Ogotai brought a guard of warriors with him, but soon enough he rode with me alone. He enjoyed my company and he trusted me. I told him about the lands and people of Europe, of the great kings that were yet to be and of the glories of the ancient empires. He was especially interested in Rome, and disappointed when I spoke of the corruption and decay of its empire.

"We would not have High Khans such as Tiberius or Caligula—they can only exist when the Orkhons are spineless. That is not the way Mongols are."

Agla did not trust the High Khan's friendship. "You are playing with fire. Sooner or later the Dark One will put a spell on Ogotai, or he will get drunk and pick a quarrel with you."

"He's not that kind of man," I said.

She fixed me with those luminous gray eyes of hers, as endlessly deep as an infinite ocean. "He is the High Khan, a man who has the power to slaughter whole cities and nations. Your life or mine does not matter to such a man."

I started to tell her that she was wrong, but heard myself say, rather weakly, "I don't think so."

Agla remained unconvinced.

The summer wore on with me still stranded on dead center, not knowing what to do or what Ahriman was planning. Messengers galloped in from the west, breathless with the news of Subotai's victory over Bela on the plain of Mohi. Weeks later, long caravans of camels and mules arrived, heaped high with armor and weapons and jewelry, Subotai's spoils from Hungary and Poland.

I never saw Ahriman. It was as if we operated in two different time-frames, two separate dimensions. He was there in Karakorum, I knew. He knew I was there as well. We both saw Ogotai almost daily—or nightly. Yet, either by the High Khan's adroit planning or Ahriman's, we never met face to face in all those many weeks.

The wind sweeping down from the north began to have an edge to it. The grass was still green, but soon the storms of autumn would begin, and then the winter snows. In the old days the Mongols would move their camp southward and collide with other tribes who claimed the same pasture lands along the edge of the Gobi. Now, with Karakorum becoming more of a fixed city every day, the High Khan prepared to stay the winter and defy the winds and storms that were to come.

The Mongols organized a hunt each autumn, and Ye Liu Chutsai summoned me to his tent to tell me that the High Khan requested my company on the hunt.

The mandarin's tent was a tiny slice of China transported to the Mongolian steppes. Solid, heavy furniture of teak and ebony, chests inlaid with ivory and gold, an air of quiet and harmony—unlike the boisterous, almost boyish energy of the Mongols. It was the tent in which I had asked him for my first meeting with Ogotai. I had not realized then that Liu lived in it. Now I could sense the philosopher's stoicism all about me: Ye Liu Chutsai slept here, probably on that cherrywood bench covered with silks, but this tent was really a home for the books and parchment scrolls and stargazing instruments of the mandarin—more precious and rare than the body of an aging Chinese administrator.

"The High Khan has shown a great fondness for you," Liu said, after sitting me down at his cluttered desk and offering me tea.

"I have a great fondness for him," I admitted. "He is a strangely gentle man to be the emperor of the world."

Liu sipped from his miniature teacup before replying, "He rules wisely—by allowing his generals to expand the empire while he maintains the law of the Yassa within it."

"With your help," I said.

"Behind every great ruler stand wise administrators. The way to determine if a ruler is great or not is to observe whom he has selected to serve him."

Cardinal Richelieu came to my mind.

"Yet, despite your friendship," Liu went on, speaking slowly, carefully, "the one called Ahriman is also close to the High Khan."

"The High Khan has many friends."

The mandarin placed his cup delicately on the lacquered tray next to the still-steaming teapot. "I would not say that Ahriman is his friend. Rather, the man seems to have become something of a physician to the High Khan."

That startled me. "Physician? Is the High Khan ill?"

"Only in his heart," said Liu. "He wearies of his life of idleness and luxury. Yet the alternative is to lead an army into the field and conquer new lands."

"He won't do that," I said, remembering how Ogotai had told me he was sick of bloodshed.

"I agree. He cannot. Hulagu, Subotai, Kubilai—they lead the armies. Ogotai's task is to remain in Karakorum and be the High Khan. If he began to gather an army together, what would the Orkhons think? There are no lands for him to conquer except those already being put to the sword by the Orkhons."

I began to understand. Ogotai literally had no worlds left to conquer. Europe, China, the Middle East were all being attacked already. He would start a civil war among the Mongols if he went marching in any direction.

But then I thought of India.

"What about the land to the south of the great mountains, the Roof of the World?"

"Hindustan?" Ye Liu Chutsai came as close to scoffing as his cool self-restraint would allow. "It is a land teeming with diseased beggars and incredibly rich maharajahs. The heat there kills men and horses. The Mongols will not go there."

Liu was wrong. I seemed to remember that the Mongols eventually did conquer India, or at least a part of it. They were called Moghuls by the natives, a name that became so associated with power and splendor that in the twentieth century it was cynically pinned on Hollywood executives.

The mandarin brought me out of my reverie by saying, "Fortunately, it is the season for the hunt. Perhaps that will cure the ache in the High Khan's soul, and he will have no need of Ahriman's sleeping draughts for a while."

CHAPTER 19

A hunt by the Mongols was little less than a military campaign directed against animals instead of men. The Mongols had never heard of sportsmanship or ecology. When they went out to hunt, it was to provide food for the clan over the bitterly cold and long winter. They organized with enormous thoroughness and efficiency.

Young officers scouted out territories of hundreds of square miles and brought reports back to the ordu so that the elders could select the best location for the hunt. Once the place was selected, the Mongols got onto their ponies and rode out in military formation. They formed an immense circle, perhaps as much as a hundred miles in circumference. Every animal within that circle was to be killed. Without exception. Without pity.

The hunt took more than a week. No actual killing was allowed until the High Khan gave the signal, and he would wait until the noose of armed horsemen had been pulled to its tightest around the doomed animals.

Between the horsemen walked the beaters, clanging swords on shields, shouting, thrashing the brush all day long, driving the animals constantly inward toward the center of the circle. At night they lit bonfires that kept the beasts within the trap. All day long we rode, drawing closer and closer to each other as the circle tightened.

At first I could see no animals except our own horses. Nothing but slightly rolling grassland, with waist-high brush scattered here and there. By the third day, though, even I could spot small deer, rabbits, wolves darting through the high grass. An air of panic was rising among the animals as predator and prey fled side-by-side from the terrifying noises and smells of the humans.

I rode on the High Khan's left, separated from him by two other horsemen, nephews of his. Ye Liu Chutsai had not been invited to the hunt, nor would he have been happy out here in the steppes. I could see that Ogotai loved it, even though the physical strain must have been hard on him. He was in the saddle at daybreak like the rest of us, but by midday he grew haggard and quiet. He would fall out of the line then, and rest through the afternoon. At night he retired early, without the long drinking bouts he led at Karakorum. But even though his body seemed stiff with age and pain, Ogotai's spirits remained high. He was free of the luxuries and cares of the court, breathing clean fresh air, away from the decisions that had weighed upon him at Karakorum.

And I felt free, too. Ahriman was far from my mind. I thought of Agla, especially at night as I drowsed off to sleep on the hard ground, wrapped in a smelly horse blanket. But all that could wait. They would still be in Karakorum when we returned: problems never go away; they simply wait or grow worse until you return. For the present I was enjoying myself hugely, and I recalled that the Persian word, *paradise*, originally meant a hunting ground.

It would ruin the whole strategy of the hunt if animals were allowed to break through the tightening circle of horsemen. For the first few days, the animals simply fled from us, but as the noose closed in on them, some of the terrified beasts tried to break out. There was no alternative but to kill them. To allow even one to escape was regarded as a disgrace.

The sour-faced Kassar was riding on my left the morning that a wolf, slavering with fear and hate, launched himself at the space between us. Kassar spitted him on his lance while I sat on my pony, too hesitant to beat him to the game. The wolf howled with agony and tried to reach around and gnaw at the lance, but three of the beaters rushed up and clubbed it to death.

Kassar laughed and waved his bloody lance high over his head, while I thought how strange it was that I could kill a man without an instant's hesitation, yet allowed Kassar to move first on the brute animal.

Later that day I found myself riding next to Ogotai. His nephews had stopped for a quick meal of dried meat and a change of mounts. The afternoon sun felt warm, although the breeze was cool.

"Do you enjoy the hunt, man of the West?" he asked me.

"I've never seen anything like this before. It's like a military campaign."

He nodded. "True. It is a chance for the younger warriors to show their bravery and their ability to carry out orders. Many a general has been trained in battle against the beasts of the fields."

So this was the Mongol version of the playing fields of Eton.

A servant rode up with some dried meat and fruits in a leather pouch, along with a silver flask of wine. Ogotai shared the meal with me as we kept on riding. Ahead of us, animals were scurrying, leaping, running in circles through the grass, more confused and terrified with each inexorable step our ponies took.

Ogotai was draining the last drop of wine, tipping the silver flask high and holding his head far back, when a boar broke out of a small thicket and

started a mad dash directly toward us. The High
Khan could not see the animal, but his pony did.
Neighing wildly, it reared back on its hind legs.

Anyone but a Mongol would have been thrown
out of the saddle. As it was, Ogotai lost the reins
he was holding loosely in his left hand. The wine
flask went flying, but he grabbed the pony's mane
and held on.

I saw all this out of the corner of my eye, because my attention was focused on the boar. I
could see its hate-filled red eyes and flecks of sa-
liva flying from its open mouth. The beast's tusks
gleamed like twin daggers, backed by a thickly
muscled neck and a strong, compact body bris-
tling with fury.

My own horse had swung around away from
Ogotai's, trying to avoid the boar's rush, so that I
could not shift the lance I carried in time to spit
the charging animal. It was heading straight for
Ogotai's pony.

Without even thinking, I dove from my saddle,
pulling the dagger from my belt as I hit the boar's
flank like a football linebacker trying to stop a
galloping fullback. We rolled over each other, the
boar squealing and squirming, as I drove the dagger into its hide again and again, my left arm
wrapped around its throat. I could hear the thud-
ding of hooves around me—my own pony or
Ogotai's, I did not know which. I remember
thinking, ludicrously, how foolish it would be to
be killed by a horse's kick while I thrashed around
on the ground wrestling with a maddened boar.

Finally the tusker shuddered and went limp. I
yanked my dagger from its hide with an effort and
got slowly, shakily to my feet. A dozen Mongol
warriors surrounded me, swords and lances ready to
attack the now-dead animal. More warriors sat on
horseback behind them, bows at the ready. Among
them was Ogotai.

For long moments no one spoke. I spat grass and dirt from my mouth. My shoulder ached, but otherwise I seemed to be all right.

"Man of the West," called Ogotai from his saddle, "is that the way you hunt boars in your country?"

The tension broke as they all laughed. I joined in, feeling suddenly foolish. If I had been a better horseman, I could have speared the animal and been done with it. Ogotai was right: I had made my kill the hard way.

A servant led my pony back to me and I swung into the saddle. Kassar grinned at me humorlessly; the wolf he had killed was tied behind his saddle. I saw that Ogotai's nephews had returned, and began to lead my pony to my usual station, between the nephews and Kassar.

"No," said the High Khan. "Stay here, beside me." He reached out and gripped my arm. "You will ride at my side now—in case we meet more boars."

I bowed my head at his compliment, then turned and gave Kassar a self-satisfied smile. He glowered at me.

Like friendships forged in the heat of battle, the bond between Ogotai and me became firm and lasting that day. We rode together for the rest of the hunt, and during the terrible day of carnage at the end, when we killed and killed and killed again until we were all delirious with blood lust, we never left each other's side.

We rode side by side at the head of the troop on the return to Karakorum. Behind us stretched a mile-long column of mounted warriors and ox-drawn carts piled high with dead game—every kind of animal from squirrel to deer, from boar to wolf.

I was anxious to see Agla, to tell her of the adventure of the hunt, to hold her in my arms once more and feel her body against mine.

Ogotai became quieter as we neared Karakorum, more somber with every step we took. He looked almost as if he were in pain, and by the time we could see the dust clouds from the corrals that marked the city's outskirts, he was obviously gloomy and depressed.

I began to think of Ahriman, and grew as downcast as Ogotai. The two of us had thrown off our problems and run away for more than a week, like schoolboys playing truant. But the problems were still there in Karakorum, waiting for us.

"My lord High Khan," I said, swinging my pony so close to his that they almost touched, "it is time for me to deal with Ahriman."

"What would you do, kill him?"

"If I must."

Ogotai shook his head. "No. I will not allow blood to be shed, not even by you, my friend from the West. Ahriman has his place in Karakorum, as all men do."

"He ministers to you," I said.

If Ogotai was surprised to learn that I knew of Ahriman's medications, he did not show it. "The man gives me a draught that helps me to sleep, nothing more."

"Have you thought, High Khan, that his purpose may be to help you to sleep—permanently?"

"Poison?" Ogotai turned in the saddle, his eyes wide with surprise. Then he laughed. He did not answer my question; he merely laughed as if I had told the funniest joke in the world.

I puzzled over his reaction and tried to draw him into further conversation, but Ogotai was finished discussing the matter. He had made up his mind that Ahriman and I would not come into conflict; he had thrown his protection over us both and produced a stalemate between us.

At least that is what I thought as we rode into Karakorum.

It was almost nightfall by the time we had dismounted in the wide open area between the High Khan's pavilion and the rest of the city to unload the tons of meat from the carts. A huge throng gathered, oohing and ahhing over the immense catch we had brought home. Ye Liu Chutsai appeared at Ogotai's side, carrying a scroll from which he read to the High Khan. The affairs of state were already being poured into Ogotai's ear, even before he had shaken the dust of the hunt from his shoulders.

I searched through the crowd and could not see Agla. She must be waiting at the house, I told myself. The boar that I had killed had been given to me by the High Khan, and now servants were hauling it off to be skinned and preserved. It would feed the two of us for many weeks.

Ahriman was nowhere to be seen, but I did not expect to find him rubbing shoulders with the mob. He was a creature of shadows and silences; he would seek out the High Khan later, when almost everyone else was asleep.

Finally the High Khan gave permission for his hunting companions to go off to their own quarters. I fairly sprinted for the house. I opened the door, expecting Agla to be waiting at the threshold for me.

She was not. I searched the two small rooms in vain. Agla was gone.

CHAPTER 20

I did not hesitate an instant. I knew what had happened as certainly as if I had witnessed it with my own eyes. Dashing out of the house, I ran through the dark, narrow, twisting pathways of the city toward the stone temple of Ahriman. Thunder rumbled overhead and streaks of lightning flicked across the dark sky. People were rushing to get indoors before the rain started. I pushed past them, seeing in my mind's eye the filthy way he had murdered Aretha. My right hand tightened on the hilt of my dagger as I ran.

Even in the darkness I found Ahriman's stone temple, as if an invisible beacon guided me to it. The night air smelled damp and crackled with electricity as I raced toward its low, dark entrance. A bolt of lightning cracked the sky in half, silhouetting the stone building for an eye-flash of a moment. Then thunder growled and rumbled across the heavens, ominously.

I burst inside, into the deeper darkness of Ahriman's lair. He stood at the stone altar, his hands raised as if in prayer, his back to me. Without an instant's hesitation, without even a thought, I launched myself at him.

He swung around, as fast as I drove at him, and batted me away as easily as a man swats at an annoying gnat. The blow sent me reeling across the stone floor. I thudded against the wall painfully and the dagger clattered out of my grasp.

"You are a fool," Ahriman hissed at me, his eyes glowering in the shadows.

"Where is she? What have you done to her?"

He drew in a deep breath and eyed me calmly. "She is out on the grassland somewhere, searching for you. Someone told her that you had not come back with Ogotai and the others."

"That's a lie!"

"But she believed it. She is out there now, in the dark, trying to find you."

"I don't believe you."

He shrugged his powerful shoulders. "She is alone. Her brave escort of Mongol warriors are terrified of thunderstorms and have left her. They fear lightning, you know. Sitting atop a pony in a wide treeless plain while wearing a steel helmet—it makes them natural lightning rods."

I had heard tales of warriors throwing themselves into rivers or lakes during lightning storms. And drowning.

"I have not harmed her, Orion," said Ahriman, his back to the altar and the symbols carved into the stone wall above it. "I have no need to."

I got slowly to my feet. "No, you've merely sent her out into the storm alone."

"Then why don't you take a pony and go out and find her? She will be overjoyed to see you once again."

"That's what you want, isn't it? You want me to leave the city, so that you can go to Ogotai and finish your work."

He did not answer.

"You're poisoning him," I accused. "And you want me out of the way so that you can kill him."

For a long moment Ahriman made no reaction whatever. Then he lifted his face toward the ceiling and began to laugh—a harsh, labored, wheezing sound that was utterly without joy. It sounded as if he were in pain; it grated on my ears and made me wince.

"I was more right than I knew," he said at last, gasping for breath. "You are a bigger fool than I thought. Kill Ogotai? Kill him?" He laughed again, and the sound was like fingernails rasping across rough stone.

Finally he grew serious and pointed to the door. "Go, find your woman. She is unharmed—by me. What may happen to her in this storm is another matter."

I had no choice. I could not fight him; he was too powerful for me. And even though I did not trust his words, the thought of Agla alone out on the steppe in the storm drove me out of his temple and toward the horse corral at the city's edge.

It began to spatter rain as I commandeered a horse from the old man tending the nearest corral. My clothing told him I was of high rank, and even in the lightning-punctuated darkness he could see that my size and strange skin color marked me as the strange emissary from the West. Theft was virtually unknown among the Mongols. If I failed to bring back the pony in a reasonable time, warriors would be sent after me. There was no place in the known world where I could hide from their relentless justice.

"But this is no time to ride out into the open land," the old man insisted as I saddled the pony. "The storm can kill a man . . ."

I ignored him and swung up into the saddle. The rain was coming down strong now; we were both already soaked. Lightning forked down like fingers searching for prey. The thunder was shattering the night now, as the storm marched toward us.

"You'll kill the pony!" the old man shouted at me. True Mongol that he was, he saved his strongest argument for last.

But he was too late. I kicked at the mount's flanks and we galloped into the wild night.

It was utterly foolish, I knew. Riding out into that storm to find Agla was like searching for a particular flower in a jungle the size of Africa—blindfolded. Yet I had to do it. I had to find her before one of those probing fingers of lightning blasted the life out of her. Strangely, I was not afraid at all of my being hit by lightning. I should have been, but I was not.

My pony was skittish, frightened, and almost bolted when a flash of lightning flicked across the sky. The thunder did not seem to bother it, though; probably it had been trained to bear up under the noise of battle. The rain became torrential, and I could barely see beyond the pony's mane. Squinting into the darkness, hunched against the icy, wet wind, I urged the animal onward, farther into the night and the storm.

But the back of my mind was churning, digesting information, sifting data. Overriding all else was my mission to prevent Ahriman from achieving his goal. But how could I stop him if I didn't know what he was trying to accomplish?

Over and over again, as I rode through the blinding rain, I tried to put all the pieces of the puzzle together. Ahriman had seemed genuinely surprised when I had accused him of attempting to murder Ogotai. Yet I knew he was giving the High Khan a potion of some kind, almost every night that Ogotai was in his ordu. If it was not slow poison, what could it be?

The pony's pace slowed to a trot, and then to a slow walk, as we pushed on against the wind and rain. Not even the bravest Mongol warrior would try to ride through this storm, I knew. But I had to. I had to.

What was Ahriman trying to achieve? If he wanted to kill me, he could have done it right there in his temple. Why send me out into this maelstrom? So that I could be killed by a lightning bolt, rather than slain by his own hand? That seemed far-fetched.

To keep me away from the city? Yes, that made some sense. Keep me away from Ogotai. But why, if Ahriman had no desire to murder the High Khan? Why would he want to keep me away?

I closed my eyes, not so much against the driving rain, but to focus my memory on the bits and scraps I had read in the twentieth century about the Mongol empire. With the clarity of perfect recall I saw page after page of history. I could read the words just as clearly as if the books were in my hands. Yet I could not remember what I had never read! How much history had I studied in my earlier life? I knew that the Mongols had never conquered Europe; Subotai had crushed the armies raised by Bela, true enough, but he had never gone further into Europe. Why?

The answer flashed before my eyes like a bolt of the lightning that was shredding the darkness of the night. I saw the line from a book I had read in the twentieth century:

"No victory in battle saved western Europe from inevitable disaster. Its armies, led by reigning monarchs as incapable as Bela or Saint Louis of France, were utterly incapable of standing against the rapidly maneuvering Mongols led by Subotai. But the war never came to a final issue. A courier from Karakorum caused Subotai to halt his victorious sweep westward and turn back toward the Gobi. The courier brought the tidings of Ogotai's death."

Ogotai's death! When the High Khan dies, all the Orkhons and generals return to Karakorum to elect a new High Khan. Genghis Khan's death had halted the Mongol expansion, for a year or so. Ogotai's death stopped the Mongol invasion of Europe—permanently.

Ahriman was not out to murder Ogotai; he was in Karakorum to protect him, to keep him alive, so that Subotai could finish the work of conquering all of Europe. Because after Subotai would come the mandarins of Ye Liu Chutsai, bringing peace and order and the law of the Yassa to the enslaved inhabitants of Europe. Bringing the same immobility and eventual stagnation to Europe that their bureaucracies had brought to China itself and the Middle East.

Europe would be homogenized by the mandarins, under the sword arm of the Mongol conquerors. The petty, boisterous states of Europe would be stamped out of existence and blended into the iron despotism of the East. The great cities would wither—or be destroyed. The Renaissance would never happen. Europeans would never discover science, never build the high technology that allowed democracies and human freedom to flourish. America would be discovered by Chinese navigators, if it all.

At last I saw Ahriman's plan clearly. By allowing the Mongols to conquer all of Eurasia, he guaranteed that the human race would stagnate and slowly, slowly die away, crushing itself under the changeless heel of Oriental tyranny. What Ye Liu Chutsai believed to be the highest civilization in the world was in fact a trap in which humankind would extinguish itself.

If Ahriman could achieve that, he would have altered the space-time continuum to such an extent that its very fabric would be ripped asunder. The continuum would shatter. Ormazd would be overthrown. The human race would perish utterly. The forces of darkness would win the long, eternal struggle.

If Ogotai lived. That is what Ahriman was trying to accomplish. That was what I had to prevent.

My mission in this time and place was not to kill Ahriman. It was to kill Ogotai.

Cursing, crying out into the thunder-racked night, I turned my pony back toward the haphazard capital of the Mongols, leaving Agla alone and defenseless in the storm, heading back toward Karakorum to murder the man who had befriended me.

CHAPTER 21

I tethered the pony under the projecting eaves of the house the Mongols had given Agla and me. The rain still fell heavily, sweeping across the cleared space around the ordu in blustery waves. The twin bonfires were dark and cold. No one was in sight. Ogotai's tent swayed and billowed in the gusting wind. I could hear the tent ropes creaking.

Every conscious thought in me urged me to ride back into the grassland to find Agla. She was searching for me there, risking her life to save mine, and I was here on a mission of murder while I left her to wander alone through the raging storm.

But something stronger than my conscious will was directing me now. Like a warrior who marches numbly into battle even though every fiber of his being wants to run away to safety, I walked toward Ogotai's sleeping tent, stiff with the icy cold of the night, hunched over against the slashing rain and wind.

I was a clever assassin. Instead of heading straight for the sleeping tent, I crossed the open space surrounding the ordu on the far side of the High Khan's main tent, away from the blackened embers of the two bonfires, where there would be no guards posted to observe my approach. I entered the big, swaying, creaking tent. It was dark and empty. The long silver table had been cleared. The

cushions where the Mongols lounged while their
slaves attended them had been removed.

Crossing the darkened tent swiftly, I crept along
the shadows of the silken hangings that shielded
the entrance which connected it to the High Khan's
sleeping tent. Two warriors stood at the entrance,
erect, awake, and fully armed. I slid back behind
the hangings and tried to gather my thoughts.

Whether Ogotai was awake or asleep, he would
no doubt have those six deaf and dumb guards in
his sleeping tent with him. My only chance to kill
him would be to rush in and strike him down
before the guards could react. What happened afterward did not matter. I told myself that several
times, and I knew that I was prepared to do it. But
the other side of my mind was begging me to run
away, to find Agla and go far from here, find a
place where death and murder were unknown, a
place where we could live together in peace and
love forever.

While the Mongols conquered the rest of the
world and inexorably snuffed out the flickering
lights of learning and growth, I heard myself
answer. While the human race sank into decay,
despotism, and despair. While Ahriman won his
eons-long battle and watched all of humanity wither
away into extinction.

I shook myself the way a dog shakes water off its
fur. "Agla," I whispered so low that I myself could
not truly hear the words, "perhaps we'll meet again,
somewhere, somewhen."

Slipping my curved dagger from its sheath, I
slowly, silently sliced a cut through the tough fabric of the tent wall and carefully stepped through
it, into Ogotai's sleeping tent. Another silk hanging was draped over the tent's side so that I made
my entrance unnoticed by those inside.

The tent was dimly lit. Through the silken fabric
I could see nothing more than shadows. But I

could hear men speaking. It was Ahriman's voice that I heard first. I froze where I stood, not even daring to breathe for fear of moving the tapestry and revealing my presence.

"Sleep will come soon, my lord High Khan," said the Dark One's heavy, tortured voice.

"The pain is bad tonight," Ogotai replied.

"It is the dampness," Ahriman said. "Wet weather makes the pain worse."

"And you make the potion stronger."

"That is necessary, to keep the pain away."

"But the pain is winning, Persian. Each night it grows stronger. I can feel it, despite your potions."

"Did you suffer badly during the hunt, my lord?"

"Enough. Your draughts kept me going. But if it hadn't been for Orion, I would be dead now."

I could hear Ahriman give out a long, growling sigh.

"You still prophesy," Ogotai asked, "that he will try to kill me?"

"He is an assassin, High Khan. He was sent here to murder you."

"I cannot believe it."

Ahriman's rasping voice took on an air of complete certainty. "The next time you see him, High Khan, he will attempt to assassinate you. Be warned."

"Enough!" Ogotai snapped. "If he had wanted to kill me, he could have let the boar do the job. He saved my life, wizard."

"And won your confidence."

Ogotai did not answer. For long moments I heard nothing but the keening of the wind outside and the creaking of the tent ropes.

"My lord High Khan," Ahriman said, in his harsh whisper, "a month from now your general Subotai will gather the strength of his army once again and march farther west, across the lands of the German princes, across the broad river called the

Rhine, and into the land of the Franks. These Franks are mighty warriors. It was they who turned back the Saracens many years ago. It is they who even today battle against the Ottomans near Jerusalem. But Ogotai will crush them utterly and destroy their cities. He will reach the wide sea and plant the yak-tail standard on its shore. You will rule all the lands between the two mighty oceans. All of Europe and Asia will be yours."

"You have prophesied all this before," said Ogotai. He sounded weary, dulled, sleepy.

"Indeed," Ahriman admitted. "But none of this will come to pass if the High Khan dies and all the Orkhons and generals must return to Karakorum to elect a new High Khan. Orion knows this. That is why he must strike you down soon, within the next few days, if he is to save Europe from Subotai's conquest."

"I understand your words, wizard," Ogotai said, slowly. "But I do not believe them."

"My prophecies have never failed you, High Khan."

"Leave me, wizard. Let me sleep in peace."

"I am . . ."

"*Leave*," Ogotai commanded.

I heard Ahriman's heavy, lumbering tread cross the tent and disappear into the night. For several minutes I remained behind the tapestry while, one by one, the lamps in the tent were snuffed out. Finally there was only one dim light flickering. It stayed lit, and I decided that Ogotai was not going to have it put out.

I stepped out from behind the hanging. The High Khan was lying atop the quilts of his bed, wearing a rough robe of homespun. His face looked haggard. He was sweating. But he was still awake, and he saw me.

So did his guards. Six swords leaped from their scabbards.

Ogotai made a motion with his hands. The guards stood where they were, swords gripped tightly in their hands.

"They see the dagger in your hand, Orion," said Ogotai, "and fear you are here to slay me."

Only then did I realize that I still held the weapon. I opened my fingers and let it drop to the carpet. Ogotai gestured to the guards and they sheathed their swords and left the tent.

The two of us were alone.

The High Khan seemed drained of all strength. His eyes focused on me, and I could see agony in them.

"Have you come to fulfill Ahriman's prophecy?" he asked. "Have you come to kill me?"

"If I must."

He almost smiled. "It is not fitting for a Mongol warrior to take his own life. But I have a devil inside my body, Orion. It burns inside me like a red-hot coal. It is killing me slowly, inch by inch."

Cancer. That was why Ahriman was providing him with pain-killers. But not even Ahriman's skills could cure cancer once it was so far advanced.

"My lord High Khan . . ."

"Orion, my friend. I cannot be struck down in battle. I am too old for that. I barely made it through the hunt. But *you* can strike me down. You can give me a clean death, instead of this lingering foulness."

The breath caught in my throat. "How can I kill a man who calls me friend?"

"Death always wins, in the end. It took my father, did it not? It will take me. The only question is when . . . and how much pain there will be. I am not a coward, Orion—" he swallowed hard and squeezed his eyes shut for a moment—"but I have had my share of pain."

I stood there by his bed, unable to move.

"You are a loyal friend," Ogotai said. "You hesitate because you know that if you kill me, the prophecy of Ahriman will not come to pass: the Mongols will not rule the entire world."

How could I tell him that this was why I *had to* murder him?

"I like your own prophecy better, Orion. Let the Mongols live in peace. Let other nations struggle and war against one another. As long as we find peace . . . and rest . . ."

His eyes squeezed shut again and his whole body arched on the bed like a man being tortured on the rack.

When he opened his eyes again, there were tears in them. "Not even Ahriman's potion is helping tonight. I weep like a woman."

My hand slid to the empty sheath at my belt.

Ogotai's breathing had become shallow, gasping. "It would not be good for the others to see me so weak. The High Khan should not appear with tears in his eyes."

I remembered that among the Mongols it was forbidden to shed blood. I turned and took a pillow from the chair beside his bed.

Ogotai actually smiled at me. "Good-bye, my friend from the western lands."

I covered his face with the pillow. By the time I lifted it from him, there were tears in my eyes.

I walked slowly out of the tent, past the guards who still stood at the entrance. The storm had blown away. Dawn was turning the sky pink. I strode back to the house, to the pony tethered beside it, mounted up and rode out of the city. Agla was still there in the wilderness, somewhere. Perhaps I could reach her before the Mongols realized what I had done.

For two days and nights I searched the grassy open plain, wondering if Agla had survived the storm, wondering if the Mongols would come hunting for me, wondering what Ahriman was doing to revenge himself for my thwarting his plan.

On the morning of the third day I saw a pony, head drooping, reins dragging on the grass, its saddle askew and empty. I had been walking my horse, but I quickly mounted up and dug my heels into its flanks. I galloped along, following the trail that Agla's mount had left in the grass, my heart racing faster than the pony's drumming hooves.

And then I saw a figure sprawled on the ground as if it had fallen from its horse or dropped with exhaustion. I bent over my pony's neck and raced toward her.

But suddenly the world seemed to drop away from me. I was falling—falling in a crazy, wild, spinning tunnel—my arms and legs flailing against emptiness as a flashing kaleidoscope of vivid colors battered at my senses. Just as suddenly I was floating in utter darkness, disembodied in a black pit of weightless, timeless suspension.

"Agla!" I screamed. But there was no sound.

How long I hung suspended, bodiless in that dark void, I have no way of knowing. Slowly I began to realize that this was Ahriman's doing, his revenge upon me for thwarting him: I was sentenced to an eternity of nothingness.

But then I saw a tiny spark of light, a distant star glimmering against the vast, indifferent emptiness, and my heart leaped. The star grew, shimmering, into a golden sphere and slowly took the shape of a glowing golden man.

Ormazd.

You have done well, Orion. I could not hear his words, for no sound existed in this blankness. But I understood what he was saying. This was *his* doing, not Ahriman's. Ormazd had taken me away from Agla, whisked me out of time once I had completed his bidding. This was my reward for stopping Ahriman once again.

But your work is far from finished, he was telling me. Ahriman still threatens the continuum. You have only deflected his evil; you have not ended it.

I felt myself falling again and heard wind whistling past me. I opened my mouth in a long primal scream of anger—anger directed not against Ahriman, my enemy, but against Ormazd, my creator.

INTERLUDE

Orion's body floated lifelessly on nothingness in an infinite void. The Golden One appeared, shimmering into radiant human form, and began to examine his handiwork.

With senses that could discern the energy levels of individual atoms, the Golden One inspected the inert form floating before him. He nodded to himself, satisfied.

"He did not need to die this time."

The Golden One did not bother to look up. "No. Yet he still resisted my summons."

"He is learning to hate you."

"He is learning that his own petty desires are sometimes in conflict with mine. And the one he hates is the godlike personage he knows as Ormazd. That is only a small part of me, as you well know."

A silver gleaming lit the featureless expanse, and the one who called herself Anya appeared, clad in metallic silver from throat to foot, her dark hair tied severely back away from her face. Her silver-gray eyes looked first at the Golden One, as they must, and then focused on the body of Orion.

"He wanted to stay where he was," she said.

"Yes. With you."

"We were happy together."

The Golden One made a gesture that might have been resignation, might have been pique. "He was not sent on this mission to be *happy*. He has a task to accomplish."

"You send him to kill the Dark One; yet he does not have the strength to do so."

"He will, eventually. He must."

"You have not made him strong enough," Anya insisted.

"No." The Golden One shook his head. "It is you who are weakening him."

"I?"

"You make him realize how alone he is. You make him desire companionship, even love."

Anya's chin rose a stubborn inch. "Have you ever considered, while you are playing your game of infinities, that *he* makes *me* desire companionship . . . even love?"

"Nonsense! You cannot . . ."

"I did love him," Anya confessed. "When I was in human form, living down there in those wretched tents, he was magnificent. I thought him a god, almost. I think he reminded me somewhat of you."

The Golden One smiled. "Truly?"

"A god," she went on, "a being of great strength, and great goodness. And . . ." she hesitated.

"And what?"

"Great need." Anya's voice suddenly became almost pleading. "Can't you see how confused, how painful, it is for him? Cast into a strange time and place, commanded to do things that are impossible . . ."

"He succeeded in his task," the Golden One said. "He has kept the continuum intact."

"At what cost?"

"The cost does not matter, my dear. Only the goal is significant."

"You would sacrifice him—you would sacrifice all of them—to save yourself."

"And you," the Golden One pointed out. "If I am saved, so are you and the others."

"And so is *he*, the Dark One. He will be saved also."

"No. He must be destroyed."

"But you cannot destroy him without destroying us."

"That is not true. I will destroy him. This creature that you dote on will do that for us."

Anya looked down on Orion's silent body. "You know he can't achieve that. He is only a creation of yours. The Dark One has powers that he cannot match."

"He will defeat the Dark One."

"He can't."

"And I say he will! We have already stopped him twice. I will keep sending out this creature to defeat the Dark One, no matter how long it takes."

"Haven't you looked around you?" Anya demanded. "Haven't you seen what's happening? Are you so egotistical that you believe you actually are winning this contest?"

"I *am* winning," the Golden One replied. "The continuum remains intact, despite the Dark One's pitiful little schemes."

Anya raised one hand, and the emptiness in which they stood was suddenly filled with vast swirls of stars, boiling cauldrons of gas that glowed pink and ultraviolet, whirlpools of galaxies sweeping out to infinity.

"Look!" she shouted over the rumble of the expanding, exploding universe. "See what is happening to the continuum."

The Golden One followed her outstretched finger and saw stars collapsing in on themselves, titanic explosions that flung out seething gases and then sucked them back in to an insatiable vortex of energy until what was once a brilliant star became nothing more than a black hole in the fabric of space-time. He saw whole galaxies succumbing to the same forces, winking out of existence, dying even as he watched.

"Do you think you are winning?" Anya demanded. "While the continuum is dying, piece by piece?"

The Golden One snapped his fingers and the starry universe disappeared. Once again they were in the calm nothingness of the void.

"Do not be alarmed by side-effects, my dear," he said. "The battle is taking place on Earth. Of all the planets of the continuum, of all the living intelligences in that universe, it is these creatures of Earth that hold the key to our struggle."

"So you believe," Anya said.

"What I believe is true," answered the Golden One. "What I believe *is* the continuum."

"For how long?" she taunted. "How long will you be able to maintain your control? He is defeating you, O mighty Ormazd. The forces of darkness are gobbling up the continuum, bit by bit."

"That will all be reversed once the Dark One is destroyed."

With a sad, unbelieving shake of her head, Anya said more softly, "So you will send him back again?"

Glancing at Orion's waiting body, the Golden One replied, "Yes. It is necessary."

"Then I will go also."

"You are very foolish," said the Golden One.

"And stubborn. I know."

"You can't actually want to be with this . . . this, creature. You can't actually desire him."

She smiled. "He reminds me of you, a little. But where you have arrogance and power, he has doubt—and courage."

The Golden One turned his back on her, and abruptly disappeared. Orion's body began to stir; his eyelids fluttered as his fingers clutched at emptiness.

Anya watched him coming to life, and slowly

she faded into nothingness. But as she dissolved the human form that she had taken, her luminous gray eyes never left the face of the creature she had known, the man she had loved.

PART THREE:
FLOOD

CHAPTER 22

My eyes opened and showed me a blue sky bright with sunshine and puffy white clouds. The memory of Karakorum, of Ogotai and the Mongols, faded from my mind like a distant, echoing song. All I could think of was Agla, the sound of her voice, the touch of her vibrantly warm skin, her beautiful face.

"Ormazd," I thought, "do you understand what suffering is? Do you know how cruel you are?"

Yet, even as I said those words to myself, I had the feeling that I would meet her again. Aretha, Agla, whatever her true name was—she was bound to me, and I to her, through all of time. No matter how many centuries separated us, we would find each other. I knew it with all my soul.

I realized that I was lying on my back. Sitting up, I surveyed my new location. It was a broad open meadow of cool grass that sloped gently down toward a distant river. Trees grew at the water's edge, the first trees I had seen in a long while. The grass itself was long and wild and matted; no blade had ever cut it, from the looks of it. Wild flowers dotted the land with color. Rocks and boulders jutted here and there; no one had ever cleared them away. The trees by the river swayed in a warm wind; they rose up from a tangle of low foliage that hugged the river's bank. There was no sign of civilization, no sign of human beings ever having been here.

A rabbit's brown, lop-eared head popped up from the grass. It eyed me, nose twitching, as I sat there, then hopped up closer, well within arm's reach. It had no fear of me at all. After a few moments of inspection, it bounded away and disappeared into the long grass once again.

I looked down at myself. My garments were a simple kilt made of hide and a leather vest. A braided belt around my waist held a small knife. I drew it from the belt and saw that it was made of a smooth stone handle and a blade of chipped flint, tied to the handle rather clumsily with what looked like dried pieces of vine.

Closing my eyes for a moment, I tried to puzzle out where and when I might be. Obviously I had been sent backward through time again. Ahriman had told me I was moving back toward The War, from the twentieth century to the thirteenth to the . . .

I looked down at the crude knife in my hand once more. I was in the Stone Age, apparently. This time Ormazd had flung me backward not mere centuries; I had traveled back ten thousand years or more.

From the tortured hell of a blazing nuclear fury to the barbaric splendor of the capital of the Mongol empire, and now to this. A calm, grassy meadow on a sweet, sunlit morning. An Eden where humans were so rare that animals did not fear them. Civilization had not yet begun. Not even the first villages had been started. The pyramids of Egypt were a hundred centuries or more in the future. Glacial ice sheets still covered much of Europe, retreating grudgingly as the Ice Age gave way to a warmer climate.

Here it was springtime. Flowers bloomed everywhere. Insects buzzed and scurried through the grass. Birds swooped and sang overhead. I must be far south of the ice, I reasoned, or in a region where the glaciers had never penetrated.

I got to my feet. It was a beautiful part of the world, serene and untouched by human hands. Yet I knew that if Ormazd had sent me here, it was because there were humans in this time and place. And Ahriman. He would be here, too. Somehow, this spot was a nexus in the space-time continuum, a pivotal location where Ahriman planned to change the course of events. My task was to stop him, at all costs, and kill him if I could.

At all costs. I could feel my face harden into a grimace of anger and frustration. What did death mean to one such as Ahriman? Or to me? Pain, the shock of separation, the grief of loss. But all that was temporary. A moment, a blink of an eye later, and centuries or millennia had melted away and we still lived, still existed, only to begin the cycle anew: hunter and hunted, prey and predator—kill or be killed. Must it go on forever, endlessly? Was there no peace in all of space-time? Was there no place for me to rest and live like a normal man?

You are Orion, a voice within my mind spoke to me. Orion the Hunter. Your task is to find Ahriman and kill him. Through all the eons of time, if need be, you must seek out the Dark One and destroy him before he succeeds in destroying all humankind. For this purpose you were created. Ask nothing more.

I knew it was Ormazd's command, and I had no choice but to obey it. I knew that asking for something more, for rest or love or simply oblivion and an end to all existence, was futile; Ormazd would never grant me any of it. I knew that I would do his bidding because I had no real choice. But I did not have to like it. Nothing that Ormazd could do to me could make me serve him happily, willingly. I did what I did out of necessity, out of a sense of duty to my fellow human beings. But not out of love, or even respect, for the God of Light.

I walked to the river. It was pleasant, at first, strolling easily under the warm morning sun. My feet were bare, and I had to smile to myself to think that now I did not even have the sandals that I had worn in the time of the Mongols—the sandals that had caught Ogotai's notice. But my smile vanished as I remembered Ogotai, his pain, and how I had murdered the man who had befriended a stranger from a distant time.

The going was more difficult along the river's bank; the brush grew thick and tangled here. Thorns scratched at my bare arms and legs as I forced my way through. At last I stood at the water's edge, with the big trees swaying and sighing above me in the gentle breeze.

The river was slow and sluggish, meandering gently through the grassy plain. I knelt down and drank from its clear water. Off to my right I saw a row of stones rippling the water's surface; they had been lined up roughly to form a path across the river. This was the first sign that human beings had been here: a ford.

I made my way across the river and began climbing the gentle slope that led up and away toward a line of low hills. As I reached the crest of the ridge line, I saw that the land became more rugged, serrated into row after row of hills, each line rising slightly higher than the one before it. And off in the distance, floating like a disembodied ghost in the bluish haze, rose a strange double-peaked mountain. One of its cones was covered with snow at the top, but the snow was streaked with dark gray, and a thin wavering line of whitish smoke snaked upward and dissipated in the clean blue sky.

A slumbering volcano. Something about the mountain's double-peaked shape stirred a faint memory within me, but I couldn't pin down exactly what it was.

With a shake of my head, I turned to go back down the hill. The river-watered meadow looked better to me than these ridges.

That's when I saw them, coming over the ridge line about fifty yards to my right. Silhouetted against the bright springtime sky, a string of thirty-some people walked single file, heading in my direction.

I blinked. For a moment I thought they might be Mongols and that I had not traveled through time at all. But they were afoot, not mounted. And they were slender, fair of skin, their hair reddish and wild and long. Their clothes were hides, like mine. They were caked with dirt and I could smell their sweat and grime on the breeze. A few mangy, bone-thin dogs accompanied them. They bared their fangs and snarled at me, but they stayed near their masters.

The red-bearded man leading them carried a pole with the skull of a horned animal fixed to its top. He raised the pole and halted so abruptly that the children, back toward the end of the line, bumped into their elders and jostled them. I almost laughed—until I saw that all of the men, and several of the younger women, carried long, slim spears tipped with blackened, fire-hardened points. Even the pole carrying the group's totem was actually a spear.

For several moments the red-haired people did nothing but gape at me, their expressions ranging from puzzlement to curiosity to fear. Hands fingered stone knives. Several of them shifted their long, knobby-shafted spears to their throwing hands. I saw that all the women were armed, at least with knives, and even the bigger children carried sticks or clubs. The dogs continued to growl menacingly.

A Stone Age hunting clan, out of the dawn of

human history. Shaggy-haired, unkempt, gaunt with
the tautness of constant hunger, and as wary of a
stranger as a bird is wary of a snake. Yet they
were human, fully; just as human as I. Perhaps
even more so.

The red-bearded leader's upraised arm still hung
poised in the air as he looked me over very carefully.
A young woman stepped up beside him. My heart
leaped inside my chest. She was redheaded, just
like the rest of them, and matted with filth. But
even from this distance I could see that was
Agla/Aretha.

She showed no sign of recognizing me, though. I
saw her lips move as she spoke to the leader, but
her tones were too low for me to hear her words.

The leader silenced the dogs with a gesture, then
turned and gestured to two of the younger men,
further down the line. They glanced at each other
in the classic *Why me?* expression, but they started
walking slowly, reluctantly, along the grassy slope
toward me, hefting their long spears as they
approached. The rest of the clan gathered around
their leader in a ragged semicircle, ready to charge
at me or run away, back over the crest of the
ridge, depending on what happened next.

The pair approaching me were teenagers, the
Stone Age equivalent of cannon fodder. They were
beardless, but their coppery hair was shoulder-
long and matted. I could almost see the vermin
living in it. Every muscle and tendon in their arms
and torsos was rigid with tension. Their knuckles
were white as they gripped their spears and held
them pointed at me. They were too skinny, hollow-
cheeked, and young to look truly fierce, but they certainly lacked nothing in grim determination.

I raised both my hands, palms outward, in what
I hoped they would understand as a sign of peace.
At least they could see that I held no weapons.
They halted a good ten yards from me—close

enough to drive a spear clean through me, if I were slow enough to allow that to happen.

"Who are you?" asked the one on the left, in a quavering, cracking adolescent's voice.

I wasn't surprised that I understood their language. Ormazd had programmed it into me, no doubt, during my brief transition from one time era to another. If I could converse with the Mongols, or the twentieth-century Americans, for that matter, why not with these primitives whose language has not been spoken for millennia?

"I am a traveler, from afar," I replied.

"What are you doing here?" asked the other one. His voice was a bit deeper, but equally shaky. He raised his spear as he spoke, ready to throw it at me.

I kept my hands outstretched from my body. I knew that I could snap both their spears and their bones anytime I chose to. But I doubted that I could handle the whole clan if they decided to rush me all at once.

"I come from far away," I said, loud enough for their leader to hear me. "I have traveled a long, long time." No lie, I told myself. "I am a stranger in your land and seek your help and protection."

"Traveled?" asked the second one. "Alone? You travel alone?"

"Yes."

He shook his head vehemently. "You lie! No one can travel alone. The beasts would kill you, or the spirits of the dead. No man walks by himself, without a clan."

"I speak the truth," I said. "I have traveled a great distance, alone."

"You belong to another clan. They are hiding nearby, waiting to ambush us."

So there was warfare here. Killing. I felt a great sadness wash over me. Even in this young Eden human beings murdered one another. But I looked past the two frightened, suspicious youths at the young woman standing by the leader's side. Her eyes met mine. They were as gray and deep as those eyes I knew so well. But there was no spark of recognition in them, no hint of understanding. She was a woman of her time, a Stone Age huntress, as savage and uncouth as the rest of them.

"I am alone," I repeated. "I have no clan. That is why I want to join you. I am weary of being alone. I seek your friendship."

They glanced back over their shoulders at their leader, then turned back to me.

"You cannot be of the Goat Clan," said the deeper-voiced one. "Who is your mother? Who is your father? They are not of the Goat Clan. *You* are not of the Goat Clan."

It was all very simple in their minds. Either you were born into the clan or you were an outsider, a threat, a danger. Perhaps you could marry into the clan, but more likely a male took his bride to his own clan. Women could be traded back and forth, but not men, I was willing to bet. And the horned skull on the leader's pole had been a goat. I smiled to myself. It was a good totem. The goat is a hardy animal, willing to eat almost anything and as tough as the flint these people used for tools and weapons.

"It is true that I am not of your clan. I have no clan. I would like to stay with you. It is not good for a man to be alone."

They wavered, uncertain, and looked back at the leader again. He was scratching his red beard, frowning in concentration. He had never encountered a problem like this before.

"I can help you," I coaxed. "I am a good hunter. My name is Orion. It means Hunter."

Their jaws fell. All of them. Not merely the two youths, but the leader and the rest of the clan gaped at me. Even the dogs seemed to become more alert.

"Yes," I said. "Orion means Hunter. What are your names? What do they mean?"

Both the lads started yelling and brandishing their spears at me. Their pupils were dilated with rage and fear as sweat broke out on their bodies and the veins in their necks began to throb furiously.

Beyond them, the whole clan surged and roared. Without a visible signal from the leader they hefted their weapons and swarmed down the slope toward me, dogs and all. The two teenagers were jabbing their spears at me, working up the courage to make a real attack.

I made a very quick, very human decision. I turned and ran. I had no desire to frighten them further or to risk being swarmed under and hacked to bloody pieces by their primitive weapons. So I ran, as fast as I could.

They threw spears at me, but I easily avoided them. There was no organized pattern to their fusillade; over my shoulder I could see the individual shafts wobbling across the sky so slowly that I could have turned and caught them if I had wanted to. Instead, I simply dodged as I ran.

They chased after me, but their speed and endurance were nowhere near mine. Not even the dogs could keep up with me. Besides, they were merely trying to chase me away; you always run better when your goal is to save your own skin. In less than a minute I was beyond the range of their spears. Their leader sent a relay of four men after me, but their endurance was pitifully short. I jogged down toward the river, crashed through the underbrush, and dove into the cold water with a huge, belly-whopping splash.

I swam to the other side and crawled up into the foliage along the bank. My erstwhile pursuers stopped on their side of the river, pointing in my general direction, yelling and shouting angrily, but never so much as dipping a toe into the turgidly flowing water. The dogs yapped, but stayed close to the men.

After a while they turned away and headed back toward the rest of the clan. I crawled out of the brush and stretched myself on the grass to let the afternoon sun dry me.

CHAPTER 23

By nightfall I had reasoned out what had upset them so badly. Names. Primitive tribes are naturally wary of strangers, and in a landscape as thinly populated with humans as this one, strangers must be extremely scarce. Primitives are also very superstitious about names. Even in the time of the Mongols no one willingly spoke the name of Timujin, Genghis Khan.

To these Stone Age hunters, a person's name carried his soul and strength with it. To give your name to a stranger is to expose yourself needlessly and to invite witchcraft and danger, like voluntarily giving your fingernail clippings or strands of hair to a voodoo priestess.

Thinking back on the afternoon's encounter, I could see that I had shocked them when I voluntarily told them not only my name but also its true meaning. And when I asked them for their names, they attacked me. Obviously they thought me a demon or a warlock. I had terrified them and made them triply afraid of me.

As the sun set behind the row of rocky hills across the river and the sky flamed into achingly beautiful reds and purples, I picked out a mossy spot next to a tree for my night's sleep. I usually need only an hour or two of rest, but I felt physically weary and even more spent mentally.

Then the distant roar of a hunting lion echoed

through the darkening evening. Reluctantly I got up from the soft moss and climbed the tree. A pair of squirrels chittered at me angrily, then scampered back into their hole. I found a sturdy notch and settled into it. The bark was rough and hard, but I fell asleep almost immediately, thinking of Agla.

But it was Ormazd who came to me in my sleep.

It was not a dream; it was a purposeful communication. I saw him shining against the darkness of night, his golden hair glowing with light and his face smiling, yet somehow neither happy nor pleased.

"You have found the tribe." It was neither a question nor an acknowledgment of success—merely a statement of fact. His robes were golden, glowing. He was seated, but on what I could not see.

"Yes, I found them," I reported. "But I frightened them and they chased me away."

"You will gain their trust. You must."

"Yes," I said. "But why? What is so important about a gaggle of primitives?"

Ormazd looked as splendid as a Greek god, radiant against the darkness. But as I studied his face more closely, I saw that he was a troubled god, weary of struggle and pointless questions from mere mortals.

"The Dark One seeks to destroy this . . . gaggle of primitives, as you call them. You must counter him."

I wanted to say no; I wanted to tell him that I would refuse to do his bidding unless he gave me the woman I loved, unharmed and safe from the wrenching separations of this endless quest through time. The thought was in my mind, the demand on my lips.

But, instead, I heard myself asking meekly, "What does Ahriman stand to gain from killing a small clan of Stone Age hunters? How would that affect human history?"

Ormazd eyed me disdainfully. "What matter is that to you? Your appointed task is to kill Ahriman. You have failed in that task twice, although you have managed to thwart his schemes. Now he is stalking this clan of primitives; therefore, you will use the clan as bait to stalk him. What could be simpler?"

"But why me?" I pleaded. "Why have I been taken from my own time to hunt down Ahriman? I haven't the strength to kill him—you must know that! Why can't you deal with him yourself? Why must I die when I don't even understand . . ."

"You do *not* understand!" Ormazd's voice was suddenly thunder, and the brightness radiating from him became too painful to look at directly. "You are the chosen instrument for the salvation of the human race. Ask no pointless questions, and do as you must."

I had to shield my eyes with my upraised hands, but I pressed on. "I have a right to know who I am and why I am being made to do this."

Ormazd's blazing eyes felt hotter than the nuclear fires that had killed me ten thousand years in the future.

"You doubt me?" he rumbled. It was not a question, it was a threat.

"I accept you. But that is different from understanding. I had a life of my own once, didn't I? If I must die . . ."

"You will die and be reborn as often as is necessary."

"No!"

"Yes. You must die to be reborn. There is no other way to step through time, not for you and your kind. For mortals there is no way to move across time except through death."

"But the woman, Agla . . . Aretha—what of her?"

For many moments Ormazd was silent, his lips drawn into a tight line. Then he spoke again, more softly. "She is in danger from the Dark One. Ahriman seeks to destroy her, and me, and all of the continuum. If you wish to save her, you must kill Ahriman."

"Is it true that you, your race—" I hesitated, then plunged on—"that you annihilated Ahriman's race, all of his kind, except for him?"

"He told you that?"

"Yes."

"He is the Prince of Lies."

That was no answer, I realized. But it was all the answer I was going to get.

"When was The War?" I asked. "What happened?"

"That is something that you must discover for yourself," Ormazd replied, his image beginning to waver and fade before my eyes. Then he added, "And for me."

I was stunned. "Wait! Do you mean that you yourself don't know what happened? You don't know what took place in The War? What your race did to his?"

But he was only a pinpoint of light now, dwindling into the all-engulfing blackness. I heard his voice calling, from far away:

"Why do you believe that my race is not the same as yours, Orion? Are we not father and son?"

With a shock I realized that I was staring at the dark night sky. Twinkling stars gazed back at me from the depth of space as I clung to the tree's rough bark and searched the bowl of heaven for understanding, for meaning. I sought out the constellation of Orion, but it was nowhere in sight.

CHAPTER 24

For days on end I trailed the Goat Clan as it marched across the Neolithic landscape. I had to get them to accept me, but they were totally xenophobic; either you were born a member of the clan or married a member of the clan—or you were an outsider, to be shunned and feared.

But Ormazd's command was clear. I must save this clan from Ahriman's plan, whatever it might be; I must use this clan to trap the Dark One.

And the woman—the gray-eyed one whose beauty could not be hidden even by layers of grime and ignorance—I knew she was the one I had known as Agla, and even before then, as Aretha. But she gave no hint of recognizing me. Was she reborn each time I was, but without any memories at all of her previous lives? Why would Ormazd do that?

I thought I knew the answer. She was my local barometer, as native to this time and place as any other member of her clan. If I could get her to accept me, the rest of the clan would.

And I wanted her to accept me. I wanted her to love me, as she had loved me ten thousand years ago, as I have loved her through all time.

But they were a superstitious, fearful troop of savages whose prime instinct was to flee from the unknown—and kill strangers.

I watched them from afar. They spent much of their days hunting, the younger women beating the bushes for rabbits, squirrels, and anything else they could find, while the men roamed farther afield, looking for bigger game and generally finding none. The older women stayed by their campfire, tending the children and gathering edible plants and berries.

By dusk they were all gathered around their fire, the women cooking their meager meals, the men chipping new tools from stores of flint they carried in leather bags or hardening their spear points in the flames. They were a self-contained, self-sufficient group, living off the land, staying just above the starvation-level as long as they did not produce too many children.

Twentieth-century ecologists despaired of "modern" man's so-called throwaway culture and pointed to primitive tribes who, they claimed, lived in harmony with nature. Here I was watching the origins of the throwaway culture. These Neolithic hunters walked to a campsite, cut down brush and stripped trees of their smaller limbs to build a fire, killed whatever game they could find and tossed their bones away when they were finished gnawing on them. They left discarded flakes of flint, tools and weapons that were no longer useful, wherever they dropped them.

The smoke from their fires did not damage the purity of the Neolithic air. Their scattered refuse piles did not contaminate the soil. Their pitiful little camps did not harm the water table, nor did their hunting endanger any animal species. But the attitudes of these simple nomadic hunters would become the ingrained attitudes of all the generations of humans that followed them. What was acceptable for a few scattered bands of primitive hunters became a major environmental problem when those hunters' descendants began to number in the billions.

But, despite myself, I had to smile as I watched

them, day after day, and thought of the absurd assumptions that twentieth-century ecological moralists made about primitive peoples.

This was not accomplishing my mission, however. After several days of observing them, mostly from hiding, but now and then blatantly enough so that they could see me and know I was trailing them, I hit upon a scheme that would get them to accept me—I hoped.

I had boasted to them of my skill as a hunter. It had been mostly empty words; the only hunting I had ever done had been at Ogotai's side in the great Mongol killing drive. But I knew that my reflexes and senses were far enough beyond theirs to give me a great advantage over them in anything that required physical exertion and skill. After watching them stalking game and building their primitive snares, and usually failing to catch anything, I knew that I could improve on their methods.

So I began taking game from the countryside and leaving it at their smoldering campfire while they slept. Innocents that they were, they posted no guards as they slept out in the open. The fire protected them from dangerous night-stalking beasts, and other human tribes must have been too far away to pose a threat to them. It was easy for me to leave a brace of fowl or a rabbit or two that I had flushed out of the brush and killed by throwing small rocks at them.

It took me several tries, but eventually I fashioned a crude bow and learned how to make arrows that would fly halfway accurately. I brought down a young doe with my new weapon, although I had to finish the job with my knife. I left the catch at their campfire just before dawn.

I watched them each morning, from a distance and always from concealment behind rocks or bushes. They were startled at first, wondering how the dead game appeared in their midst. They discussed it for hours at a time, some members of the clan apparently believing that others had done the deed. But no one admitted to it, and after a few mornings of finding the gifts by their campfire, they began to realize that it was the work of an outsider.

That made them fearful, even though they ate the offered gifts just as though they had caught it themselves. But they started to post sentries through the night. At first they were drowsing youths, and I managed to slip past them easily enough. Then a few of the adult men stood guard, but it was a rare night when they stayed alert enough to prevent me from leaving a gift near the smoldering campfire.

Gradually I began to let them see me, but always at a distance. I would hold a fowl in my upraised hand or carry a young buck across my shoulders. They would huddle together and stare at me in awe. In the dark of night I would sneak in close enough to their crackling fire to listen to their talk, and before morning streaked the sky, I would leave the prize that they had seen me with the previous day.

Soon enough they turned me into a legend. Orion was eleven feet tall. His eyes darted flame. He could leap across rivers and stop spears in midair merely by glancing at them with his fierce countenance. He was a mighty hunter who could bring down a mastadon single-handedly.

Their talk of mastadons intrigued me. Apparently the clans came together, later in the year, and hunted down truly big game together. The elders—who may have been all of thirty-five years, or even forty—told tales of grand hunts where they chased entire herds of mighty tusked behemoths over the edge of a cliff and then feasted on their carcasses to bursting.

I listened also to the names they called themselves, and I learned that the red-bearded leader was Dal and the teenager with the cracking voice was Kralo. The woman I had loved in other times was known as Ava—and she was Dal's woman, I soon realized. That hurt. For days I wandered away from the clan, feeling alone and betrayed by a woman who had none of the memories I had, whose only sight of me had been that first day when I had surprised and terrified the entire clan. What did you expect? I raged at myself. These savages don't have the time or the resources to allow women to go unmated. Did you think she would wait for your arrival? She didn't even know you existed until a few weeks ago. Even now she thinks you are a demon or a god, not a man who loves her and wants to possess her.

Still I moped and sulked, filled with self-pity and a smoldering anger at Ormazd, who could put me into this situation without a thought about my feelings.

After three days away from them spent nursing my aching heart, I realized that I was not doing myself or them any good. I decided to return to the task that had been set before me. In truth, there was nothing else that I could do. I was a pawn in Ormazd's game, and the emotions of a pawn are not important to the chess master.

I sneaked back to their camp that night and listened to them asking themselves why the mighty Orion had abandoned them. What had they done to offend the great hunter? It took all my self-control to keep from laughing. How quickly the miraculous becomes common-place! The gifts of food that had frightened them, at first, they now considered quite normal. It was the *absence* of the formerly wonderful gifts that troubled them.

I decided to give them a real gift. First I thought back to the marches they made each day, the dis-

tances between one night's camp and the next.
They were obviously moving through this springtime with a definite objective in mind. I calculated
where they would camp two days hence and made
for that spot. To my pleasure, I saw that the area I
arrived at had obviously been used as a campsite
before: beside a shallow, swiftly gurgling brook
there was a patch of earth already blackened by
the fires of countless earlier camps and a mound
of weathered bones where they had tossed their
garbage.

I spent that night and all the next day *really*
hunting. With my rickety bow and with a sling I
had devised for throwing rocks, I amassed a huge
pile of slain meat for the clan: rabbits, birds, deer,
even a succulent young boar. I left the food at the
intended campsite, spending almost as much time
defending the cache against wild dogs and other
scavengers as I did in hunting down more game.

The dogs were my biggest difficulty. These were
not the half-tamed companions of the humans;
they were more like wolves than pets. They were
ferocious and intelligent. They hunted in packs,
and they would have dragged me down and killed
me if I had not been fast enough and smart enough
to outwit them. I hated to do it, but I had to kill
several of them before they finally gave up on my
horde and left the area.

I guarded the cache of meat through that long
night and most of the following day. Finally, as
the late afternoon shadows lengthened toward
sunset, I saw the vanguard of the clan approaching from over the grassy horizon—two of the teen-
agers whom Dal often sent out ahead of the rest. I
splashed across the rushing brook and hid in the
foliage on its other side.

The boys saw the pile of game first and began
leaping into the air and yelling madly. The rest of
the clan hurried toward them, gaped, and then ran

for the campsite. They were ecstatic. Never had they seen so much food in one place before. They gathered around the cache, swishing their hands through the air to shoo off the flies, and simply stared in awe at the pile of meat.

From my hiding place in the bushes I heard their leader, Dal, say gravely, "Only Orion could have done this."

"Can it be all for us?" Ava asked.

"We are his people," replied Dal. "This has been our clan's camp since before even old Makar can remember. It is Orion's gift to us. He has returned to his people. He is no longer angry at us."

I let them build their fire and settle down to feasting as the evening slowly pulled its violet blanket over the cloudless sky. I slipped away, went upwind along the bank of the stream, and where it eddied into a wide pool, I saw a fine solitary stag dipping his antlered head to drink.

Unlimbering my bow, I slowly walked toward the stag. It saw me, but it was so unused to humans that it allowed me to get within deadly range of it. I felled it with a single shot through the neck, then slit its throat swiftly and cleanly with my stone knife. I felt a twinge of conscience, the memory of a later century when human hunters stalked such beautiful animals for sport, not for food. With a determined shake of my head, I lifted the carcass onto my shoulders and headed back toward the clan's camp. It was heavy, and I walked slowly, carefully, through the gathering dusk.

Just as the first star showed itself in the dark sky, I stepped into the flickering light of the clan's camp with the stag across my shoulders. They were still eating, stuffing themselves as only people accustomed to long hunger can do, their fingers and faces greasy with meat, the campfire blazing hot and shining in their eyes.

I stepped into their midst and dropped the stag with a heavy thunk at Dal's feet.

No one spoke a syllable. For several moments the only sound was the hissing of spitted meat burning on the fire.

"It is me," I said at last. "Orion. I bring you another gift."

They were victims of their own propaganda. They had puffed up their stories about me so far out of proportion that now they seemed terrified of my presence. None of them moved. Their faces were rigid with fear and surprise. They probably expected me to strike them with lightning, or something equally drastic, I suppose.

Ava recovered her wits before any of the others. Rising slowly to her feet, she extended both her arms toward me.

"We thank you, O mighty Orion. What can we do to show our gratitude?"

She was filthy, her face and hands stained with the bloody, charred meat she had been eating. But in the firelight I saw the calm gray eyes that I had known and loved in other eras, and it took all my self-control not to clasp her in my arms.

I took a slow, calming breath and tried to speak in the somber manner they would expect of a demigod.

"I grow weary of solitude," I said. "I wish to be among you for a while."

That sent a murmur through them. Dal got to his feet and stood slightly behind Ava.

"I will teach the ways of hunting that I use. I will show you how to catch more game than you ever thought possible."

They remained unmoving, Dal and Ava standing, facing me, the rest of them still sitting in a semicircle around the crackling, hissing fire. I could see the conflict warring in their grimy faces. They were scared half out of their wits by me. Yet, to be able to hunt down animals like that! It was a tempting offer. Which would it be, their fear or their bellies?

Ava stepped closer to me and studied my face in the dancing firelight. I suppose I was none too clean myself, shaggy and unkempt.

"Are you a man or a spirit?" she asked boldly.

She was as beautiful as I remembered her. Tall and slender, almost my own height, taller than most of the men of the clan. Yet her strong, lithe body was completely female; the skins she wore could not hide that. Her bare arms and legs were dirty, scratched here and there. A scab covered one knee. Her matted filthy hair was reddish, like the others, instead of the darker tones I remembered. But she was the same woman—beautiful, intelligent, courageous—the woman I loved.

I made myself smile. "A man," I answered. "I am only a man."

Dal moved from behind Ava to examine me more closely. There were no weapons in his hands, but he was clearly being protective of her.

"You look like a man," he said. "Yet . . ."

"I *am* a man."

"But you do things that no man can do."

"I will teach you how to do them."

Ava asked, "What clan were you born to, if you are a man?"

"My clan lives far from here. I have traveled for a long, long time."

"Can everyone in your clan hunt the way you do?"

"Some can," I said. "Some hunt better than I."

For the first time, a smile curled her lips. "They must be very fat, then."

I laughed. "Some of them are."

"Why are you alone?" Dal asked, still suspicious. "Why have you come to us?"

"My clan is far away, and I have been separated

from it for a long time. I was sent here to help you,
to show you how to hunt and to protect you from
your enemies. I have been alone for more days
than any of you can count, and I am weary of
loneliness. You are the clan that I have sought.
You are the people I wish to be with."

As I spoke the words, I realized the truth that
lay in them. I had been alone all my life, except for
those few brief months with Agla, so far in the
future of this time.

"It is not good for a man to be alone," said Ava,
with surprising warmth and understanding in her
voice. "Even the mightiest hunter needs a clan
and a family."

Like all humans facing a difficult decision, they
finally settled on a compromise. Dal spoke ear-
nestly with the two elders of the clan, then with
all the adults, male and female. They agreed to
let me join them and show them my tricks of
hunting. But they insisted that I had to sleep by
myself, away from their campfire. Many of them
were not convinced that I was not some form of
a supernatural being, and they wanted to take as
few chances with me as possible.

I accepted their decision. I had to. No one brought
up the question of what to do about me *after* I had
shown them all my techniques of hunting. These
people did not think much about their future; they
lived in the present, like all animals, and only
dimly perceived that tomorrow might be different
from yesterday.

I was content with their decision, for the time
being. It fulfilled Ormazd's command. And it
brought me closer to Ava.

CHAPTER 25

Dal and Ava stayed close to me at all times as the clan continued its migration across the green, flowering land.

Dal was a good leader, who took his responsibilities seriously. Nearly as tall as I, although much slimmer, he was well-muscled and had keen, alert eyes. He watched me carefully every minute of the day. Dal had no fear that I might be a spirit who posed a supernatural threat to the clan. His worries were very practical and matter-of-fact. He feared that I might be a spy from another clan, an infiltrator who would somehow lead the clan into an ambush.

At first I didn't realize this. But after a few days of his suspicious, wary watch over me, I began to piece it together. At night, when the elders told their tales around the campfire, I heard enough singing over blood and battle to realize that even in this demi-Eden, where human clans were so thinly spread that contact between them was rare, war and killing were still common enough, and still glorified.

Apparently they met other clans on these migration routes, and when they did they generally battled over control of the hunting grounds. Although to me it seemed that the territory was teeming with game, to these nomadic hunters, territorial rights were vital to their survival. It took many square miles of ground to provide enough game to feed even the smallest of clans, because they depended on hunting for most of their nourishment. And the hunting was never good enough to support them very well.

From what I heard from Dal and the others, several clans that were related by marriages generally lived in the same area during the summer. We were heading for the summer camping grounds now, up in the hills that lay close to the big double-peaked volcano that dominated the landscape. The clans would spend the summer together, close enough to each other for regular visits, courting, marriages, and exchange of stories and information. In the autumn they would break up and go their separate ways toward their winter campsites, far to the south.

Ava had her suspicions about me, also. But her fears all centered on the supernatural. She was the clan's shaman, a combination of herbal physician, priestess, psychologist, and advisor to Dal, the clan's leader. It almost amused me to realize how early in human history the roles of priest, doctor, and power-behind-the-throne had come together.

She walked beside me nearly every day, but her interest in me seemed purely professional. She wanted to make certain that if I did turn out to be a demon, she would know about it and be able to do something about it before I could hurt the clan. She questioned me endlessly about where I came from and what my clan was like. I didn't mind; I was happy to be with her, even though I knew that each night, when I had to move far from the campfire, she bedded down with Dal.

I had expected that the clan's shaman, or witchdoctor, would have been an old woman, a crone who had either outlived her mate or never attracted one. It surprised me, at first, that someone as young as Ava would fill the role while she was mated to Dal. Then I realized that there were no old women in the clan. No woman over thirty or so, as far as I could see. The two elders, both men, could hardly have been much more than forty; their shaggy beards were just starting to turn gray. But there were no gray-haired women in the Goat Clan. And of the eight children, only three were girls, one of them an infant still being carried on her mother's back.

I asked Ava what happened to women as they grew older.

"They die," she said calmly. "Their spirits leave their bodies."

"How do they die?" I asked.

She shrugged her slim shoulders. "Many times they die in childbirth, or soon afterward. Some become too sick or weak to keep up with the clan as we march."

"And you leave them?"

Her gray eyes flashed at me. "Of course not! We let out their blood so that their spirits can remain with us. We would not let the spirit of one of our people roam the world all alone."

"I see," I said, and let the subject drop. No need asking her about selective female infanticide. I could see that it was being practiced simply by counting the children.

Women were a liability in this rugged hunting life. They were necessary for procreation, of course, but too many women meant too many babies, too many mouths to feed. So female children were weeded out at birth. Conversely, once a woman was no longer capable of bearing children, her usefulness to the clan was finished and they apparently got rid of her. Not that the men lived much longer: disease and accidents took their toll, and if they were not enough, there was always war. Long before human beings learned to tame the wild ponies that they hunted for food, the Four Horsemen of the Apocalypse kept human numbers in balance with the rigors of the Neolithic landscape.

Without consciously deciding to do so, I was changing that balance. It took me many weeks to realize that it was so. But as I taught the clan how to make bows and arrows, how to dig pits and camouflage them so that animals would fall into them, I began to realize that I was altering—ever so slightly—the ecological balance of this era. For it was not preordained that humans should live in small, scattered hunting groups and survive on the ragged edge of starvation. Only their lack of knowledge, their lack of proper tools, kept these hunters weak and vulnerable. Given more knowledge, better tools, they would become the masters of this world.

And eventually build nuclear bombs and vast cities choking in their own filth, I knew. Yet, as I woke up each morning in this dawn of human history and watched these people get ready to work another day with little more than their bare hands, I realized that my choice was the only one I could make. They were part of me, I knew, as human as I was. For me to refuse to help them would be the same as for me to refuse to breathe. No matter what the consequences, I had to choose life over death, knowledge over ignorance, humankind over all the other forms of life in the world.

And then I would see Ava walking gracefully among her people, sipping water fom a gourd, tending to a crying infant, and I realized that all my fine thoughts were merely excuses. I did what I did to help this clan because she was here, and I could not face the idea that one day, when she grew too slow to stay up with them, her clansmen would open her veins and let her spirit leave her body.

My own knowledge of Neolithic technology was shadowy, at best, but I remembered seeing pictures of spear-throwers, long, grooved handles that effectively extended the length of the throwing arm and allowed one to fling a spear twice the distance that he could unaided. I experimented for the better part of a week and finally taught myself how to make one and use it.

Dal's suspicions of me almost vanished when I showed him how to throw a spear farther than any man had before. The bow and arrow he had regarded with misgivings, mainly because I was far from expert at feathering the arrows and they were consequently far from accurate. But the spear-thrower fit into his experience and expectations beautifully. The first day he used it he brought down a gazelle that fed the whole clan for two nights. I was instantly besieged with requests for more of them. I made three, under the watchful eyes of the men and boys. Then they started making them, and within a week they were building better ones than I could.

Each night I gazed up at the stars longingly, searching their eternal patterns for some sign of where on Earth I might be. Most of the constellations looked familiar. I recognized Boötes, Andromeda, Perseus and the Little Dipper. Clearly, I was in the Northern Hemisphere. The Big Dipper looked strange, lopsided, its stars rearranged. If instinct had not done so already, that would have convinced me that I had moved many millennia through time.

The double-peaked volcano that loomed ahead of us seemed strangely familiar, but I could not place it. When I asked Dal what its name was, he gave me a strange stare. Either this clan did not name mountains or the name was too sacred to be spoken casually.

The landscape was rising now, and we climbed grassy slopes that grew steeper with each passing day. After almost a week of that, the land flattened out into a broad plateau covered by a dark and gloomy forest. Huge boles of pine and spruce alternated with groves of birch trees and mighty oaks. Beneath the trees the undergrowth was sparse, but it grew thick and tangled wherever the green canopy overhead thinned enough to let sunlight filter through to the ground. Dal kept us on a trail that meandered through the shadows of the trees—bare ground, softened by fallen pine needles. Easy hiking.

The forest was rich with game. Every morning the men and older boys went out to hunt boar, door, and whatever else they could find. Often a few of the women went with them. The other women and younger boys stayed at the campsite, some of them trapping smaller game. I became expert at the sling and could usually kill a couple of rabbits or squirrels in an hour or so. The clan ate well in the forest. I wondered why they ever left it.

I asked Ava, one afternoon when she had stayed in camp instead of going off with the hunters.

"We go to the valley, to our camping place for the summer," she told me. "There we will meet other clans. There will be marriages and feasting."

I sat with my back against the bole of a huge oak, while she knelt on the thin grass, sorting out the roots and herbs she had spent all morning collecting.

"Why don't the clans meet here in the forest?" I asked. "There's more game here than anywhere else I've seen."

She gave me the kind of patient smile that a teacher might offer a struggling student. "The valley is better. There is plenty of game there. And other kinds of food as well. Here in the forest . . ." She looked around the gloomy shadows cast by the trees, highlighted here and there by shafts of ghostly sunlight filtering through the leaves overhead. "Here there are dark spirits, dangerous and foul."

I knew of a dark spirit that was very real. I wondered if Ahriman was lurking in these dreary woods.

"And enemies who can ambush us," Dal's strong voice broke into our conversation. "The forest is an easy place for enemies to trap us."

He strode up to us, strong and confident and smiling through his coppery red beard. Over one shoulder he had slung a young boar, its hind legs tied together by a thong.

Ava jumped to her feet, so obviously happy to see him that I felt instantly jealous and resentful. "Why are you back so soon?"

Letting his catch drop to the ground, Dal pointed and said, "We found a new watering place, further up the hill. All the animals go there to drink. It wasn't there last year; something has dammed the stream to make a big pool. At sundown we can take enough game to carry us through the rest of the way to the valley!"

By sundown the whole clan was staked out by the watering spot, a large, still pool fed by a tiny stream that trickled through the woods from far above, where the snows still lay on the mountainside. Only the two elders, the babies, and the four oldest women had been left behind. Dal brought everyone else and carefully supervised our placement around the pool and on either side of the trail that led to it.

He was confident enough of himself to direct even me to a hiding place. I accepted his orders with a smile; Dal no longer feared me, and I felt good about that. I had been accepted.

We waited, hunkered down into the ground, covered with leaves and foliage, hoping that the wind would not change and give away our hiding positions to the animals that would come to the pool for their evening drink.

The afternoon light faded. Birds chattered and swooped through the trees. A procession of ants marched two inches in front of my eyes as I lay on the ground, itching and sweating despite the coolness of the forest shadows. Three spears lay beside me. A leafy oak branch lay over me. On either side of me I could see other clan members, similarly hiding and camouflaged. We were all to wait until Dal made the first move.

We waited. The shadows grew darker. The calls of the birds slackened and stilled. But no animals came to the pool. I began to wonder if something had gone wrong.

Then I heard a snuffling noise from behind me. I dared not turn around to look. I stayed absolutely still, barely breathing. I could hear my heart thumping in my ears. My palms were sweaty. I was as excited as any of these Neolithic hunters—perhaps even more excited than they.

Singly, in pairs, animals came warily down the trail to drink at the pool. Deer, boar, a strange kind of goat, others that I could not identify. They came warily, knowing full well that hunting dogs and wolves lurked in the woods. But they were not aware of the predators who lay hidden in their midst.

With a paralyzing scream Dal leaped to his feet and threw a spear at the biggest of the deer, hitting the doe just behind the forelegs. It fell, splashing, at the pool's edge. We all leaped up, roaring with pent-up passion, and began killing.

Ava was the wildest one of all, absolutely fearless and as fierce as any demon out of hell. She nailed a fawn with her first spear, then jumped out onto the trail to block the animals' easiest escape route. A tusked boar charged at her, head down, eyes burning with hate. Ava spitted it on her other spear, but the beast's furious charge wrested the weapon from her grasp. I came up beside her and pinned the animal's hindquarters to the ground with my remaining spear. Without an instant's hesitation, Ava straddled the boar's squirming back and slit its throat from ear to ear.

Blood spurted over us both as she leaped to her feet, arms upraised, brandishing her bloody stone knife in the air and screeching like a wild beast herself.

I stood there, suddenly transfixed by this vision of primitive ardor, the death-lust unmasked, unbridled, soaked with the blood of the prey. The killing was still going on all around us, filling the air with screams and the stench of blood. Ava flung her arms around my neck, laughing and sobbing all at once.

"Blood-mates!" she shouted. "We killed it together. We have shared a death."

I wanted to share love with her, not death. But, to her, the passions seemed much the same.

We carried and dragged the slaughtered beasts back to the campsite, where the elder men and women oohed and ahhed appropriately. All of us were smeared with blood, stinking with the lust of killing and the disembowelled entrails of our prey. None of us had been seriously hurt; one of the teen-agers had been gashed on the calf, but it did not look serious.

I was still trembling by the time we got back to the camp. I had hunted before, alone. I had hunted with Dal and others of the clan. But this evening's work was something different, something wild and passionate that stirred the savage killer-instinct within us all. We killed far more than we could eat; most of the game would rot before we could get to it. But like sharks in their feeding frenzy, we killed everything we could, sparing only those beasts that were fast enough or lucky enough to escape our spears.

Dal eyed me suspiciously as we made our way back to camp. But he was not worried that I was a spy from another clan or a spirit who would steal his soul. He was simply a jealous human male. He had seen Ava embrace me, and it did not please him at all.

The two elder males insisted that the clan perform a blood ritual to thank the gods for such a miraculous catch. They even wanted me to take part in it, as a representative of the gods. Dal adamantly refused.

"Orion has told us that he is a man, not a spirit," he insisted.

"But we never had such good hunting before he came to us," countered the eldest. "Whatever he says, out of modesty or the wisdom of the gods, he has still brought us incredible good fortune."

I stayed out of the argument, knowing that it was better to allow them to make up their own minds while I kept silent—out of modesty or wisdom.

But Ava spoke up. "Orion helped me to kill the boar. We are blood-mates. He should take part in the celebration."

Which, of course, set Dal's mind even more firmly against me. The clan was a rough sort of democracy. Dal was not an absolute ruler. But like most democracies, a strong-willed minority can usually prevail over the wishes of the majority. Dal was firmly set against allowing me to participate in their tribal ritual. His purpose was reinforced by jealousy and suspicion. The others had only fairness and good will to support them. Dal won.

So I sat alone in the darkness, far from the blazing campfire, as the clan danced wildly and split the night with their strange whoops and cries. All around me the tree trunks loomed black and unyielding. They made me think of Ahriman, brooding dark and evil, as he plotted our extinction.

For hours I watched them dancing, listened to their howls and screams as I told myself that I was glad that I was not one of them, glad to be more civilized than these savages, glad to be separate and apart from them. I told myself that, over and again.

The eerie cries at last dwindled to silence and the glow of the fire sank to a sullen glower of red among the black pillars of the trees. I finally lay back on the pine needles and closed my eyes to sleep.

Glad not to be one of them. The thought swirled around and around in my mind until I almost became physically sick. I was not one of them. I was alone, totally alone, thousands of years away from the nearest friend, my memory so blocked that I did not even know if I had a friend anywhere in the whole long continuum of time and space.

It was then that Ava came to me. Even in the darkness I could smell the blood and entrails that smeared her naked body.

"You could not come to the ritual," she whispered, her voice still breathless with excitement, "so I have brought the ritual to you."

Part of me was disgusted with her and her primitive blood-lust. Part of me knew that Dal would never forgive me for making love with his woman. Part of me was repelled at the thought of taking her in my arms and wallowing in her stench and passion. But with a suddenness that overwhelmed every thought in my mind, I became as wild and fierce as she was, and at least for a little while I was alone no longer.

CHAPTER 26

The next morning we resumed our trek northward, each of us staggering under a heavy load of dead game. We traveled under clouds of flies, and the smell of meat decaying in the warmth of the day was enough to make me sick. But no one else seemed to mind it; they all seemed happy with their burdens.

Ava walked up at the head of our little column, beside Dal. If he knew what we had done the night before, Dal gave no sign of it.

Nor did Ava. When I awakened that morning, she had already left me and returned to her usual sleeping place, I supposed, beside Dal. She gave me no sign that our relationship had changed. I began to think that what happened under the maddened passion of the clan's blood ritual was a sort of privileged event, not to be considered by the same rules as everyday life, not to be remembered or regretted once the sun arose again.

Two days later we emerged from the brooding forest and started across a broad, sunlit upland where the grass was green and sweet and dotted with flowers. Wild grains sprouted here and there, and lines of trees showed us where streams flowed. The people seemed to grow happier and lighter of heart with every step now. They knew this territory intimately, and they remarked on each and every jut of rock, bend of a stream, stand of grain that we passed.

Ava dropped back to walk with me one hot afternoon. I had taken to remaining toward the rear of the procession. For some unfathomable inner reason I had the uncanny feeling that we were being followed, watched. But, whenever I looked back, I could see no one, nothing, as far as the horizon. Yet the feeling remained, prickling the back of my neck.

"Soon we'll be at our valley," Ava told me, smiling.

"*Our* valley?" I asked.

She nodded, looking as pleased as a traveler who was at last making her way home.

"The valley is a good place. Others will come there to share it with us. Plenty of water and grain and good hunting. Everyone is happy in our valley."

When we finally reached it, nearly a week later, I saw that it was truly a lovely, sheltered Eden.

We stood by the bank of a gently meandering stream that afternoon, looking down across the valley. The stream dropped down in a series of terraced stone steps to the floor of the valley, then made its way along its length and disappeared into the cliffs at the other end. I saw that those cliffs actually formed the base of the big, double-peaked mountain that smoked quietly, far up at the top where snow still lay glittering white under the late springtime sun.

I could see why the clan was so happy to be here. The valley was sunny and green. From its U-shaped cross section I could tell that it had been scooped out by a glacier, probably from the looming mountain, which had now melted away. It was a very snug niche, quite defensible against invaders. The only easy access to the valley was down the stone terracing of the waterfall, the way we were entering. The trail was slippery, but not terribly difficult to get down. On the other sides the valley walls rose fairly steeply to heights of at least several hundred feet.

Our clan was the first to arrive that year. Dal's people raced down the wet stone terraces, laughing and happy, to the valley floor. Before the day ended they had felled some trees and chased some game. By nightfall they had erected a few primitive huts with mud walls and tree branches and hides for roofs. The huts were dug into the ground, more underground than above it, but to Dal's people they seemed like palaces.

One note of sadness touched us that night. The boy who had been injured in the hunt sank into a fevered coma. I had thought at first that the gash on his leg would heal soon enough, but it had become infected despite all that Ava could do in the way of poultices and bandages made from leaves. By the time we had reached the valley, the poor youngster could barely walk; his leg was swollen and inflamed. That night he was delirious, burning with fever. Finally he grew quiet and still. His mother sat at his side all night long. At dawn her keening cry told us all that her son was dead.

The clan buried him that afternoon, with Ava leading a ritual that included lining his shallow grave with all the possessions that the lad had accumulated in fourteen summers: a few stone tools, a handful of smooth pebbles, the winter furs that he had still carried with him. Each member of the clan dropped a flower into the grave while his mother stood quietly and watched. Her weathered cheeks were dry; she had finished her crying. Ava told me later that the boy's father had been killed two years earlier, and the woman—whose name was Mara—had no other living children. She was too old to expect to find a new husband. She would probably not survive the next winter.

I wondered how they would get rid of her, but didn't have the courage to ask.

The following morning I walked the length of the valley, following the stream that ran through it. The land must have been tilted by an earthquake, because the stream ran in what seemed to me to be a backwards direction: from the end of the valley where we had entered, it splashed down the stone terraces and ran toward the base of the double-peaked mountain. I would have thought that water would flow from the mountain's snow-cap outward, in the opposite direction.

As I walked slowly back toward the collection of mud huts that the clan had built, I saw Ava off among the flowering bushes by the base of the steeply rising valley wall. I angled off my original path and went toward her. I could see that she was gathering herbs and roots for her store of medicines. Little good that they did for Mara's son, Ava's cures were all that these people had to counter disease and injury.

"Hello," I called to her.

She looked up from the foliage she was studying. "What's the matter?" she called back.

Striding through the knee-high brush, I answered, "Nothing's wrong. I was walking down by the stream and I saw you here."

Ava's smile was more puzzled than welcoming. Apparently the idea of taking a leisurely stroll and stopping off to chat with a friend was not commonplace among these folk.

"You're gathering herbs for medicines," I said.

"Yes." Her smile faded. "I wasn't able to save Mara's son. The devil within him was too powerful for me. I must find stronger medicine."

Twenty thousand years later, I knew, medical researchers would still be hunting along the same trail.

"You did everything that was possible to do," I said gently.

She eyed me. "You did nothing to help."

"Me?"

"You are a man of great powers, Orion. Why didn't you try to help the boy?"

I was shocked. "I . . . my skills are in hunting, not medicine."

Those deep gray eyes of hers seemed to see straight through to my soul. "You have great knowledge; you know things that none of us know. I had thought that your knowledge included healing."

"It doesn't." I felt awkward, apologetic. "I'm sorry, but I just don't have that knowledge."

She pushed a strand of coppery hair from her face, still looking unconvinced.

"I told you before," I said, "I'm only a man."

Ava shook her head. "I don't believe that. You are different from any man I have ever seen."

"How am I different?" I spread my arms, as if to show her that I was built the same as anyone else.

"It is not your body," she said. "I have tested your body; I have taken your seed. You are strong, but your body is not different from Dal's or other men."

My blood ran suddenly cold. So our night of lovemaking had not been wild passion on her part, but a carefully considered experiment. Within my mind I heard a self-mocking laugh: She merely wanted to see what you were made of.

"Your difference," Ava was saying, "is in your spirit, your soul. You *know* so much more than we do!"

"I know some things, true enough," I said, trying to ignore the laughter ringing within me. "But there is much that I do not know."

"Teach me!" she blurted. "Teach me all the things you know!"

That took me by surprise. Suddenly she was eager for knowledge, avid.

"There are so many things I must learn, so many

things I don't know. Teach me. Share your knowledge with me," she pleaded.

"I can teach you some things, Ava," I replied. "But much of what I know would make no sense to you. It wouldn't be useful to you or to the clan."

"But you will teach me?"

"If you wish."

"I do!" Her eyes were wide with excitement.

"But why do you want to learn?" I asked.

She stared at me, momentarily speechless. "Why? To know, to understand—that is the important thing. The more I know, the more I can help the clan. If I had known enough about healing, I could have saved Mara's son."

It was my turn to fall silent. Beneath her unwashed skin and rude clothes, Ava was as fully human as Marie Curie, and as inquisitive. More than that, she realized that knowledge was the key to power, that understanding the world around her would help her to learn how to manipulate that world to her own ends.

But she misinterpreted my silence. Haltingly, she said, "There is nothing I can give you in return for your knowledge . . ."

So the idea of trading sex for power had not occurred to her. I almost smiled at the realization that the world's oldest profession had not yet been invented.

"There are things you know that I don't," I replied. "We will exchange knowledge for knowledge. Fair enough?"

"Yes!" She was almost breathless with enthusiasm.

"All right," I said. "To begin with, tell me what the names of these flowers are and what healing properties they have."

We spent the afternoon walking through the shrubbery and trading information. I told her that there were substances called metals which could make better tools than the stones and flints the clan used. She explained her wildflower apothecary to me. Gradually I began to lead the conversation toward a discussion of the other clans who came to the valley and the tribes who were their enemies.

"Do all the clans have hair the color of yours?" I asked.

"No, not at all. Some have dark hair, such as your own."

"And the color of their skin? Are they all the same as ours?"

She nodded. "In the summer sun the skin gets darker, but in the winter it lightens again."

"Have you ever seen a man whose skin is the color of the ashes that remain when a fire burns out? A man who is almost as tall as I am, but much wider, with enormously strong arms and eyes that burn red?"

She backed away from me. "No," she said fearfully. "And I hope I never do."

"Have you ever heard of such a man?" I pressed. "Sometimes he is called Ahriman. Sometimes he is called the Dark One."

Ava was clearly afraid of the very idea. "He sounds like a demon."

"He is a man. An evil man."

She looked at me with a new suspicion in her eyes. "A man. Just as you say you are a man."

I let the matter drop. She did not press it. Instead, we began talking about the valley and how much the clan enjoyed spending their summers here. I casually mentioned that they could spend the whole year here, if they prepared for the winter properly. She was instantly curious, and I began to describe how to make warm winter clothing from hides and fur pelts.

She knew about that. But: "What would we eat

during the time of snows? All the game animals move to the warmer places. We follow them."

"Instead of killing them," I explained, "you could trap some of them and keep them in fenced-off areas. Let them breed young for you, and you will have meat all year round, without moving away from this spot."

Ava laughed. She knew a crack-brained theory when she heard one. "And what will the animals eat during the winter? The grass dies."

"Cut the grass and grain that the animals eat during the summer, when it is high, and store it in huts during the winter to feed to the animals."

Her laughter stopped. She didn't accept the idea; it was too new and fantastic to be swallowed at one sitting. But she accepted the possibility of thinking about it. And that was more important.

We had walked to the face of the cliffs that formed the base of the double-peaked volcano. I decided it was my turn to ask a question.

"Does the mountain have a name?"

"Yes," Ava replied, squinting up into the bright sky to scan its rugged, snow-covered peaks.

"Is the name too sacred to be spoken?"

She turned her gaze back toward me, a new respect in her eyes because I understood the concept of sanctity.

"The smoking mountain can make the ground tremble when its spirit grows angry. The elders tell us that many, many years ago, before they themselves were born, the mountain spilled fire upon the people who lived in this valley and drove them away."

"But they came back."

"Not until long years had passed. They feared the mountain, and they taught that fear to their children and their children's children."

I glanced up at the snowcapped peaks. For the

first time since I had originally seen them, no
smoke came from the volcano.

"It seems to be resting now."

Ava grinned. "Yes, sometimes it rests. But it can
still breathe fire when its spirit grows angry."

"Would it make the mountain's spirit angry to
tell me its name?" I asked.

Her beautiful face pulled itself into a slight frown.
"Why do you want to know?"

Smiling, I replied, "Like you, I am curious. I
seek answers to questions."

She understood that, the drive to learn, to know.
Ava took a step closer to me and whispered the
name of the mountain:

"Ararat."

CHAPTER 27

Dal was not happy with us when Ava and I returned from our long walk. And he grew increasingly unhappy over the next few days as the two of us spent more and more time together.

At night I took Ava away from the lights of the clan's fires—each family had its own small cooking fire in front of its hut now, instead of one single campfire. Off in the darkness I showed her the stars and began to teach her how the constellations formed a vast celestial clock and calendar.

She grasped the concept quickly, and even noted, after a few nights, that at least one of the stars seemed to have moved slightly out of place.

"That's Mars," I told her. "It is not a star like all the others you see. It is a world, something like our own world here, but incredibly far away."

"It is red, like blood," Ava murmured in the darkness.

"Yes," I agreed. "Its soil is red sand. Even its sky is pink with reddish dust, almost the color of your hair."

"The people there must be angry and warlike," she said, "to have made their whole world the color of blood."

My heart sank at the thought that I was helping to invent astrology. But I consoled myself with the notion that such ideas did not occur only once, in a single time and place. Concepts as obvious as astrology would be invented time and again, no matter how ludicrously wrong they may be.

That night we stayed up until dawn, watching the stars wheel across heaven in their majestic cosmic clockwork. And when Venus arose, the Morning Star shining as brilliantly beautiful as anything human eyes could ever see, I heard Ava's sigh of pleasure in the predawn darkness.

I wanted to take her in my arms and kiss her. But she must have sensed what was in my mind, and she moved slightly away from me.

"I am Dal's woman," she whispered. "I wish it was not true, but it is."

I wanted to tell her that I loved her, but with a shock I realized there was no word for such a concept in their language. Romance was yet to be invented. She was Dal's woman, and women did not change mates in this early era.

We walked back to the huts and the embers of the cook fires. Dal sat on the ground in front of his hut, looking miserable, angry, worried and sleepy, all at the same time. He scrambled to his feet when he saw us, and Ava smiled at him and took his arm. They ducked through the low entrance to their hut without either of them saying a word to me.

I stood there alone for a few moments more, then turned and went off to my own dugout, which Dal had insisted the clan build for me—a good hundred yards away from the nearest hut of a clan family.

When I stepped down to the entrance and ducked through it into the shadowy interior of the single room, I immediately sensed that someone else was already inside. Dawn was just beginning to tint the eastern sky, and there were no windows in the hut—nothing but the open doorway to let in light or air. But I knew that I was not alone in the inky shadows of the dugout. I could feel a presence, dark and menacing. I could hear a slow, deep, labored breathing.

"Ahriman," I whispered.

Something moved slightly in the darkest corner of the room. My hand went to the stone knife at my waist. A silly, useless gesture, I knew, but my hand moved of its own accord.

"You expected me to be here, didn't you?" His harsh, tortured voice sent a chill along my spine.

Stepping to one side of the doorway, so that I would not be silhouetted against the growing light outside, I replied, "You've been trailing us for many weeks."

"Yes."

I could barely make out his form, bulking darkly in the shadows. "You plan to bring harm to these people?" I probed.

He moved slightly. "What harm can I do? I am only one man, against your entire race . . ."

"Don't call yourself a man," I snapped.

He gave out a wheezing, gasping sound that almost sounded like laughter. "Orion, you fool! Don't call *yourself* a man."

"I am a human being," I said, "not one of your kind."

"You are not one of my kind, true enough," Ahriman said, each word labored and grim. "I am the only one of my kind left. Your cohorts killed all the others."

"And you seek vengeance."

"I seek justice."

"Even if it means destroying the continuum of space-time."

"That is the only way to obtain the justice I seek. To tear down the pillars that support the world. To bring it all to an end. To destroy the one who fashions himself as the Golden God."

"Ormazd."

"Yes, Ormazd. The master slaughterer. *Your* master, Orion. Your creator."

"You can't touch him; he's too powerful for you, so you take out your spite on these poor ignorant savages." I could feel hatred boiling inside me.

He countered, "You call yourselves humans. You think you own this planet."

"We do! This is our world."

"Temporarily," Ahriman's voice rumbled darkly. "Only temporarily. He built you to conquer this planet, but I will see to it that you are destroyed— utterly and forever."

"No," I said. "I have already stopped you twice. I will stop you here, as well."

He paused, as if gathering his forces before speaking again. "Twice, you say? We have met *twice* before?"

"Yes."

"Then it's true," he muttered, more to himself than to me. "You are moving back toward The War."

I kept silent.

"The Golden One is very clever. He is moving you backward through the continuum. You have not seen The War yet. You don't know what took place then."

"I know that my task is to hunt you down and kill you, finally, for all time."

I sensed a ponderous shaking of his head. "For all time. I wonder if you realize what that means. None of us, not even Ormazd, can grasp all of time in his hands."

"That is my task," I said.

He made that ghastly chuckling sound again. "Then why don't you do your duty, here and now? Kill me."

I hesitated.

"You are afraid."

"No," I answered honestly. Fear never touched me. I was calculating how to get to him. I knew that he was far stronger than I. With nothing but the pitiful stone knife in my hand, how could I hope to attack him?

"I grow weary of waiting," Ahriman said.

The shadows exploded. His vast bulk suddenly leaped at me and I was smashed against the mud wall of the dugout, Ahriman's powerful fingers at my throat. We crashed through the flimsy wall and the makeshift roof of leafy branches fell in on us as we struggled in the dust. I slashed wildly at him with the knife, to no avail.

I saw his face inches from mine, a wide leering grin pulling his lips apart, his teeth gleaming wickedly, a brutal snarl growling up from his throat, his eyes blazing with triumphant fury. The strength was seeping out of my muscles. My arms grew weak, my attempts to fend him off feeble. Darkness started to cloud my vision, and I knew that I was about to die.

Something thudded into the ground close to me. Then I felt a muffled shock, as if a hard object had hit Ahriman's body, atop me. His fingers around my throat slackened and I heard him growl. His weight rolled off my body. My vision cleared slightly as I drew in a deep, welcome breath of cool air and I saw him standing above me, a spear dangling from his side, blood oozing from the wound, snarling defiance.

Another spear hurtled through the morning air and he caught it with one hand. Turning, I saw that Dal had thrown it. The other men of the clan were running up toward where he was standing, more spears in their hands. Their faces showed more surprise than fear; as long as their leader was willing to stand up to this strange intruder, they would too—at a distance.

Ahriman flipped the spear around in his hand and pulled his arm back to throw it at Dal. I kicked at his legs and toppled him. The men gave a blood-curdling screech and charged at us.

I scrambled to get on top of the Dark One, but he cuffed me to my knees with a tremendous backhand blow, yanked the spear out of his bleeding side and threw it at the attacking clansmen. Even so haphazardly thrown, it had the force to go right through one of the men, chest to back, lift him off his feet and throw him cruelly to the ground.

That stopped the men of the clan dead in their tracks. All except Dal, who rushed in barehanded except for his puny knife and leaped at Ahriman. The Dark One knocked him away, lumbered to his feet, and staggered off toward the cliffs.

For several moments no one moved. I pulled myself painfully up onto my hands and knees. Dal sat up slowly, shaking his woozy head. A bruise was welling up along his jaw, where Ahriman had hit him.

The other men stood as if transfixed, staring now at the two of us, now at the body of their slain comrade. Ahriman had disappeared into the shadows of the cliffs, where the dawning light had not yet reached.

"Who was that?" Dal asked, at last. He ran two fingers over the lump on his jaw and winced.

"An enemy," I said.

The other men came up to us, all of them chattering at once. Ava pushed her way through them and knelt at Dal's side. She inspected him in the brightening sunlight and concluded that no bones were broken. Then she turned to me.

"I'm all right," I said, getting to my feet. My throat burned, though, and my voice was hoarse.

The others were staring at me.

"Your throat bears the marks of the enemy," Ava said, examining me. "I can see the print of each of his fingers." She put her hands to my throat. "His hands are enormous!"

"Who is he?" Dal wanted to know.

"The enemy of all men," I replied. "The enemy of every human being. He is the Dark One, an enemy whose only desire is to kill us all."

They had all seen Ahriman, but I described him as closely as I could. I did not want them to begin thinking of the Dark One as a spirit or a demon who was beyond human resistance. I praised them for driving him away, for wounding him and saving me from his choking hands.

"We can follow his spoor and track him to his lair," Ava said, pointing to the bloodstains Ahriman had left on the grass.

The men showed a distinct aversion to the idea. Even Dal, so fearless a few moments earlier, backed away.

"No," I said. "He will have gone deep into the caves by now. We wouldn't be able to find him. He might even have set traps for us. Better to stay here in the sunlight. He won't come back." Not for a while, at least, I added silently.

The rest of the men gathered around their fallen comrade and lifted him tenderly from the ground to carry him back to his hut. I could hear Ahriman's size and ferocity growing as they talked among themselves, and their own courage and strength increasing to keep pace.

Dal lingered near me, Ava at his side.

"You saved my life," I said to him. "I thank you."

He shook his head, troubled. "You are one of us. I did what had to be done."

"It was more than any of the others did."

"I am their leader."

I remembered an aphorism: From those to whom much is given, much is expected. Dal was a true leader, and a good one. But still he looked troubled.

"Ahriman is no more of a spirit or a demon than I am," I said. "He is a man, like me."

"He took a spear in his side and pulled it loose as if it was nothing more than a burr annoying him."

"He has great strength," I admitted.

Reflexively Dal touched the bluish bruise on his jaw. "That is true. He drove that spear through Radon even while he was on his back."

"But he ran away." I didn't want Dal to fear Ahriman more than was necessary.

His troubled eyes locked on mine. "You did not tell me that you were being pursued by an enemy."

"I didn't know he was here," I half-lied. "I thought I had left him far away from here."

Sensing the beginning of an argument, Ava stepped between us. "Come and eat with us. The sun has already climbed over the hills. It will be a beautiful day."

But now Dal eyed me with new suspicion, even though I felt a bond of respect and admiration for the man who had attacked the Dark One with reckless courage, and thereby saved my life.

CHAPTER 28

The next few weeks were peaceful enough. Three more clans filtered into the valley, a total of a hundred and six additional people. Roughly two-thirds of them were adults, the remainder children ranging from nursing babies to gawky pre-adolescents. In this Neolithic society where life was so short, teen-agers became adults as soon as they reached sexual maturity. Twelve-year-olds bore children. Forty-year-olds were often too feeble and toothless to hunt or eat and were tenderly slain by their clansfolk.

"We stay here in the valley," Ava told me, "until the grain turns to gold. Then we harvest it and carry it with us for the winter." Frowning, she added, "Unless the snows come before the grain ripens."

And in a flash of understanding I knew why Ahriman was here and what he planned to do.

This was another of the crucial nexus points in human history. These clans, these ragged, dirty, wandering hunters, were going to make the transition from hunting to farming. They were going to create the Neolithic Revolution, the step that turned humankind from nomadic savages to civilized city-builders. Ahriman was going to try to strangle that development, prevent it from happening.

If he could keep these primitive hunters from

254

taking that step, he could eventually wipe out all of the scattered human tribes who wandered across this Neolithic landscape. I had no doubt of that. He could annihilate the human race, clan by clan, tribe by tribe, until the Earth was scoured clean of the last human being. Then he would be triumphant.

But if humankind made the transition to agriculture, if humans began the vast population explosion that led to the civilizations of Egypt, Sumeria, the Indus Valley and China, then not even Ahriman with all his powers could hope to wipe out the entire race. Humankind would be on the path toward mastery of this planet, no longer a few scattered half-starving tribes of nomadic hunters, but settled prosperous farmers with a steeply growing population.

Would agriculture be invented here, in this valley where Dal's clan and his allies spent the summer? I could not believe that if Ahriman prevented that invention here, it would not occur elsewhere, in some other clan, at some other favored spot. But then I realized that, with his mastery of time, Ahriman could visit each and every spot where the invention was about to take place and stamp out the idea each and every time it arose. With a growing weariness hanging like a heavy weight around my soul, I realized that Ormazd would send me to each of those times and places, to do never-ending battle against the Dark One.

Contemplating that was more than I could bear. Almost. I consoled myself with the thought that since Ahriman was *here*, this must be the place where the idea of agriculture truly originated. If I stopped him here, there would be no need to fight him elsewhere—in this era. Obviously we had met at least once more in an earlier time. Perhaps during The War that he referred to.

Dal's new suspicion of me quickly spread to the rest of the clan, and the other clans that joined us in the valley stayed well clear of me. I was regarded as something between a god and a human, feared and respected. They all knew that I could teach them wonderful things, but although they came to learn how to make bows and arrows and spear-throwers, and even how to pen game animals against the cliffs and begin herding them instead of simply killing them immediately, they still kept me away from their day-to-day social lives.

All except Ava. She spent long hours with me, learning whatever I could teach her about the stars, about spinning and weaving the wool from goats and sheep, about simple rules of cleanliness and infection.

But each evening she would return to Dal's hut and cook his supper. She invited me to join them often enough, but Dal made it clear that he was uncomfortable with me and more than a little jealous of the time Ava spent with me. I usually ate alone, outside my rebuilt hut, cooking the meat and vegetables the clanspeople gave me in exchange for my lessons on tool-making and animal husbandry. It would have been funny if it hadn't been so tragic, to think of these primitives learning from me. Actually, all I did was expose them to ideas that had not occurred to them. Once the basic idea got into their minds, they went off and did things much better than I ever could have. They taught themselves to make accurate arrows, to build corrals, to spin wool. I merely planted the seeds; they cultivated them and reaped the harvest.

Life in the valley was pleasant and easy. The days lengthened into golden summer, but without oppressive heat and humidity. The grain grew tall and ripened, filling the valley with golden fronds that swayed in the gentle summer breezes. The color of Ormazd, I thought, and realized that it was good. The nights were cool and often tossed by sighing winds. I spent hours showing Ava the phases of the Moon, the paths of the planets, the rise and fall of the constellations. I pointed out the Summer Triangle of stars high in the night sky: Deneb, Altair, and Vega. She learned quickly, and the questions she asked showed that she was eager to learn more.

Dal accompanied us during those nights. At first it was because he did not trust me alone with Ava, and I could hardly blame him for that. But despite himself he began to grow interested in the lore of the sky.

"Do you mean you can tell when the seasons will change *before* the change really begins?" He was skeptical.

"Yes," I replied. "The stars can tell you when to plant seed and when to harvest the grain."

He frowned in the moonlight. "Plant seed? What do you mean?"

That brought us to long nights of talk about how plants grow. I think I might have been the first human being to explain the similarity between the birds and bees, plant growth and human sexuality. But I did it in reverse of the way twentieth-century parents gave the explanation to their children: I used human sexuality—which Dal and Ava understood perfectly well—to explain how plants grew from seeds.

Like children, they found the idea difficult to accept. "Do you mean that if we put some tiny seeds into the ground, a whole field of grain would grow there?"

When I said yes, Dal merely shook his head in disbelief. But Ava looked thoughtful, her gray eyes focused on the future.

Except for that one blood-crazed night of the hunting ritual, Ava and I had hardly touched each other. Not that I did not want her. But she was Dal's woman, and her interest in me was the kind for which a word would not be invented for another hundred centuries: Platonic. Ava sought knowledge from me, not love or even companionship.

One afternoon, while Dal was leading a hunting party out toward the far end of the valley, where they could trap animals against the cliffs easily, I saw Ava staring soberly at the ripening fields of grain. She had filled out a bit, as had everyone. Now that we no longer had to trek each day, and as game was plentiful, we had all gained weight.

But Ava's face was knotted into such a serious frown that I decided to ask her what the trouble was.

"Ava, what bothers you?"

She seemed startled. "What? Oh—it's you."

"Is something wrong?" I asked.

"Wrong? No . . . not really." She turned her gaze back to the grain, swaying gently in the summer breeze beneath the golden sun.

"You don't believe what I told you a few nights ago," I guessed, "that you can plant the seeds of the grain and grow crops from them."

With a wan smile, she said, "No, Orion. I *do* believe you. What you say makes sense to me. I was just thinking that . . ." she hesitated, and I could see from the concentrated expression on her face that she was struggling to put her ideas in order.

I waited in silence. Her face was beautiful, and I longed to take her in my arms. But she had no desire for me, and I knew it.

"Suppose," she began again, slowly, haltingly,

"suppose we really could do it . . . grow grain the way you said. Suppose we stayed here in this valley—all the time, winter and summer. We could grow the grain; we could pen up the animals against the cliffs. We wouldn't have to go out each day and hunt. We could stay here and live much more easily."

I nodded. The transition from hunting and gathering to a settled agricultural life had begun, at least in the mind of one Neolithic woman.

"But suppose the grain didn't grow?" she asked me.

"It grows every year, doesn't it? It's always here when you return to this valley."

She agreed, but reluctantly. "It begins to grow when we are away. If we stayed here all the time, would the grain still grow the way it does now?"

"Yes," I said. "You will even find ways to make it grow better."

"But doesn't the grain's spirit need to be alone? Won't the grain die if we stay here always?"

"No," I assured her. "The spirit of the grain will grow stronger if you help that spirit by tending the grain, by killing the weeds that choke it, by spreading the seed to new parts of the valley, where the grain does not yet grow."

She wanted to believe me, I could see. But the old superstitions, the ingrained ways of thought, the stubborn fear that change—any change—would bring down the anger of the gods, all were struggling within her against the bright promise of this new idea.

"I'm going to take a walk," I said, with a sudden inspiration. "Will you come with me?"

She agreed and I started out across the waist-high field of golden grain, toward the cliffs that the glacier had scooped out on the far side of the valley.

We talked as we made our way to the base of the cliffs, Ava going over the whole idea of agriculture and herding, again and again, trying to find out where the weak points were, where there might be a hidden flaw in the scheme, a trap that could bring ruin to the clan.

I could have told her that once the clan stopped its roaming and gave up hunting, it would lead to settled farming villages, to an hierarchical society of peasants and kings, to class divisions between rich and poor. I could have told her that the occasional tribal clashes she was familiar with would escalate into wars between villages, then between cities, and ultimately wars in which all the world was bathed in blood. I could have told her about teeming cities and pollution and the threats of overpopulation, nuclear holocaust, environmental collapse.

But I said nothing. Here in the bright morning of human civilization, I remained silent and let Ava examine the new idea for herself.

We reached the base of the cliffs. I squinted up toward their top, outlined against the bright summer sky.

"I think I'll climb up to the top. Want to come with me?"

"Up there?" She laughed. "No one can climb up those cliffs, Orion. You are teasing me."

"No, I'm not. I think we can make it to the top."

"It's too steep. Dal tried it once and had to give up. No one can climb these cliffs."

I shrugged. "Let's try it together. Maybe the two of us can get to the top, whereas one man alone would fail."

She gave me a curious stare. "Why? Why do you want to climb where no one has climbed before?"

"That's just it," I said. "Because no one has done it before. I want to be the first. I want to see how the world looks when I'm standing in a place where no one has ever stood before."

"That sounds crazy."

"Haven't you ever done something simply because you wanted to do it? Haven't you ever had the desire to do something that no one has ever done before?"

"No," she said. But not very convincingly. She looked up the face of the cliffs and her gray eyes were filled with wondering. "We always do things the way they have always been done. .That's the best way, just as our fathers and their fathers did it."

"But somewhere, sometime, one of them must have done a thing for the first time. There has to be a first time for everything."

She looked sharply at me. I was challenging the safely ordered routines of her world, and she was not altogether happy about it.

But her expression softened and she asked, "Do you really think we could reach the top?"

"Yes, if we work together."

She turned back to look at the cliffs again. They were steep, all right, but even an amateur climber could handle them, I knew. With utter certainty within me, I was sure that Ormazd had programmed me with much more than an amateur's strength and skill.

Ava tore her gaze away from the looming cliffs and turned to look back at the golden fields of grain we had crossed. The afternoon breeze sent a swaying wave through them. She grinned at me.

"Yes!" she said eagerly. "I want to see what's at the top of the cliffs, too!"

We used vines for ropes, and our bare, travel-hardened feet had to do without climber's boots. But the cliffs were nowhere near as forbidding as they had seemed at first glance. It was a two-hour struggle, but we reached the top at last, panting, sweaty, weary.

The view was worth it.

Ava stood puffing, grinning broadly, and wide-eyed, as we looked far to the east and west and saw valley after valley, river after river, all running southward through golden fields. Above us loomed Ararat, towering high into the cloudless, brilliant sky, its snowy cap glistening in the sun, a thin stream of smoke climbing from the higher of its two peaks. And beyond, farther to the north, the land dazzled with ice, glittering like a vast diamond that hurt the eyes if you stared at it too long. That vast glacier still covered most of Europe, I knew, although it was retreating northward as the Ice Age surrendered to a more humane climate.

"There's so much to see!" Ava shouted. "Look at how small our valley seems from here!"

"It's a big world," I agreed.

She gazed down into the valley again and slowly her face lost its exultant happiness. She began to frown again.

"What's wrong, Ava?"

Turning toward me, she said, "If we lived away from the others, if we found a valley for ourselves where no other clan lived . . . just you and I together . . ."

I felt my jaw go slack. "What are you saying?"

There were no words in her language for what she was feeling.

"Orion," she said, her voice low, trembling, "I want to be with you; I want to be your woman."

I reached out to her and she fled into my arms. I held her tightly and felt her strong, lithe body press against mine. For an eternity we stood there, locked in each other's arms, warmed by the summer sun and our own passionate blood.

"But it cannot be," she whispered so softly that I could barely hear her.

"Yes, of course it can be. This world is so large, so empty. We can find a valley of our own and make our home in it . . ."

She looked up at me and I kissed her. I didn't know if kissing had been invented yet by these people, but she took to it naturally enough.

But when our lips parted there were tears in her eyes.

"I can't stay with you, Orion. I am Dal's woman. I can't leave him."

"You can if you want to . . ."

"No. He would be shamed. He would have to organize the men of the clan to hunt us down. He would have to kill you and bring me back with him."

"He'd never find us," I said. "And even if he did, he'd never be able to kill me."

"Then you would have to kill him," Ava replied. "Because of me."

"No, we can go so far away . . ."

But she shook her head as she gently disengaged herself from my arms. "Dal needs me. He is the leader of the clan, but how could he lead them if his woman deserts him? He is not as confident as you think; at night, when we are alone together, he tells me all his fears and doubts. He fears you, Orion. But he is brave enough to overcome that fear because he sees that you can be helpful to the clan. He places his responsibility to the clan above his fear of you. I must place my responsibility to the clan above my desire for you."

"And me?" I asked, feeling anger welling up inside me. "What about me?"

She looked deep into my eyes. "You are strong, Orion, with a strength that no ordinary man has. You were sent among us to help us, I know that. Taking me from Dal, from the clan, would not be a help. It would destroy Dal. It could destroy the clan. That is not why you have come among us."

I could have replied. I could have simply picked her up and carried her off. But she would have run back to her clan the instant I relaxed my hold on her. And she would have hated me.

So I turned away from her and glanced at the sun, low on the western horizon.

"It's time to start back," I mumbled. "Let's go."

CHAPTER 29

The grain grew taller than my shoulders, and the people of all the clans grew more excited and impatient to harvest it with each passing day.

I stayed aloof from them. I had taught them all I could. Now I waited, just as they did. But not for the time of harvesting. I waited for Ahriman. He would return; he was planning his attack on these people, on me, on the whole future existence of the human race. I waited with growing impatience.

I combed the valley, poked into the caves among the rocky cliffs, seeking the Dark One. All I found were snakes and bats, clammy, cold dampness and dripping water. And one cave bear that would have crushed my skull with a swipe of its mighty paw if I had not been fast enough to duck out of its way and scramble out of its cave before it could get to me.

I knew he was there, somewhere, biding his time, picking his point of attack. All I could do was to wait. Ormazd did not appear to me again to give me more information or even the slight comfort of showing me that he still existed and still cared that I existed. I was alone, placed here like a time bomb on a buried mine, waiting to be triggered into action.

Ava kept her distance from me. And the less I saw of her, the more I did of Dal. He came by my hut almost daily now. At first I thought he was trying to work up the nerve to pick a fight with me. But gradually, as he tried to strike up a conversation in his halting, pained way, I realized that he was trying to work up the nerve for something else, something that was far more difficult for him than merely fighting.

"The grain will be ready to cut soon," he said, late one afternoon. I was sitting on the ground in front of my hut, fitting a new flint blade to the stone hilt of my knife. One of the clan's elders was an artist when it came to making sharp flint tools; that was why he was allowed to remain with the clan even though he was too old and slow to hunt.

Dal squatted down on his haunches beside me, forcing a smile. "If it doesn't rain in the next two days, then we can cut the grain."

"That's good," I said.

"Yes."

I looked up at him. "What's troubling you, Dal?"

"Troubling me? Nothing!" He said it so sharply that it was clear he was deeply bothered.

"Is it something that I've done?" I asked him.

"You? No, of course not!"

"Then what is it?"

He traced a finger along the dirt, like an embarrassed schoolboy.

"Is it about Ava?" I asked.

His glance flicked up at me, then down to the ground again. I tensed.

"It concerns her," Dal said, "and the things you've been telling her. She thinks we should stay here in this valley . . . all the time."

I said nothing.

"She claims that you said we could pen the animals against the cliffs and stay here even when the snows come," he gushed out rapidly, as if afraid of stopping, "and next spring we can plant seed from the grain all across the valley and make more grain than anyone has ever seen before."

He looked at me almost accusingly.

"I told you these things, too," I replied. "I told you both."

Dal shook his head. "But she really believes them!"

"And you don't."

"I don't know what to believe!" He was honestly confused. "We live well here, that's true. We could move into caves when the snow comes. As long as we have fire we can stay in the caves and keep them warm and dry."

"That's true," I said.

"But our fathers never did this. Why should we stop living the way our fathers have always lived?"

"Your fathers have not always lived this way," I told him. "Long ages ago your ancestors lived far from here, in a land where it was always warm and they could pick fruit from the trees and live a life of ease and happiness all year long."

His eyes showed that he did not want to believe me. But he asked, "Why did they leave such a paradise, then?"

"They were driven out," I replied, "by a change in the climate. The trees withered. The land changed. They had to move elsewhere. They began to roam the land, as you do, following the herds of game."

"But each year the herds get smaller," Dal said, his mind focusing on the present and dismissing old legends that he only half believed "Each year we must travel farther and our kills are harder to make."

I gestured toward the fields. "But the grain grows high. And there are enough game animals here to feed all the gathered clans, if you keep them penned up and let them breed. They will provide you with all the meat and milk and wool you need, if you learn how to take care of them."

He was truly perplexed. It was a gigantic hurdle for him.

"The grain is good," he admitted slowly. "We make food from it—and a drink that makes you feel as if you're flying."

Bread and beer, the two staples of farming. I wondered which offered the bigger lure in Dal's mind and swiftly decided that beer would be more important to him than bread.

"Then why not stay here, where the grain grows so well? You can store it in the caves after you've cut it. If you grow enough grain, you can even feed some of it to the animals you keep."

With a deepening scowl, Dal wondered aloud, "But what would the spirits of our fathers do if we stopped following the game trails? How would they feel if we turned our backs on their ways?"

I shrugged. "They will probably rejoice that you have found a better way to live."

"The elders say that the grain won't grow if we stay here all year long."

"Why wouldn't it grow?"

"Its spirit would wither if we watched the fields all the time."

I wondered if the elders were groping toward the idea of environmental pollution. But I said, "The grain grows just as the sun shines and the rain falls. It is all completely natural, and it will happen whether you are here to watch it or not."

"Hunting is good," Dal muttered. "Hunting is our way of life."

And I'm going to destroy that way of life and turn you into farmers. In my heart, I could see that Dal's every instinct was urging him away from the strange new ideas I had planted in his mind. For untold thousands of generations human-kind had been hunters. Their minds and bodies were shaped for hunting; their societies were built around it. Now I was telling them that they could live fatter, easier lives by giving up their hunting ways and turning to farming and herding. It was true; farming would be the first step toward total domination of the planet by humankind. But they would have to turn their backs on the "natural" lives they now led; they would have to abandon the freedom they had, the rough democracy in which each clan member was as good as any other.

For an instant I wondered if I was doing them any good. But then I realized that it was not a choice between lifestyles; the choice these people had was between farming and eventual extinction. They would have to pay a bitter price for survival, but it was either pay that price or die.

Is this part of Ormazd's plan? I wondered. Does Ormazd have a plan? Or is he merely determined to keep himself safe from the Dark One, no matter what it costs? As I sat there studying Dal's face, so deeply etched with doubt and concentration, I was tempted to tell him to forget the whole thing and keep on living as he had always lived. But then I thought of the boy who had died of a simple infection. I thought of how lean and ragged these people were when they were following the game trails and living off what they could catch each day. I remembered that their elders were at an age that would be considered still youthful in later centuries. I realized that the clan's hunting life kept them just barely alive; they lived constantly on the edge of extinction. Ahriman would not have to push hard to wipe out the human race.

"Hunting has been your way of life, it is true," I said to Dal, "and a good way of life for you and the clan. But it is not the only way. It is not the best way."

He looked unconvinced and very troubled. Dal was an honest, forthright man. He did not know what to believe, and he was too honest to make up his mind before he was convinced, one way or the other.

"Ava wants to stay," he muttered, "but the elders say we must not."

I put a hand on his shoulder. "Talk to the clan. Talk to all the people who have come to the valley. Tell them what I have told you. If you like, I will speak to them myself and tell them how the grain grows. The spirits of your fathers will not be angry with you; they will be pleased that you have found a better way to live."

He smiled slowly. "Do you really believe they will be pleased?"

"Yes. I'm sure they will be."

Dal rose to his feet and stretched his cramped legs. Nodding his head, he told me, "I will talk to the clans. I will tell them what you have told me."

He felt relieved. He didn't have to make the decision. He would put it to a vote. That lifted the burden from his shoulders. Or so he thought.

Even in this simple Neolithic society, with fewer than a hundred adults to deal with, it took three nights before Dal could assemble all the people to listen to him. I was fascinated to watch a primitive bureaucracy at work. Each clan had to discuss the idea of such a meeting within itself, with the elders going into painstaking detail on how such clan conferences had been arranged in the past, where their clan sat in relation to other clans, who was responsible for building the fire, who would speak and in what order. For these supposedly unsophisticated folk, the occasion of a clan gathering was an event, an entertainment, as well as a serious time of decision-making. They savored the arrangements and the protocol, fussing over the details for the sheer enjoyment and excitement of having something to fuss over.

At last the clans gathered around a big central bonfire that had been built closer to the Goat Clan's huts than any other clan's. The elders of each clan spent the first few hours of the night retelling their

most important stories, each old man establishing
his clan's history and stature by sing-songing legends that each person sitting around the fire knew
by heart, word for word. But they all sat through
each tale of monsters and heroes, gods and maidens,
bravery and cunning and seemed to enjoy themselves thoroughly—or at least as much as a twentieth-century family would enjoy spending an evening watching television.

Finally it was Dal's turn to put his proposition
to the assembled multitude. It was fully dark now,
the night well advanced. Overhead, despite the
glowing fire, I could make out the stars that pre-
saged autumn: my namesake Orion was climbing
above the saw-toothed horizon, looking down at
me. He seemed different from the way I knew him
from other eras, still easily recognizable, but
vaguely lopsided. And there were four bright stars
in the Belt, instead of just three.

Dal was no orator, but he spoke in a plain, clear
way about the idea of staying in the valley through
the winter. He hemmed and hawed a little, but he
got across the basic idea that the clans could pen
the animals against the cliffs and slaughter them
at their leisure instead of tracking them down,
that they could live off the grain which grew in the
valley and could even grow more grain than sprang
up naturally.

Everyone listened patiently without interrupting,
although I could see many of the elders shaking
their heads, their gray beards waving from side to
side in perfect stubborn unison.

Finally, Dal said, "And if you want Orion's words
about it, he will be glad to tell you. This is all his
idea, to begin with."

A man Dal's age, from the Wolf Clan, jumped to
his feet. "We are not meant to stay in one place!
This valley is prepared for us each year by our
spirit-fathers. How can they prepare the grain if

we stay here watching all year long? The spirits will go away and the grain will die!"

Dal turned uneasily toward me. I had been sitting to one side of the Goat Clan's area, placed off at the end so that I was almost by myself, in a space between clans. I got to my feet and took a single step closer to the fire so that they could all see me well. I wanted them to see for themselves that although I was a stranger, I was a man and not one of the forty-armed monsters the elders had sung about earlier.

"I am Orion," I said, "a newcomer to this part of the world. I love to hunt as much as any man here. But I know that there is a better way to live, a way that will bring all of us much pleasure, much comfort—a way that will keep us well fed all year long. Babies will be fat and healthy even in the winter's worst cold and snow. We will all be able to . . ."

That was as far as I got. An explosion of blood-curdling screams shattered the night, and flames seemed to burst all around us.

Everyone jumped every which way. A spear thudded into the ground near my feet. Screaming and yelling erupted from everywhere as men and women toppled, spears driven through their bodies. The bonfire hissed as blood spattered onto it. The clanspeople ran for their huts, terrified.

But not Dal. "They're burning the grain!" he roared. "Get your weapons!"

Through the flickering flames I saw naked men painted in hideous colors dashing toward the huts. Some held torches, others spears.

"Demons!" Ava screamed. And they did look unhuman, the way they were painted, with the firelight glinting off their glistening bodies.

Dal had already yanked a spear from the body of a fallen clansman and was running toward one of the enemy warriors. Ava dashed in behind him, scooped up a fallen spear, and advanced to his side. Another spear whizzed past my head. A trio of the strange warriors dashed into one of the huts. Screams of pain and terror wailed from it.

All this happened in seconds. I rushed for my own hut, knocked down two warriors who tried to stop me, and grabbed my bow and a handful of arrows. I could hear more shouting and sobbing outside, and Dal's voice clear and commanding over the din of confusion and battle.

As I ducked back into the night air outside my hut, a painted warrior sprang at me, his spear leveled at my chest. I sidestepped and floored him with a lethal chop to his neck. Over his body I stepped, out into the flame-filled screaming furor of the battle, my reflexes accelerating into overdrive, every sense alert and sharpened to its finest pitch. I felt a wild exhilaration: the waiting was over, the battle had been joined.

I notched an arrow and sent it through a warrior's skull. Dal and Ava were off to my right, using their spears to fend off four spear-wielding warriors. I knocked off one of them just as Dal ripped another's belly open. Ava dropped to one knee as a warrior charged her and spitted him from below. The screaming man fell atop her, but she wriggled out immediately, took his spear and rejoined the fight. By that time I had put an arrow through the neck of the fourth warrior.

In the light of the blazing grain I could see many of the clanspeople on the ground. But there were more of us on our feet, fighting. The invading warriors were falling back now, throwing their torches at us to slow our pursuit.

Sheer maddened anger drove me forward. I raced at them, bellowing mindlessly as I fired my remaining arrows into them and then took a spear from a fallen warrior and charged them with all the fury that had been pent up inside me, waiting for this release. I knocked down the first one to stand before me with a sidelong swipe of my spear against his skull, using the weapon like a quarterstaff. Another loomed to my side, and I drove the spear point into his guts. He screamed as I yanked it free and slashed it across the face of the next one.

It seemed longer, but within mere seconds my spear was bloodied along its whole length, slippery in my grasp, as I slaughtered anyone who came within reach. The remaining warriors bolted, wide-eyed with newfound fear, and I raced after them, killing, killing, killing again as I caught up with them, one by one. Behind me I could hear the shouts of Dal and the others growing fainter.

I followed the retreating warriors toward the distant cave-dotted cliffs. One of them stumbled and fell in front of me; I drove my spear through him and felt it bite into the dirt. He shrieked with his last breath. Tugging hard, I yanked it free again and resumed my chase after the others.

The invaders were scattering in all directions, their weapons thrown away as they ran for their lives to escape my bloody rage. I slowed and turned. Far behind me, Dal and the others had turned their attention to the fires that the invaders had started in the grain fields. I saw Ava, smeared with blood of her enemies, standing triumphantly and waving both arms over her head, urging me to come back.

But I pressed onward, toward those caves, where I knew Ahriman lurked. It was the Dark One who had organized this raid, no one else. He was there, and I moved relentlessly to find him, my hands already soaked in the blood of his cohorts. Like an automaton running wild, I stalked the Dark One, longing with every ounce of my being to add his blood to that which was already darkening my spear.

It was black by the base of the cliffs; not even the glow from the burning field cast much light there. But in that hushed gloom, where even the insects and beasts of the night lay silenced and frightened by the rush of fighting men, I heard breathing and the soft tread of bare feet on stony ground.

There were three of them, off to my left, waiting to attack me—and another two, further to my right, ready to circle behind me and close the trap.

I moved forward, as if unaware of their presence. But the instant they leaped toward me, I whirled around and swung my spear at their legs like a scythe, cutting the three of them down. As they fell in a jumbled heap, I hefted the bloody spear in my right hand and threw it at the nearer of the two who were circling behind me. The solid *thunk* of it hitting his chest was louder than the desperate little gasp he gave out as he died. I killed the three on the ground quickly, with my bare hands, while the only remaining warrior fled for his life.

I took all three of their spears and headed toward the nearest cave. I had no way of telling if Ahriman was there; all I knew was that I was certain he would be.

The cave was pitch dark inside, not a single glowing ember lit its yawning blackness. But I plunged into it anyway, hot with reckless fury.

It was the cave bear's warning growl that saved my life. If the beast had been as intent on killing as I was, it would have waited until I had blundered into its grasp and then crushed me with its mighty paws. But it was only an animal defending its lair; it had none of the malicious hatred that human beings carry within them. It growled before it slashed out at me. I lunged forward at the sound with all three of the spears bundled together in my grip. I was lucky. I hit the bear's heart or lungs. One of the spears snapped in my hands, but the other two penetrated and the animal died with a hideous shriek of agony.

Suddenly the blood lust cooled within me. I was dripping with sweat, covered with blood from head to toe, trembling with physical exertion and emotional exhaustion. Killing other humans had meant nothing to me, but killing the bear had snapped me out of my battle fury. There, in the utter darkness of the beast's cave, I doubled over, hands on knees, panting and almost weeping with shame and regret.

For several minutes I remained there. Gradually my strength returned, and with it my resolve. Ahriman was here, I knew it. I could *feel* it. The bear might have been one of his defenses, to be used against me as he had used the rats in a man-made cave to kill the woman I loved.

I wrestled one of the spears from the bear's still-warm body, stepped over the carcass, and started to grope my way into the ever deeper darkness of the dank cave. Eyesight was useless in this black pit, but all my other senses were fully alert, stretched as far as they could reach.

But just as I could see nothing, I heard nothing. Not a sound, except my own ragged breathing and the almost inaudible padding of my bare feet on the cave floor. My left hand slid along the rough stone wall; my right held the spear. I advanced cautiously, probing the darkness like a blind man, seeking the enemy that I knew lurked somewhere up ahead of me.

The sudden glare of blinding light paralyzed me, and then a tremendous blow to my head thrust me into darkness once more.

CHAPTER 30

I felt the chill of death, and when I opened my eyes, I saw that we were in a cave of ice. Cold, glittering, translucent ice surrounded us. The floor and walls were smooth, polished, blue-white. The ceiling, high above, was craggy with frozen stalactites. I could see my breath puffing from my open mouth. I shivered involuntarily.

We were far underground, beneath the rocky surface of Ararat. A natural hiding place for the Dark One. Ahriman sat, incongruously, behind a heavy, broad slab of wood, like a thick slice taken from a full-grown tree. The top of the slab was burnished down to a gloss so fine that I could see the reflection of his dark, brooding face and powerful neck and shoulders in it.

I was sitting up, my back propped against an outcropping of stone. My head thundered from the blow I had received, but with a conscious effort I eased the tension in my neck muscles and directed the capillary blood flow to reduce the swelling. The pain began to slacken.

Behind Ahriman's menacing bulk I could see a dully gleaming canister. It seemed to be made of wood also, but a dense, black wood that almost looked like metal. Its top half was hinged open. It looked to me more like a coffin than anything else.

Ahriman sat silently behind the wood slab of a desk, staring into its gleaming surface as if he could see things in it that I could not. I shifted slightly, testing my reflexes. I was not bound; my arms and legs were free and seemed to respond to my commands with no difficulty.

He looked up at me, his eyes glaring. The Dark One wore a skintight suit of metallic fiber, sealed at the throat with a gleaming stone whose colors changed and shifted even as I watched. The metallic suit glittered in the cave's soft lighting. I looked up, but could see no lamps, only a glow that seemed to be coming from the ice itself.

"Bioluminescence," Ahriman said. His voice was a grating, painful whisper.

I nodded, more to test my aching head than to agree with him. The pain was receding quickly.

"Your people put out the fires quickly enough," he said. "The grain is rich with moisture. I should have waited a week, it would have been drier then."

"Where did you get those warriors?" I asked.

A grim smile flickered across his almost lipless face. "That was easy. There are plenty of tribes of your people who are eager for the chance to murder and loot. They think of it as glory. They go back to their miserable hovels with a clutch of heads they've cut off and tell their wives and children what powerful men they are."

"You tempt them to do so."

"They don't need much temptation. Killing is a part of their way of life; it's built into them."

"You're going to fail here, you know," I told him. "We will meet again."

"Yes, you told me. You have met me twice before."

"Which means you will fail here. You will not succeed in preventing these people from developing agriculture . . ."

He raised a single massive hand to stop me in mid-sentence.

"How certain you are," Ahriman whispered

harshly. "How absolutely sure that you will triumph, that you are right, that the Golden One represents truth and victory."

"Ormazd is . . ."

"Ormazd is not even his true name, any more than mine is Ahriman. They are merely fabrications, lies, inventions, simplifications that are necessary because your mind was never made to grasp the entire truth in all its endless facets."

Anger began to warm me from within. "I know enough of the truth to understand what you intend."

"The destruction of your kind is what I intend," Ahriman said, "even if it takes all of time to accomplish it. Even if it means tearing apart the continuum and destroying the whole universe of spacetime. I have nothing to lose. Do you understand that, Orion? *I have nothing to lose.*"

His red eyes were burning at me. I felt the power of his anger, his hatred, and something more—something that I could not identify, something that felt like sorrow, eternal and everlasting.

But I spat back, "You'll never win! No matter what you do, it's you who'll be destroyed."

"Really?"

"You will fail here, just as you failed in other times. You can't stop the human race."

He leaned his powerful arms on the tree-slab desk and hunched forward, looming before me like a dark thundercloud.

"You pitiful fool, you don't understand the nature of time even yet, do you?"

Before I could reply, he went on, "Just because we have met before, in other centuries, in other places, does not mean that you will defeat me here. Time is not a railroad track that's laid down in place, one section at a time, and fixed solidly, unmovably. Time is like a river, or better yet, an ocean. It moves, it shifts; it washes away a bit of the land here and throws up a new island there. It is not immutable. If I succeed here, the eras in which you and I have already met will dissolve back into primeval chaos, as if they never happened."

I stared at him for long, silent moments. Then I said, "I don't believe you. You're lying."

He shook his head slowly, ponderously. "I can win here, Orion. I will. And all of the space-time will be disrupted. The continuum will crumble, and those times and places where we met will cease to exist."

"It can't be true!"

"But it is. And you know it is. I will destroy all of you, you who call yourselves *Homo sapiens sapiens*. All of you who are Ormazd's creations. You and he will dissolve into nothingness together, and my people will triumph at last."

"Never," I said, but so softly that I barely heard it myself.

Ahriman ignored me, gloating, "Your little band of savages will not make the transition from hunting to agriculture. Nor will any other of your tribes. Your people will remain a small, weak, starving collection of scattered hunting tribes—*with the instinct for war built into you*."

He stressed that last phrase, savored it, hissed it at me as if it were a justification for everything he had done, every life he had taken, every evil he had committed.

"It will be easy enough to get your bloodthirsty tribes to slaughter each other, given enough time," Ahriman went on. "All that I need do is lead them into collision courses, bring two tribes together unexpectedly. Your own savage instincts will do the rest for me."

"The clans don't always fight when they meet," I argued. "They're working together in the valley . . ."

"Only because they know each other. And only because food is plentiful in the valley. But they are

such wasteful, wanton fools. Already they have
thinned out the game herds and driven some beasts
into extinction. Food will become scarcer for them,
I promise you."

"If they don't turn to agriculture," I muttered.

"They won't. And when one of your wandering
bands of hunters bumps into a strange group, they
will annihilate each other."

I shook my head stubbornly, refusing to believe
him. "There are too many human tribes for you to
destroy them all. They're spread out all across the
world . . ."

"Not so," Ahriman said. "The glaciers cover a
good part of the northern hemisphere. And even if
they did not, what difference does it make to me? I
have all the time in the world to kill off your
wandering tribes of savages. Think of it! Centuries,
millennia, eons! A long, delicious feast of killing."

His pain-red eyes glowed with the thought. I sat
still, silently calculating my chances for leaping
across the desk and crushing his throat before he
could stop me.

"And in the end," Ahriman went on, his face as
close to happiness as it could ever be, "when your
primitive blood-drinkers have finally slaughtered
each other, the wrenching of the continuum will
be so severe that the Earth, the sun, the stars and
galaxies themselves will all collapse in on themselves. A temporal black hole. The end of everything,
at last."

I jumped for his throat. But from the expectant
leer on his dark face I realized that he had made
the same calculation that I had, and placed himself just far enough from me to give himself time
to block my lunge. I saw his powerful hands clench
into fists and launch themselves straight at my
face. Pain exploded in my brain. I blacked out
again.

I awoke to the sound of trickling water. I lay on

hard stone, in utter darkness. It took a long time before the throbbing in my head stopped, even though I exerted every effort to control my nervous system and shut off the pain.

When I tried to sit up, I bumped my head against solid rock. I probed upward with both hands and found that I was tucked into a narrow cleft of stone. I felt a blank rock wall on my right; on my left, an edge that dropped off into nothingness.

Ahriman was gone, I knew. Off to accomplish his task of either driving the clans out of the valley or killing them altogether. I had to get free and prevent him from winning.

Vision was useless; there was no light at all. The trickling water noise came from below me. Carefully, I turned myself over onto my stomach and groped down along the ledge as far as my arm would reach. No bottom. I poked around for a loose pebble, found one, and dropped it over the edge. Straining my ears and concentrating all my attention did no good. I waited for what seemed like hours, but heard no splash. I found a larger piece of rock and tried it again. The seconds moved slowly, slowly—and then I heard a faint *plonk.* There was water down there, far below.

I began inching forward, not knowing if I was moving in the right direction. The rock seemed to slope slightly upward, but that did not necessarily mean it was heading toward the surface, I knew. But there was nothing else I could think of. So I crawled, blind as a mole, inching along without knowing where I was heading. No sounds reached me except my own breathing and the scrabbling noises of my body scuffing along the rock ledge, and the far-off murmur of running water.

Slowly I began to realize that the rock was getting warmer. It reminded me of the underground cell that Ahriman had trapped me in the first time we had met. But this was a natural cave, not a bubble of captured energy. The heat was coming from a natural source. Magma from the volcano, I reasoned. Perhaps I was moving deeper underground, rather than toward daylight.

I stopped, panting in the dank, heavy air, and tried to think it out. That got me nowhere; I simply did not have enough information. Then I tried to put myself in Ahriman's place. What was he going to do?

Destroy the Goat Clan, came the answer.

How? I asked myself. The attack on the clans had failed. They would be on guard now. Instead of driving them out of the valley, the attack probably made them realize how precious the grain fields were. They might well have decided by now to stay in the valley year-round, to protect the grain against marauders.

But Ahriman is no fool, I told myself. He would have foreseen that.

Then the true purpose of the attack must have been to entice the clans into staying in the valley. But that did not make sense—unless Ahriman planned to destroy the clans and the valley itself, together!

How? Earthquake? Could the Dark One control tectonic forces? I didn't know. But the answer came to me soon enough, as I lay there in my lightless prison of rock. I heard a loud, slapping, sloshing noise from far below me. A wave was surging through the underground river that flowed down there in the darkness.

"A flood," I said aloud, my voice strangely hoarse and muffled against the close confines of rock. My thoughts raced. Underground heat to melt the underground ice. The stream that runs through the valley will burst out of the mountainside in an uncontrollable flood. The clans will never have a chance of getting out. The valley will be drowned, together with everyone in it.

Even as I lay there, it was beginning to happen. The water was lapping noisily below me, getting closer, rising to where I lay trapped in this prison of stone. I would be the first one to drown. Ahriman had planned well.

Going through death and being reborn does not make you eager to face death again. Ormazd was in control of my destiny, I knew, but the more I learned about the Golden One and his powers, the more I became aware of his limitations. If he had the power, he would have dealt with Ahriman directly, without need of me or any intermediary. He had power enough to pull me through death and project me into another time and place—at least twice. But what assurance did I have that he could do it again, or would do it again, or even that he knew where I was and what I was facing?

I felt totally alone, facing the choice of waiting for the water to rise up and drown me or plunging down into it and trying to find a way back out to daylight. Time was vital. If I survived at all, it was crucial that I get to Dal and Ava in time to warn them of the flood.

I made up my mind, took a deep breath, and rolled over the edge of the rock and dropped like one of my tossed stones down toward the water. There was plenty of time for me to be frightened; the fall was a long one. I oriented my body feet-downward, the best way to take such a dive. I found myself wondering how deep the water was; I might break my neck before I drowned.

The water felt like cement when I finally hit it, and then I was plummeting deep, deep down in icy black water, every nerve shocked numb, no sensory input except a painful bubbling in my ears.

I bobbed to the surface at last, took a deep, happy breath, and half swam, half rode the current wherever it was leading me. I had the feeling

it was in the direction opposite to the one in which
I had been crawling.

After what seemed like hours, I banged my flailing arms against solid rock. The river swirled and
surged against a blank wall, but I could feel from
the undertow that it dipped into a deeper tunnel
and kept flowing on. There was no airspace in that
tunnel, I realized, but I had no choice except to
follow it. I filled my lungs and then dove under,
letting the current carry me along.

The oxygen in my lungs was soon exhausted; yet
the river still flowed in its natural tunnel. I began
to squeeze oxygen from the spare cells of my body,
consciously shutting down whole muscle systems
and organs that I didn't need, taking their stored
oxygen to feed to my heart and brain and limbs. I
began to die, bit by bit, like the lights of a city
winking out in a power failure, one section after
another. Desperate, I slowed down my heartbeat
and brought myself into a virtual catatonic trance,
passively flowing along the underground river,
starving for oxygen, not knowing if I would ever
see the light of day again.

It seemed like months went by, but finally the
darkness around me began to brighten and I floated
to the surface of the river.

Air! Real, breathable air. It tasted wonderful as
my body returned to life and I gulped in huge
lungfuls of the most precious substance on Earth.

The river was emptying itself into a huge cave,
turning it into a vast underground cistern. I dragged
myself up onto dry, rocky ground, every part of
my body jangling from lack of blood circulation.
Sunlight filtered from an opening in the vast cave,
far overhead. I was much too weak even to try to
reach it.

CHAPTER 31

For hours there was nothing I could do but lie there on the rock-strewn dirt and try to recover my strength. But every moment of that time, the water behind me rose higher, splashing and gurgling as it filled this natural underground cistern. Soon enough it began lapping at my feet as I lay stretched prone on the damp ground.

I forced myself to stand and began scrabbling up the sloping wall of the huge cave, toward the opening where the sun's light streamed in. The bare earth was loose and pebbly, difficult to climb. With each step forward I was in danger of sliding all the way back. But I struggled upward and finally pushed myself through the narrow fissure of rock and out into the daylight.

Looking back, I saw that the underground river was filling up the cave. When it reached the rock ceiling, the water would have nowhere to go but outward, exploding through the rock that held it back, gushing down into the valley below with the force of a tidal wave that would sweep everything before it.

I staggered down the steep slope of the valley wall, my legs weak and rubbery from exertion. Through blurring eyes I could see the valley spread out below me in the late afternoon sun, beautiful, peaceful, vulnerable. I had to get down to Ava and Dal and warn the people.

Tottering with exhaustion, I made my way toward the grain fields. People were at work there, cutting down the long golden stalks with their flint knives. I made my way to them.

"Look!" came a shout from one of the men. "It's Orion!"

"He's come back from the dead!"

They dropped their work and gathered around me, keeping a respectful distance.

I raised my hand in greeting, but before I could utter a word to them, exhaustion and hunger took their inexorable toll. I blacked out.

Ava's taut, lovely face was staring at me when I opened my eyes again.

"You are alive," she said gravely.

"Yes," I croaked. "And starving."

Looking around, I saw that I was in my own hut, lying on the matted grass that we used for a pallet. I could see a crowd of clanspeople pressing at the doorway, peering in. Food of every description was piled high in the middle of the room—gifts from the people, I supposed.

Ava turned from me momentarily. Within seconds one of the other women had pushed her way into the hut, bearing a gourd of steaming broth. I sipped at it, burning my tongue. But it felt good and strengthening as it slid down my innards.

"Where's Dal?" I asked, my voice more normal. "We've got to get the people out . . ."

"Eat first," Ava crooned. "Get your strength back."

I put the gourd to my lips and gulped down all of the broth. She tried to get me to lie back again, but I gently pushed her hands away.

"I've got to see Dal."

"Were you in the land of the dead?" asked the woman who had brought the gourd.

I shook my head, but her eyes were round with

awe. "What was it like? Did you see my son there? His name is Mikka, and he was four summers old when he died of a fever."

Ava shooed her away, then came back to me.

"You were in the land of the dead, weren't you?" she asked softly.

I saw that the people cramming my doorway believed that, no matter what I said. Ava did too, with that mistaken simplicity of logic that says: Dead people are buried underground; Orion has been underground; therefore, Orion has been in the land of the dead.

"Dal," I whispered urgently. "I must talk to Dal. We've got to leave this valley. Quickly!"

"Leave? Why . . . ?"

"There is going to be a flood. We'll all be drowned if we stay here. Find Dal and bring him here. Now!"

She turned and told one of the men to bring Dal. Looking back at me, Ava said, "Dal was wounded in the fighting three nights ago."

"Badly?"

"His leg was slashed by a spear, just above the knee."

Infection, I thought.

"It's not a very bad wound, but I've made him stay on his pallet to rest. I've kept the wound covered with leaves and poultice."

I got to my feet and headed for the doorway. The people melted away from me, almost in a panic. I had been in the land of the dead and then returned. There was fear in their eyes, and a desperate curiosity to know what lay beyond death. Grimly I strode through their midst toward Dal's hut, thinking to myself that their primitive superstition was truer than they knew: I have been through the land of the dead, more than once.

In the slanting late-afternoon light I could see that the stream cutting through the valley was already broader, noisier, and moving faster than it ever had before. And its direction had reversed. It was flowing from the base of the cliffs out toward the waterfall at the other end of the valley, where the two flows met to form a growing, frothing pool.

Off in the distance I heard a low rumble and felt the ground shudder. All the clanspeople looked toward Ararat's smoking crest.

"Orion walks and the mountain speaks to him," I heard a woman say.

The others mumbled agreement.

I said nothing. For the moment, their awe-stricken respect for me was useful; I was going to give them commands that they had to obey swiftly.

Two of the clan's teen-aged boys were helping Dal to his feet when I stepped into his hut, Ava trailing a step or two behind me. His leg did not seem swollen, beneath the leaves that she had plastered over his wound. Perhaps he would survive, after all.

"Let him sit," I told them, and they lowered Dal back onto his pallet.

He looked me over in the gloomy shadows inside the hut. "We thought you were dead. But we could not find your body."

"I am still alive," I said. "But we will all be killed if we don't get out of this valley right away."

Dal winced as if I had slapped his face. "What? Leave the valley? But I thought . . ."

"There is going to be a flood," I said. "Soon. Very soon. Perhaps only a few hours from now. It will drown this whole valley and everything in it."

"But the stream has never . . ."

"Dal," I snapped, "have I ever lied to you? There will be a flood. I know! If we stay here, we will all be killed. We must leave. *Now!*"

He looked up at Ava.

"There's no time for argument," I said. "We

must tell all the people, all the clans, and move out now, this hour."

"Up the steps of the waterfall," Ava said.

I realized that would be impossible. The first stage of the flood was creating an ever-deepening pool at the base of the waterfall. We could not get out of the valley the way we had come in.

"No," I said. "We must go up the cliffs along the side of the valley."

Dal looked shocked. "No one can climb those cliffs!"

"I will show you how to do it," I said.

"But it can't be done. We're only ordinary people; we can't fly!"

"We can climb," Ava said firmly. "Orion and I climbed the cliffs one day, more than a month ago."

He stared at her, began to object, then shook his head. It was more new information than he could take in, I thought. But when he looked down at his leg, stiff and tender from the spear wound, I realized that Dal was worried about his own survival.

A roar of thunder shook the ground. But it did not come from the heavens. The sky to the north flared an angry red, and I could hear fearful moans from the people outside the hut. The volcano was smoldering, preparing to erupt. Ahriman was flexing his muscles.

"There is no time to lose," I said. "We must leave now."

With a nod, Dal said, "Go ahead. Ava, you direct the clan. Call the elders in here; I'll tell them that you will be in charge until they can pick another leader."

"But you're coming too!" she said.

He pointed to his wounded leg. "How can I? I couldn't even climb those cliffs when both my legs were whole."

I was terribly tempted to agree with him. It

would be difficult enough to get more than a hundred men, women and children, none of whom had ever climbed before, to make it safely up the face of the cliffs. A man with a bad leg could slow us down to the point where the flood waters would overtake us before we reached safety. And if Dal stayed behind, I would have Ava to myself once we had put the flood behind us.

My eyes locked on his. He was clearly afraid; he believed me and knew that if he stayed behind he would die. Yet he was willing to sacrifice his life for the safety of his clan. Bravery or stubbornness or just plain stupidity—whatever was driving him, I simply could not leave him there to die.

So I bent down and hauled him to his feet. Moving to the side of his bad leg, I grasped him firmly around the waist.

"Put your arms across my shoulders," I commanded, "and lean your weight on me."

"You can't . . ."

"Don't argue with me!" I snapped. "There isn't enough time."

Ava beamed at me as we hobbled out of the hut. Dal began shouting orders to the people. Teenagers were sent scampering off to warn the other clans. Women collected whatever food they could from their huts. Men gathered their tools and weapons.

"The grain!" Ava realized. "What's going to happen to the grain?"

"It will be swept away by the flood," I said.

"No!" she said. And she ran off toward the field, gesturing two of the teen-aged girls to come with her.

Ararat grumbled again, making the earth tremble. Hot steam was boiling up from the volcano's cone now, and I knew that worse would soon follow. The gentle stream that meandered through the valley was rushing and roaring now, already overflowing its banks here and there and edging into the grain field as it burbled the length of the valley and splashed into the lake that was growing at the base of the waterfall. The waterfall itself was angrier, more powerful, pouring an ever-stronger torrent down the stone terraces and into the widening lake. Mist rose from the lake and caught the slanting rays of the dying sun in a diabolically enticing rainbow.

"This way," I shouted as the people began to gather around Dal and me; they were frightened, confused, casting terrified glances at the angry stream and the angrier volcano.

"Do as Orion commands!" Dal told them. "Only he can save us. Do not anger the spirits of the dead by failing to obey him."

That calmed them a little. Tell us what to do; give us a direction, lead us—anywhere, just as long as you seem to know what you're doing. That's all it takes to stop a frightened crowd from turning into a panic-stricken, self-destructive mob.

We headed toward the cliffs, away from the flooding stream. I hauled Dal along, his weight dragging against me as he hobbled along on his good leg. Over my shoulder I saw the people of the other clans streaming after us, following blindly. But I could not find Ava's face in the growing crowd.

We made it to the base of the cliffs at last, and I sat Dal down on a rock. Picking two of the wiriest teen-aged boys, I lashed us together with ropes made from vines and took the lead in scrambling up the cliff face. The boys were young enough so that they did not know what was impossible, unlike their elders. They followed me with barely a false step.

We made it to the top, where the setting sun was still above the horizon. Looking below, I could see that most of the valley was in shadow now. And the stream was spreading its growing fingers in all directions, rapidly flooding the grain fields and edging toward the huts the clans had built. The waterfall at the far end of the valley was lost in mist now, and I could hear its thundering roar even from this distance.

Working quickly, we tied the ropes to trees and dropped them down to the people waiting below. I ordered the boys to remain where they were, then rappelled down the cliff and started the others climbing upward.

Dal watched with unabashed admiration as the people hauled themselves up the steep rocky wall, pulling hand-over-hand along the ropes.

"Have you seen Ava?" I asked.

"No . . ."

"Here we are!" she called.

I looked up to see her and the two girls carrying big leather sacks on their backs, grinning wearily as they neared us.

"We've got as much of the cut grain as we could carry," she said happily. "All the seeds that you told us about, Orion. And roots and berries, everything we could find. We're bringing it with us. We'll plant the seed next spring."

I could feel myself smiling broadly. Glancing up at the smoldering volcano, I thought that Ahriman had lost. The idea of agriculture had found good soil here, and it had taken root. And the legends that would be handed down from generation to generation for hundreds of centuries before writing was invented would garble the story of Ararat: it was a woman, not Noah, and she saved the species of grain and fruits that would feed the human race, not of animals who could escape the flood under their own power. Mythology was usually based on a kernel of fact, but what distortions the male-dominated tribes would make of this story!

All through the deepening twilight the clanspeople worked as they had never worked before. The volcano's rumblings grew stronger, angrier, and it began to spout black smoke streaked with red flame. The sky turned black, and flashes of lightning strobed the darkness, frightening the people even more. By ones and twos and threes they climbed, scrabbled, groped, inched their way up the ropes we had set out along the cliff face, and hauled themselves up to the safety of the top. The sturdiest of the teen-agers and young men helped the older and less agile. Babies rode on men's backs. I made the journey up and back down again several times, helping everyone I could.

Dal sat on the rock at the base of the cliff, keeping the people organized down there, calming their fears and holding their panic at bay.

Ararat was growling at us now, and its sullen red glow lit the evening hours for us. I could see boulders the size of a house flying up out of its crater, and burning tongues of lava spilling over the lip of the volcano's cone. The ground trembled with each roar of the mountain, but there was no true earthquake—not yet.

Slightly more than half the people had made it to the top of the cliff when the flood burst upon the valley. The rock wall where the stream had been gushing forth exploded in a mammoth shower of water and steam, hurling boulders halfway down the valley. The cistern where I had been earlier that day had not only reached its overflow point, but the heat from the tectonic forces that Ahriman had unleashed had turned the cistern into a mammoth tea kettle. The water had finally come to a boil and the expanding steam blew open the side of the mountain like a kiloton charge of explosives.

A wall of white water blasted down the valley, roaring like all the demons of hell let loose at once. Steam hissed into the dark sky and a hot rain began to fall on us.

I was halfway down the cliff, returning to help another pair of people up to safety, when it happened. I could see it all clearly, despite the darkness, and I saw the people still down at the base of the cliff standing frozen in terror as that all-consuming wave hurtled toward us.

"Move, move, move!" I bellowed, letting go of the rope and jumping the rest of the way down the cliff, landing with a shock on the balls of my feet and rolling over twice to absorb the impact.

The people jerked to frantic life, dozens of men and women suddenly scratching up the cliff to save their lives. Others clambered down from the top, risking their lives without a moment's thought to help their friends and relatives.

Dal got to his feet and leaned heavily on a spear. He was staring at the angry flood of frothing hot water as it surged toward us, swallowing everything in its path.

The volcano erupted truly now, and the ground shook hard enough to knock people loose from the ropes as they climbed up the cliff. They fell; bones broke. Screams of agony and terror pierced the darkness over the roar of the flood and the volcano.

I helped those I could, racing among the fallen to set them on their feet and start them up toward the top again. Teen-aged boys scrambled down to help others.

Then I saw Dal standing there watching us, his face set in a stubborn mask of self-control. He neither frowned nor cried for help. He leaned on his gnarled spear shaft, his injured leg held out stiffly, as he watched his people climbing to safety. Behind him, the raging hot waters of the flood roared and thundered closer, closer.

CHAPTER 32

With a yell, I grabbed one of the dangling vine ropes and ran for Dal. He raised one arm to protest, but I grabbed him and looped the rope under his shoulders before he could stop me.

"Hold on to the spear," I shouted over the roar of the approaching flood. "Use the strength of your arms to make up for your bad leg."

"I can't make it!" he shouted back. "Save yourself, Orion!"

"We'll both make it. Come on!"

I half-carried, half-tugged him to the base of the cliff and gave him an upward shove. Whoever was on the other end of the rope, up at the top, understood what I was trying to do and began hauling in the rope. Dal used his spear like a crutch as I scrabbled up the cliff beside him. The rain was making the rock slippery, and I nearly fell more than once.

We were barely a quarter of the way up the cliff face when the flood smashed against the base of the rocks, splashing boiling hot foam against me and sending Dal spinning on the end of the rope. He lost his spear and screamed with sudden pain. I automatically clamped down on my own pain receptors as the boiling water seared my legs. Grabbing Dal, I pushed and grunted and shoved the two of us higher. The water clawed at us, trying to drag us down into its steaming clutches.

I got one hand on the rope and gripped Dal around the shoulders with my other arm. Slowly, slowly, we inched up the cliff as the water rose behind us, seeking us, pulling at us, cooking the flesh of our legs as we desperately climbed toward safety.

Suddenly I heard Ava's voice shouting commands, and we were lifted by what could only be the strength of many hands. Miraculously, it seemed, that strength hauled us roughly up the cliff, out of the water's boiling grip, and landed us wet, burned, exhausted at the top of the cliff.

I lay there like a fish hauled out of the sea, squinting up through the hot rain at a ring of faces peering down.

"Are you all right?" Ava asked over and over. "Are you all right?"

It was Dal that she was talking to. I sat up, wincing, as I allowed the pain receptors in my legs to resume their normal function. Both legs were scalded, but the damage did not seem too serious. Ava was kneeling beside Dal, already smearing some kind of ointment over his reddened legs.

He turned to me. "You saved me, Orion."

"As you once saved me."

"I owe you my life," he said.

With a shake of my head, I said, "No, you owe your life to your people. Lead them well, Dal. Find another valley and make it your own."

Ava turned to me. "We will. We will live as you told us to live, Orion. We will start a new life."

I should have felt happy, but there was nothing inside me except the pain of realizing that Ava would go with Dal, that she had to, and that I would be left alone once again.

I turned to peer through the darkness at the flood surging below us. It frothed and lapped at me, as if angry that I had escaped and trying to reach higher to get at me.

"You'd better take the clans to higher ground," I said, "until the flood goes down."

"Up the mountain," Dal agreed.

"But it's shaking, burning," Ava said.

"That won't hurt us," said Dal, sure of himself once again. "When the flood is over, we will find a new valley to live in."

"Good," I said. The rain was slackening, but I could still hear the flood waters boiling below us. "You'd better get going now, without delay."

"But what about you?" Ava asked.

"I'll stay here. You don't need me any longer."

"But . . ."

"Go," I commanded.

Reluctantly, they left. They made a litter for Dal and said a brief little prayer for those who had been killed, and then the band moved off, many of them limping, toward higher ground.

I sat there, willing my scalded legs to heal, waiting for the inevitable. I looked out across the valley in the deepening darkness, lit now only by the surly glow of the volcano's fiery grumbling. The flood waters hissed and growled below me. I could feel the steam wafting up from their surface. The whole valley had been turned into a boiling cauldron. Ahriman had done his work well—but not well enough.

"You think you've won." It was his labored, rasping voice in the darkness.

Turning toward him, I said, "I know I've won."

His ponderous bulk seemed to congeal out of the shadows to loom over me as I sat on the ground, my legs poking straight out awkwardly.

"Nothing will grow in that valley for a long, long time," he said. "Your superstitious little band of hunters will be so afraid of returning to it that . . ."

"They won't have to return," I interrupted. "They've brought the seeds of their grains with them."

His red eyes flashed. "What?"

"And they have the seed of a new idea in their heads," I went on. "You've lost, Ahriman. Those hunters will survive. They'll turn into farmers and flourish."

He did not bother to argue or to deny the truth of what I had told him. He did not rant or shout with rage. He stood there in silence for a long time, thinking, calculating, planning.

"It's checkmate, Dark One," I said. "There's no way you can stop them now. You've done your worst, and they've stood up to it."

"Because of you," he rumbled.

"I helped them, yes."

"For the last time, Orion." He strode swiftly to me and picked me right up off the ground, his powerful hands squeezing my ribs like a pair of steel vises. He held me up in the air, my legs dangling uselessly.

"For the last time!" Ahriman shouted, and he threw me over the edge of the cliff, down into the boiling water below.

But in that last instant I grabbed him around his bull neck and held on with all my strength. For half an instant we hung there on the edge of the cliff, the two of us teetering there in the darkness, and then we toppled together downward into the raging water.

The boiling water was a shock of agony as we plunged into its depths. We've beaten you again, I exulted silently as the water hissed and bubbled all around me. And maybe this time is the final encounter; maybe this time I've finished you once and for all.

The water surged over me, dragging me down

into its hot depths, boiling me, flaying the flesh from my bones. I gave way to pain and death, my last hope being that this would truly be the end of it all.

INTERLUDE

The gray-eyed goddess who called herself Anya took on her human form and stood at the crest of an ice cliff, her body encapsulated in an invisible bubble of energy that protected it from the frigid cold of this frozen world.

Far below her she could see an army of humans and their robots working furiously, scurrying like ants across the iron-hard plain, as they built the fragile towers that soared high into the inky sky.

Turning, she saw the mammoth bulk of Saturn hanging overhead, resplendent in its gaudy colors and impossibly beautiful rings. The sky was as clear as the pristine vacuum of space itself, and she could see three of Saturn's smaller moons etched boldly against the star-strewn blackness of the heavens.

She felt the Golden One's presence before his human form materialized beside her. She held her seething anger in check until he completed the transformation and stood on the ice cliff's edge in solid flesh, clad in a radiant golden robe decorated with starbursts that shimmered with all the colors of the spectrum when the robe moved.

"You kept me separated from him," Anya said, unable to hold back her temper any longer.

The Golden One did not look at her. Instead, he watched the work of the builders far below them.

"My creatures have learned how to build creatures of their own," he murmured, almost as if talking to himself. "But how limited their robots are. How clumsy."

Anya knew that she could not touch him, but she stepped in front of the Golden One, confronting him. "You forced me to stay apart from him. I lived a whole lifespan with those savages . . ."

"Did you enjoy it?"

She spat an exasperated sigh into the frigid night.

The Golden One smiled. "You said you loved those creatures. You were willing to live hundreds of lifespans among them."

"With him! With Orion."

"No," said the Golden One. "You were becoming too attached to him. And he to you. I told you that you were weakening him. I cannot allow that."

"It was cruel of you," she said, her voice sinking lower. "To be so close to him and yet unable to truly love him. It was *very* cruel to treat him that way."

"He has a mission to accomplish. I created Orion for that goal. I can't have him sidetracked by the hormones that pump through the body I gave him."

Anya began to reply, but hesitated and then fell silent. The Golden One turned back to watch the work proceeding on the plain below them.

"They call this world Titan. They think of it as a frigid wasteland, dark and dangerous. If they didn't wear those ludicrous suits and helmets, they would die instantly."

"But you are the one who forced them to come here, to build those towers."

"Yes, and when they're finished with that, I'll get them to alter the atmosphere enough to make it opaque to their space probe instruments. They must not discover these towers too soon."

Anya stared at him, puzzled.

"The creatures down there are from a period

much closer to The End," the Golden One explained. "They are the distant ancestors of the humans who will discover these towers and puzzle over their meaning."

"What are the towers for? Why are they being built?"

"Why, to please me, of course."

She gave him an angry glare. "Your ego grows larger and larger. You really think you are a god, don't you, O mighty Ormazd?"

His smile faded only slightly. "The machinery in those towers will make subtle alterations in the climate of Earth. The planet will experience what my creatures will call an Ice Age. It's all part of my plan. The Dark One can manipulate rivers and volcanoes? I will manipulate the output of the Sun and the climate of Earth for hundreds of thousands of years!"

"And you will keep that knowledge from your own creatures?" she asked.

"Yes. They are not prepared to understand."

"You have not prepared them."

"Look," he said, pointing. "The tide is beginning to come in."

Anya knew he was deliberately changing the subject, cutting short any chance of argument. But, despite herself, she stared out, fascinated, as the ammonia sea rose like a living beast and hurled itself up along the broad frozen plain. Driven by the immense gravitational pull of Saturn, the ammonia sea slithered halfway around Titan with each spin of the satellite around the ringed planet. Now it was sliding up, frothing, rushing toward the site where the humans and their robots worked frantically to build the towers.

The Golden One watched, fascinated, with Anya at his side as the ammonia sea hurled itself across the sloping plain and then stopped, as if exhausted, just short of the ringwall that protected the building site. The sea seemed to shudder within itself as its farthest tendrils lapped against the foot of the curving stone ringwall. Behind it, the humans and their robots worked ceaselessly.

"I'm going to him," Anya said at last, breaking their silence. "You can't keep me from him."

"I cannot allow you to weaken him," said the Golden One. "His mission is to kill Ahriman."

"I will help him," she promised.

"How? By luring him to some half-baked paradise where the two of you can frolic like primitives while the Dark One destroys us all?"

She stood up straighter in front of the Golden One, her fists clenched, her eyes blazing. "I will help him to find the Dark One and kill him. You have not made him strong enough to do that by himself. But the two of us together can achieve what you want."

The Golden One gazed at her for long moments, pondering.

"I will go to him whether you wish me to or not," Anya threatened.

"Even if you do, I can see to it that you remain apart."

She weakened. "Let me help him. Let me be with him."

"I don't like the attachment for him that you've allowed yourself."

"I'll come back to you," she said softly. "After we've killed the Dark One. I will return to you, if that's what you want."

"That is what I demand."

"Then that is what I will have to do, isn't it? I don't really have a choice."

"No, you don't."

Her voice so low that he heard it only as a whisper in his mind, Anya pleaded, "Let me be with him one more time. One more lifespan."

"I will allow you to go only because you can help him to conquer the Dark One."

"Yes. We will. Together."

"And then you will return to me."

She nodded.

The Golden One folded his arms across his chest. His robe swirled and the starbursts on it flared and glittered against the darkness. The two of them winked out of sight, like fireflies on a summer night. Down below, on the plain, the space-suited humans and their robots worked as blindly as ever, driven by needs they could not begin to understand.

PART FOUR:
THE WAR

CHAPTER 33

From the searing heat of hell I plunged into a cold so bitter that it felt like burning. I opened my eyes to find myself crouched against a raging wind, snow flying in my face, the ground covered with ice and heavy banks of snow.

The wind howled and roared. I could feel my face freezing as I closed my eyes to slits against the snow that pelted me like stinging darts.

Stumbling, sliding, stooping low against the biting wind, I groped toward the only protection I could find—a looming snow bank that reared up massively in this bewildering blizzard of white.

I sank down on my haunches and leaned my back against its protection. The cold was inescapable, but at least I was protected from the slashing force of the wind. Looking down through lashes already thick with ice, I saw that I was dressed in what looked like white armor, from throat to foot, although the material seemed to be plastic rather than metal. I realized that, except for my freezing head, I was protected and comfortably warm. The suit was heated. My hands were sheathed in gloves so thin and flexible that they might have been another layer of skin, but they kept my hands warm, nonetheless. Somewhere there must have been a helmet that went with this outfit, but now it was lost in the howling blizzard that was covering the world with featureless white.

I sat there, puzzled and slowly freezing, for what seemed like hours. I shifted the blood flow in my capillaries to keep my head as warm as possible, but that merely postponed the inevitable. In this sub-zero blizzard I was merely using up my body's internal store of energy to delay frostbite and eventual death. I had to find shelter.

But where? The snow blanketed everything. I could not even tell where the horizon might be; all was blurred in endless snow and ice.

And what era was this? Everything that had happened to me so far told me that I was moving backward in time toward The War. If so, I should be in an era that preceded the Neolithic. The blinding storm raging around me made me suspect that I had been sent back into the Ice Age. But my clothing told me differently. I was wearing the products of a highly sophisticated technology—minus the helmet, of course. The midsection of my armored suit was studded with plastic pouches that contained elaborate electronic equipment that I could not even begin to understand. Always before, I had been dressed in a manner appropriate to the era in which I had been placed, but this was no Ice Age hunter's furs.

Where was I? And *when*?

Those questions were secondary, though, to the problem of survival. One by one, I tried the various pieces of equipment from the pouches around my waist. Most of them made no sense to me at all. One looked vaguely like a telephone or communicator of some sort; it was palm-sized, with a small grill at its base and a tiny plastic oval at the top that looked suspiciously like a miniature video screen. I tapped the three pressure pads that ran across its middle, one by one. They were color-coded red, yellow, and blue. Nothing happened.

In my haste to examine the equipment I put the communicator down on the snow beside me, alongside the other gear I had pulled out of the pouches. I went on yanking them out, trying to determine what they were for, how they worked—to no avail.

Except for the last one. That one was obvious. It was shaped like a pistol and holstered at my right side. Its barrel was a crystal rod circled by metallic cooling fins. Its grip bulged slightly in my hand and felt warm to the touch; no doubt a power pack of some sort was built into it. I curled my finger around its trigger, pointed the gun straight up, and squeezed slowly. It hummed softly for a moment and then fired out a blood-red beam so bright that I had to turn my eyes away from it. For several moments the afterimage burned in my vision. I almost welcomed it, a relief from the deathly white that covered the world around me.

I tried it again, this time averting my eyes from looking directly at the beam as it lanced through the snow-filled air. The beam disappeared in the gray clouds. I got the impression that it could bore a hole through the armor I wore, or through a mountainside, for that matter.

As I slid the gun back into its holster I heard a chirping sound which quickly turned into a steady little whistle. I pulled out the gun again and checked it over; it was neither vibrating nor making the noise. For a moment or two I thought it might have been my ears, perhaps the aftereffect of firing the pistol. But then I glanced down at the various bits of equipment scattered in the snow around me. Already the freshly falling snow was covering them with white—all except the communicator, I saw.

I snatched it and brought it to my ear. Not only was it slightly warm, but the tiny electronic wail was coming from it. The red pressure pad was glowing! Someone was trying to make contact with me!

I punched those buttons and jabbered into the

little device for what seemed like hours. No use.
All I could get out of it was that steady shrill
whistle. I got to my feet, thinking that perhaps
voice or picture transmission was being blocked
by the snow bank I had huddled against. No
difference, except that when I turned around, the
whistle changed its pitch.

Squinting against the howling wind, I slowly
turned a full circle. The whistle whined up and
down the scale, strongest in the direction I had
been originally facing, weakest and almost inaudible when I was turned exactly away from that
direction.

A directional beam, I told myself. Or, with a
thrill of hope bubbling inside me, a direction *finder*.
I knelt down to scoop up the rest of the equipment
from the snow, stuffed it into the various pouches at
my waist, and then headed off in the direction that
the electronic signal indicated, bent almost double
against the raging, icy wind.

I trudged through drifts that almost reached my
armpits. Fortunately the suit I wore kept me warm
and dry. The hair on my head was a brittle mass
of ice and I could barely see through the icicles
that closed my eyes to slits. All feeling had left my
cheeks, my ears and nose. But I could still breathe,
and I pushed on, hour after hour, growing hun-
grier and weaker with each painful, plodding step.

The storm did not let up in the slightest. If
anything, it seemed to be growing in strength. But
through the swirling snow I began to make out the
dim gray form of a massive bulk of rock. The
directional beam was leading me toward it, and as
I struggled through the blinding snow, I could see
that it was a looming cliff of granite, scoured clean
of snow by the furious wind, jutting stubbornly
up from the snow-blanketed landscape, standing
jagged, raw, and dark against the gray, snowy sky.

I floundered through deep drifts, stopping only

to check my communicator every few minutes, to make certain I was still following its electronic guidance. My strength was ebbing fast. The cold was seeping into me, leaching the energy of my muscles, numbing my will to press on. Each step became more difficult. My booted feet felt as if they were shod with lead and weighed a ton apiece. All I really wanted to do was to lie down and rest in the soft, comforting snow.

I remembered seeing pictures from some distant era of Eskimo sled dogs curled up happily in little holes they had dug for themselves in the snow, their bushy tails wrapped around their noses, their dark eyes peeping out from a world of white and cold. I stopped for breath and turned to look back at the trail I had broken through the deep snow. Already my tracks were being filled in, obliterated, by the howling storm. The stern gray bulk of the mountain frowned silently down at me as I stood lost in a world of white, totally alone in the universe, as far as I knew. It was time to rest, time to lie down and sleep.

Even my fingers were growing numb, despite the gloves and the suit's overburdened heating system. I let the tiny communicator slip from my fingers. It landed in the snow, its one red square glowering at me accusingly.

"You can glare all you want to," I said to it, in a voice raw with pain. Each breath I took was agony now; the air was so cold that it was burning my lungs.

"I've got to rest," I said to that red light.

It stared back at me, unblinking. The tiny electronic wail cut through the blizzard's howling.

"All right," I rasped. "I'll take ten more steps. Then, if there's no shelter in sight, I'm going to dig a hole for myself and get some sleep."

I forced myself through ten more steps. Then ten

more. Then five. The granite cliff seemed as far away as ever. The storm grew in fury.

"There's no point to it," I said to the inanimate little box in my hand. "There's no point . . ."

A blinding red pencil-beam of light lanced past my head. I plunged down into the snow instinctively and fumbled for the gun at my hip.

The beam streaked out again, and I could hear the air around me crackle.

Friend or enemy? I asked myself, and then almost laughed at the ridiculousness of the question. The enemy was this storm, the cold, the bitter agony of the ice that surrounded me. Anyone who could fire a gun must have heat, and food.

I raised my pistol and fired it straight overhead. That eye-hurting brilliance ought to be visible for miles, even through the storm.

Peering toward the granite cliff, I saw an answering beam angling up into the clouds. I headed for it, adrenaline pumping through my aching body and my limbs flailing through the snow with every last ounce of energy in me.

I saw, up ahead, a dark cleft in the rock, the mouth of a cave. Several people were standing there, clad in the same kind of white armor that I wore. They saw me, too, and began waving frantically, encouragingly. But they did not leave the safety of their shelter.

I plunged ahead, waving my own arms foolishly over my head, yelling hoarsely to them.

"Come on, you can make it!" one of them called.

"Only a few more yards," yelled another.

I staggered toward them, wondering far in the back of my mind why they would not come out of their cave to help me through those last few yards. But that question was swamped by the joy I felt at finding others like myself in this endless desert of ice and snow.

The storm winds had sculpted the snow banks

around the base of the cliff into smooth ramps of white. I slithered down one of them, sliding and slipping on the ice until I staggered into their welcoming arms.

They grabbed me, held me up, grinning and laughing happily at me. Beyond them, deeper in the cave, I saw crates of equipment and a big electric radiant-heater glowing red and warm.

"Hey!" one of them said. "He's not from our unit!"

Their laughter froze and their grins disappeared as they held me in their arms.

"Just who the hell are you, anyway?"

"What unit are you with?"

"I didn't know there were any other units operating in this sector."

"Come on, buddy—who are you and what are you doing here?"

I had no real answers for them. My body sagged in their arms, every last bit of energy totally spent. My eyes closed and the world went dark.

CHAPTER 34

When I opened my eyes, I saw the ceiling of the cave, rugged slabs of granite, far above me. I flexed my fingers and toes, then turned my head slightly. I saw that I had been stripped to the waist; my armor suit was gone and I wore nothing but a pair of briefs.

But I felt *warm*. The sensation was delightful. I reveled in it for a few moments, then propped myself up on my elbows to take a better look around.

They had placed me on a cot that seemed to be suspended in midair. It felt like a hammock; it swayed with every move I made. But I could see no supports holding it up. The others were grouped together deeper inside the cave, gathered around what looked like a desk. I could only see their backs. Most of them had removed their suits of armor, and I could see seven men and five women dressed in gray coveralls. Someone was seated at the desk, but I could not tell whether it was a man or a woman, because the others were clustered around so tightly.

"How are you feeling?"

I turned at the sound of a woman's voice, so quickly that the hammock's swaying nearly dumped me to the floor of the cave.

"I'm all right . . . I think."

She was a good-looking woman with blonde hair

and a pert little nose. She grinned at me. "I thought you'd be in for a fierce case of frostbite when you staggered in here, but the computer checked you out fine."

"I feel fine," I said, realizing that it was true. I felt warm and safe. I was not even hungry.

As if she could read my thoughts, the woman said, "I pumped a couple of vials of nutrients into you while you were sleeping. Whatever happened to your helmet? Good thing you had the emergency communicator. And using your pistol as a distress signal! What put that idea into your head? What unit are you from, anyway?"

I stopped her staccato questions by raising one hand and saying, "I think I can get up, if you'll hold this thing steady for a second."

She laughed and grabbed one end of the floating cot. "It looks great back at headquarters; all you need is a grav disc and a length of fabric. Travels light. But none of the desk jockeys ever tried to sleep on one of these monstrosities!"

I got to my feet, glad to be off the cot. I saw that a tiny metal disc lay on the floor beneath it. Somehow it canceled gravity and allowed the cot to float in midair.

"My name's Rena," said the woman, proffering her hand. "Technician and biowarfare specialist. Naturally, they made me the squad's medic."

I shook hands with her. She was barely as tall as my shoulder and as slim as an elf. She looked at me expectantly with eyes as blue as a distant snow-clad mountain.

"Orion," I said. "My name is Orion."

"Unit? Specialty?"

I shook my head. "None that I know of."

Her smile faded into a look of concern. "Maybe I ought to run the diagnostic computer over you again. It has a neuropsych program . . ."

"Rena, put some clothes on him, for god's sake!"

A man strode up to us. His coveralls bore silver emblems on the collar and a nameplate sewn above the heart: Kedar. On the shoulder of his left sleeve was the symbol of a bolt of lightning. His face was grim. He had the strong, lean build of an athlete, but I noticed that he limped slightly.

"Yes, sir," Rena said, snapping her hand to her brow in a military salute. I thought there was just enough emphasis on the *sir* to make it slightly mocking.

She pointed me farther back in the cave, where stacks of plastic cartons stood lined in neat rows.

"Clothes in here." She yanked open the side of one carton and I saw a pile of gray coveralls. "Helmets and equipment in those rows back there. Help yourself. One size fits all."

I took a pair of the coveralls from the bin. They looked much too small for me as I held them in my outstretched hands. But I shrugged and tried them on. They seemed to mold themselves to my body, stretching as necessary to fit comfortably without being too snug.

Rena peeled the blank nameplate from the chest of my uniform and took a light pen from her pocket.

"Orion," she said, tracing my name onto the fabric. As she handed it back to me, she whispered, "Be careful of Kedar. Just because he's a power tech he thinks he's above the rest of us."

I nodded my thanks and slapped the nameplate back where it belonged, just above my uniform's breast pocket. Then we went shopping for a new suit of the white plastic armor that Rena said they all wore outside the cave. And a helmet.

I felt a little like the squire to a medieval knight, carrying a double armload of armor and equipment as I followed Rena back toward the front of the cave.

Kedar intercepted us. "Well, at least you're properly outfitted," he said, eying me up and down.

"Come on, Adena wants to ask you a few questions."

For an awkward moment I stood there, my arms full, not quite knowing what to do. Rena solved my problem by taking the stuff I was carrying. She could barely peep over the top of it once I had loaded it all on her. But she gave me a friendly wink as she staggered off toward the area where the cots were.

Kedar led me to the desk where the others had been clustered before. A woman stood at it, her back to me, bent slightly over the desk as she studied a map displayed on her video screen.

"Here he is, Adena," said Kedar.

She turned, and the breath caught in my throat. It was she. As young and vibrantly beautiful as I had first seen her, so many long ages ago. Her hair was cropped short now, shorter even than mine. But it was thick and shining black, curling around her ears and across her brow. Her eyes were the same profound gray, warm and deep and knowing.

She flicked a glance at the name stenciled on my breast.

"Orion?" Even her voice was the same rich resonance.

I nodded. "And you are Adena." The insignia on her shoulder was a clenched fist.

"What are you doing in this sector? What unit are you with?"

"I don't know," I answered. "I found myself lost in the blizzard out there. I can't remember anything further back than a few hours ago." Unless you want to count other ages, other lifetimes, I added silently.

She frowned at me.

Kedar said, "Obviously he's not from the transport team."

"Obviously not," Adena replied. Looking back at me, she asked, "What's your specialty?"

I had no answer.

"Biowar? Chemicals? Energy weapons? Power? Communications?" Her voice rose slightly as I stood there mute and befuddled.

"You've got to have *some* specialty, soldier," Kedar snapped.

"I'm on a special assignment," I heard myself reply. "I'm an assassin."

"A what?" Kedar glanced at Adena, his brows arching almost up into his scalp line.

"My assignment is to find Ahriman and kill him," I said.

"Ahriman? Who in the name of the twenty devils of the night is Ahriman?"

Adena's voice was softer. "There's no one in this unit by that name."

"Ahriman's not one of us," I said. "He's a different kind of creature, intelligent but not truly human, dark and powerful . . ." I described the Dark One as closely as I could.

Their faces grew more surprised and nonplussed with each word I spoke.

When I stopped, Adena said, "And your special assignment is to find this person and kill him?"

"Yes. That's why I was sent here."

"By whom?"

"Ormazd," I said.

They looked at each other. The name obviously meant nothing to them.

"Do you know of Ahriman, the Dark One?" I asked. "Do you know where I can find him?"

Kedar's expression turned into a bitter smirk. "Just stay here for another day, Orion. As soon as this blizzard ends, you'll see more men like the one you described than you'll ever want to see in your entire life."

"I don't understand."

"Don't you know that we're at war with them?" Adena asked.

"War? With . . . with whom?"

"The man you described," she said. "This whole planet was covered with people such as he. We're here to eliminate them."

"But we're cut off from our other units," Kedar added before I could draw a breath. "They're gathering out there in the snow—hundreds of them. Maybe thousands. They're going to attack as soon as the storm stops. They're going to eliminate us."

But his despairing words barely registered on my attention. Within me, my mind was racing. The War! This must be The War!

CHAPTER 35

Adena and Kedar soon turned me loose. There was not much they could do with a man who was obviously either insane from battle or feigning insanity to avoid battle. They turned their attention to defending the cave against the attack that they knew was coming as soon as the storm died down.

I made my way to the mouth of the cave, feeling the eyes of the other soldiers on my back. The wind still raged out there, bitterly cold. I shivered and retreated back to the warmth of the radiant heaters.

Rena took me in tow once again and led me to a small circle of men and women who were heating prepackaged meals in what looked to me like a portable microwave oven. We ate in gloomy silence. One by one, the soldiers got up and went back to the ridiculous floating cots, where they grimly checked out their weapons.

The only halfway-cheerful person in the squad was a youngish man who introduced himself as Marek, communications specialist. He showed me the portable consoles and screens that were his responsibility.

"The brutes are jamming all our outgoing transmissions, somehow," he said in a pleasant voice, almost as if he were describing how the equipment worked. "I don't know how they do it, but they're doing it damned well."

"The brutes?" I asked.

Nodding, he replied, "The enemy, the guys with the gray skins and red eyes." He hunched forward, pulling his neck down and raising his shoulders, then shuffled a few steps, scowling as mightily as he could. For a slim human youngster it was a fairly good imitation of the one I knew as Ahriman.

"Anyway," Marek went on, relaxing again, "they're jamming our outgoing calls, so we can't tell the commanders up in the orbiting ships where we are or what we're up against."

"We're cut off," I said.

He bobbed his head again, seemingly as unconcerned as a man who faced nothing worse than an annoying equipment breakdown.

"We're getting most of the incoming transmissions. The orders from Up Top—" he jabbed a finger toward the ceiling of the cave—"are reaching us just fine. And the weather maps. And the multispectral scans that show us where the brutes are massing their forces."

He pointed to a video screen and tapped a few pads on its keyboard. The screen glowed to life, showing me a wild, sweeping circle of clouds, a gigantic cyclonic storm as seen from the cameras of an orbiting satellite.

"That's us, that spot where the cursor is." Marek tapped a flickering green dot on the lower left corner of the screen.

I could feel my eyes widening as I stared at the picture. The storm clouds covered about half the screen, but where the ground was clear, I could make out geography that looked tantalizingly familiar. A long peninsula jutted out into a large sea; it looked to me like Italy, except that the shape was subtly wrong and the "toe" of what I remembered as the Italian boot was definitely connected to what would someday be the island of Sicily. Above that one recognizable shape the ground was a featureless expanse of white. Glaciers covered most of Europe. This was truly the Ice Age.

Marek prodded me. "Seen enough? Ready for the bad news?"

I nodded.

He tapped at the keyboard again and the storm clouds disappeared from the screen, showing the ground—or rather the ice fields—beneath them. The view seemed to zoom down closer to the surface, until I could make out a few gray peaks of granite jutting above the snow.

"That's our cave," he said, gesturing at the flickering cursor again. "And here—" he touched a single key—"are the brutes."

A forest of red dots sprang up against the whiteness of the ice and snow. There must have been at least a thousand of them, arranged in a ragged semicircle that faced our cave.

So we were cut off from the rest of our own forces and hugely outnumbered as we waited for the enemy—the brutes—to attack.

Young as they seemed to be, the soldiers around me were veterans of many battles. They wasted no time in worrying. They ate; they checked their weapons, and soon enough they began to stretch out on their wobbly cots and go to sleep.

"Might as well grab some sleep while you can," Marek told me, as pleasantly as if he had not a worry in the world. "The storm won't let up for another six hours, and the brutes won't attack until it does."

"Are you sure?"

His grin changed only slightly. "How long have we been fighting them? Have you ever known them to attack during a storm like this?"

I shrugged.

"Besides, we've got the field out there covered

with scanners. When they start to make their move, we'll have plenty of warning."

But I noticed that he stayed by his equipment, fiddling with it, checking it over, searching for a way to break through the jamming and tell the commanders in orbit where we were and what we faced.

I saw Adena standing alone up by the entrance to the cave, already dressed in armor, her helmet masking her lustrous dark hair. Most of the others were either asleep or pretending to be. The cave was quiet except for the hum of electrical equipment and the louder, more ominous moaning of the storm wind outside.

Kedar was crouched beside a set of squat, heavy green cylinders. From the cryptic lettering stenciled on them, I knew they were the electrical power packs that supplied the energy to run the squad's equipment. He cast a suspicious glance at me as I walked slowly toward Adena, but he said nothing and remained where he was, checking his power packs.

Before I could say anything to her, Adena spoke to me. "You'd better get some rest."

"I don't need much sleep," I replied. "I'm all right now."

"Waiting is the worst part," she said, her eyes peering out at the wind-driven snow. "If I had more troops, I'd go out now and attack them now, while they're still getting themselves ready."

"You don't remember me?" I asked.

She turned to face me, her gray eyes troubled. "Should I? Have we met before?"

"Many times."

"No." She shook her helmeted head. "I would recall it if we had. And yet . . ."

"And yet I look familiar to you."

"Yes," she admitted.

"Think," I urged her, feeling a burning intensity

blazing inside me. "We *have* met before. Long ago—in the future."

"The future?"

"A primitive hunting tribe, in the springtime that will follow this age of winter. The capital of a barbarian empire, thousands of years afterward. A giant metropolis, centuries later . . ."

She looked startled, troubled. "You're insane," she whispered. "Battle fatigue, or the shock of exposure to the storm."

"*I think!*" I insisted. "Close your eyes and see what comes into your mind when you think of me."

She gave me an odd look, part disbelief, part distrust. But slowly she squeezed her eyes shut, and I concentrated with every ounce of my will power.

"What do you see?" I asked her.

For long moments she did not respond. Then: "A waterfall."

"What else?"

"Nothing . . . trees, a few people . . . and . . . strange animals, four legs . . . I'm riding on its back . . . and . . . *you!* You're riding next to me . . ."

"Go on."

"One of the brutes. A big one. In a cave . . . No, it's some kind of tunnel . . ." She gasped and her eyes flicked wide open.

"The rats," I realized.

Adena's trembling hands reached up toward her throat. "It's horrible . . . they . . . they . . ."

"We both died in that era," I said. "We have lived many lives, you and I."

"Who are you?"

"I am Orion, the Hunter. I seek Ahriman, the Dark One, the one who turned the rats on you. I have been sent to all those different ages to find him, and kill him."

"Sent? By whom?"

"Ormazd," I answered.

She closed her eyes for the span of a heartbeat, and the air around us seemed to glow with a cold, silvery radiance. The cave, the storm outside, dimmed and almost disappeared. Out of the corner of my eye I could see Kedar frozen in time, his outstretched hand as still as a statue's. Adena opened her eyes again, and all the knowledge of the continuum shone in them.

"Orion," she said. "Thank you. The veil is lifted. I can see clearly now. I remember—more than you can."

We were alone in a sphere of energy, beyond normal time, just the two of us in a place that she had created. My heart was hammering in my chest.

"Adena, I lied to you a moment ago . . ."

She smiled, quizzically. "Lied? To me?"

"Perhaps not so much a lie, as not telling the full truth. I said I was sent to hunt down Ahriman."

"That is true, I know."

"But not the whole truth. The whole truth is that although Ormazd has sent me to kill the Dark One, the real reason I am here—the reason that drives me—is to find you. I've searched through a hundred thousand years to find you, and each time that I do, he takes you away from me."

"Not this time, Orion," she said.

"I love you, Adena . . . Aretha . . . whatever your true name is."

She laughed, a low bubbling sound of joy. "Adena will do, for now. But you are always Orion, always constant."

Shrugging, I replied, "I am what I am. I can't be anything else."

"And I love you, love what you are and who you are," she said. "I will love you forever."

I wanted to leap out into the raging storm and outshout the wind. I wanted to howl my triumph to Ormazd, wherever and whoever he was, and tell him that despite all his powers I had found my love and she loved me. I wanted to take her in my arms and hold her and feel the warmth of her love.

But, instead, I simply stood before her, almost paralyzed with happiness. I did not even reach out to take her hand in mine. I was content to glow in the happiness of having found her.

"Orion," she said, speaking low and swiftly, "there is much that you don't yet know, much that is still hidden from you. The one you call Ormazd has his reasons for the things he's done to you . . ."

"And to you," I said.

She smiled briefly. "I insisted on coming here. I made myself human, mortal, on his terms. What has happened to me is my own doing."

"And Ahriman? What of him?"

Her face grew somber. "Orion, my love, when you learn the entire truth, it will not make you happy. Ormazd may be right in keeping it from you."

"I want to know," I insisted. "I want to know who I really am and why I've been made to do these things."

She nodded. "Yes, I can see that you do. But don't expect everything at once."

"Start me with *something*," I half-begged.

She pointed out toward the storm. "Very well. We start with here and now. This squad of troops is part of an army of extermination. Our task is to annihilate the brutes, to rid this planet of them."

"And once that is done?"

"One task at a time, my love. Before anything else can happen, before you and I can meet each other at the foot of Mt. Ararat or make love together in Karakorum, before we can meet in New York City—we must annihilate the brutes."

I took a deep breath. "Ahriman is among them?"

"Yes, of course. He is one of them. One of their mightiest leaders. And he knows, by now, that if he can prevent us from achieving the task Ormazd has set before us, he can win the ultimate victory."

I puzzled in silence for a few moments. "You mean that if we fail to annihilate the brutes, then we humans—you and I—will be the ones to be wiped out?"

"If we fail to annihilate the brutes," she replied, "the human race—your species, Orion—will die out forever."

"Then the continuum will be broken. Space-time will collapse in on itself."

"That is what Ormazd believes," Adena said. "There is some evidence that it is true."

"Some evidence?" I snapped. "We're neck-deep in a war of annihilation, based on *some evidence*?"

She met my angry question with a smile. "Orion, I told you that there is much you still don't understand. Forgive the words I used. I wouldn't ask you to fight this battle if it wasn't necessary."

My anger melted away, although the confusion in my mind remained. "Who are you?" I heard myself ask. "What are you? And Ormazd, what is he . . ."

She silenced me by placing a finger on my lips. "I am as human and mortal as you are, Orion. I was not always so, but I have chosen to be. I can feel pain. I can die."

"But then you live again," I said.

"So do you."

"Does everyone?"

"No, not everyone," she said. "The capability is there. Every human has the capability to live beyond death. But very few realize it; very few can succeed in actually bringing that capability to fruition."

"You can."

"Yes, of course. You cannot, though. Ormazd must intervene for you. Otherwise, you would live only one lifespan and die just like the others of your kind."

"My kind. Then you're *not* of my kind. You said you chose to make yourself human. That means you're . . . something else."

Adena's smile was sad with the knowledge of eons. "I am what your people will someday call a goddess, Orion. They will build temples to me. But I want to be human; I want to be with you—if Ormazd will permit me to be."

CHAPTER 36

I stood there gazing into her gray eyes and saw whirlpools within whirlpools, wheels within wheels, the entire continuum of stars and galaxies and atoms and quarks spinning in an endless cycle of creation and change. I did not understand, could not understand, what Adena was telling me. But I believed every syllable that she spoke.

I was in love with a goddess, a goddess who would someday be worshipped by human beings, human beings who were created by the gods. The cycle of creation, the wheel of life, the continuum of the universe.

And this was the continuum that Ahriman sought to destroy.

The silver aura surrounding us faded away, and a blast of icy wind sent a shudder through me. I heard its howl, then the muted voices of the soldiers inside the cave. Kedar's hand closed around the tool he was reaching for. We were back in normal space-time.

"The wind has shifted," she said. "The storm will be passing by in another few hours. They'll attack then."

I focused my attention on her, on the here and now. "Can we hold out against them?"

"As long as our power holds. Once the battery

packs are drained, though . . ." She let the thought
dangle.

"There are others," I probed, "other units in the
area, aren't there? Can we get help?"

Adena hesitated a moment, then said, "This is
the last battle, Orion. The brutes that are gathering out there are all that's left of them."

"And us? You mean that we're all that's left of
the human army?"

"We're all the humans there are," she said.

"What about the commanders, up in the orbiting ships?"

With a single small shake of her head, Adena
replied, "There are no ships, no commanders. The
transmissions that Marek is receiving come from
Ormazd. He doesn't want us to know it, but we
are quite alone here. There will be no help for
us."

"I don't understand!"

That bitter smile touched her lips again. "You're
not supposed to understand, Orion. I've already
told you far more than Ormazd wants you to
know."

She stepped past me, no longer the goddess now,
but the human commander of a lost, trapped, ex-
pendable detachment of human soldiers. I stood at
the cave's entrance, letting the icy wind slice
through me, almost enjoying its bitter cold. The
thoughts spinning around in my head led nowhere,
but out in that waning storm, I knew, waited the
ultimate enemy. This tiny group of men and women
carried the fate of the continuum in their hands.
Soon the battle would begin, and the victor would
inherit the world, the universe, all eternity.

"Orion?"

I turned and saw Rena standing there, an appre-
hensive little frown on her elfin face.

She tried to smile. "The commander says we

should all get into our armor now and check weapons."

I nodded and followed her back to the area where the cots floated in ragged rows. The others were pulling on their armor suits. I found mine and followed Rena's example: the bodyshell first, then the legs, the boots, the arms, the magically thin gloves, and finally the equipment belt. I hefted my helmet; it had a two-way communicator built into it and a visor that could slide down to cover the face completely. The visor was completely transparent from the inside but opaque from the outside. Once the troops had them on, I could not see their faces. Only the insignias emblazoned on their shoulders and the names stenciled on their chests told me who they were.

Once we had checked out the suits, Rena led me to the power packs that Kedar was nursing so tenderly and we charged up our suit batteries. Then we joined the others as they lined up for weapons issue.

Adena watched as Ogun, the squad's burly, sour-faced armorer, grimly handed each soldier a pair of weapons: a long-barreled, rifle-like gun and a pistol that plugged into the suit's battery pack.

When I stepped up before him, Ogun scowled at me and turned to Adena.

"Give him a pistol," she said. "He will work the heavy gun, with me."

The pistol was like the one I had found on me when I had been stranded here out in the storm. I hefted it in my gloved hand.

"It has its own battery," Rena said, "but regulations are that you plug it into the suit. That extends its range and duration."

I glanced down at her and nodded. She looked strange in armor and helmet, almost like a child playing at war. But this was no game, as I could tell from the sober expressions on the faces around me.

They were an experienced squad. Once armed, they moved out toward the cave's mouth and took up positions where they could cover each other with protective fire while at the same time raking the sloping field of snow that led up to the cave.

I stood uncertainly in the middle of the cave, watching the soldiers and not knowing what I should do. Rena gave me a fleeting smile and hurried to a large metallic crate that rested at the side of the cave. She touched a few buttons on its top and it levitated several inches from the floor and followed her like a dutiful pet dog as she joined the others at the cave's entrance.

"You can help me," Ogun said. His voice, like his looks, was surly. He headed back toward the deeper recesses of the cave. I followed him.

"Rena's biowar," he told me, without my asking a question. "Her equipment checks what the brutes are throwing at us in the way of viruses and microbes. We lost a lot of good people before we realized what they could do with those little killers. Instant poisons. Paralyze you, tear your guts inside-out, make you blind, choke you—they got some beauties."

"They work instantly?" I asked.

"Faster than you can blink your eyes," he said as we ducked through a low passageway worn in the rock. "That's why you got to keep your visor down and locked and breathe nothing but the suit's air until Rena gives us the all-clear. Understand?"

"Yes, sir."

His face contorted in what might have been a grin. Despite his sour looks and demeanor, Ogun was a man who cared about the others around him.

"Well," he huffed, "there it is. Let's get it into position."

It was a heavy-looking mass of tubes and coils that looked to me vaguely like a cannon. Ogun activated its gravitic lifters and it floated up off the cold rock floor. We nudged it down the shadowy passageway toward the front of the cave, with him warning me every other step of the way to be careful not to bang it against the stone wall.

"Are you sure that there's only one entrance to this cave?" I asked as we guided the heavy weapon toward the entrance.

Ogun nodded. "We've been holed up here six days. The commander had us explore every inch. All those passageways end in blind alleys, except for the one that drops down into the water. Damned near fell into it myself. It goes *deep*. Nobody's going to come at us from that direction."

He was absolutely certain of himself. But I wondered, remembering Ahriman's ability to alter space-time and his fondness for darkness and the deep.

"Maybe we ought to place a sensor there, just in case," I said. "You're probably right, but if they do find a way to get at us from down there, it'd be better if we had a warning, don't you think?"

We had pushed the weapon as far as Kedar's line of green power packs. Ogun grimaced as he straightened up and let Kedar take up the cannon's heavy cables and plug them into two of the green cylinders.

"I'm the armorer, not the commander. I'm not supposed to think. I just take care of the weapons and follow orders." He stretched his heavily muscled arms toward the rugged ceiling of the cave. "Besides, if they find a way to come at us from down there, we're cooked, no matter how much of a warning we get."

Kedar shot him an inquisitive glance.

"He wants to put a warning sensor down by the well," Ogun explained. "Just in case."

The power specialist turned his gaze to me, and for the flash of an instant I thought I might have been looking at Dal, shaved clean of his red beard.

"I'll ask the commander about that," he said. "It might be a reasonable thing to do."

"Reasonable." Ogun mumbled and muttered to himself.

The three of us pushed the cannon up to the mouth of the cave. The other soldiers had left a cleared space for it, and now they busily began lifting loose rocks and planting them in front of the heavy weapon to form a rough sort of protective wall. I helped them, while Ogun and Kedar ran their checks on the equipment.

I found myself hauling rocks with Marek. We made an effective team, although I suspect I did most of the real work. He grinned at me as we sweated away at it, and cocked his head toward Ogun and Kedar.

"Officers," he whispered.

I almost laughed. It was the same in all armies, in all organizations. Some worked with their muscles; some worked with their brains.

And there was always one who directed them all. With us, it was Adena.

"The wind's dying down," she called out to us. She was standing a few yards out in front of the cave's mouth, fully armored and helmeted, but with her visor up, off her face.

I looked up and saw that the snow had stopped. It was knee-high just outside the cave, where she stood, but farther off, outside the lee of the cliff, it had drifted many feet deep. The gray clouds were scudding along the sky, as if hurrying to get away from the carnage that was to come.

"The sun will break through soon," Adena said, almost cheerfully. "We'll have a blue sky to fight under."

The soldiers stirred and tinkered with their weapons. Pure instinct, I thought, produced by merciless training.

Ogun gave me a rapid run-through on the workings of the heavy cannon. It was an energy-beam weapon, an extremely powerful kind of laser that made the fusion-laboratory lasers I had known in the twentieth century seem like children's toys.

I wondered, as we crouched behind the massive gun, how these people and their advanced weaponry could have been brought into the Ice Age. I knew that Ormazd could play with time and space at will. So could Ahriman. But, for the first time since I had arrived at this bewildering place, I wondered how humans could exist in what must have been the Pleistocene Epoch, a hundred thousand years before the pyramids were erected in Egypt, with such sophisticated technology. There was no archeological record of it in later centuries.

And who was our enemy? Who were these creatures we were fighting against? The brutes. Ahriman's people. Where had they come from? Why were they here on planet Earth?

There was much that I did not yet know, Adena had told me. And she had said that I would not be pleased with the knowledge, once it was revealed to me.

Was this little band of human beings part of an army that Ormazd had sent back to the Ice Age from some distant future era? Had he sent us here to drive out the brutes, the invaders who were trying to destroy the human race? But Marek had spoken about command ships in orbit. Why would the commanders of this army be in ships orbiting the Earth? Why not in cities or command posts in their native lands?

A horrifying thought struck me. What if *we* are the invaders? And the brutes—Ahriman's people— are the ones defending their homes against us?

I almost cried out aloud with the pain of that idea. But my thoughts were stifled by Adena's calm announcement:

"Prime your weapons. Here they come."

CHAPTER 37

"Visors down."

I reached for my helmet in response to Adena's order and slid the transparent visor down until its lock clicked in place against the neck ring of my armor.

The clouds were breaking up and patches of blue were spreading across the sky. The snow glittered under the wintry sun, a featureless expanse that rolled out as far as the eye could see. Not a tree or a rock broke the ocean of white.

I stood up, peering out from behind the laser cannon, to study the field in front of us. Adena, I noticed, was crouched just inside the cave's entrance, her eyes glued to the small display screen of a gray metal box that rested on the rocky ledge where she had posted herself.

At first I could see nothing out there. Then, gradually, I began to make out the tiny specks of moving forms trudging slowly, inexorably, across the snow, heading at us.

"They've got bears in the vanguard," Adena's flat, emotionless voice called out to us. "And smaller game scouting ahead—wolves, it looks like."

I strained my eyes to make sense of what she was saying. Gradually I realized that the forces marching toward us were mostly animals, rather than the humanoid brutes. Gray wolves were at their front, with silver-furred foxes slinking among

338

them. Farther back I could see the lumbering shapes of great bears, some of them white, most of them cinnamon brown. They were huge and muscular, trudging toward us on all fours.

Eagles, hawks, and smaller birds filled the sky. Smaller animals—raccoons, badgers, wolverines—became visible against the glistening snow. It was as if the whole planet's fauna had united to attack us.

Now, as they approached to point-blank range, I could see the humanoids behind them. Gray-skinned, powerfully muscled men dressed in skins. Smaller, slimmer females among them. Each of them carried long, spear-like weapons in their hands.

"Hold steady," Adena told us, in an expectant whisper. "Pick your targets. Leave the animals to the cannon crew."

I crouched behind the transparent plastic shield that curved across the front of the cannon. My assigned task was to monitor the power being used by the laser and warn the firing crew when the energy drain became dangerous. It was a job a monkey could do; all that was necessary was to watch the gauges on the power conversion panel that was built into the cannon's main console.

I looked up from the panel and stared at the advancing army of beasts, fascinated. How could Ahriman's people control them? As I watched, the animals seemed to hesitate for the span of a heartbeat, and then they broke into a running, galloping charge, heading straight for us.

"Fire!" Adena snapped, and the cave was suddenly filled with the hum and crackle of blazing energy weapons.

A hideous roar arose from the icy field outside, and I looked up to see the gleaming virgin snow turned into a sea of flame as the heavy laser cannon swept out an arc of raw burning energy, boiling the snow, roasting the beasts that were charging at us, filling the air with noisome oily smoke.

The soldiers were firing their individual weapons through the clouds of smoke and flame. What they were aiming at, I could not see. But a few of them pointed their guns upward, against the falcons and other birds that were swooping down toward the cave's mouth. An eagle smashed into one of the helmeted troopers, knocking him off his feet and killing itself with the impact.

I could see snarling wolves dashing across the snow toward us, leaping across the smoldering arc of blackened snow and burning animal flesh that the cannon had left. As we swung the laser to one side of the field, the animals would charge at us from the other side. The gunners shortened the range of their beam and roasted the beasts in their tracks, but more kept coming at us, closer and closer. The other troopers were picking them off, but always they got closer.

Suddenly a bear loomed right at the mouth of the cave, frighteningly huge, snarling and slavering, towering over us on its hind legs. It smashed a heavy clawed paw into one of the troopers, ripping the soldier in half and sending him sprawling bloodily against the cave wall. Four troopers blasted at it with their laser rifles, burning its guts open and nearly severing its head from its body. But the giant beast lumbered into the cave, screaming with pain and rage, striking blindly, bowling people over as it staggered forward on sheer inertia.

Without even thinking of what I was doing, I leaped out from behind the cannon's shield and threw myself in a rolling body block at the beast's legs. It felt like hitting the concrete pillars of a towering skyscraper, but the huge bear toppled and fell to the floor of the cave. A half-dozen laser blasts killed it; I felt the sizzle of their heat, smelled

the burning hair and flesh as the beast died with a
final strangled scream.

There was no time for congratulations. I snatched
up the rifle from the fallen trooper and saw from
her shoulder insignia that it was Rena. Her helmet
visor was spattered with blood, her broken body
plainly lifeless.

"They're infiltrating along the wall of the cliff!"
Adena shouted to me.

I shouldered my way past the visored troops
who were still firing into the advancing army of
animals and stepped halfway out of the protecting
mouth of the cave. Out of the corner of my eye I
saw Adena doing the same thing on the other side
of the entrance.

A dozen yards in front of me, a sleek gray wolf
was edging its way along the face of the cliff,
pressing its flank against the rock wall so that we
could not see it from inside the cave or detect it
with our sensors. Behind it, in single file, I could
see a mountainous gray-white bear and more
wolves.

The wolf stopped when it saw me. For an instant
we looked into each other's eyes. I saw an intelligence there, and a burning red hatred that shocked
me. The beast snarled and leaped for my throat. I
squeezed the trigger of the rifle and burned it from
jaw to crotch. It was dead when it hit me, and I
staggered back a step under its impact but did not
fall. The bear roared up onto its hind legs and
came at me. I shot it through its fanged mouth; I
could see the red beam of the laser emerge out of
the roof of its skull. As it fell ponderously at my
feet, I blazed away at the rest of the beasts. Wolves,
foxes, badgers—whatever they were they scattered
in all directions and ran away.

For just an instant I stood there, breathing
heavily, feeling exultant. Then I spun around and
saw that Adena was doing an even better job on

her side of the cave entrance. Several dead beasts littered the ground around her, and she was picking off the others as they fled from her.

The area directly in front of the cave's mouth was a sickening carnage of charred bodies and glazed ice. The snow had been boiled instantly by the laser's power and then refrozen in the frigid air.

I suddenly realized that the battle had stopped. The only sound I could hear was the soft sighing of the wind. The clouds had blown away, leaving a crystalline blue sky marred only by the wafting black smoke from the smoldering bodies of the beasts.

"Get back inside the cave," Adena's voice commanded in my earphones. I could not see her face through the visor, but she sounded as if she was smiling at me.

I trudged inside and lifted my visor. The others were either clustered around Rena's dead body or checking the cannon and power packs.

"Is that it?" I asked Adena. "Is it over?"

She shook her head. "That was merely the first attack. They're regrouping. They'll be back in a few minutes."

"But . . . it's a slaughter," I said. "We've killed hundreds of them."

"We haven't killed anything but animals," Adena countered. "The brutes are fighting a war of attrition against us. They send in the animals to make us use up our power. Then, when our guns are out of energy, they make their *real* attack."

It took a few moments for the meaning of her words to sink in on me. "You're saying that they'll keep sending those animals against us until our weapons run out."

"That's what they've always done in the past," Adena said.

"Then what chance do we have of winning?"

Her smile came back, but it was the grim smile of a woman who appreciated irony, even when the joke was on her. "It all depends on whether they run out of beasts before we run out of power."

I must have looked unconvinced.

"It happens, Orion. Ahriman's people are not invincible. They're just as desperate as we are. That's the last group of them out there. If we can kill them, there will be no others to bother us."

"And if they can kill us . . ."

She nodded. "They win. For all eternity."

I was about to reply when one of the troopers called out, "Here they come again."

We rushed back to our battle stations. Rena's corpse was left on the bare rock floor, deeper back in the cave. Every man and woman took their assigned posts. Without being told, I hefted Rena's rifle and placed myself at the edge of the cave's entrance, where I could guard against infiltrating animals that could not be detected from further inside the cave. It was an exposed position, but the enemy had to come to within grappling distance to do me harm, I reasoned. As long as my rifle held out, I was safe enough.

"Visors down," came Adena's calm command. I obeyed and looked out at the approaching army of beasts.

Four times in as many hours the animals charged at us. Each time we beat them back: energy beams against fang and claw. The air became sickeningly heavy with the stench of burning fur and flesh. Dark clouds of death smeared the blue sky as the pale sun climbed across the heavens and began to throw lengthening shadows across the blackened, body-strewn field of snow and ice.

Every muscle in my body ached. My head buzzed wearily. The cave itself seemed dank with human sweat and the cloying odor of ozone. Marek made his way through us, handing each trooper a pair of yellow capsules. Food pills, he told me. Enough nutrition to sustain a man for twelve hours or more. I almost laughed. Less than a hundred yards from us was more meat than the sixteen of us could devour in a month, and we were subsisting on capsules.

Marek was speaking quietly with Adena, his face somber. I caught her eye, and she seemed to indicate that I should join them.

"How many more attacks can we handle?" she was asking him as I came up and stood beside her.

He gave me a suspicious look before answering, "Two, at least. Maybe three."

Adena glanced at the sensor screen, still resting slightly crookedly on the rock ledge near the cave's entrance. "They still have enough animals for three attacks or more."

"Then we can't stay here," I blurted.

Marek glared at me. But Adena said, "What do you propose?"

"That we stop fighting dumb animals and carry the attack to the real enemy."

"Do we invite them to come here to the cave?" Marek asked sarcastically. "Or do we walk out into the snow and go to their camp?"

"The latter," I said. "We send out two or three volunteers to make their way into the enemy camp and attack them there."

He snorted. "They'd be torn to pieces by the beasts out there before they got close . . ."

"Not if they could get out of this cave undetected and circle around the beasts," I said. "They could attack the enemy from the rear."

"How could you get out of here undetected?" Adena asked.

"I'd go right now, and follow along the cliff wall until I'm beyond the flanks of their army of beasts. Then I'd cut across the snow field and make for their camp."

"That would take hours and hours, even if they didn't spot you," Marek said.

"Yes, I know. It would be nightfall before we even got near their camp."

"Suppose you waited until nightfall before you started," Adena said, "and then attacked at dawn. We could lay down a bombardment on them from here in the cave, with the cannon. That would take their attention off you."

Marek shook his head. "They have the advantage at night. They have animals out there that can see in the dark, where we can't."

"We have sensors that are as good as any beast's," Adena said. "And they never attack at night. You give them too much credit, Marek. We have the advantage in the darkness."

"I don't believe it."

"But I do," she said. "Orion, we're going to try your plan. It's worth the risk. I'll pick two troopers to go with us."

"Us?"

"I'm going with you."

"You can't do that, Adena!" Kedar snapped.

"I've got to. The others won't follow Orion; he's a stranger. But they'll obey my orders without hesitation."

"But the danger . . ."

"I would never send any of my troopers on a mission that I wouldn't undertake myself," Adena said. "Never."

I could see by the fire flashing in her eyes that there was no sense trying to change her mind. And, to be truthful, I was glad that she would be coming with me.

"But what about the rest of us?" There was real fear in Kedar's voice.

"You will be in command here," she told him. "Start a bombardment against the beasts at the first light of dawn. We should be in position to attack the brutes' camp by then."

"And if you're not?"

She grinned at him. "No matter. If we're not ready to attack them by dawn, it will be because we're dead."

CHAPTER 38

Whether or not my plan would have worked, we never found out. The brutes attacked us before we had a chance to try it.

Adena picked two troopers to go with us: Ogun, the burly armorer who looked at the world from behind a scowl, and Lissa, a tall, lithe, dark-haired beauty whose specialty was explosives.

"If we catch the brutes asleep in their camp," Adena explained to me, "Lissa can rig her grenades to destroy them with a single blow."

The lowering sun had dipped behind the cliff in which our cave was set, throwing the blackened and littered field in front of us into deepening shadow. Adena ordered the four of us to sleep, since we would be on the move once true night covered the area.

I have never needed much sleep, but I commanded my body to relax as I stretched out on one of the floating cots. I closed my eyes and within minutes I was drowsing.

If I dreamed, I do not remember. But I was awakened by a strange, cloying odor that tingled in my nostrils and made me feel as if I were choking. I opened my eyes and tried to sit up. The cot tilted beneath me and I slid to the stony floor with a thump.

Adena lay asleep on the cot beside mine, her arms and legs limp, her face turned in my direction, utterly relaxed. I started to gag on the strange odor; it was like having your face pushed into a thicket of exotic tropical flowers.

I staggered to my feet, only to see that all the other troopers were asleep, too. No one was on guard. *Gas!* I realized. Somehow they were filling the cave with a gas that had knocked everyone unconscious. The only sound in the cave was the soft hum of the power packs, which kept the lights on.

Lurching, gagging, I battled my way past the fallen bodies of the troopers and out into the fresh air beyond the cave's entrance. It was black night, clear and frigid, the stars shimmering coldly in the icy air. I filled my lungs once, twice, as my head cleared.

They must be about to attack us, I thought. Unless the gas is lethal.

I plunged back into the cave, holding my breath as I dashed to my cot and the helmet that rested beneath it. I pulled the helmet on, slid down its visor, and pressed the stud at my waist that activated the suit's life-support system. A tiny fan whirred to life, and I felt clear air blowing against my face. I breathed again.

Quickly, with one eye on the cave entrance, I pulled Adena's helmet over her head and put her on suit air. Then I went to the cave entrance to be on guard there.

"What happened?" I heard Adena's voice in my earphones, wobbly, confused.

Looking back into the cave toward her, I began to explain. But out of the shadows deeper in the cave I saw one of the brutes looming, a long, pointed shaft of crystal aimed at Adena's back.

"Look out!" I shouted as I grabbed for the pistol holstered at my side. Adena ducked instinctively as the brute rushed toward her. I fired and hit him in the face. He howled and went down, the crystal spear shattering as it hit the cave floor.

There was no time for more explanations. More of the enemy were rushing at us from out of the darkness at the rear of the cave. Adena picked up a rifle and cut them down. I covered her with my pistol. The two of us stood them off for what seemed like hours, but actually was no more than a few minutes. Suddenly their attack melted away into the shadows. Four of the hulking brutes lay dead at our feet.

"They've found a way to get into the cave from the rear," I said, forcing my breath and heartbeat back to normal.

"Or made one," Adena replied. "We don't have much time. They'll be back."

I felt trapped. And outsmarted. The brutes had us surrounded now; our cave was no longer a shelter—it was a confining, constricting cell of solid stone in which we were unable to move, unable to escape. The walls seemed to be closing in on me. My hands started to shake.

But it was not fear that racked me. It was anger. As I looked around at the bare stone walls of the cave, realizing that it could well become a coffin for all of us, I was seized with fury. At myself. How could I be so stupid? The chamber deep beneath the ground that Ahriman had created in the twentieth century, the dark stone womb of a temple he had built at Karakorum, the caves he had dwelled in back in the Neolithic—caves and darkness were *his* places, *his* sources of power. Why didn't I see it before? Why did I let these poor doomed soldiers stay in this trap? I should have known better.

As I berated myself, I worked with Adena to revive the others. Swiftly she told them what had happened.

"They thought they would find us all unconscious, and easy to kill. Now they know differently. They'll be attacking from the front and rear, any minute now."

The sensors up at the entrance to the cave showed plainly that more animals were moving about in the darkness of the night. Adena kept the cannon pointed outward toward the open field of snow and ice.

"Orion," she commanded, "you, Ogun and Lissa must cover the rear of the cave. Try to find where the enemy is coming from. It looks as if they can't bring a large number of fighters through that way at the same time. If the three of you can't hold them, call for help."

I could not see Ogun's face behind his visor, but I easily imagined the sour grimace on it. Lissa hauled a crate of grenades with her, towing it on a leash wound around her fist as it floated on its anti-gravity disc a few inches above the ground.

"I can give you explosive forces from mild concussion to the kiloton range," she said, her voice sounding almost cheerful in my helmet earphones.

"It looks too confined in here for explosives," I said as we pushed deeper into the cave's narrowing recess.

"Yes, I'm afraid you're right," she answered glumly.

Leaving the bodies of the slain brutes behind us, we inspected the narrowing rock tunnel by the lights set into our helmets. It soom became too tight for the three of us to walk abreast. Ogun took the lead; I followed, with Lissa a few steps behind me.

"We checked out this area when we first came to this cave," Ogun grumbled. "There's no way out of . . ."

"What is it?"

He had stopped dead in his tracks. I looked past his shoulder and saw an opening in the cave floor in front of him.

"That wasn't there yesterday," Ogun muttered. He knelt on the rocky ground and picked up a few loose pebbles in his gloved hand. "This is new. They must have been digging all the time we were being attacked."

"Why aren't they guarding this shaft?" Lissa wondered. "Have they just abandoned it?"

I peered down into it. The light from our helmets was swallowed up in a well that seemed bottomless.

"They'll be back," Ogun said. "When they're ready to attack again, they'll come swarming up here."

But something about the shaft bothered me. Lissa was right: if this was their avenue to attack us from the rear, why had they abandoned it?

"Let's move back," I said.

"Back?" Ogun's voice sounded puzzled. "Why?"

"I can booby-trap the shaft," Lissa suggested. "If they try to use it again they'll blow themselves to pieces." I couldn't get over how happy she sounded when she talked about blasting people to death.

"It's a fake," I said, just as surprised as they were to hear the words coming out of my mouth. "A feint. Maybe they used this shaft earlier, but they're probably digging a new one right now, between here and the main chamber of the cave."

"They'll cut us off," Ogun said.

"And surprise the rest of the troop from the rear," Lissa added.

I nodded, then realized they could not see it through my helmet visor. "Come on, quickly!" I said.

We scrambled back as quickly as we could toward the spot where the bodies of the dead brutes lay. Once there, with the lights and activity of the other troopers at our backs, I took off my helmet and pressed my ear to the rock wall. Sure enough,

I could hear a crunching, tapping sound. Someone, somewhere, was digging.

Adena must have seen us, for she appeared at my side and asked why we were not back in the deeper recess of the cave, as she had ordered us to be. I explained:

"They're digging another entrance into the cave. They'll attack as soon as they break through."

She looked skeptical until I invited her to listen to them at work. Then she nodded her understanding.

"We'll be ready for them," she said grimly.

Waiting was the most difficult part of it. The sensors at the cave's mouth showed the enemy's buildup of beasts quite clearly, despite the blackness of the night. Marek attached seismic sensors to the cave walls back where we were, and their flashing lights showed every blow the brutes were striking against the rock. As they came closer to the cave, the sensors began to triangulate their location. Soon we knew where they would break through. But we had no way of knowing when.

We kept our helmets on, visors down, gripped our weapons and waited.

Nerves stretched taut. Fingers tapped on gunstocks or fiddled with equipment. I strained my eyes at the blank rock wall, trying to see *through* it to the enemy working so patiently, so laboriously to reach us. How they must hate us, I thought. How they must be focusing every ounce of their strength and hatred against us, sixteen men and women, alone, abandoned, trapped in a time and a place far from their own, waiting for a battle that can end only in extermination of one side or the other.

The sensor lights went blank. They've stopped digging, I thought. Why?

"Here they come!" came a shout from the cave's

mouth. I inadvertently turned to glance in that direction. . . .

The wall of the cave in front of me exploded, knocking all of us back onto the ground. I rolled over, my rifle still in my hands, and saw a half-dozen of the brutes charging at us out of the smoke and rubble. They were big, powerful, their broad, red-eyed faces snarling with fury and crystal spears in their raised hands.

I fired pointblank at them. The rifle's beam cut the first two in half, but their momentum carried them into me and they fell beside me as I rose to one knee and fired again. Ogun was firing too, but one of the brutes reached him with a crystal spear. It barely grazed his helmet, but a shower of sparks erupted and I heard Ogun scream in my earphones. His body spasmed, arched, then fell dead.

I ducked under the spear that was aimed at me and jammed the muzzle of my rifle into the brute's midsection as I pulled the trigger. His body burst into flame, and he shrieked hideously as he bounced away from me and into the others behind him.

Lissa had recovered her wits now and was firing into the brutes who were emerging from their newly dug tunnel. I lost count of how many there were; we fired and dodged and fired again at them, killing them left and right until their bodies jammed the entryway that they had blasted out of the rock.

Lissa leaped onto the barricade of flesh and lobbed a grenade into the tunnel. Its explosion shook the whole cave—stones fell from the ceiling; smoke filled the area.

I staggered back a few steps, turned and glanced at the front of the cave. A huge gray-brown bear was rearing on its hind legs, roaring and swinging its clawed paws at the troopers ringed around it like midgets. A dozen rifles blasts hit it, but the bear stalked forward, into the cave, as the soldiers fell back. Behind it I could see wolves and slinking great cats with saber fangs.

The cannon fired its searing beam of raw red energy into the bear's chest, blasting the beast in two, blood and bone and flesh splattering in every direction. As it toppled to the cave floor, already slippery with blood, the soldiers turned their weapons on the wolves and saber-toothed cats.

I looked back at the tunnel mouth we were guarding. Lissa was busily rigging explosive charges, sitting on the floor, her back to the barricade of dead bodies, her rifle on the ground beside her.

I went to her and peered into the murky darkness of the tunnel.

"There don't seem to be any more of them coming from this direction," I said.

I could sense her nodding inside her helmet. "This will seal off the tunnel." She lifted with both hands a set of grenades that she had wired together. "Then we can seal off the other one, farther back."

I agreed to her plan. Quickly she dropped her explosive package into the tunnel. We flattened out against the solid rock wall as she counted off five seconds. The blast jarred me almost to my knees, but when the smoke cleared, Lissa shone her helmet light into the tunnel and laughed lightheartedly.

"It'll take them awhile to dig through *that*," she said triumphantly.

Within minutes she had blasted the other tunnel shut, and we joined the others at the front of the cave.

Wave after wave of animals attacked us, and we battled them back. Huge, ferocious bears, snarling wolves and smaller dogs, saber-toothed mountain lions. We killed them by the dozens, by the score, by the hundreds. The nighttime darkness was lit by the glow of our energy weapons; the stars themselves faded from the sky in the blood-red light of

our killing beams. Through the padding of my
helmet and earphones I could hear the screaming,
howling, shrieking roars of pain and fury as the
animals were driven at us by Ahriman's diabolical
powers, only to be slaughtered by the blazing energies of our guns.

Off in the distance, barely seen against the flickering shadows, I could now and then glimpse one
of the brutes, skulking among the poor savage beasts
that they were commanding. But they never came
close enough to kill; they stayed their distance, as
if they knew that what had happened to their
comrades at the tunnel would happen to them.

I heard a voice in my head calling to them,
daring them, challenging them: Come and fight us
yourselves! Leave these poor dumb beasts alone
and take up the fight, face to face. Come and meet
the death you hand out so freely to others.

But they hung back, keeping to the shadows.

After long hours of fighting, I realized that the
cannon had gone silent. The lights in the cave
were out; we fought by the light of our weapons
and the lamps built into our helmets now. My own
rifle finally quit on me, and I began to use my
pistol, instead.

As dawn tinted the sky with a grayish pink, the
attacks stopped. The ground in front of the cave,
once smooth with pristine snow, was a blackened,
bloodied shambles of dead beasts, shattered limbs,
bodies ripped open, flesh torn apart.

I looked around me. Four soldiers were down,
their helmets and armor broken, blood-soaked.
Counting Ogun, back by the tunnel, we had lost
five. There were only eleven of us left alive, and
three of them were wounded, including Kedar. His
leg had been broken when a bear charged into the
cave and made it almost to the power packs.

Lissa and several others began tending to the
wounded. I went to Adena, who was surveying the

battlefield with a powerful pair of electronically boosted binoculars.

"They're leaving," she said, as if she knew I was beside her. "The brutes are moving off to the south."

"We've won," I said.

She handed the binoculars to me. "Not until we've killed the last one of them."

I looked out toward the south. Through the magnification of the binoculars I saw eight people like Ahriman shambling through the snow. There was no sign of any animals with them. No tracks except their own. Not even a dog accompanied them.

"They've thrown everything they have at us," I said, "and we beat them off. They've lost."

Adena's visor was up, and I could see that her face was set in grim determination. "No, Orion. We may have won this battle, but the war is not finished. Our task is to exterminate them."

"Those eight . . ."

She nodded. "Those last eight brutes must be killed, Orion. We have to go out after them."

"Is that Ormazd's command?" I asked her.

The corners of her mouth curved slightly in the beginning of a smile. "It is *my* command, Orion. It is what must be done."

CHAPTER 39

She gave orders quickly, efficiently. Kedar and the other wounded would remain in the cave. The rest of us started out after the fleeing enemy, without pausing for rest. We gulped down food capsules as we slogged through the knee-deep snow, following the trail left by the brutes, under a clean blue morning sky. The air was cold but still, as chilled and delicious as wine.

"Eight of us against eight of them," I said as I marched beside Adena. "Ormazd arranges things neatly."

She gazed at me, her gray eyes gleaming in the reflection of the morning sun against the pure white snow.

"You mustn't think that Ormazd is doing all this for his entertainment, Orion," she said. "We are dealing with the fate of the universe here, the maintenance of the continuum."

"By hunting down a handful of people . . ."

"*Ahriman's* people," she corrected. "Our enemies."

"Whose most powerful weapon is some sort of electrostatic wand, while we have laser guns that can cut them down at a thousand yards."

"Do you think it would be fairer if we fought them hand-to-hand?" She almost seemed amused. "The power packs that heat our suits and energize our weapons will be drained soon enough. The main power packs back in the cave are completely

357

drained. We'll be fighting them hand-to-hand soon enough, Orion. Will that please you?"

I had to admit that it did not.

"They must be exterminated," Adena went on, her face utterly serious now. "Every last one of them, including Ahriman. Especially Ahriman. You understand that, don't you?"

With a reluctant nod, I replied, "I understand that Ormazd wants it so. I understand that Ahriman wants to exterminate us. But I don't like it."

She gave me a strange, almost pitying glance. "Orion . . . we are not here to enjoy what we do. We do what must be done. We have no choice."

I started to reply, but thought better of it and held my tongue.

We pushed on through deepening snow, walking in the tracks made by the enemy band. The sun shone brightly but without much heat out of a cloudless sky of perfect blue. Adena headed our little column; I walked beside her. Due south the tracks headed, through a featureless expanse of dazzling white snow. After long hours of marching, with nothing to do except plant one foot in front of the other and watch my breath puffing out in tiny clouds of steam, I saw a forest of huge pine trees rising on the horizon, their deep green a startling, welcome contrast to this world of white.

The brutes' trail led straight into the woods, and I began to think about what might be waiting for us in the shadows of that forest.

"That's a fine spot for an ambush," I said.

Adena nodded agreement. "But as you say, we have weapons that outdistance theirs. If they're foolish enough to attack, they'll be doing us a favor."

"They'll throw more animals at us. There must be wolves and other predators living in that forest."

Adena asked, "What do you think we should do?"

"Circle the forest. If they're in there waiting for us, we can make them come out in the open."

"And if they're not, we'll lose half a day's march on them. Perhaps more."

"Does that matter?"

"We mustn't let them get away."

"If we go straight into those woods, we'll be ambushed and probably killed."

"That doesn't matter . . ."

"Perhaps it doesn't matter to you," I said, "or even to me. But what about them?" I cocked my head to indicate the other soldiers. "They may not have as many lives as you or I. Death for them is very real, and very permanent."

Her eyes looked troubled. "I had forgotten that."

"If we've got to kill the enemy down to the last man, at least let's try to preserve the lives of our own people."

"But you don't understand, Orion."

"I don't care," I said, keeping my voice low but putting as much strength into it as I could muster. "You've taken these men and women out of their own time, torn them away from their homes and families and flung them into this distant age of cold and ice to do Ormazd's bidding . . ."

"To do what must be done," she insisted. "To save the human race from extinction."

"Whatever the reason, they deserve a chance to get through this alive. They shouldn't be thrown away like a handful of pawns."

"But that's exactly what they are," Adena said. "Don't you see? They *are* pawns. They were created to be pawns."

"They're human beings, with lives of their own that are precious to them, families, friends . . ."

"No, Orion, you are wrong. You don't understand." Adena's face was sad, her eyes searching mine.

"Then tell me, explain it to me."

For long moments she said nothing, as we trudged through the snow, each step bringing us closer to the looming, brooding dark forest.

"I'm afraid," she said at last. "If I tell you the entire truth, you will hate me."

"Hate you?" I felt shocked. "How can I hate you? I've gone through death three times to find you, to be with you."

She lowered her eyes. "Orion, we are all pieces in a game. We all play our assigned roles."

"And the gameplayer is Ormazd," I said.

"No. It's not that simple. Ormazd plays his role, just as I do. And you." She hesitated, then added, almost in a whisper, "And these . . . pawns, who march with us."

"You're not a pawn," I said.

"Neither are you," she said, with a sad, resigned smile. "You are a knight. I am a bishop, perhaps."

"A queen."

"Not that powerful."

"My queen," I insisted. Then I realized, "And Ormazd is the king. If he is killed . . ."

"We all die. Permanently. The game ends."

"So that's what it's all about."

"Yes."

"And these men and women with us?"

"As I said, they are pawns. They were made for this task, and no other." She looked weary, miserable. "You spoke of their being wrenched out of their own time, separated from their friends and families. Orion, they have no families! No friends. They know of no other time except this. They were created by Ormazd precisely for this task of exterminating Ahriman's people. For this task, and none other."

It was as if I had known this all along. The truth did not surprise me. Instead, I felt a terrible hollowness within me, an emptiness as deep as the pit of hell.

I glanced back over my shoulder at them, marching along through the frigid Ice Age afternoon without a complaint, following Adena's orders, each step bringing them closer to death—either their own or their enemy's. And they did not seem to care which.

Lissa smiled at me. She was toting a heavy sack of grenades and other explosive devices on her back. I thought back to her lighthearted eagerness just before the battle in the cave. To the killing frenzy of Dal's clan that night they were attacked. To the grim efficiency of the Mongols as they wiped out the armies of Bela the Hungarian. Even to the crowd of demonstrators in front of the fusion laboratory in Michigan, so quick to violence.

"Yes," Adena said, as if she could read my thoughts. "Violence has been programmed into them."

"They are machines, then? Robots?"

With a single small shake of her head she answered, "They are flesh and blood, just as you yourself are. But they were created by Ormazd and their minds were programmed for this task of killing."

"Just as I was," I realized.

"Now you know the truth," she whispered, her gray eyes filled with sorrow.

"I was created by Ormazd to kill Ahriman, and for no other reason."

"Yes."

"That's why I couldn't remember my past, back in the twentieth century. I had none. I am a puppet, and Ormazd pulls the strings."

The hollowness I felt inside me grew to engulf the universe. I was a machine! We were all machines, made of organic molecules and DNA, of bone and nerve, but machines nonetheless, programmed to do Ormazd's bidding: puppets, marionettes, remotely controlled killers.

"Orion." Vaguely I heard Adena's voice calling me, summoning me back to this instant in time, this place on the vast chess board that Ormazd controlled.

"Orion," she said again. "You were made to serve Ormazd, but you have grown beyond the purpose for which he created you."

"Have I?" My voice sounded utterly weary, defeated, even to my own ears. "Then why am I here, if it isn't to twitch whenever Ormazd pulls my strings?"

Adena's beautiful face eased into a smile. "Why, I thought you were here to find me. That's what you told me."

"Now you're teasing me."

"Not at all." She grew serious again. "You were created for a single purpose, true enough. But even from the first you acted on your own. You are a human being, Orion. As fully human as Socrates or Einstein or Ogotai Khan."

"How can I be?"

"You *are*," she said. "How could I love you, if you were not?"

I stared at her for long moments as we trudged steadily through the snow toward the gloomy forest. Its huge conifers reared before us like the battlements of a fortress.

"You do love me," I said.

"Enough to make myself human," Adena answered. "Enough to share in your life, your fate, your death."

"I love you. I've loved you through a hundred thousand years, through death and resurrection."

She nodded happily, her eyes suddenly misty.

"But we must face death again, mustn't we?" I said.

"Yes, but we'll face it together."

"And these others?"

She grew somber again. "Orion, they *are* pawns.

They have no past. They know nothing but how to fight."

"Even pawns have a right to survive," I said.

"Our task is to exterminate Ahriman and his kind. There is no other goal for us, no other path. If we fail in that, we die forever, Orion. Oblivion for us all."

I knew she was telling the truth; yet I could not accept it.

Adena halted abruptly and grasped me by the shoulders. The others stopped a respectful few paces behind us.

"Orion, if you love me, you must be willing to sacrifice these pawns," she whispered fiercely.

I gazed into her gray eyes for what seemed like an eternity. With an effort I turned my face away, toward the looming dark forest that awaited us, and then back to the men and women who followed us. They stood at rest, shouldering their weapons, waiting for the next command.

"I don't want them to die," Adena said, her voice low, almost pleading with me. "It may not be necessary for them to die. But if we delay, Ahriman and his band will get away."

"If we march straight into those trees, we will be ambushed."

"That doesn't mean that we will all be killed. Our weapons are far superior to theirs."

"While they last."

"We've got to be willing to make the sacrifice," Adena insisted. "You risk your own life, and mine. Why draw the line at theirs?"

"Because they don't understand what's at stake."

Adena turned away from me and glanced up at the lowering sun. Already the trees were throwing long shadows toward us, like fingers reaching for our throats.

"Check your weapons," she called to the handful of troops. "We're moving into the forest. The brutes will probably spring an ambush in there. Be on the alert."

They nodded and began checking their guns and power units. Within a minute we were all marching forward again, without a protest or even an instant's hesitation from any of them. If anything, they looked glad to be coming to grips with the enemy.

There was nothing I could do. Nothing I *should* do, I kept telling myself, except move forward and find Ahriman. But deep inside my mind a voice was telling me that there was more to the world, far more, than hunting and killing.

It made no difference. Adena was right, we were all players in a cosmic game, and we all had our roles to fulfill. I stayed at her side, pistol in my hand, and peered into the shadowy hollows between the trees as the forest swallowed up our meager little band of warriors.

Birds called back and forth among those dark trees. Small furry animals chittered at us and scrampered up to the higher branches, as if they knew that danger surrounded us. The sunlight was mottled and weak. It grew colder the deeper into the woods we tramped, cold and still as death.

The ground beneath the thickly clustered trees was barely touched by the snow that had drifted so thickly out in the open, but we could still see the trail that the brutes had left, as clearly as if they had deliberately laid it down for us to follow.

A squirrel, the biggest and reddest squirrel I had ever seen, jabbered angrily at us as we neared the tree on which it was standing; all four paws gripped the bark of the pine's huge bole. When it saw that we would not turn away, it raced up the tree trunk toward the safety of a lair high up in its branches.

I saw a shadowy form move up in those branches, something as big as a man.

I reached out and touched Adena's arm. "They're up in the trees," I whispered.

She barely had time to look up before they attacked. Mountain lions leaped out of those branches, their saber fangs huge and glittering white. Adena had no time even to shout an order, but the troops automatically formed a circle as they shot the beasts in midair. One snarling, spitting cat landed in our midst and I blasted his skull open with a burst from my pistol.

"Wolves!" somebody yelled.

They came loping through the trees, eyes gleaming balefully as they charged at us. We gunned them down by the dozens.

I searched the trees as we fought the howling, roaring, bloodthirsty beasts. The saber-toothed cats lay dead in our midst, and the bodies of wolves ringed our tiny defensive perimeter. But I was looking for Ahriman and his kind. They were up there in the trees, I knew, waiting for the moment when our weapons ran out of power. Already four of our troopers had dropped their rifles and were using pistols, which were powered by the suits' power packs.

I called to Lissa. "Let me have some grenades!"

She was scanning the trees, too, looking for more cats to kill. The wolves were skulking out in the deepening shadows for the moment, working up the fury for another attack. We could see their eyes glittering in the darkness.

"What kind?" Lissa called back, cheerful as ever. "Concussion, fragmentation, gas . . ."

"Concussion," I answered.

She rolled four of them to me, shouting instructions on how to set the fuse's time delay. I picked one up, turned the timer to five seconds, then reared back and threw it high into the trees in front of me.

The blast was much smaller than I had expected,

but a shower of snow and shattered branches rained down us. Adena looked up sharply.

"What are you . . ."

I silenced her with an upraised hand. A howl of pain echoed through the trees; it was not an animal's howl either.

"They're up there!" Adena realized.

As I picked up another grenade, the brutes launched their real attack, swinging out of the concealing branches of the trees on long, thin ropes and slashing at us with those crystal spears of theirs.

We fired at them as they fell upon us, but they were wearing glittering crystal armor that splashed our laser beams harmlessly away. Out of the corner of my eye I saw that the two troopers who still had rifles in their hands were the first to be swarmed under by the brutes. I fired at them but my pistol's beam could not penetrate their armor.

Their electrostatic spears, though, were deadly effective. Both our riflemen were cut down in showers of blue sparks, and the beasts turned to charge at the rest of us.

Lissa threw herself at four of them, grenades in each hand. Twin explosions tore all of them apart and knocked the rest of us down. Groggily, I clambered to my knees, threw my useless pistol into the face of the nearest brute and kicked the legs out from under him. I grabbed his spear and jammed it into his neck, where his crystal armor did not protect him. He screeched and died in a blast of electrical agony.

Adena was on one knee, coolly shooting one of the brutes through the head as two others rushed at her. She turned slightly and shot at one of them, who raised his armored forearm over his face to deflect her shot. Her pistol went dead.

I leaped at the two brutes, knocking them both away from her.

They snarled at me, spears raised in their hands. I parried the first thrust that the nearer one made, then rammed the butt of the spear into the head of the other. Someone's pistol blast took the head off the first one as I killed the second with the spear's electrical bolt.

Suddenly the fighting was over. Four of our people lay dead at our feet, and seven of the brutes.

"One got away," Adena said.

"Ahriman." I knew.

"We must find him. We mustn't let him escape."

"I'll go after him," I said.

"No," Adena countered. "We all will."

CHAPTER 40

For two days we followed Ahriman's trail southward, until another storm darkened the skies and began to pelt us with grainy snow driven by a fierce, howling wind.

I led Adena's little band back to the relative shelter of the pine forest as quickly as I could. Our suit packs were running out of power, one by one. We had only a handful of food capsules remaining. If we'd stayed in the raging blizzard, we would have starved and frozen.

I showed them how to make a lean-to shelter from the pine boughs and how to make a fire. We used the last ergs of energy in the pistols to cut the tree limbs for the shelter and to start the campfire. When the last power pack finally was exhausted, our little troop was suddenly plunged into the Stone Age. None of the equipment they had with them would work anymore. We had to make do with what we could take from the land itself.

The storm moved off after three hungry days, and we started back toward the cave where we had left Kedar and the other wounded. Adena let me become the leader, and I remembered from my time with Dal's clan how to make primitive spears and how to find small game hidden in the snow. We did not starve, although we were a ragged, hungry, lean and very cold straggle of soldiers by the time we got back to the cave.

For the next several days we were all busy every waking moment. I showed them how to survive in the wilderness, how to start a fire by the friction of rubbing two sticks against each other, how to flush out the hares and squirrels that lived unseen in the snow-covered fields, how to skin and cook them over the open fire.

And at night, while the others slept, I stood watch—alone with my thoughts.

The shock of the battles and their aftermath was wearing away. I began to *feel* what had registered on my conscious mind, but not yet penetrated to my inner self. I saw Lissa's goodhearted grin as she handled her deadly cargo of explosives, as innocent as a child when she spoke of them and what they could do. And I saw the exultant look on her face, eyes wide and mouth agape with a scream of triumph, as she rushed the enemy with those live grenades in her hands.

I stared up at the stars, glittering coldly in this Ice Age night, and began to realize that Ormazd never intended that these soldiers would survive their battle. They were put here to defeat Ahriman's people, to annihilate them, and once that task was done, they were meant to self-destruct, to die here in the cold darkness, their purpose accomplished, their value reduced to zero.

"Ormazd," I muttered to the silent, grave stars, "wherever you are, whoever you are, I offer you this vow: I will find Ahriman for you, and I will kill him if I can. But, in exchange, I am going to take these people to a place where there is no snow, where they can survive and live like decent human beings. And I will do that first, before I seek out Ahriman."

"You bargain with your creator?"

I turned to see Adena smiling at me. "I can't leave these people here to die," I said. "Can you?"

"If it's necessary," she said.

"But it's not. We can take them south, to a land they can live in. I can show them how to survive."

Her smile broadened. "You have already shown them so much. Their children will create legends about you, Orion. You will become a god yourself. Is that what you want?"

"I want you," I said, "in a land and a time where we can live together in peace."

"For how long?"

"For a lifetime," I replied.

"And then?"

I shrugged. She was not teasing me. Her smile was not one of amusement.

"Orion," said Adena, "when you can live beyond death, you must try to see further than a single lifetime."

"But I won't live beyond my next death." I knew. "Ormazd won't revive me once I've killed Ahriman."

Her gray eyes fixed on mine, pulled me to her. "Do you think, my beloved, that I would want to face eternity without you?"

"Then what . . ."

"I will see that you survive death. And if Ormazd prevents me from doing so, then I will live your one lifetime with you and die with you at the end of it, gladly."

"I can't ask you to give up . . ."

She placed a finger on my lips, silencing me. "You have not asked me. You did not need to ask. I make my own decisions."

I took her in my arms and kissed her as if we would never be able to touch each other again, as if this night were the last night of the world, as if the stars were blinking out forever.

"Now lead them, Orion my love," she whispered. "Lead them to a land where they can live in peace."

The following morning we started our long trek southward, Kedar and the two other wounded forcing us to move slowly across the glittering fields of snow. No animals attacked us. If Ahriman were nearby, he did not show his presence in any way.

We became a band of primitive hunters, stalking game for food and furs. Piece by piece we discarded our useless equipment, replacing laser pistols with wooden spears, plastic armor with the hides of foxes, hares, and mountain goats.

Southward we trekked, away from the snow and ice. Within a week we found an open stream, gurgling toward the southwest, its glacier-fed water as cold as the dark side of the moon. We followed the stream through hilly, wooded country. The snow grew thinner on the ground, the sun brighter, the air warmer.

One of the wounded died, and we buried her in the bank of that unnamed stream. Kedar grew stronger, though, and we made better time despite his limp.

At last we entered a land of softly rolling hills, covered with grass, teeming with game. Trees tossed their leafy branches in the warm breeze. Huge, lumbering beasts trumpeted at us from the undulating horizon—mammoths, I guessed, from their size and their trunks.

I had no idea where we were, but we found a large, dry cave and made it our own. The ten of us had become quite skilled at survival by now. The men set off to catch meat; the women began gathering shoots and berries from the plants that grew in profusion all around us.

"We can stay here awhile," I said as I started a fire. "This might be a good place to stay."

Adena sat beside me and stared into the crackling flames. The sun was low in the west and the heat from the fire felt good, comforting.

"Now you can begin to search for Ahriman again," she said, without turning her head from the flames.

I nodded wordlessly.

"Do you think he's far from here?" she asked.

"No. He's near us, I'm sure. He still wants to exterminate us. He hasn't given up, not yet."

"When will you leave?"

I squinted up at the setting sun. Thick clouds were gathering in the sky, turning the sunset into a blaze of reds and golds and violets.

"Tomorrow," I answered, "unless there's a storm."

Adena smiled and leaned her head against my shoulder. "I'll pray for rain."

CHAPTER 41

It did begin to rain. As darkness fell and the men came straggling back to the cave, a strong wind arose and thunder boomed across the sky. Kedar, the last of the hunters to return, limped sullenly into the cave, wet to the skin, his hair plastered down over his head, grumbling to himself.

As we feasted on rabbit and woodchuck, the men began talking about the bigger game they had seen farther downstream—antelope and bison, from the sound of their descriptions. And, of course, there were mammoths and horses and all sorts of other animals abounding in this Ice Age landscape. I told them as much about them as I could, knowing that I would be leaving them soon.

"And there are wolves out there, too," said Kedar. "I saw a pair of them as I was heading back, in the rain."

"There must be bears, too."

"They won't bother us here in this cave as long as we have a good fire going," I said.

"Unless the brutes control them."

"There's only one brute left," I said to them as we sat around the fire. Their faces, lit by the flickering flames, were smeared with dirt and dinner. "And I'm going after him, as soon as the storm ends."

For a moment no one said a word. Then Kedar began to talk about going out after antelope.

I glanced at Adena and let them make their plans. Already they were more concerned with their bellies than with continuing their war.

The storm grew in fury as the night wore on, its raging wind slashing into the cave, driving raw wet coldness and rain that nearly drenched our fire. We grabbed up burning firebrands and moved farther back into the cave, beyond the reach of the rain.

Thunder racked the night, and lightning flashed out in the darkness. The others tried to sleep on the cold rock floor, but something kept me staring out into the night, into the storm.

Ahriman, I realized. He is here. He is reaching for us. This is *his* storm, his doing.

Adena was stretched out on the ground, sound asleep. I smiled at her, my sleeping goddess who had taken on human form. Her breath was slow and regular, her beautiful face even more exquisite in repose. I wondered how she could make the transition to being so completely human. I wondered how Ahriman could make the transition to being superhuman.

He must have started life just like any other of his kind. Even now, here in this time and place, he had shown no evidence of superhuman powers. In other eras he had whisked himself—and me—through space-time as easily as a man steps through an open doorway. How did he acquire those powers? When?

A flash of lightning lit the world outside the cave for a brief instant of time, and I saw something that startled me. It happened too quickly to be certain of it, but I closed my eyes for a moment and reviewed the scene in my memory.

Frozen in place by the lightning's strobe glare, it was the hulking form of Ahriman I saw, not more than a hundred yards beyond the entrance of the cave. And beside him, standing on all four legs, a huge bear that dwarfed Ahriman's powerful figure. He was facing the bear, one thickly muscled arm raised, a blunt finger pointing, as if he was giving the beast instructions.

Guided my Ahriman's intelligence, driven by his hatred, that bear could kill us all. I scrambled to my feet and drew two blazing branches from the fire, one for each hand, and hurried to the cave's entrance.

As I approached, a jagged fork of lightning streaked across the sky and the bear's massive, fearsome form reared up in the cave's entrance, blotting out the storm outside, its roar of rage blending with the boom of thunder to shake the ground itself.

It advanced toward me, forepaws raised, claws the size of hunting knives glinting in the light of the fire, gaping jaws armed with fangs that could tear off a limb with ease.

Instead of retreating, I yelled as loudly as I could and jabbed the burning end of one of my torches at it. The bear roared back and swung a mighty swipe that ripped the torch out of my hand. I feinted with the other torch, tossed it from my left hand to my right, and then drove it into the beast's midsection. It bellowed with pain and anger, staggered back a step.

My body went into overdrive, every sense hyperalert, every nerve reacting faster than any normal human could move. Out of the corner of my eye I could see the others awakening, getting to their feet as if in slow-motion, taking up firebrands.

They circled to the bear's left and right, dancing close and then away, jabbing at him with the blazing torches. The bear screamed fury at them but would not back out of the cave. Ahriman's control was iron-bound.

I saw that we were at a stalemate that could end only with the bear's killing one or more of us.

Then a burning stick whistled over my head and hit the bear on the shoulder.

"Drive him out!" Adena shouted, and I knew it was she who had thrown the stick.

But the bear had other ideas. Instead of retreating it moved straight at me, utterly disregarding the others and the torches they jabbed at it. I could see the poor beast's coat blackening from the flames, smell seared fur and flesh, yet still the bear forced itself forward, toward me.

It was like a nightmare where everything happens slowly, as if time itself was winding down; yet even so you cannot escape the terror that is relentlessly engulfing you. The torch in my own hand seemed puny as a matchstick as the bear's eight-foot height towered over me, its bellowing roar blotting out the shouts and cries of the soldiers, its hate-reddened eyes fastened on mine.

I saw the blow coming, but I had backed up so far that I could not retreat any further without stumbling into the fire. I could feel its heat singing the backs of my legs as the bear's mountainous paw swung slowly, inexorably, at me. I tried to duck under the blow, and almost made it.

The paw cuffed me on the back of the head as I ducked, hitting me like a boulder dropped from a great height. I went sprawling; everything went fuzzy and black spots danced before my eyes.

I don't know how long I lay stunned, probably only a moment or two. I found myself on my back, my vision blurred. But I could see Adena leaping at the beast, both hands gripping firebrands, and the bear cuffing her away. It knocked down two more of the troop, then loomed over me. I saw those fangs reaching for me, and I was unable to move out of their way.

The first shock of pain went through me like a bolt of electricity. I could hear my bones crunching as the bear bit into my shoulder and roughly jerked me up off the floor. I pawed feebly at its snout with my free hand and saw, vaguely, dimly, the others still jabbing uselessly at it with their torches. The bear swatted another soldier to the ground and shambled out of the cave, into the night and the cold rain, with me dangling like a limp doll from its jaws.

The last glimpse of the cave I got, through eyes blurred by blood and pain, was of Adena clambering to her feet and starting out after us. But Kedar and another soldier restrained her. They held her there, struggling, and watched the bear carry me off.

The beast dropped to all fours as the rain pelted down on us. Lightning danced through the black sky. The fire-lit mouth of the cave became a distant glow, a speck of warmth as remote as the farthest star.

The bear dropped me, at last, unceremoniously, in a muddy puddle and then trundled off to lick its own wounds. I lay there on my back, the cold rain sluicing down my face and torn body. The pain had reached the point where numbness was setting in. I was too far in shock to even think of trying to control it. My right shoulder was useless, the arm dangling by a few ligaments and scraps of torn, bleeding flesh.

I coughed and shivered. So this is how Prometheus was created, I thought, half delirious. The demigod who gives humankind the gift of fire only, in return, to be horribly punished by the gods. I think I must have laughed as I lay there bleeding to death. Not a dignified way for a demigod to die.

Another stroke of lightning split the darkness and I saw Ahriman's brooding form hulking over me.

"I've beaten you," he said, in that tortured whisper of his. I could barely hear him over the moaning of the storm wind.

"You've killed me," I agreed.

"And them. They'll die off soon enough, without their weapons and their energy generators."

"No," I said. "They will live. I've taught them how to survive. They have fire. They will master this world and populate the Earth."

In the darkness I could not see the expression on his face, only the anger and hatred radiating from his red-rimmed eyes.

"I will have to strike elsewhere, then," Ahriman muttered. "Find the weak points in the fabric of the continuum . . ."

It took all my strength to shake my head as I lay there in the mud. My voice was growing weaker; each breath I drew in was more difficult, more painful.

"Ahriman . . . it won't do you any good," I gasped. "Each time you try . . . I am there . . . to stop you."

For long moments he said nothing, merely standing there, looming over me like a dark, ominous destiny.

Finally: "Then we will go back to the very beginning. I will kill you for all time, Orion. And Ormazd with you."

I wanted to laugh at him; I wanted to tell him that he was a fool. But I had no more strength left in me. I could do nothing but lie there as my blood mingled with the rain and mud and the life seeped out of my body.

Ahriman raised his powerful arms to the stormy night sky, threw his head back, and gave out a harrowing, blood-chilling, howling cry, like a beast baying at the moon. Twice, three times, he cried out, his thick blunt fingers reaching toward the black clouds that blotted out the stars.

Lightning strokes flickered through those clouds and then began lancing down to the ground all around us. My failing eyes widened as one bolt after another sizzled to the ground, scant yards from us, and stayed there, crackling and blistering the air around us until we were surrounded with a cage of electricity. The rain-sodden ground bubbled where the lightning danced. The sweet, burning smell of ozone filled the air.

Ahriman stood outlined against the blue-white glare of the lightning, his arms still straining upward, reaching, his baying, yowling cry the only sound I could hear over the simmering blaze of electricity.

Then a tremendous stroke of lightning shattered the world, engulfing Ahriman, turning him into a glowing demon of pure energy, overflowing onto me, screaming along every nerve in my body until there was nothing in the universe but pain.

And then darkness.

PART FIVE:
THE CYCLE OF ETERNITY

CHAPTER 42

I never lost consciousness. I felt nothing, as if my body had gone numb, encased in a cocoon of transparent gossamer that held me immobile and perfectly protected from everything outside. Neither heat nor cold, pain nor pleasure, joy nor fear penetrated the cladding that covered me.

But I could see. The night storm and the Ice Age landscape wavered and slowly dissolved, like a castle of sand being washed away by the incoming tide. Beside me stood Ahriman, still encased in the bluish-white shimmer of energy from the lightning bolt, frozen immobile just as I was. His red eyes glared at me, and in them I could see not only hate and anger, but fear as well.

Slowly, by degrees, it grew darker and darker until vision was useless. I could see nothing. I was alone in a well of darkness, suspended in time and space, not knowing where I was or where I was heading.

Strangely, I felt no fear—not even apprehension. Even though I could no longer see him, I knew that Ahriman was beside me. I knew that Adena and her tiny band of remaining soldiers would survive the cold of the Ice Age and raise their children to tell them of the demigod who taught them how to make fire. I realized now that Dal's hunting clan and all the other humans of every age were the descendants of those few soldiers, lost and abandoned after the last battle of The War.

And I knew that Ormazd was near. And with him would be the goddess whom I loved when she deigned to take human form.

The darkness began to pale. Faint flickers of light, almost like stars in the night sky, began to show themselves. Then, like a slow, reluctant dawn, the blackness around me softened, became a pearly gray, a softer pinkish hue.

Light and warmth slowly washed over me, thawing the cocoon that held me. I could flex my fingers, move my arms. Gradually I felt all constraints melt away from me. I could move and feel once again.

But Ahriman remained trapped in an invisible web of energy—glowering at me, but unable to move. I should have felt glad at that; instead, I felt something close to pity.

"There's nothing I can do," I said aloud, knowing that he could not hear me. I shrugged elaborately to show him that I was helpless. His baleful stare never left me.

I turned away from him to examine the place where we stood. It was a featureless expanse of clouds. Not a hill, not a tree, not a blade of grass in sight. Nothing but a cloudscape extending in every direction as far as the eye could see. Not even a horizon, in the usual sense of the word; merely soft, puffy white clouds drifting slowly, one after the other, endlessly.

My feet seemed to be standing on something solid; yet, when I looked down, I saw nothing more substantial than wisps of cloud tops. Overhead the sky was clear, and far up at zenith the blue was dark enough to show a few twinkling stars.

I remembered flying in jet airliners through cloudscapes such as this, where no trace of the ground could be seen and there was nothing below except the tufted tops of a thick, soft carpeting of dazzling white clouds.

I grinned to myself. "So this is heaven, is it?" Raising my hands to cup my mouth, I shouted as loudly as I could, "I don't believe it, Ormazd! You'll have to do better than this!"

I looked back at Ahriman. He stood like a statue of implacable enmity, the only substantial landmark in this fairyland of cloud and sky.

Something drew my eyes up toward the zenith, where those few stars looked down at us. One of them seemed to burn brighter than the rest. It glowed and shimmered and seemed to grow as I watched it. Like a bubble of light it expanded and blazed brighter until it was too brilliant to look at. I threw my arm over my eyes as the glare from that golden sphere flooded everywhere.

The glare subsided, and I looked up again to see the human form of Ormazd, splendidly adorned in a uniform of gold, his thick golden mane framing his handsome, smiling face.

"Well done, Orion," he said to me, beaming. "You have succeeded at last."

I felt an overpowering satisfaction at his words, the kind of emotion a puppy must feel when its master pats it on the head. Yet, deep within me, there was a nagging resentment.

"My duty was to kill Ahriman," I heard myself say.

Ormazd waved a self-confident hand. "No matter. He is as good as dead. He can't harm us now."

"Then . . . my task has been accomplished?"

"Yes. Quite fulfilled."

"What happens to me now? What happens to *him*?"

Ormazd's satisfied smile faded. "He remains here, in this stasis, safely out of the stream of the continuum. He can do us no harm now. The continuum is safe, at last."

"And me?" I asked.

He looked slightly puzzled. "Your task is finished, Orion. What would you have me do with you?"

My throat froze. I could not speak.

"What is it that you want?" Ormazd asked me. "What reward can I give you for your faithful service?"

He was playing with me, I could see. And I could not find the courage to tell him that I wanted Aretha, Agla, Ava, Adena—the gray-eyed goddess whom I loved and who loved me. Suddenly I wondered if she hadn't been a part of Ormazd's plan, a stimulus to move me through the pain of death in my hunt for Ahriman, an unattainable prize to lure me through space-time in the pursuit of Ormazd's goal.

"Well, Orion?" Ormazd asked again, grinning at me. "What is it that you desire?"

"Is she . . . does she really exist?"

"Who?" Ormazd's grin became feline. "Does who really exist?"

"The woman—the one who called herself Adena when she led a squad of your troops in The War."

"Adena exists, certainly," he replied. "She is as real as you are. And as human."

"Ava . . . Agla . . ."

"They all exist, Orion. In their own time. They are all human beings, living their lifespans in their own particular times."

"Then she's not . . ."

The air beside Ormazd began to shimmer, as if a powerful beam of heat had suddenly been turned on. It wavered and sparkled. Ormazd edged back a step as the air seemed to congeal, to take on a silvery radiance and then solidify into the form of a tall, slender, beautiful woman, clad in glittering metallic silver.

"Stop toying with him, Ormazd," she said sternly.

Then she looked at me, and our eyes met. "I exist, Orion. I am real."

The breath froze in my lungs. I could not utter a word.

But Ormazd could. "Is she the one you meant? Have you fallen in love with a goddess, Orion?" He laughed.

"You find it ridiculous that your creature should love me?" she asked, cutting through his laughter. "Then how amusing it must be to think that I love him."

Ormazd shook his head. "That is impossible."

"Is it?"

I found my voice at last. "Your name . . . what is your true name?"

Her tone softened as she told me, "I am all those women you have met, Orion, in each of the times you have found yourself. Here, I call myself Anya."

"Anya."

"Yes," she said. "And despite the scoffing of your creator, I do love you, Orion."

"And I love you, Anya."

"Impossible!" snorted Ormazd. "Can a human being love a worm? You are a goddess, Anya, not one of these creatures of flesh."

"I became one of them. I have learned to be human," she said.

"But you are *not* human," he insisted. "Any more than I am." Ormazd's form shimmered, blurred slightly. "Show him your true self."

Anya shook her head slightly.

"You refuse? Then look upon me, Orion, and see your creator as he truly exists!"

Ormazd's body flowed and blurred and began to burn with an inner golden light so powerful that I could not look directly at it. It cast no heat at all; if anything, the air around me seemed to grow colder. But the brilliance was painful. I had to lower my eyes, bow my head, put my arms up to shield my vision from that overpowering glare.

"I am Ormazd, the God of Light, the creator of humankind," his voice bellowed.

Through nearly closed eyes I saw a great shining globe of light, radiant as the sun, hovering in the place where the golden-maned man had stood moments before.

"On your knees, creature! Worship your creator!"

I could feel the power of his brilliance pushing against me like a palpable force, like the pitiless blasting radiation from the fusion chamber, so many centuries away.

But Anya gripped my arm and held me steady. She looked straight into Ormazd's glowing form.

"He has served you well, Ormazd," she said. "This is no way to treat him."

The glowing globe dimmed, shrank, and became a human form once again.

"I wanted him to realize," Ormazd said, in a tone as calm and conversational as you might hear in a quiet church rectory, "with whom he is dealing."

Anya smiled grimly. "And you should realize, O God of Light, with whom *you* are dealing. I have seen Orion's courage. You cannot overawe him."

"I built that courage into him," he snapped.

"Then stop trying to overpower it!"

"Wait!" I said. "Wait. There's so much to this that I don't understand."

"How could you?" Ormazd sneered.

I glanced back at Ahriman, who watched us with pain-filled eyes.

"You created me to hunt down Ahriman and kill him," I said to Ormazd.

"Yes. But removing him from the continuum's time stream is just as good. He will remain here, safely held in stasis, forever."

"In each of the eras I was sent, I found a woman— the same woman—it was you, Anya, each time."

"That is true," she said.

"But Ormazd told me that each of those women was as human as I, and lived a human lifespan in that particular time . . ."

"He doesn't understand the difference between time flow and stasis," Ormazd said.

"Then we should explain it to him."

"Why?"

"Because I want to," Anya said.

Ormazd made a disgusted face. "Why bother with explanations to a creature that has outlived his usefulness?"

CHAPTER 43

Outlived my usefulness. I realized that if Ormazd had created me, had placed me in all those different eras to hunt down Ahriman, had brought me through death many times over—he could also end my existence, totally and forever.

I stared at him. "Is that the reward you will give me? Final death?"

"Orion, try to understand," he said, almost placatingly. "What you desire is truly impossible. Anya is not a human being, no more than I am. We take on human form to make ourselves familiar to you."

"But Adena . . . Agla . . ."

"They *are* human," Anya said. "Adena was created in a time that is far in the future of any era you have known . . ."

"Fifty thousand years in the future from the twentieth century," I said, recalling what Ormazd had told me when I had first met him.

"Exactly," Anya said. "She was created at the same time you yourself were."

"Then . . ."

"And the others, Aretha, Ava, Agla—they were born of human mothers, just as all humans have been, since Adena's band of soldiers struggled to survive in the Age of Ice."

"But they were you."

"Yes. I inhabited their bodies for their entire lifetimes. I became human."

"For me?"

"Not at first. In the beginning it was merely . . . curiosity, a novelty, a chance to see what Ormazd's handiwork was like. But then I began to feel what *they* feel—the pain, the fear—and then I found you, and I began to understand what love is."

I turned to Ormazd. "You would prevent us from being together?"

His taunting grin had long disappeared. He seemed deeply concerned now, somber. "I can give you a full, rich lifetime, Orion. Many lifetimes, if you wish. But I cannot make you into one of us. That is impossible."

"Because you refuse to make it possible," I replied, bitterly.

He shook his head. "No. It is impossible because not even I can accomplish it. I cannot transform a bacterium into a bird. I cannot turn a man into a god."

Turning back to Anya, I pleaded, "Is he telling me the truth? There's nothing that can be done?"

"Try to understand, Orion," she said gently.

"How can I understand?" I felt rage boiling within me. I glanced at the imprisoned form of Ahriman and knew a little of the hatred burning in his eyes. "You haven't allowed me to understand. You created me to do a job for you, and now that it's finished, you're finished with me."

"No," Anya said. "That's not . . ."

But Ormazd overrode her. "Accept what cannot be changed, Orion. You have done well. The human race will worship you, through all of time, in one form or another. They will forget about me, but they will always remember Prometheus."

"Why?" I asked. "Why did you create me? Why create humankind? Why fight The War against

Ahriman's people? Why did you cause all this agony and bloodshed?"

Ormazd fell silent. His golden radiance gathered around him almost like a protective cloak as he lowered his head and refused to answer me.

But Anya's gray eyes flashed with silver flame. She stared at Ormazd until he lifted his eyes to meet hers.

"He deserves to be answered, God of Light," she said, in a voice I could barely hear.

Ormazd did not reply. He merely shook his head slowly in refusal.

"Then I will tell him," Anya insisted.

"What good will it do?" Ormazd said. "He already hates me. Do you want him to hate you, too?"

"I want him to understand," she said.

"You are a fool."

"Perhaps I am. But he deserves to know the entire truth."

The golden glow of Ormazd's aura began to pulsate and redden at its fringes. The light grew brighter, brighter, until it was impossible to look directly at him. His human body faded into the brilliance and the radiant golden sphere, a miniature fiery sun, then rose above our heads and dwindled in the featureless distance until it was no more than a star-like point of light against the far sky.

I turned back toward Anya.

"Are you prepared to see the truth, Orion?" she asked. Her eyes held all the sadness of time in them.

"Will it mean that I must lose you?" I asked.

"You must lose me in any case, Orion. Ormazd spoke truthfully: you cannot become one of us."

I was tempted to ask her to end it all right there and then, to put me out of existence, out of pain. But, instead, I heard my voice replying, "If I must exist without you, then at least let me know why I was created."

"You were created to hunt Ahriman," she answered.

"Yes, but *why*? I don't believe the story Ormazd told me. Ahriman couldn't possibly destroy the universe. It's all nonsense."

"No, my love," Anya said gently. "It is all quite true."

"Then show me! Let me understand."

Her beautiful face was utterly serious as she nodded to me. "You will have to enter the time stream again. I must send you to a place in space-time that is before the Age of Ice, before human beings existed on Earth."

"Very well, send me. I'm willing."

She drew a slow, hesitant breath. "I will not be there with you. Not in any form. You will be alone—except for . . ."

"Except for whom?"

"You will see," Anya said. "Suffice it for now to know that there will be no other human beings on Earth, no creatures like yourself."

I realized. "Ormazd won't have created them yet."

"That's right."

"But there will be others there," I guessed. And then a flash of recognition lit my mind. "Ahriman's people! *They* will be on Earth!"

Anya did not reply, but I could see in her eyes that it was true. I turned my gaze from her to Ahriman, imprisoned in his web of energy, and saw his eyes burning with a fury that could destroy worlds, if ever it got free.

CHAPTER 44

Anya instructed me to close my eyes, and not open them again until I felt the wind against my skin. For a moment I stood there, unmoving, my gaze fixed on her lovely, somber face.

This would be the last time I'd see her, I knew. There would be no return from this journey.

I wanted to take her in my arms, to kiss her and tell her for one last time that I loved her more than life itself. But she was a goddess, not a human woman. I could love her as Agla the witch, or Ava the huntress. I could love Aretha, whom I barely knew, or Adena, as she led her troops in battle. But this silver-clad goddess was beyond me, and I knew it. Ormazd had been right: a bacterium cannot become a bird; a goddess cannot fall in love with a monkey.

I closed my eyes.

"Keep them closed until you feel the wind against you," her sweet voice told me.

I nodded to show her I understood. Then I felt the softest touch against my cheek. Her fingertips, perhaps. Or perhaps the faintest brush of her lips. I burned for her, but found myself paralyzed. I could not unclench my fists, could not move a step. My eyes would not open even if I willed them to.

"Good-bye, my love," she whispered. But I was unable to answer.

For the briefest instant I remained locked in frozen darkness, deprived of all sensory inputs. I could see nothing, hear nothing, feel nothing.

My hearing returned first. A soft, sighing sound came to me, the whisper of something I had not heard for so long that I thought I had forgotten it: a gentle breeze rustling the leafy limbs of trees.

I felt that breeze on my face, warm, kind, loving. Opening my eyes, I saw that I stood in the midst of a forest of gigantic trees—sequoias, from the looks of them. Their immense boles were wider than a house, and they stretched up toward the blue, cloud-flecked sky like the pillars of a giant's cathedral.

Except for the sighing of the breeze, the forest seemed silent to me. But as I stood there lost in wonder beneath the shade of those gigantic leafy boughs, I began to recognize the sounds of life in the background: bird calls echoing through the forest, the gurgling of a fast-rushing stream off in the distance, the scampering of a small furry creature through the sparse underbrush between the enormous tree trunks.

What a world this was! How Dal and Ava and their clan would have loved it here. Even Subotai and the High Khan, crusty old warriors though they were, would have happily settled themselves here. Everything a man could desire was here—except other people.

I wandered through the forest for hours, picking berries from a bush, drinking from that noisy brook, reveling in the peace and joy of a world untainted by war and killing.

Slowly I began to wonder if Anya had not sent me here to get rid of me as gently as she could. It was a good world, an easy place to live in except for the absence of companions. Was this her way of exiling me, removing me from her presence? A pleasant Coventry? A warm and lovely Siberia? I would live out my solitary existence here in comfort, and when I finally died, I would no longer trouble her. Like putting a pet to sleep when you no longer need or want it.

I shook my head. No, she would not lie to me. She sent me here so that I might understand the whole scheme of things. She placed me here for a reason, not merely to get me out of her way, I told myself. I insisted to myself. I had to believe that. There was nothing else for me to cling to.

The sun was setting behind hills that I could barely make out, far off in the distance, through the stout columns of the trees. The shadows lengthened into dusk, but the air was still warm and fragrant with flowers. I wore a sleeveless shirt and knee-length pants made of hides. My feet were shod with thonged sandals of leather. Yet, even as twilight deepened into night, I did not feel cold. The ground was mossy and soft; I stretched out on it and fell asleep almost at once.

In my dreams I saw this early Earth as a god might see it, as Anya and Ormazd undoubtedly saw it, a beautiful blue sphere set against the cold darkness of unfathomable space, decked with bands and swirls of clouds that gleamed purest white. I recognized the rough outlines of Europe and Africa, the Americas and Asia, set against the glittering deep blue of the oceans. The Atlantic seemed narrower than it should be, and Australia was not yet an island, but this was Earth, clearly enough.

The Arctic was clear of ice, its waters as blue and inviting as those girdling the Equator. Antarctica was dazzling white, though. Nowhere did I see cities, or roads, or the gray domes and sooty plumes of human habitation.

It was an Earth empty of human life, devoid of intelligence—almost.

I awoke feeling physically refreshed, yet puzzled to the point of worry. There had to be people here; if not the human creations of Ormazd, then Ahriman's people. That was why Anya had sent me here: to find them and see them for what they truly were.

I got to my feet, washed in the cold stream and ate a breakfast of berries and eggs. I could not bring myself to kill any of the animals that chattered and called through the echoing forest. I had no tools, no weapons, and no inclination to start making them.

Instead, I began walking along the stream's bank, up the gently rising ground, surrounded by the skyscraper trees that threw dappled patterns of sunlight and shadow across the mossy ground. The stream gurgled and splashed across rocks. On the far side I saw a doe and her two fawns watching me, ears twitching and eyes so big and liquid brown.

"Good morning," I called to them. They did not run away. They merely watched me until, satisfied that I was no threat, they returned to browsing on the shrubbery that grew by the stream's edge.

As I walked further upstream, more deer came into view, stepping carefully on their slim legs, gazing at me with their innocent eyes. There must be predators somewhere nearby, I thought. Yet I had not heard a cat's roar nor the growling and baying of canines during the night.

Although the ground was rising as I walked upstream, the going was quite easy. Undergrowth was sparse, and the ground was covered with green, springy mosses and needles from the trees. More and more groups of deer and smaller animals clustered by the water's edge, where the shrubbery grew more thickly. It almost seemed to me like a park, a deliberately designed game preserve. Built by whom? I wondered. For whom?

By mid-morning I found the answer to those questions.

Birds were chattering and rustling up in the limbs of the giant trees. I looked up and saw them gathering, flocking, birds of every kind and color: brilliant red cardinals, bluebirds, brown sparrows, red-shouldered blackbirds, glossy crows, robins, wrens, birds of yellow and green and white. Hundreds of them, thousands, sitting and jabbering on the branches, swooping back and forth. Not a predator among them. No hawks or falcons, no ravens or eagles.

As I stood among the trees, my head tilted back in amazement, they all became still and quiet. As if expecting something. And then, one by one, they began gliding down from their lofty perches, wings outspread and hardly flapping at all, gliding down toward the ground, and swooping right past me.

I followed their flight with my eyes and saw, off in the distance, where they were heading.

Several men stood in a small clearing among the massive trees, reaching into pouches they wore slung over their shoulders and tossing handfuls of their contents onto the ground.

Human beings! I was staggered. Anya had said there were no humans here, and yet there were three—no, four of them, feeding a forest full of birds!

I approached them slowly, staying in the shadows of the trees, partly to get out of the way of the stream of birds swooping down toward the feeding area, partly because for some instinctive reason I did not want to startle them by revealing myself too soon.

As I came nearer, I saw who they were, and my heart sank. Ahriman's people. The ones that Adena's troopers called the brutes. They did not seem terribly brutal, sprinkling birdseed on the ground around them, letting birds perch on their broad shoulders, laughing as they fed the multihued flocks.

I studied them from the cover of a giant tree trunk. They were Ahriman's people, not my own kind. Broad faces with high cheekbones and thin, almost lipless mouths. Wide, thick, well-muscled torsos. Heavy arms and legs.

Suddenly my insides seemed to go hollow. I realized who they were, what they were. Neanderthals.

I sank to my knees and leaned my head against the smooth bark of the mammoth tree. Neanderthals. The other race of intelligent primates who had lived on Earth during the Ice Ages.

Squeezing my eyes shut to concentrate, I tried to recall what little I knew of twentieth-century anthropology. The Neanderthals were regarded as quite human, and just as intelligent as my own kind of human being. The scientists had named them *Homo sapiens neanderthalensis* as opposed to our own *Homo sapiens sapiens*.

The Neanderthals had evolved out of the four-million-year-long line of primate apes, replacing the earlier hominids such as *Homo erectus*. And then, quite abruptly, the Sapiens appeared—my own line of human beings, the ones whom Ormazd claimed to have created—and the Neanderthals became extinct. No anthropologist could explain why they disappeared; it happened very abruptly, as evolutionary time goes. Before the Age of Ice, Neanderthals were the highest and most widespread primates on Earth. When the glaciers melted, they were gone, and the high-domed, slim-bodied Sapiens were the only intelligent species on the planet.

I knew what had happened. As I knelt there in that primeval forest, the knowledge made me sick.

It can't be, I told myself. There must be more to it than you think. Anya would not have sent you here merely to show you the horror of genocide. Not even Ormazd could be that callous.

I did not want to believe what I knew to be true. I gathered my strength and pulled myself to my feet. There must be something else, something still hidden from me, something that I had yet to learn.

I have always been able to control my body,

down to the most peripheral nerve cell. I have never lacked courage—most probably because I never had the imagination to see, ahead of time, what pain and danger I was facing. Action has always been easier for me than reflection.

Yet the most difficult action I ever had to take was to step out from behind the concealment of that tree and show myself to the four young Neanderthal men who were in the clearing, feeding the flocks of birds.

I took a deep breath, calmed my racing heart, and began walking toward them. They were youngsters, probably no more than teen-agers, their hair dark and full, their faces smooth and unlined. They were laughing and whistling to one another as they tossed birdseed around the mossy ground. One of them was holding out both his hands and half a dozen birds perched on them, pecking at the seeds in his palms.

The birds noticed me before the lads did. With a great swirling, fluttering, flashing of colors they flew off in all directions as I approached. Not a peep out of them; no sound except the beating of frightened wings.

The four young Neanderthals, suddenly alone except for a few drifting feathers, turned to gape at me.

I held up both my hands, palms outward, as I approached.

"I am Orion," I said. "I come in peace."

They glanced at one another, more puzzled than frightened. They made no move to stop me from coming nearer, nor did they seem in any way inclined to run from me. They whistled back and forth among themselves, low, musical sounds not unlike the calls of birds—or the whistling language of dolphins.

I stopped and let my hands fall to my sides. "Do you live nearby?" I asked. "Will you take me to your village?" I knew that they could not understand my words, any more than I could interpret their whistles. But I had to establish at least the beginnings of communication.

The four of them looked me up and down, then walked around me as if I were a clothing display. In utter silence. Yet I had the feeling that they were conversing with one another, without the need for sounds.

They were more than a full head shorter than I, all four of them, although already their barrel chests and powerful arms were much bigger than my own. I felt puny beside them. The tallest one, who almost came up to my chin, grinned at me. There was no hint of fear or distrust in his deep brown eyes. Merely curiosity.

He stared at me in silence for several moments, and I could almost hear the questions in his mind: Who are you? Where do you come from? What are you doing here?"

Like an English tourist, I spoke slowly and loudly in my effort to make him understand. "My name is Orion. Orion." I touched my chest with a forefinger and repeated, "Orion."

"Ho-rye-un," the youngster said, in the same painful whisper that I had heard so often from Ahriman.

"Where is your village?" I asked. "Where do you live?"

No response.

I tried a different tack. "Do you know Ahriman? Where is Ahriman?"

The lad's eyes flicked to his comrades and I could *feel* some form of mental communication vibrating from one to another. *Ahriman* echoed in my mind. *Ahriman*.

After a moment or so, the teen-ager stared into my eyes and frowned in concentration. I concentrated, too, trying to receive whatever mental message he was trying to send. I got nothing but the vaguest impression of the forest around us, big trees and not much else.

With a very human shrug, the lad whistled a few notes to his companions, then gestured for me to come along with him. The five of us started along a well-worn trail that began in that clearing and headed deeper into the woods.

CHAPTER 45

The Neanderthals' "village," it turned out, was in the trees. Not among them, but actually inside the giant boles of those tall, massive sequoias. They had carved out elaborate living quarters for themselves, high above the ground, with long ladders made of vines hanging inside the trunks and leading up to their rooms. The broad, sturdy branches that radiated outward some forty or fifty feet above the ground served as patios and verandas for these dwellings.

At first I thought that their technology was pitifully limited. I could see nothing more sophisticated than stone axes and chisels, and smaller tools made of flint or quartz. But they had fire; they had as much intelligence as an Einstein or a Buddha, and they had a form of mental telepathy that allowed them to live in harmony with the world of animals and plants around them.

Where we Sapiens invent a machine to do work that our arms are not strong enough to do, the Neanderthals tamed, trained, or developed an animal or plant. The vine ladders that they scampered up and down on were one example. They were living, growing vines, with roots imbedded in the soil and broad green leaves spreading in the sunlight along the high branches of the giant trees.

They did not hunt, nor did they farm. They had no need of either. They were gatherers, in the ultimate sense. They *controlled* herds of animals mentally, and led the oldest and weakest to their ritual deaths by some form of telepathic inducement. They kept pets such as dogs, but even there the link between Neanderthal and dog was a mental one.

They had no spoken language; their throats were not built for speech. They communicated among themselves by an elaborate combination of telepathy, whistling, and gestures. I tried as hard as I could, and after several weeks of living among them, I began to be able to make a crude, tentative form of mental contact. The ability was built into my brain, as it was built into theirs by evolution, but it would take a long period of training before I could communicate as easily as their babies did.

The Neanderthals had no fear of strangers. Warfare and conflict were virtually unknown to them. At first I thought that might be because their telepathic abilities made it impossible to attack someone without his sensing it beforehand and being prepared to retaliate. I was wrong, although I had been on the right track.

They were peaceful because their telepathic abilities allowed them to *understand* each other much more thoroughly than speech permits true understanding. It was not that they constantly read each others' minds, I gradually learned. But the Neanderthals were trained from birth to communicate their feelings, their emotions, as well as rational thoughts and ideas. When a Neanderthal was angry or upset or afraid, everyone around him knew of it instantly, and they all did their best to get to the cause of the problem and solve it. Similarly, when a Neanderthal was happy, everyone knew it and shared in the joy.

How alone we Sapiens are! Locked inside our skulls with our individual personalities, we make feeble attempts at communication through speech, where the Neanderthals shared their thoughts as naturally as warmth flows from a fire. There were no psychotherapists among them—or, rather, they were all psychologists.

They were a gentle people, in spite of their powerful muscular bodies. Their innocent brown eyes reminded me of the doe and fawns I had seen my first day in this time. They did not, probably could not, dissemble. Even their method of slaughtering the weakest members of their herds was so gentle that the word slaughter hardly applies: they merely exerted enough mental control over the animal to stop its heart. The animal collapsed and died within moments, painlessly.

The days lengthened into weeks as I dwelled among them, living with the family of the tallest teenager of the four who had first encountered me. Their home, like all the others', was some forty feet above the ground, inside a sturdy sequoia. The family consisted of the parents, Tohon and his wife Huyana, their son Tunu, and their daughter, Yoki, who was about five or six years old. They had accepted me as a guest, after the whole village—some hundred or so people—gathered in a clearing at the base of "their" trees to discuss what they should do with me.

It was an eerie, unsettling feeling to be standing in the midst of all these Neanderthals, knowing that they were talking about me, but unable to hear a word. Except for a few whistles and an occasional wave of a hand or shake of a head, the discussion was carried out in complete silence.

I could not listen to them, so, instead, I studied their faces. They were not at all like the shambling, beetle-browed savages that twentieth-century Sapients depicted the Neanderthals to be. Their faces were broader than mine, their brows heavier, their chins less prominent, but the totality of their facial features were not all that different from my own. They were no hairier than I was. The men's faces were beardless, and I learned after several painful attempts at shaving with a flint knife that the Neanderthals removed facial hair with an ointment they obtained from the leaves of a shrub.

Apparently they decided that I would live among them, and Tunu's father accepted the obligation—or, for all I knew then, they might have considered it an honor.

I saw that very first day how they managed to carve living quarters out of the tree trunks. After Tunu painfully introduced himself and his family to me, pointing to each in turn and carefully pronouncing each name several times in his labored, dry whisper, his father led me to their home.

I followed Tohon up the sturdy ladder of vines to their main room, a spacious womb-like chamber set in the living wood, with a round window on one side and an open doorway that led out onto a branch that was broad enough to allow all five of us to stand on its flattened surface at the same time. Their furniture consisted of stools and table-like things that looked oddly out of place, yet strangely familiar. Then I realized that they were actually giant mushrooms, toadstools, that had been shaped to serve the Neanderthals. It was then that I began to understand that they altered the world around them, vegetable as well as animal, to suit their needs.

Tohon took me out on that broad, green veranda and showed me how they enlarged their living quarters to make room for a guest. He sent Tunu scampering out along the big branch toward a smaller limb where thick clusters of needles grew. The lad came back with a wooden bowl filled with a thick, syrupy liquid that must have been some form of tree sap.

I followed Tohon inside and watched him begin to paint the sap onto the wall of their main room. It smelled of pine resin, but stronger. Off to one

side, I could see Huyana and Yoki silently studying an array of herbs and leaves that they had
spread across the floor: a lesson in botany, or more
likely, nutrition.

And all this was being done in nearly total silence.
I had never realized how much we Sapients take
for granted our constant chattering. Noise is our
companion from our first birth cries to our last
dying words. The Neanderthals lived in a world of
quiet, broken only by the natural sounds of wind
and rustling leaf, of bird song and animal call. As
the time went on and I grew accustomed to this
hushed way of life, I began to wonder if the
Neanderthals' lack of violence was associated with
their lack of noisemaking equipment.

As I stood watching Tohon's handiwork, that
first day, I could feel my eyes widening with surprise as the liquid he smeared onto the curved
wall of the room began to eat into the wood. At
first it etched the smooth surface of the wall slowly,
giving off the faintest hissing sound and a slightly
acrid smell. Then the wood seemed to dissolve; it
just began to melt away.

Tunu grinned at me, his nearly lipless mouth
pulling back to show a wide expanse of gleaming
teeth. I must have looked very surprised; I'm sure
my jaw was hanging open.

Tohon gestured urgently to his grinning son, and
the two of them began smearing the syrupy liquid
with great vigor against the sides and back of the
niche that had just been created. Why the stuff
melted away the wood and yet seemed to have no
effect at all on their bare hands, as they stuck
them into the bowl and spread the liquid against
the wood, was a mystery to me.

Within a few minutes Tohon seemed satisfied
with their work. Tunu took the nearly empty bowl
back out along the branch while his father sat

cross-legged on the floor and gestured to me to sit beside him.

Huyana served a meal of boiled vegetables and fresh fruit. Their kitchen, I soon found out, was a level below this main room. By the time we finished eating, the acidic sap had done its work, and there was a small but comfortable room for me, literally eroded out of the living wood of the tree trunk, connected to the main room by a short corridor that curved so that my room could not be seen from the main room. No need for doors; privacy was maintained by geometrical arrangement.

Tohon inspected the new room, and for a moment seemed somewhat agitated. Without moving or making a sound, he wrinkled his heavy brow in concentration. Tunu came back with the bowl and wordlessly painted a small round window for me. Tohon nodded, satisfied that the job was completed.

I thought that they had forgotten about my asking for Ahriman, that first day. As the weeks rolled leisurely by and I became accustomed to this almost silent life among the Neanderthals, I nearly forgot about him myself. I spent most of my time trying to learn how to communicate with them, mentally, and gradually I began to get the hang of "speaking" without making sounds. My abilities were ludicrously poor, but I found that some of the Neanderthals were better communicators than others. Tunu, the grinning, cheerful teen-ager, was the easiest for me to converse with. So were many of the other youngsters. I had more trouble with the adults, perhaps because they were more withdrawn and circumspect. And the Neanderthal women, even little Yoki, were virtually a complete blank to me, as far as telepathic communication was concerned. I was certain that this was by intent; well enough for the men to converse with this spindly stranger, but the women decided they would keep their distance, physically and mentally.

Not that Huyana or any of the other Neanderthals, of whatever age or gender, were anything but unfailingly kind and courteous to me. The women merely stayed beyond my reach, as far as communication of any sort was concerned.

At night, as I lay stretched out sleeplessly on a bed of spongy moss, I wondered what Anya was doing and why she had sent me here and how long she would keep me among the Neanderthals. I began to form paranoid fears in my head: Ormazd had decided to keep me here permanently, even though Anya wanted to bring me back to her. Or worse yet, the two of them had agreed to keep me in this sylvan exile; they were laughing at me, alone and helpless among people I could not even speak to.

I thought about Ahriman, and how Ormazd intended to keep him imprisoned in that shell of energy, alive in a timeless stasis, but trapped, smothered, helpless. Ormazd was doing the same thing to me, I knew it. And there was nothing I could do about it. Not a thing. Each night I searched every molecule of my mind for a way to escape this idyllic prison, and each dawn I admitted defeat. There was no escape. Not unless, or until, either Anya or Ormazd decided to allow me to return.

I began to lose track of the days. They were all pretty much the same. A heaven of peace and plenty, without anger, without murder, without war. Yet I could not accept it; I could not rest content.

Then one morning, after I had climbed down the vine ladder from Tohon's dwelling and stepped out onto the open ground, Tunu came running up to me, breathless with excitement.

"Ahriman!" he gasped aloud.

I blinked with surprise. "Ahriman?" I asked. "He's coming here?"

Tunu bobbed his head up and down. "Yes, he is

coming up the trail." I was so excited that I did not realize he was speaking telepathically and I was understanding him clearly.

He gestured for me to follow him. I saw that the whole village was pouring out of their tree homes and gathering in the clearing, jostling one another slightly, low whistles flicking back and forth, staring expectantly down the trail. I picked up enough of their telepathic vibrations to understand that they were all quite excited. Ahriman was one of their greatest leaders, a man of high intelligence and accomplishment, a poet and philosopher whose fame was known wherever the Neanderthals lived.

It can't be the same Ahriman that I have known, I told myself. The mental image I was getting from the crowd was very different from the dark, tormented, angry, vengeful Ahriman that I knew.

But when I saw him, walking on the trail, smiling at the crowd that had gathered to greet him, I saw that it was indeed the same man.

Ahriman. A younger Ahriman than the one I had known, but unmistakably the same one. Taller than any of the other Neanderthals, more powerful in physique, his eyes held the intelligence that I had seen in them in other ages. But they were not yet the reddened, hate-filled eyes of the Ahriman who sought to destroy the continuum. This was the face of a man in his prime, happy with life, content with his environment and his place in it. He had not learned to hate. He had no need for vengeance—not yet.

The crowd gathered around Ahriman as he strode the final yards toward the center of the clearing. I could not make out specific words or meanings from their mental chatter, but I felt an urging from them, a pleading for him to do something—I did not know what—that would please them.

He smiled and nodded his assent. The crowd

immediately sat down on the ground, excited, anticipating. I remained standing.

Ahriman's eyes met mine. His smile did not change. His eyes betrayed no hint of anger or enmity. Nor surprise. Obviously, the others had already told him that there was a stranger in their midst. They must have told him my name as well. And, just as obviously, my name, my appearance, my presence meant nothing to him. He was not afraid of me. He was not enraged. The only emotion I caught from him was a gentle curiosity.

Slowly I sat, too, between Tunu and another teen-aged boy. I closed my eyes and concentrated as hard as I could to catch whatever it was that Ahriman was going to say, telepathically.

There was no need for me to work so hard. He was the most powerful telepathic "voice" I had encountered. I could understand him with almost no effort at all.

He sang.

Not with words or musical sounds as we Sapients use. Ahriman sang with thoughts, mental conceptions that released colors, shapes, memories, impressions in my mind. My eyes flew open and still my head filled with beauty and harmony that I had never known before. I could see the Neanderthals around me, staring blankly, enraptured by the beginning of Ahriman's song.

I closed my eyes once again, but this time it was only to shut out the conflicting view of the world around me, so that I might share more fully the vision that Ahriman was projecting directly into my mind.

It was a song, a poem, a speculation, a history, a report—all in one. I saw the many places that Ahriman had traveled through since the last time he had been to this village. I realized that he was a wanderer, a nomad who linked the scattered settlements of the Neanderthals the way we Sapients eventually learned to link our communities with electronic circuitry.

I saw all the other Neanderthal villages, in ice cliffs far to the north, along balmy seashores, huts built of mud and straw clustered together in the open treeless steppes. I felt the oneness of all these communities, the linkage among their men and women, the common bonds of blood and affection that they all shared. And Ahriman showed us more; he began to tell us of his own thoughts, the ideas and questions that filled his mind when he gazed up at the star-filled night sky. He showed us the harmony of the stars, the rhythms of the planets as they swept among the fixed points of nighttime fire, the glory of the sun as it was created out of cold dust and gained its strength by bringing all the myriad motes together into one fiery, loving embrace.

Ahriman took us among the stars and helped us to wander in realms of breathless beauty. Then, slowly, with enormous reverence and gentleness, he brought us back to Earth, to this clearing in the forest, to this moment in time.

I saw, as I opened my eyes, that Neanderthals cannot weep. But the tears were streaming down my cheeks as Ahriman ended his song.

CHAPTER 46

The Neanderthals did not applaud. Such noise-making was not their way. But I, with my dim telepathic ability, could sense the enormous wave of approbation and thanks that swept through the gathered villagers. A few low whistles and grunting mutters accompanied the telepathic appreciation. Ahriman nodded a few times, accepting their approval. Then the crowd broke up and everyone went back to their business.

I got to my feet, after wiping away the tears that had blurred my vision.

"You are Orion," Ahriman said, silently.

We were alone in the clearing now. All the others had dispersed. He looked at me without any emotion except curiosity. He had never seen me before this day. I was the one with the memories, not him. I recalled how I felt when I had first met him, in that chamber he had created deep underground in the twentieth century. How confused I had been then; he had known everything, and I, nothing. Now I knew of all our encounters, The War and its aftermath, and he was as innocent as a newborn. Yet I still felt confused, uncertain.

"I enjoyed your song," I said, aloud, knowing that he could understand the meaning of my sounds.

"Thank you."

I wondered what I should say next. I wondered how deeply into my mind he could probe. The other Neanderthals had apparently been unable to read my thoughts, my memories. It had been difficult enough for me merely to communicate ordinary conversation to them. But Ahriman's powers of telepathy were many times greater.

"Where are you from?" he asked, and I felt genuine concern. Either he could not search my mind or he was too polite to try.

"Far from here," I answered. Then I added, "Farther in time than in distance. I come from the future, from thousands of years in the future."

His heavy brow knitted with puzzlement. "The future?"

"You can see that I am not one of your kind."

"That is true."

"I came into being more than a hundred thousand years from now, and have been sent to this time."

I caught a vague, fleeting thought to the effect that I must be insane, but it passed quickly.

"It is quite true," I said. "I don't know how it is done, but I have been sent to this time and place."

"Sent by whom? For what purpose?"

Ignoring that, I went on, "Somehow you will learn how to transport yourself through time and space. We will meet many times, in different eras . . ."

"I will travel into the future?" He seemed genuinely fascinated by the possibility.

"Yes."

"With you?"

With a shake of my head, "We will not travel together, not as companions. But we will meet in the future, time and again."

His heavy-featured face broke into a wide smile. "Travel into the future! Can time be bent and turned the way a man can knot a length of vine?"

"Ahriman!" I had to tell him. "In that future—in those times to come—we will be enemies."

His smile vanished. "What? How can . . ."

"Whenever we meet in the future, I will try to kill you. And you will try to kill me."

"That's impossible." And I could feel that he really meant it. The thought of violence was so repugnant to him that I shared the shuddering revulsion he unconsciously broadcast.

"I wish it were impossible," I said, "but it has already happened. Many times. We have met; we have fought. More than once, you have killed me."

He stared into my eyes. In my mind I felt the gentlest questioning touch. I nodded and relaxed and allowed him to see what I had experienced: The War, the flood in the Neolithic, the barbaric splendor of Karakorum, the technological glory of the fusion reactor.

"No," Ahriman whispered, in that labored, tortured, rasping voice that I had come to know so well. "No . . ."

He trembled. This mighty hulk of a Neanderthal shook from head to toes, so repulsed and sickened was he by the scenes he saw in my mind. I heard his thoughts just as easily as if he were blaring at me through an electric bullhorn:

"It can't be . . . that can't be me . . . not me . . . he's mad, his mind sick and perverted . . . no one could possibly . . . the killing, the sick, sadistic horror . . . not me. Not me!"

Ahriman turned his back to me and walked rapidly, almost ran, away from the clearing where I stood.

I closed my eyes and tried to clamp down on my thoughts. When I looked again, Ahriman was nowhere in sight, but several of the Neanderthals—men and older boys—stood around the edge of the clearing, staring at me with troubled eyes. Had they caught my thoughts, or Ahriman's reaction to them? What would they do to me if they knew that I was created to kill the best man among them?

Slowly, reluctantly, I returned to Tohon's house.

Tunu was at the base of the tree, conversing with a few of his friends. He gave me the same cheerful smile as always, and with a few gestures told me that his father was down by the stream, where the fruit trees grew, gathering food for the feast that would honor Ahriman tonight.

I nodded my understanding, then climbed up the vine ladder to the house. Huyana was humming softly to herself as she cooked a spicy-smelling brew over the small fire in the kitchen. The pot was a tough, hollow gourd, larger than any I had ever known to grow naturally. The fire pit was a hollow in the kitchen floor, lined with flat stones and ventilated through a narrow shaft overhead.

Exhausted mentally and disgusted with myself, I barely nodded hello to Huyana. On rubbery legs I made my way through the short curving corridor to my own room and threw myself onto the spongy moss of my bed.

I awoke to Tunu's gentle shaking. He gave me a quick skirling whistle and pointed to my window. It was almost dark.

"The feast," Tunu said wordlessly.

I wondered if Ahriman would show up for the celebration in his honor, or had the terrifying visions I had shown him driven him away?

He was there, sitting cross-legged among the elders of the village as I arrived. The big ceremonial bonfire in the middle of the clearing bathed everything in a hot red flickering light. The massive trunks of the giant trees ringed us like the pillars of temples yet to be built, throwing their shadows back into the forest so that the clearing was a circle of light set in the midst of utter darkness.

Unconsciously I had expected drumbeats, music, dancing figures leaping against the lurid light of the huge fire. Instead the Neanderthals were quiet, almost silent, except for a background murmur of mumbles and grunts and occasional low whistles.

In their minds, though, they were laughing and chattering back and forth, exchanging stories, singing happily. I could catch the edges of their communications, like a man with a weak radio receiver catching fragments of broadcasts from a hundred different stations as he turns the dial.

But when I tuned in to Ahriman, I got nothing but a vast and dark silence. I studied his face as he sat there in the firelight. He was as impassive as a statue made of granite. The elders on either side of him did not seem troubled, though. They respected his need for silence and privacy, I understood; they expected him to favor us with another song later in the night.

The bonfire was strictly ceremonial. All the food had been prepared by the women in their individual kitchens. There was no roast venison, no suckling pigs on spits, no tales of bravery and cunning in the hunt. Instead, the Neanderthals ate mostly vegetables and eggs, nuts and berries, and drank fruit juices or clear water brought cold from the stream by the best runners among the youngsters. The little meat they had, which came from the animals they culled from their herds, was offered as a delicacy, a special treat in honor of their guest.

Ahriman gazed at me from his place among the elders. I sat with Tohon and his family, a dozen yards away in the arc of Neanderthals who half-circled the bonfire. I felt the heat from the flames on my face, and I began to sweat—but it was not entirely because of the hot fire.

Through the meal I caught fragments of conversations, back and forth, but nothing from Ahriman. Yet, every time I looked his way, his eyes were on me. The expression on his face was more than somber: it had the pall of death upon it. He had made up his mind about me. He knew that I was not insane, that I had told him the truth. The question now was, what would he do about it?

Finally, when everyone had had enough to eat, the murmuring rose and they all turned toward Ahriman. In my mind I heard them asking, pleading, for another song. For many minutes he merely sat there, his head bowed, as if trying to avoid their demand. But they merely begged harder, even though it was all done in almost total silence. The mental chorus grew stronger, moment by moment; the villagers were not going to allow Ahriman to leave without performing again.

He raised his head at last, and their silent importuning stopped as abruptly as if it had been chopped off with a guillotine. Ahriman looked at me bleakly, then slowly, painfully got to his feet.

The villagers drew in a collective breath of anticipation. For many of them, it was the last breath they ever took.

A pencil-thin red beam from a laser rifle lanced out of the darkness among the trees past Ahriman's head. He threw his arms across his face and jumped sideways. More laser bolts flashed out from the trees, and I heard the yelling roar of attacking soldiers—Sapients—and saw their white-armored forms rushing toward the clearing.

They were firing pointblank into the Neanderthals, their beams ripping men, women, and children apart the way a honed razor would slice through a rag doll.

I learned that Neanderthals can scream. Pain and terror brings out the same wild animal screeches from them that it does from us.

There were only a dozen or so Sapient soldiers, but they were armed with laser rifles. The Neanderthals scrambled to their feet and ran in all directions, as those searing red beams slashed them apart. Tohon reached for his daughter as a soldier turned his visored, helmeted head toward us. He

hesitated an instant, no doubt stunned to find a
fellow Sapient among the brutes he had come to
slaughter. I was empty-handed and, worse, my
mind was a blank, too. I did not know what to do,
where to turn.

Tohon began running with Yoki in his arms. The
soldier snapped out of his hesitation. He gunned
them both down. Their bodies sprawled to the
ground, spurting blood.

"No!" I screamed. "Stop!" I waved my arms and
ran toward the soldier, yelling and ranting like a
maniac. He tried to step aside and get a clear shot
at Huyana, who stood paralyzed beside the dead
bodies of her husband and daughter. I grabbed for
his rifle, and as he tried to pull it back from me,
Tunu leaped at the soldier and knocked him off his
feet.

I took the rifle as Tunu, his eyes wide and blazing with new-found hate, seized a rock in his two
hands and smashed it down on the soldier's helmet.
The plastic armor dented, then cracked, as Tunu
pounded at it again and again. Blood oozed from
the smashed visor and the trooper went rigid and
inert.

I wheeled about and saw the carnage that the
soldiers had created. Neanderthals lay sprawled
grotesquely everywhere; the survivors were running toward the relative safety of the trees and
darkness. The fire burned hot, casting glinting high-
lights off the white armor of the soldiers. I held a
laser rifle in my hands, my finger curled around
its trigger.

Yet I could not fire it. I could not shoot at those
troopers. Behind those featureless visors might be
Marek, or Lissa, or even Adena. I could not fire at
them, even to save the defenseless Neanderthals.

Or were they defenseless? One of the troopers
was on the ground, a pair of savage dogs viciously
snapping at him. Ahriman had grabbed another

from behind, pinning his arms to his sides with a mighty bearhug, while another Neanderthal ripped off the soldier's helmet and choked the life out of him. Then Ahriman took up the soldier's rifle and began firing at the other troopers.

The Sapients scattered into the shadows of the trees and disappeared as quickly as they had come. For several eternally long minutes we simply stood there, panting with fear and anger. I counted thirty-eight dead, their blood soaking the ground. Tossing the rifle away, I leaned down and took the smashed helmet off the trooper who lay dead at my feet. Her hair billowed out, blonde, matted with her own blood.

Tunu knelt at her side, his mind a keening, shuddering wail of grief and agony. I could not find Huyana at first; then I recognized her body, sliced neatly in two by a laser beam, at the edge of the clearing.

Ahriman strode through the field of dead, a rifle in one mighty hand, until he stood face-to-face with me. His eyes were red with pain.

"Your people, Orion," he said, in his tortured whisper. "Why?"

I had no answer. There was nothing that I could say or do. I turned away from him, away from the carnage, and began walking into the darkness of the forest.

CHAPTER 47

The black night engulfed me completely. With each step I grew colder, shuddering with the horror within me. The forest was absolutely silent—not an owl's hoot, not a cricket's chirp. Nothing but silence, darkness, and cold.

I have no idea of how long I walked, alone, heading nowhere. I could not return to the village, to the accusing faces of the Neanderthals. I could not bear to see Ahriman, to watch him learn how to hate, how to kill, how to make vengeance the only thing he lived for.

I thought it was dawn, when I first saw the light glimmering up ahead of me. But as I walked toward it, miserable with remorse, I saw that the trees were fading away, literally disappearing, and the light was a golden, sourceless radiance that illuminated a flat, featureless expanse that stretched in all directions toward infinity.

In the distance I saw a lone figure standing, waiting for me, clad in gleaming silver. It was Anya, I knew. I walked steadily toward her, unable to quicken my step, unwilling to hasten the final moment.

As I approached, I saw another figure, darkly brooding: Ahriman, still encased in his prison of energy, his eyes blazing fury at me. He looked much older than the Ahriman I had just met. Hatred and pain had aged him more than time ever could.

I searched Anya's face as I came up to her. I saw the sadness of eternity in her luminous eyes.

"Now you know," Anya said to me.

Nodding, I replied, "I know everything except the most important answer of all—why?"

"For that you must ask Ormazd."

"Where is he?"

She made a little shrug and smiled joylessly. "He is here; he can see us and hear us."

"But he's too ashamed to show himself, is that it?"

Anya looked almost startled. "Ashamed? Him?"

I lifted my head to the blank golden dome that shone above us. "Present yourself, Ormazd! It's time for the final reckoning. Show your face, murderer!"

The emptiness seemed to gather in on itself, to contract into a golden bubble, a sphere of gleaming radiance that floated down toward us.

"I am here," said a voice from that globe.

"In human form," I demanded. "I want to see a face; I want to be able to watch your expression."

"You presume much, Orion," said the golden sphere.

"I've served you well enough. I deserve a little consideration."

The sphere shimmered and faded into nothingness, leaving the tall, golden form of Ormazd standing before us. His smile was part amusement, part tolerance of a lower creature's insolence.

"Does that please you, Orion?" he asked.

I glanced at Anya. There was nothing in her face but fear.

"Why?" I asked Ormazd. "Why slaughter the Neanderthals? They were harmless . . ."

"Precisely so. Harmless. Inoffensive. Beautifully

adapted to their environment." He spread his hands in an ancient gesture of resignation.

"Then why destroy them? Why start The War?"

"Because they were an evolutionary dead end, Orion. They would never progress beyond the stage in which you found them."

"How can you know that?"

He laughed at me. "Orion, pitiful creature. I know! I have examined all the possible paths of the continuum. The Neanderthals would live their idyllic existence for their allotted time, and then be snuffed out like the dinosaurs were."

Ahriman's face was contorted with agony. He could hear what we were saying, even though he could not move a muscle to reach us.

"Believe me, Orion," Ormazd went on, "I examined every possibility. I even transplanted some of the Neanderthals to a different planet, to see if they would evolve at a more efficient rate. The differences were negligible."

"But that doesn't justify . . . killing them!"

"Doesn't it?" he snapped. "They would all die anyway, Orion. Sooner or later, the blind forces of nature would have wiped them out. I merely substituted a *directed* force. I hastened their demise. I helped them out of their misery. More efficiently than nature would have done."

"They weren't in misery."

Ormazd gave me a coy grin. "Orion, allow me a metaphor, please!"

"Who gave you the right to perform genocide?" I demanded. "Who made you the giver of life and death?"

He raised a hand, and the golden radiance around us darkened and sparked with jagged bolts of lightning.

"I have the power," he said, his voice thundering. "That gives me the right."

Anya put up both her hands and the lightnings vanished. The featureless golden expanse re-formed itself.

Ormazd made a little bow to her. "Of course, others have some power, also. Not as much as mine, but enough to do a few simple tricks."

Anya looked from him to me. "Ask him why he decided to eliminate the Neanderthals, Orion. Don't let him mislead you. Ask him why he did it."

"Yes," I agreed. "I want to know why."

"Because I chose to."

"That's no answer," I insisted.

"Your scientists argued about evolution for more than a century," Ormazd said. "Well, I am evolution, Orion. I direct the comings and goings on your little world."

I glanced at Anya; she gave me a small nod of encouragement.

Ormazd was not finished. "Take a promising little planet called Earth. It is populated by a race of bright, two-legged creatures. They can communicate with each other directly, mind to mind. They can control the lower animals around them and the plants. They have adapted themselves perfectly to their environment. Dull, Orion. Very dull and pointless. They will never progress."

"Why do they have to . . ."

He ignored me and continued. "So I wipe the slate clean. It may seem cruel, but it is necessary. I create a race of warriors, soldiers, to do the bloody work of eliminating the natives. You are of that race, Orion. You—all of you Sapients—were designed for killing. You all take delight in it; when you can't find a reason to kill each other, you go out and slaughter the helpless beasts around you. Mighty hunters, Orion, all of you."

I remembered how easily, how callously I had killed others of my own kind. And the hunts, where we had covered ourselves with the blood of helpless animals. I trembled with shame, and with anger at the god who made us this way.

"So I set you to the work of eliminating the Neanderthals. I had others of your kind build vast machines on a world you call Titan, a moon of Saturn, machines that can alter the output of the Sun enough to cause Ice Ages on Earth. The glaciers finish the job of scouring the planet clean of its natives—and of the murderous creatures whom I created."

"But that's not the way it happened."

"No, Orion, it isn't." He seemed amused by it all. "You helped them to survive. You showed that final little squad of bloodthirsty warriors how to live on Earth. Instead of a self-destructing army of killers, I got a self-perpetuating race of *Homo sapiens sapiens*. Thanks to you, Orion."

"We were supposed to die in the Ice Age." The knowledge hollowed out my insides, made me feel as if I were falling from heaven to hell.

"Yes. Of course. I was going to create a truly superior race! You can't even imagine the creatures that I would have fathered. Not in your most ecstatic dreams! The angels that your kind fantasize about are *nothing* compared to what I would have created!"

Anya interrupted his ranting with a voice as cool and hard as silver. "But the Sapiens lived, and took over the Earth. And you made such excellent warriors of them that you could not dislodge them."

"Yes," Ormazd admitted, glaring at me. "And at the same time I became aware that *this* one—" he tilted his golden-maned head toward Ahriman's dark, imprisoned form—"had survived the slaughter and somehow gained powers almost equal to my own."

"So you created me," I realized.

"I created you to hunt down Ahriman before he found the way to destroy all that I had built. Yes, I created you—too well."

My head was spinning. "But if you knew all this, if you could examine all the pathways of the continuum and foresaw what would happen . . ."

"Linear thinking, Orion," said Anya. "Events happen in parallel, not in sequence. What you experience as time, as a progression from past through present into future, is really all happening simultaneously. Cause and effect are interchangeable, Orion. Tomorrow and yesterday co-exist."

"I still don't understand . . ."

"It's not necessary for you to understand," Ormazd said. "In your own stumbling way, you *have* done what I wanted done. Ahriman is trapped here, forever. The continuum is safe."

"You are safe," Anya said to him.

"And you," he countered.

She turned to me again. "You still have not found out why he has done all this, Orion. He constantly outwits you about the ultimate question."

I felt utterly helpless.

"Shall I tell him?" she asked Ormazd.

He folded his arms across his chest. "You will, no matter what I say."

Anya's smile was bitter, rueful. "Orion, he created you—he created what you call the human race and used it to destroy the Neanderthals, because without the humans, we gods would never have come into being."

I heard her words, but the meaning was just as opaque to me as if she had said nothing.

"Ormazd saw that the Neanderthals would eventually die away, leaving nothing. So he created the Sapients to eliminate them, to scour the Earth clean and prepare the way for a new race . . ."

"Better than angels," I mumbled.

"But what actually has happened," she went on, "is that you humans learned how to manipulate your own evolution, learned how to engineer the genes of your cells. You took control of your own destiny and eventually, after many millennia, you metamorphosed into—us."

"We became gods?"

"You evolved into creatures such as we are," Anya said. "Creatures of pure energy, who can control and manipulate that energy to take whatever form we wish. Creatures who understand the innermost workings of the continuum, who can move through time and space as easily as you walk through a forest."

I turned back to Ormazd. "We became you."

He frowned at the two of us.

"We *created* you!" I shouted.

"Now you understand why Ormazd determined to destroy the Neanderthals. If they lived, if you humans had never been created, we ourselves would never have come into existence."

"But you *do* exist!"

"Yes, and we are bound by the same inexorable rules that bind all the continuum. Ormazd had to do what he did; otherwise, this continuum, this universe, would collapse and perish."

They could both see the utter confusion that had my mind reeling. Past and future, life and death—it was all a vast dizzying whirl, the entire universe spinning wildly, galaxies forming like eddies in a swift stream, spawning stars and planets and creatures who struggle and die . . .

"It is the truth, Orion." Anya's calm voice cut through my agitation.

"You can see the necessity of it," said Ormazd.

"The Neanderthals had to die so that we could live, and evolve into you."

Ormazd nodded grimly. "That is not the way I

had planned it, at first. But it worked out well enough."

I could not look at Ahriman, not now. Instead, I asked Ormazd, "And what is to become of me?"

His expression lightened. He almost smiled at me, like a benign, generous creator. "I will grant you the gift of life, Orion. A full, rich, human lifespan in any era you choose."

"And then death."

His brows arched. "If you choose the right era, a human lifespan can be very long indeed. Centuries."

"And you?" I asked Anya.

Before she could reply, Ormazd said, "We have evolved out of humankind, Orion. We are not human, any more than you are a hominid ape."

"So I would live on Earth without you," I said to her.

"I can give you more than one lifetime," Ormazd said. "You can live for thousands of years, if you desire to."

My heart felt like a stone sinking to the bottom of the deepest ocean trench. "One lifetime or many—without you, Anya, what good is it?"

She took a step toward me, held out her hand.

But I turned toward Ahriman, glowering helplessly in his eternal prison. "For this I helped to annihilate his entire race. For this I've led him into this living hell."

"You saved your own race," Ormazd said.

"I saved *you*, and your kind." Turning to Anya again, I said, "Free him! Use the power you have to set him free."

She gaped at me.

"What are you saying?" Ormazd cried.

"Let Ahriman go free," I said. "Kill me if I've outlived my usefulness, but give him back his life, his people."

"Never!" Ormazd snapped.

But I was pleading to Anya. "Even if it means the end of everything, do it! Free him! Let him and his people have their time on Earth. Let him live."

"That would mean the destruction of us all!" Ormazd roared. "I won't allow it!"

"If we can't live together," I said to Anya, "then let us die together."

Her gray eyes struck sparks off my soul. She looked from me to Ormazd, and then turned to Ahriman.

"No! Don't!" Ormazd screamed. "Telepathy . . . he knows all that *we* know, now. He has seen what's in our minds; he has taken in our knowledge of the continuum!"

"Yes," Anya said. "He has."

"He'll use that knowledge to rip the continuum apart!" Ormazd's voice was a frenzied shriek. His image was wavering, shimmering.

"Orion is right," Anya replied, as calmly as if she were discussing abstract philosophy. "Ahriman's people deserve their moment of life. We have existed long enough."

"I won't let you!" Ormazd bellowed. He became a shining globe of golden radiance again, but Anya remained in her human form and stretched her hands out toward Ahriman.

Lightning flashed blindingly. I heard Ormazd's voice roaring as I squeezed my eyes shut and felt my flesh bubbling from the tremendous energy flow being released. The radiance burned through my closed lids, boiled my eyes away, seared so deeply into my brain that I sensed nothing but flaming hot light as the very atoms of my body exploded into showers of ephemeral bursts of energy.

Without eyes, without body, I could see the continuum collapsing in on itself, all the material and energy of the whole universe rushing together in one titanic, dark whirlpool of space-time, a convoluted, multidimensional black hole into which planets, stars, galaxies were sucked in, flayed, dismembered and digested into a primeval fireball.

And then it all exploded in a soundless, measureless spasm of new creation.

EPILOGUE A

I am not superhuman.

I do have abilities that are far beyond those of any normal man's, but I am just as human and mortal as anyone of Earth.

Yet I am a solitary man. My life has been spent alone, my mind clouded with strange dreams and, when I am awake, half memories of other lives, other existences, that are so fantastic that they can only be the compensations of a lonely, withdrawn subconscious mind.

As I did almost every day, I took my lunch hour late in the afternoon and made my way from my office to the same small restaurant in which I ate almost every day. Alone. I sat at my usual table, toying with my food and thinking about how much of my life is spent in solitude.

I happened to look up toward the front entrance of the restaurant when she came in—stunningly beautiful, tall and graceful, hair the color of midnight and lustrous gray eyes that held all of eternity in them.

"Anya," I breathed to myself, even though I had no idea who she was. Yet something within me leaped with joy, as if I had known her from ages ago.

She seemed to know me as well. Smiling, she made her way directly to my table. I got up from my chair, feeling elated and confused at the same time.

"Orion." She extended her hand.

I took it in mine, and bent over to kiss it. Then I held a chair out for her to sit. The waiter came over and she asked for a glass of red wine. He trundled off to the bar.

"I feel as if I've known you all my life," I said to her.

"For many lifetimes," she said, her voice softly feminine. "Don't you remember?"

I closed my eyes in concentration and a swirl of memories rushed in on me so rapidly that it took my breath away. I saw a great shining globe of golden light, and the dark brooding figure of a fiercely malevolent man, a forest of giant trees and a barren, windswept desert and a world of unending ice and snow. And her, this woman, clad in silver armor that gleamed against the darkness of infinity.

"I . . . remember . . . death," I heard myself stammer. "The whole world, the entire universe . . . all of space-time collapsed in on itself."

She nodded gravely. "And rebounded in a new cycle of expansion. That was something that neither Ormazd nor Ahriman foresaw. The continuum does not end; it begins anew."

"Ormazd," I muttered. "Ahriman." The names touched a chord in my mind. I felt anger welling up inside me, anger tinged with fear and resentment. But I could not recall who they were and why they stirred such strong emotions within me.

"They are still out there," Anya said, "still grappling with each other. But they know, thanks to you, Orion, that the continuum cannot be destroyed so easily. It perseveres."

"Those other lives I remember—you were in them."

"Yes, as I will be in this one."

"I loved you, then."

Her smile lit the world. "Do you love me now?"

"Yes." And I knew it was so. I meant it with every atom of my being.

"And I love you, too, Orion. I always have and I always will."

"But I'm leaving soon."

"I know."

Past her shoulder, I could see through the restaurant's window all the gaudy crescent of Saturn hanging low on the horizon, the thin line of its rings slicing through its bulging middle. Higher up, the sky of Titan was its usual dull orange overcast. The starship was parked in orbit up there, waiting for us to finish our final preparations and board it.

"We'll be gone for twenty years," I said.

"To the Sirius system, I know."

"It's a long voyage."

"Not as long as some we've already made, Orion," she said, "or others that we will make someday."

"What do you mean?"

"I'll explain it during the voyage." She smiled again. "We'll have plenty of time to remember eveything then."

My heart leaped in my chest. "You're going too?"

"Of course," she laughed. "We have endured the collapse and rebirth of the universe, Orion. We have shared many lives and many deaths. I'm not going to be separated from you now."

"But I haven't seen you at any of the crew briefings. You're not on the list of . . ."

"I am now. We will journey out to the stars together, my beloved. We have a long and full lifetime ahead of us. And perhaps even more than that."

I leaned across the table and kissed her lips. My loneliness was ended, at last. I could face anything in the world now. I was ready to challenge the universe.